Deconstructing East Germany

Studies in German Literature, Linguistics, and Culture

Edited by James Hardin
(*South Carolina*)

DAVID W. ROBINSON

DECONSTRUCTING EAST GERMANY

CHRISTOPH HEIN'S LITERATURE OF DISSENT

CAMDEN HOUSE

Copyright © 1999 David W. Robinson

All Rights Reserved. Except as permitted under current legislation,
no part of this work may be photocopied, stored in a retrieval system,
published, performed in public, adapted, broadcast, transmitted,
recorded, or reproduced in any form or by any means,
without the prior permission of the copyright owner.

First published 1999
by Camden House

Camden House is an imprint of Boydell & Brewer Inc.
PO Box 41026, Rochester, NY 14604–4126 USA
and of Boydell & Brewer Limited
PO Box 9, Woodbridge, Suffolk IP12 3DF, UK

ISBN: 1–57113–163–9

Library of Congress Cataloging-in-Publication Data

Robinson, David W., 1958–
    Deconstructing East Germany : Christoph Hein's literature of
dissent / David W. Robinson.
      p.   cm. – (Studies in German literature, linguistics, and
culture)
    Includes bibliographical references and index.
    ISBN 1–57113–163–9 (alk. paper)
    1. Hein, Christoph, 1944–   —Political and social views.
2. Germany in literature. 3. Cold War in literature. 4. Germany
(East)—Politics and government. 5. Germany (West)—Politics and
government. 6. Germany—History—Unification, 1990. I. Title.
II. Series: Studies in German literature, linguistics, and culture
(Unnumbered)
PT2668.E3747Z87   1999
838'.91409—dc21   99-27607
                                                                                CIP

A catalogue record for this title is available from the British Library.
This publication is printed on acid-free paper.
Printed in the United States of America.

Christoph Hein's 4 November 1989 speech on Alexanderplatz in Berlin
is reprinted by permission.

This book is dedicated to Caren Town, who came along for the ride.

Contents

Acknowledgments	ix
Introduction	xi
1: A Playwright Turns Chronicler	1
2: Individuals in the Slough of History: Hein's Early Short Stories and *Passage*	30
3: Power and Repression in *Der fremde Freund*	75
4: Hein's Historians: Fictions of Social Memory	125
5: Chronicling the Cold War's Losers and Winners	181
Works Consulted	221
Index	233

Acknowledgments

MANY PEOPLE AND INSTITUTIONS CONTRIBUTED to the making of this book. Heidrun Wimmersberg, now of Bäyerischer Rundfunk, first introduced me to Hein's writing and has kept me supplied with research materials. Peter Graetz introduced me to Hein himself. My attendance at the New Hampshire Symposia on GDR Studies in 1987 and 1989 was invaluable. A Fulbright grant in 1988 allowed me to spend six months in the German Democratic Republic reading, writing, traveling, and learning: in retrospect, precious time spent in a republic that was about to vanish. I was fortunate to have one of Hein's important East German critics, Frank Hörnigk, serve as my *Betreuer* (a term which can be construed as either mentor or minder) during that stay, along with Elke Hansen, who grew from an advisor into a friend. Georgia Southern University, through faculty development grants as well as financial support from the Department of English and Philosophy, helped fund my further travel to the GDR in 1989 and to the expanded Federal Republic of Germany in 1991, 1992, 1994, and 1998. Thanks go as well to Christoph Hein, who has been generous with his time and commentary, and to my editor at Camden House, Jim Walker.

D. W. R.
June 1999

Introduction

IN THE AUTUMN OF 1989, I WAS TO DELIVER a talk at Georgia Southern College on my then-recent visits to the German Democratic Republic, including six months in 1988 and a month the following spring. As the date approached, I found myself writing version after version of the speech, trying to keep up with the torrent of events that the world was watching on television: thousands fleeing the GDR in packed trains, demonstrations at Berlin's Alexanderplatz, beatings of innocent people by the East German secret police, candlelight marches in Leipzig, and, climactically, the opening of the Berlin Wall on the evening of November 9. By the time I gave the talk, a revolution had been accomplished. Afterward, as the GDR faded away into "the new federal states," I endured a modest amount of ribbing from colleagues who wondered whether I still had a field to work in: how, after all, could one be a scholar of GDR life and letters without a GDR?

The question of the place and significance of GDR studies, including GDR literature, is an important one, because by historically and critically accounting for this strange, forty-year episode in German history, we are also accounting for ourselves, that is, the modern age, the West, and, of course, "Germany." The urgency of this accounting was made evident by the early efforts after 1989 to evade or deny it, to close the book on the uneasy balance of terror and moral conviction that has marked the twentieth century. In America, State Department analyst Francis Fukuyama created a furor by suggesting that the end of the Cold War amounted to the "end of history." In Germany, parallel controversies erupted among literary critics and historians, with the *Kritikerstreit* resulting from attempts to denounce and dismiss GDR literature as propagandistic tripe, and the *Historikerstreit* from revisionist efforts to "move beyond" the German atrocities of the Nazi era. German popular politics bore a similar stamp of hostility toward remembering and assimilating the past, as West German Chancellor Helmut Kohl successfully campaigned on a platform dismissing the East German past as a criminal aberration and promising immediate and seamless integration of the East into the West. Obviously, these efforts to escape history have not fared well over the last last ten years, and it has again become clear that a sober understanding of the past is needed for even a rudimentary understanding of the present. In the field of literary studies, East Germany now represents both a closed period and a still-vital movement of writers with a distinctly East German voice or viewpoint. The questions raised in and by this literature have lost nothing of their currency — questions concerning the moral responsibilities of individuals in modern society, the social costs of advanced capitalism, the nature of freedom, the roots of oppression. The analysis here of the writings of Christoph Hein, the most successful of the GDR writers who professionally survived the post-1989 transition to a unified Germany, will delve into all of these areas.

Hein embodies the predisposition of East German writers to seek ways of escaping the confinements of ideological thinking (whether their own or others'). This effort was not a trivial one, for it helped prepare the way for the collapse of the communist regime in 1989, a bloodless revolution that could easily have been a bloody replay of Tienanmen Square, had not the GDR leadership lost faith in its own ideology, and with it, the rationale for its rule. However much the GDR's geopolitical significance may have boiled down to serving as a buffer state between the Soviet Union and the West, it also bore an ideological meaning for its founders, its ruling class, and even its beleaguered populace. East Germany was at least a partial realization of Marx's dream of socialism on German soil, symbolizing a vindication of the German communist movement that failed during the Weimar years, a repudiation of the crimes of the people and leadership of fascist Germany, an assertion of the rights of all people to food, shelter, and employment, and a step toward a communist utopia. Not just in the rhetoric of its leaders but often enough in the hearts of its citizenry, the GDR was a civilized alternative to the society based on greed and exploitation that began immediately to the West. The justification for its existence, in short, was a degree of moral superiority to the West that was proclaimed by official ideology in the face of all economic, social, and political facts to the contrary. Throughout the GDR's existence, the moral force of its Enlightenment ideals (liberty, equality, fraternity) was used to distract attention from those facts, and from the responsibility of Leninist centralism for causing them, and for corrupting the ideals themselves. The legitimacy of the socialist regime, with all it warts, rested on the shaky basis of a vast system of taboos, of truths that could not be spoken, least of all in the national literature that was supposed to be helping the Party build socialism. Christoph Hein's artistic response was to find ways of stating the obvious, and thus to break through the deceptions of self and others that allowed the society to continue functioning. Speaking the unspeakable became for Hein a strategy for deconstructing the dominant ideology (revealing the gaps in its logic, laying bare the interests at work in it) in order to recover the Enlightenment ideals in whose name it pretended to function. And in a country as saturated by ideology as the GDR, this rhetorical strategy was tantamount to hurling bombs at the state itself. Deconstructing ideology was a means of undermining the state; though a less dramatic form of dissidence than street demonstrations, hunger strikes, and prison-house martyrdom, it was no less effective in bringing down the edifice of power. The conformist, true-believing GDR fell first, not Poland or Czechoslovakia with their cynical leaders and high-profile dissident movements. Hein, with other leading artists and intellectuals, was an important contributor to the mood of disgust and disappointment that erased the GDR from the map of nations.

This book, as an essay in literary criticism, approaches Hein's works by focusing on a number of key thematic concerns, with discussion of historical, political, and other sorts of backgrounds when they are central to an understanding of the works. Among these concerns are the role of political ideology in social and private behavior, the mirroring of political oppression and violence in intimate relations, the impact of history (war, tyranny, revolution) on individual lives, the human costs of modernity, and the nature of social responsibility, especially for intellectuals. Against the continuing tendency, particularly in western Germany, to read everything eastern as politically corrupted, culturally backward, and morally deficient, my critical gesture is to treat Hein's works as worthy of close reading and interpretation in their own right, not merely as keys to a Cold War political landscape, or as veiled protests against a now-defunct state.

A concentration on intrinsic aspects of Hein's fiction may seem strange in view of the topicality of so much of Hein's writing, especially the fiction, which strives to reflect a true, unbiased image of everyday GDR reality. Yet, paradoxically, Hein's response to the reality of life and thought in the GDR is revealed precisely in his stylistic striving toward authorial detachment, which is better understood as a flight from ideological distortion than a confident assertion of some personal worldview. Worldviews are cheap, especially in this ideological century. Hein's subject matter, therefore — the object of all his purported objectivity — is really of less political moment than the stance of detached objectivity itself. Hein assumes responsibility for telling his stories, as Tacitus (the first chronicler of the Germans) promised in the *Annales*, "sine ira et studio" (I.1), without passion or prejudice. This is a stance that is logically untenable but ethically necessary: untenable because pure, detached objectivity can never be more than an ideal, and necessary because in Hein's fictive world, the alternative to the search for truth is the embrace of every kind of falsehood, whether political or personal. And though Hein resists characterization as a moralist, his work everywhere attests to a moral sense that values social engagement, honesty, courage, and endurance. He describes his moral and artistic stance in an early-1990 interview:

> I understand myself to be a chronicler, one who describes with great accuracy what he has seen. Thus I stand in an honorable tradition running from Johann Peter Hebel to Kafka. But the writer is not a preacher, someone adding his own commentary to the facts of the case. I avoid preaching, but my own position is sufficiently clear. You can't write and remain concealed at the same time. Without backbone, writing is impossible. ("Die alten Themen" 38)

Hein's resistance to the label "preacher" or "moralist" stems from his rejection of the pedagogical (that is, moralizing, propagandizing) role forced upon East German authors by Socialist Realist dogma, which enlisted writers in Stalin's project of engineering human souls. Rather than telling his readers what to think, Hein tries to provoke them into thinking their own thoughts, just as the protagonist of his play *Die wahre Geschichte des Ah Q* (The True Story of Ah Q, 1983), who yearns to make an earth-shaking pronouncement, ultimately confesses that he has no message for the audience. His companion remarks, "They should think of something themselves" (107). In a society marked by *Bevormündung*, paternalistic guidance in all aspects of life, this modest aesthetic renunciation announces a moral position amounting to political dissidence. In adopting such a position, Hein participates in a skeptical, anti-ideological project undertaken by many GDR writers, most notably Heiner Müller and Christa Wolf. Hein's own distinctiveness lies in his passionate belief in the power of facts to speak for themselves if only given the chance.[1]

My emphasis on Hein's fiction comes somewhat at the expense of his plays, which are dealt with more cursorily, but there are both pragmatic and critical reasons for such an approach. I am cognizant of the fact that Hein's plays remain largely untranslated and unperformed in the United States and (to a lesser degree) in the United Kingdom, whereas two of his novels have been published in the United States in English translations. Hein's renown in German-speaking countries has also followed more from his fiction than from his plays. Specifically, Hein's novella *Der fremde Freund* (1983, translated as *The Distant Lover*, 1989) won him inter-German and international fame.[2] This preeminence of Hein's prose over his dramas is likely to remain true in the English speaking countries, if only due to differences between the theatrical traditions of East Germany and Anglo-America; Hein's spare, disquieting narratives have proved to be far more easily transferable across cultural boundaries.

The chapters that follow deal with the entire range of Hein's thematic concerns. The introductory chapter 1, "A Playwright turns Chronicler," sketches the social and political contexts of Hein's work, surveys the most important among his early plays, and prepares for his transformation from a playwright into (primarily) a fiction writer. Such plays as *Schlötel oder Was solls* (Schlötel or What's the Use?, 1974), *Cromwell* (1980), and *Lassalle fragt Herrn Herbert nach Sonja. Die Szene ein Salon* (Lassalle asks Herr Herbert about Sonja. The Scene a Salon, 1980) break with received Socialist Realism while dissecting the personalities of both historical and fictitious reformer-idealists. By representing the collapse and dissolution of initially idealistic revolutions through the disintegration of the individuals that lead them, Hein began to map out the relations between public and private that absorb his later efforts. This culminates in *Ah Q*, where Hein parodies the alleged guiding role of reformer-idealists in historical movements (something already deconstructed in the earlier plays) and lays out the problematic of social engagement versus social withdrawal that will dominate the longer fiction, beginning with *Der fremde Freund*.

Chapter 2, "Individuals in the Slough of History: Hein's early Short Stories and *Passage*," shows the emergence of Hein's trademark stance as a "chronicler," depicting ordinary people in the ordinary madness of twentieth-century German life. Central to this is the story group "Aus: Ein Album Berliner Stadtansichten" (From: An Album of Berlin Postcards, 1980), where, drawing on Kleist and Hebel as models, Hein perfects his detached, documentary method. Closely related is the play *Passage* (1987), which can be seen as a dramatic treatment of the moral puzzle haunting the early stories: What is the responsibility of individuals caught up in historic forces that no individual can reasonably hope to change, amid circumstances leaving no room for hope?

Chapter 3, "Power and Repression in *Der fremde Freund*," is an extended discussion of what probably remains Hein's most perfectly realized work. The seductively reasonable first-person narrator gradually reveals an emotionally sterile interior life that represses and reenacts the political and sexual brutality she has endured, a life totally disengaged from society, though eminently "successful." A perfectly adapted and perfectly conforming modern woman, she is an indictment of the many readers who find her worldview alarmingly familiar. The chapter also provides a detailed sample of East German critical discourse, illustrating the ideological context alluded to in earlier chapters and showing how the cultural establishment dealt with challenging works.

Chapter 4, "Hein's Historians: Fictions of Social Memory," presents the development of Hein's ideas about history and literature, as worked out both in his essays and in works of fiction, including "Einladung zum Lever Bourgeois" (Invitation to the Lever Bourgeois, 1980), *Horns Ende* (Horn's Fate, 1985), and *Der Tangospieler* (1989; translated as *The Tango Player*, 1992). Acknowledging that all historical narratives are personal, partial, slanted, and flawed, Hein argues for a multiplicity of such fragmentary viewpoints, where no single view dominates, and truth may be inferred through comparison, contradiction, and competition. This is what Hein means by his call for *Öffentlichkeit*, the free and open discussion of ideas, a prerequisite for true culture and something still missing from the GDR during its last decade of existence. The works discussed are all explorations of the potential for courage, cowardice, folly, and cynicism inherent in the key social role of chronicler/historian. "Einladung," an early effort in this vein, consists of an imagined monologue by the French dramatist and court historian Jean Racine, revealing the cost of his personal compromises with absolutist power. *Horns Ende* was the GDR's first honest look at the reality of everyday life in an ordinary provincial town under Stalinism in the 1950s, including its connections and continuities with the Nazi years and before. The central event — the suicide of a historian named Horn, who has been accused of espionage — is told from various contradictory perspectives, such as those of the apparatchik mayor, an embittered local physician, a young boy, and so on. The problem of how to tell the truth about history (and the many reasons for not doing so) becomes the theme of the book, and is debated explicitly and implicitly among the different narrators and characters. *Der Tangospieler* is a satirical account of an apolitical historian's ups and downs in the political situation of the late-sixties GDR. The ultimate point appears to be that the more detached, cynical, and opportunistic a person may be, the better suited he is to the needs and methods of a totalitarian society. The central character is the perfect anti-historian.

The book's concluding chapter 5, "Chronicling the Cold War's Losers and Winners," looks at Hein's literary contribution to the GDR's collapse or *Wende* (change of course), and at new directions suggested by his narrative and dramatic work in unified Germany. The chapter discusses the so-called *Wende*-play *Die Ritter der Tafelrunde* (1989; translated as *The Knights of the Round Table*, 1995), which depicts the court of King Arthur as a gang of corrupted idealists with more than a passing resemblance to the GDR's Politburo; the first post-*Wende* play, *Randow* (1994), which paints a bleak picture of exploitation and opportunism in the new united Germany; and the first post-*Wende* novel, *Das Napoleon-Spiel* (The Napoleon Game, 1993), which provoked irritation in the West for its unflattering portrait of a West Berlin psychopath. Finally, I discuss Hein's two most recent books. The first is *Exekution eines Kalbes* (Execution of a Calf, 1994), a collection of short stories spanning two decades and a dizzying variety of styles, from additional "Berliner Stadtansichten" and dramatic monologues to surrealistic tales that seem to announce a new direction for Hein. The second, *Von allem Anfang an* (From the very Beginning, 1997), is a "fictive autobiography" set in the mid-1950s rural GDR. Its setting notwithstanding, the book shows Hein applying his chronicling methods for the first time in a totally post-*Wende* context. In general, the old Hein, critical of Western excess, smugness, and rapacity is still in evidence, but his notion of "chronicling" seems to be undergoing revision. While it was subversive *simply to state the facts* in the GDR, Hein's latest writings have shown signs of a move toward indirection, allegory, and ironic self-positioning within German literary and political history. In the brave new world of unified Germany, Hein may be finding Kafka an even better model than his much-admired Kleist.

Notes

[1] The term "ideology" is not used here just to mean "political beliefs" or "political doctrine," though it was often used in this way by East Bloc Marxist philosophers (with little sanction from Marx's own writings). Instead of this rationalistic definition, I have in mind the more complex notion formulated by Louis Althusser, who refines Marx's definition of ideology as false consciousness in order to explain its positive relation to objective reality. "Ideology represents the imaginary relationship of individuals to their real conditions of existence," Althusser asserts; while ideological illusions do not accord with reality, "they do make allusion to reality" (162), and thereby constitute the very basis of what an individual living within the ideology experiences (falsely) as the real, the true, and the obvious (171–172). Thus when I refer to GDR authors who resist ideology, I have in mind the struggle to escape the limitations of one's own belief system, not merely to see through the claptrap printed in the government newspapers. The most important lesson from East German literature may be that one is always personally implicated in ideology, and that the great danger is to see one's ideology as the truth.

[2] Confusingly, *Der fremde Freund* was published in the Federal Republic under the title *Drachenblut*, an allusion to the Siegfried story. The English title reflects the original German title, which is now also the title of the post-1989 editions from Aufbau Verlag.

Abbreviations

Christoph Hein's novels and story collections will be cited parenthetically using abbreviations, accompanied by a page number, based on the following editions:

NUFM	*Nachtfahrt und früher Morgen. Prosa.* Munich: Deutscher Taschenbuch Verlag, 1987.
DFF	*Der fremde Freund. Novelle.* Berlin (East) and Weimar: Aufbau, 1982.
TDL	*The Distant Lover. A Novel.* Trans. Krishna Winston. New York: Pantheon, 1989.
HE	*Horns Ende. Roman.* Darmstadt and Neuwied: Luchterhand, 1987.
DT	*Der Tangospieler. Erzählung.* Berlin (East) and Weimar: Aufbau, 1989.
TTP	*The Tango Player.* Trans. Philip Boehm. New York: Farrar, Straus and Giroux, 1992.
DN	*Das Napoleon-Spiel. Ein Roman.* Berlin and Weimar: Aufbau, 1993.
EEK	*Exekution eines Kalbes und andere Erzählungen.* Berlin and Weimar: Aufbau, 1994.
VAAA	*Von allem Anfang an.* Berlin: Aufbau, 1997.

Other short stories, plays, essays and interviews will be cited in accordance with MLA style.

Substantial quotations from Hein's fiction and plays are rendered in both the original German and in English translation; quotations from the essays and interviews are presented only in translation. Quotations from secondary sources (i.e., critics) and from non-literary authorities (such as Sigmund Freud and Walter Benjamin) are also rendered in English. All translations are my own unless otherwise noted.

1: A Playwright Turns Chronicler

Christoph Hein and the German Democratic Republic

IN 1978, IN THE DEPTHS OF THE GDR'S LAST major crackdown on uncooperative or uncomfortable artists, the 34-year-old playwright Christoph Hein told an interviewer for the East German journal *Theater der Zeit* that "the contemporary stage is a splendid opportunity for writing fiction" ("Ein Interview" 101) — that is to say, opportunities for getting plays produced were virtually non-existent. Hein's characteristically acerbic remark points to some hard facts about the GDR literary scene of the time. First, Hein was alluding to the chill that had marked official cultural policy since the exile in 1976 of political singer/songwriter Wolf Biermann. Second, he was describing the besieged position of dramatists in the heavily politicized East German theatrical establishment, which had as its most sensitive responsibility the management of large public assemblages of citizens who were always ready to view dramatic performances as political allegories, and thus as an alternative to the enforced monotony of public discourse. In the face of these realities, Hein embarked on a course that would issue in the stories and novels of the 1980s that brought him critical acclaim and enormous popularity in both Germanies. In the cramped political culture of the GDR, printed literature no less than the stage was seen by the public as a forum for real political discussion, yet it was frequently accorded a modest degree of ideological freedom by the authorities, perhaps because of the less social, more private manner of its consumption. Hein was therefore able to carry on his challenge to moribund Stalinism by means of fiction as the 1980s arrived, while most of his plays languished unstaged, at least in the GDR.

As one of the small number of dissident authors in the GDR who managed both to live and to publish within their homeland, Hein participated in the remarkable subculture of writers and readers which, operating with handed-along, sometimes smuggled books, through public readings, through theatrical performances, and through the letters of readers to authors, constituted the GDR's closest approximation to free public discourse. (The churches played a parallel role during the late eighties, providing a haven for political discussion and protest.) Operating from the idiosyncratic position of the quasi-sympathetic political outsider, or better, as an anarchist detesting the ideological mystifications that reinforce the power of any political system, Hein established himself as one of the most important of a handful of internal left-wing critics of the GDR. And like Christa Wolf and Heiner Müller, Hein has also been a trenchant critic of Western capitalism, most explicitly in his numerous essays (collected in 1987 as *Öffentlich arbeiten* [Working Openly]), but also in his novels, where the West is generally painted as alien and unappealing, full of rapacious entrepreneurs and intellectual charlatans. He is particularly harsh in his assessment of Western leftist intellectuals, whose inconsequential moralizing about socialism and capitalism contrasts with the clarity of vision forced on East Bloc leftists by lived confrontation with their own ideology. In response to leftist cause-mongering, with its tendency to take up false utopias and then toss them aside when they prove disappointing, Hein asserts:

> My struggles here are not so easy. For us, Cuba is a story that *isn't over*. We haven't yet been able to file away China, Vietnam, or Cambodia. All of the problems and hardships of these countries and of my country will remain my problems and hardships. We are backward enough here to think that Stalin still has some life in him.
> ("Linker Kolonialismus" 152)

Hein's contempt for intellectual vacuousness in the West and his rage at brutality in the East remained in evidence after the events of Fall 1989, when the East German border was opened and the country began moving toward unification with West Germany. Although Hein declined to join any new group or party, he was among the artists and intellectuals who hastened the collapse of the communist regime by denouncing the police violence that marred the GDR's fortieth anniversary celebrations, and by speaking out at the mass demonstration on Alexanderplatz the weekend prior to the abrupt opening of the German-German border. After the opening of the Wall, Hein used his new status as a pan-German media figure to argue for a socialism worthy of the name, telling *Neues Deutschland*, the official Party newspaper, "We have now been granted the enormous opportunity to build, for the first time, real socialism on German soil" (December 2/3, 1989; quoted by Andress 164). He continued to call for a democratic and socialist society distinct from West Germany well after it was clear to him that a majority of his fellow citizens wanted only quick unification.

The so-called *Wende* or political turnabout of 1989 and the German unification (on wholly West German terms) in October 1990 abolished a Byzantine world of balanced ideologies and well-honed strategies of opposition, and it plunged the dissident artists of the GDR into severe political and artistic confusion. An early and spectacular event of this new order was the pillorying of novelist Christa Wolf by the West German press after the publication of *Was bleibt* [What Remains, 1990], a fictionalized account of her surveillance in the late 1970s by the Stasi, the East German secret police. Since Wolf had been a prominent member of the ruling Socialist Unity Party and had declined to criticize the government publicly before 1989, she was accused of seeking political absolution in the new, post-communist Germany.[1] Despite the crudeness of the attacks against Wolf (they had little to say about the book itself or about her 25 years of steady resistance to the GDR's conformist philistinism), an important question was raised: What was to be the function or niche of writers of the former GDR (to say nothing of the literary-historical assessment of their earlier works) now that they were no longer able to define themselves artistically in relation to a communist regime with whose ideals they had identified, but whose practices had been abhorrent to them? Since for many of these leftist authors there was no question of embracing Western-style capitalism, what, as Wolf had asked, really *did* remain for them? The answer to this question about the future lies in the GDR past, which nurtured not just a repressive ideology, but also intellectual and artistic strategies of resistance. The writings of Christoph Hein illustrate the continuing power of those strategies.

Born in 1944, Hein was a member of the middle generation of GDR writers who grew up wholly within a socialist society in the act of creating and defining itself. Unlike the previous generation, which had lived through the barbarism of the Nazi years, or the generation that came of age in the late 1970s and 1980s, knowing only the stagnation and hypocrisy of the GDR's decline, Hein and his contemporaries possessed a taste for idealism, which, once disappointed, fostered a bitter sense of irony about the distance between theory and practice, and a resolute skepticism toward the blandishments of either Cold War ideology. The literature that resulted was a continual testing of the material consequences of socialist ideology against the promises of socialist ideals. Therefore Hein's politics and the role he played in the cultural struggles of the GDR elude easy categorization. Hein's father was a Lutheran minister who settled with his family as war refugees in Thuringia; put at an educational disadvantage by his religious background, Hein was forced to live in West Berlin to attend a *Gymnasium*; and after being forbidden through most of the 1960s to attend a university (in retribution for the West Berlin sojourn, despite the fact that he had chosen to return to the GDR after the Wall was built), he was eventually permitted to study logic and philosophy in Leipzig and later Berlin. In the years that followed, his biography resembles that of many other East German non-conformists: barred from pursuing his real interests, he worked construction, attended a trade school, and clerked in a bookstore, all the while writing occasional journalistic pieces and working without pay as a director's assistant (McKnight, *Understanding Christoph Hein* xiii). As for his political education, Hein says that his final disillusionment with Soviet-style socialism came in August 1968, when Warsaw Pact troops crushed the Dubček regime in Czechoslovakia ("Kennen" 56). In the early 1970s, Hein rose to prominence at the East Berlin Volksbühne, working as dramaturge and house playwright under artistic director Benno Besson. This association placed him at the heart of the GDR's theatrical tradition; Besson, one of the most respected and innovative directors of his time, had collaborated with Bertolt Brecht as a director at the Berliner Ensemble in the 1950s, and his dramaturgical staff at the Volksbühne [People's Stage] included Heiner Müller, the most important neo-Brechtian playwright. Unlike many colleagues who were effectively hounded out of the country, Hein stayed on in the GDR even during the dark days following the Biermann affair, when politically-motivated staffing changes at the Volksbühne (including the dismissal of Besson) and the effective proscription of his plays propelled him into a freelance career in prose fiction (McKnight, *Understanding Christoph Hein*, xiv).

The Socialist Realist milieu

Hein's earliest original dramatic works emerged from a neo-Brechtian tradition in more or less open conflict with the conservatively propagandistic requirements of Socialist Realism, which, despite vigorous academic debate throughout the fifties, sixties, and early seventies, was never entirely abandoned as the official cultural-political dogma. The doctrine, though rooted well back in Russian literary history, was first promulgated (at the instigation of Stalin himself) as official Soviet policy in the Constitution of the Union of Writers of the USSR in 1934, which demanded from writers "a true and historically concrete depiction of reality in its revolutionary development. Moreover this true and historically concrete artistic depiction of reality must be combined with the task of educating workers in the spirit of Communism" (quoted in James 88n). Socialist Realist art was expected to embody *narodnost* (people-ness, that is, rootedness in the proletarian masses), *klassovost* (class-ness, class-typical character), and *partiinost* (party-ness, *Partei-*

lichkeit in German, meaning commitment to the programs and goals of the Communist Party). By thus exhibiting popular appeal, class consciousness, and political and ideological orthodoxy, Socialist Realism was not to be not a mere materialistic reflection of reality, but rather a reflection of it with an explicitly pragmatic, pedagogical slant, as explained by any of countless East German publications elucidating the nature of socialist art in close conformity with Soviet dicta, as this list of objectives from a 1957 article illustrates:

> To know life in order to represent it faithfully. To understand how to expose the essential aspects of life. To represent life not scholastically, not dead, not simply as "objective reality," but instead as reality in a process of revolutionary development. To bind artistic representation to the ethical task of educating people in the spirit of socialism, providing them with artworks that will put them in a position to affirm the New in life and to build on it actively. (Liebmann 326)

Among the characters in a Socialist Realist work should be clearly-drawn heroes who, as representatives of the New Socialist Man, could serve as role models to the readers, while self-interested or politically immature characters functioned as foils.[2] Socialist Realist art was conceived as offering "a new content, new hero, new social ideal, and a new relation to reality" (Romanowski 161), all guided by the narrowly pragmatic question, "How does art serve the establishment of socialism?" (Liebmann 326). Artists were recruited as educators and propagandists working for socialist transformation in the ideologically-charged context of worldwide class struggle. "The struggle for art that concretely and historically reflects socialist reality in its revolutionary development," reads one fervent East German pamphlet, "that simultaneously exerts its educational influence and its mobilizing effect on people so as to propel this development forward — this is in fact the main task for art in the socialist cultural revolution, to facilitate the parallel task of fighting every form of bourgeois-imperialist decadence" (John 8)." The paradoxical requirement that Socialist Realism depict reality even as it pursued a utopian agenda is itself a version of Maxim Gorky's concept of "revolutionary romanticism," which was to be art that "embodies the 'pathos' of the creation of a new society and of the vision that urges people on . . . , not idle dreaming but a vision of the future based on an understanding of reality and the processes of development" (James 91). Gorky's idea in turn resembles Lenin's belief that "dreaming" was a crucial aspect of socialist transformation, that is, of revolution (James 25).[3]

Of special importance for the construction of plot in dramatic or narrative literature was the putatively unique nature of socialist society and its profound ontological difference from capitalism, a distinction elaborated theoretically in the doctrine of "antagonistic" versus "non-antagonistic contradictions," terms based ultimately on Marx's description of the destabilizing contradictions that riddle capitalist society. According to one political manual, *Marxistische Philosophie. Lehrbuch*, published in 1967, the distinction can be understood as follows:

> By antagonistic contradictions we mean *above all* those contradictions which express *class* antagonisms, i.e., social relations based on the exploitation of one class by another, on class oppression, on the relation of masters to slaves. Contradictions are termed non-antagonistic when they express class relations characterized by the fundamental commonality of interests among different classes and levels (which by no means excludes oppositions in a few fundamental questions), or by the emerging political-moral unity of a people liberated from exploitation.
> (Quoted in Kuczynski 1271)

Non-antagonistic contradictions, such as will arise in socialist society, may be resolved by the "synthesis of the two sides of the contradiction," whereas antagonistic contradictions can be resolved only through the "annihilation" [*Vernichtung*] of one of the sides (1272). Moreover, the only antagonistic contradictions to be found in a socialist society are, according to doctrine, ones persisting from the pre-revolutionary period, or resulting from external stresses on the socialist state. Similarly, the only literary works containing evidence of antagonistic contradictions would be those still suffering from the residual influence of bourgeois social relations ("Thesen zum sozialistischen Realismus" 130). In an unhappy application of ideas from Marxist political economy to literary criticism, made possible by the preexisting (and unrelated) literary concept of "conflict," these terms became convenient tools for critics bent on vilifying politically contrary works. With "conflict" (in life or in art) understood as the microcosmic manifestation of a macrocosmic social contradiction, it becomes possible to gauge the political soundness of a work by observing how effectively it resolves the "conflicts" that it introduces.[4] Depictions of socialist society, in short, had better not contain unresolved conflicts that imply the presence of antagonistic contradictions. It was not only an objective aesthetic error for an artist to leave conflicts unresolved, it was prima facie evidence of a "Mangel an Parteilichkeit" (Adling and Geldner 97), a lack of partisan loyalty, and so a political transgression, since the Party is by definition the self-aware voice of the proletariat as well as the arbiter of objective reality. By such casuistry as this, politics overrode the East German theater's progressive, oppositional, and dialectical Brechtian roots (in which problems are presented as real, and spectators are expected to struggle with them toward an uncertain outcome) in favor of a drastically vulgarized and undialectical Aristotelianism that requires all conflict to be neatly resolved before the audience leaves the theater. The fatal insensitivity to artistic nuance and ambiguity fostered by such a position is typified by Adling and Geldner's earnest but stupid attack on the growing mid-60s tendency, specifically as exemplified by Heiner Müller, "to deliberately avoid resolving dramatic conflicts" (99).

Breaking with the Party Line

When viewed against this background of politically charged aesthetic norms, Hein's dramatic works can be understood as the radical acts of intellectual liberation that they are. In the mid-1980s, with the battle won, Hein contrasted his literary practice with the by then antiquated norms of the fifties and sixties. Socialist Realism rested on a conception of the artist as an educator, as a political activist *through* art, and it is in this light that the censoriousness and condescension of the critics ought to be judged:

> I believe that the [critics] back then meant well. They thought that they could really help. But I reject that, because I see the arrogance behind it, the idea that I have something to say to the masses, to the nations. But I think that has probably changed in all of the socialist countries. And this literature, therefore, that wanted to say how things ought to proceed, that constantly painted this picture of the future — that belongs, I think, to the past . . . . Criticism is lagging behind, it still has a lot to learn. It still has familiar models, familiar patterns, for instance the positive hero. It assumes that the writer really has to say everything and functions as a higher authority, whereas I and others have long since come to trust that my reader is also my partner, and brings along his own experiences. ("Wir werden es lernen müssen" 53)

Hein's position clearly is an oppositional one, despite his somewhat disingenuous stance of unassuming intellectual modesty. The Leninist insistence on partisan ideological loyalty and its Stalinist adumbration in the realm of art leave little room for the inherent anarchism of independent thinking, and anarchy is indeed a significant theme for Hein, whose characters live at the political margins, dangerously wavering between radical independence and complete irrelevance. To think independently, without ideological guidance and interpretation, was to strike at the heart of the GDR's political order, and for an artist to cast off the role of ideological mentor to the masses was a supremely hazardous gesture (one also made by Hein's slightly older contemporaries, Wolf and Müller, among others).

If the Party's mentorship in political and artistic matters is discounted, then the arcane formulas for assessing "contradictions," like the canons of Socialist Realist art, become superfluous — except as a departure point. Hein's early plays and stories show the marks of a Socialist Realist-trained artistic sensibility, but one turned against itself, subverting precisely the principles that Socialist Realism was created to promote. On the fundamental question of social contradictions, Hein deliberately blurs the sophistries of "antagonistic" and "non-antagonistic" categorizations by arguing that *all* societies contain the seeds of contradictions within themselves, and that these contradictions are often irresolvable. In a discussion of his 1984 novel *Der fremde Freund* Hein claimed as his central theme

> our current state of civilization. That may be what makes the book interesting outside our borders, even though it is thoroughly rooted in the GDR. It examines the costs associated with our lifestyle, which are necessitated by our form of industrial production. An automobile is necessary, but it carries a cost: a few traffic fatalities, a certain amount of landscape. Round-the-clock shift work is necessary, but that means we need small individual apartments, so that individual workers won't be burdened by a grandmother — that means the shattering of the extended family. The trend began under capitalism, then we adopted it and we won't be turning back. This has given rise to a corresponding lack of interest in the extended family among individual middle Europeans. Society is set up so that I can put my old grandma into a home. That's all part and parcel, it's very pleasant and wonderful and it carries a price, and that price is what I am talking about in this book. To that extent, alienation and violence are only consequences of what we have abandoned. We have abandoned a kind of intimacy, with good reason: the sacred cow, progress. And we pay for it. ("Ich kann mein Publikum nicht belehren" 69)[5]

Hein's denial of the possibility of closure, of utopia, in socialist society inevitably parallels his preference for ambiguity, detachment, and paradox in his writing.

Hein's early plays

All of Hein's work reflects a sense of place, of East German citizenship and the determination to hold on to it despite official harassment. His plays, and later his fiction, address the problems that present themselves in his particular time and place, even when the nominal setting of the play is exotic. Unlike other prominent East German dramatists of the 1960s, seventies, and eighties (people like Heiner Müller, Volker Braun, and Peter Hacks), Hein seldom employs allegory or myth to disguise his critiques of contemporary East German or capitalist society. Rather, he writes (with some exceptions that invite ironic readings) in a flat, unadorned, realistic style about situations set either in twentieth-century Germany, or in more remote, but still historic, times and places that suggest clear analogies to the present. (Even the one exception to all of this, Hein's comedy *Die Ritter der Tafelrunde*, still bears no resemblance to the somber reworkings of mythic material so frequently encountered in East German drama.) The dramatic emphasis is always on the subjective experience of the characters: Hein favors enclosed, claustrophobia-inducing settings for his plays, writing with few exceptions *Kammerspiele*, intimate plays with interior settings that focus attention on the closed, circumscribed, personal world of the characters, while history, though exerting a steady pressure on the action, happens outside, somewhere else.

From his first play, *Schlötel oder Was solls*, through his best known play, *Die wahre Geschichte des Ah Q*, and the other plays of the 1980s, including his last play from the GDR period, *Die Ritter der Tafelrunde*, Hein has explored the relation between individual political and moral choices and the pressures exerted by the state toward conformity. Sometimes, as in *Schlötel*, this struggle manifests itself as the predicament of the intellectual in a society whose ideals are appealing but whose reality is determined by political cynicism or corruption; sometimes, as in *Cromwell* and *Die Ritter*, passionately held political ideologies lead to unanticipated outcomes, turning on their partisans and destroying them; and sometimes, as in *Ah Q*, the option of withdrawing oneself from society is exposed as a pernicious illusion that only perpetuates oppression. *Lassalle fragt Herrn Herbert nach Sonja: Die Szene ein Salon* examines the intersection between the political and the personal in the life of Ferdinand Lassalle, the pioneering German labor leader. *Passage*, which describes the efforts of a group of refugees to escape from Vichy France into Spain during the Second World War, takes up the theme of individual political responsibility in the most extreme, disempowered of circumstances, invoking ultimately the power of visionary hope.[6]

While my discussion of the later plays will be pursued in subsequent chapters, an examination here of the most important early plays — *Schlötel, Cromwell, Lassalle*, and *Ah Q* — will serve to map the artistic and political directions that the fiction will ultimately take. The break with Socialist Realism and the exploration of the contradictions within what the GDR regime smugly termed "real existierender Sozialismus" (actually existing socialism — as opposed to the more attractive imaginary kind) begin already with *Schlötel*. The play shows more clearly than any subsequent one the importance of Hein's cultural-political context: it appears formally to be a typical "factory" or "production" play, a Socialist Realist sub-genre employed extensively by German dramatists (and similarly by prose fiction writers) in the fifties and early sixties.[7] Typically, idealistic heroes struggle against the self-interest of opportunistic or counter-revolutionary fellow workers and the cautious careerism of Party functionaries, triumphing in the end with greater proletarian self-awareness and higher productivity. In Hein's version of the formula, all of the ingredients are present in the central characters: there is a dedicated hero (Schlötel), a careerist Party secretary with petit bourgeois characteristics, and fellow workers more interested in their love affairs and garden plots than in their work or the good of society. Yet the particulars belie the superficial typicality of the piece. Hein lays bare the time-wasting political indoctrination that steals production time and the cynical manipulations of the Party leadership as it attempts to have an incentive-oriented wage reform introduced "from below." And as for Schlötel, he is not just any worker, but a learned man, "a genius" (24) whose headstrong personality propels him from a position in an academic institute into the ranks of factory workers. But nobody wants geniuses there, either. His determination to introduce more efficient labor practices earns him the hatred of his fellow workers and the ire of the management and the Party; even when he is in technical agreement with the leadership, his arrogance makes him a disastrous ally. Schlötel is the very type of a *Schwärmer* or fanatic, someone deficient in normal feelings, and motivated instead, robotlike, by an excessively clear vision of truth. Ignoring a colleague's sage (if cynical) advice that "You can't change the world" (40), Schlötel declares to his wife (whom he is effectively abandoning):

> [Die Kollegen] haben sich an die Verhältnisse gewöhnt, ich nicht. Sie strotzen von Selbstzufriedenheit, ich will ein wenig mehr. Mein Leben ist zu kurz und zu wichtig, als daß ich alles schlucken werde. Praktizisten, Anpasser, Leisetreter, Karrieristen, ich werde ihnen noch zu schaffen machen. (63)

> [(My colleagues) have gotten used to the way things are, but I haven't. They are full of self-satisfaction, but I want something more. My life is too short and too important for me to simply swallow everything. Embezzlers, conformists, pussyfooters, careerists — I'll shake them up yet.]

When Schlötel hectors and threatens the Party secretary, the workers standing by are astonished and amused to see the stereotypes of Socialist Realism acted out before their eyes, as when one remarks, "Pinch me, I think I'm at the movies" (59). Behavior such as this in real life can only have one meaning: "The man is insane [wahnsinnig]" (59). In the real GDR, everybody knows that heroics are always a staged event, and that everything gets done along the path of least resistance. Idealism is for fools. By embodying a version of the "New Socialist Man," and giving up everything for the improvement of society, Schlötel, as far as ordinary GDR citizens are concerned, simply eludes classification: "Was ist das für ein Mensch. Ob dem was fehlt?" [What kind of man is that? Is he one brick shy of a load?: 61]. After being dismissed from his job, Schlötel really does go crazy, lodging unfounded accusations of sabotage against his superiors, strangling a colleague's prize-winning rabbit in a fit of anti-bourgeois rage, and finally throwing himself into the Baltic Sea. Schlötel provides a diagnosis for his condition — complete alienation from society with resultant self-alienation — when he raves at some puzzled strangers, "Meine Herren, Sie täuschen sich in mir. Ich bin ein anderer, sehen Sie. Ich habe nichts mit mir zu tun" [Gentlemen, you have mistaken me for someone else. I am another person, you see. I have nothing to do with myself: 81].

Hein's satire stresses the gap between the reality and the rhetoric of the GDR, suggesting that the New Socialist Man, like Jesus, would only be crucified if he actually showed up on earth; but it is hard to say whether Schlötel ultimately earns more contempt or admiration. The other characters really *are* petit bourgeois cynics and conformists, even if Schlötel really *is* a fanatic and, ultimately, a madman. Hein can already be seen working out his essential problematic: what is the role of the individual in a society that, realistically, *cannot* be changed, that crushes non-conformists and idealists? The commonsense answer is, of course, to keep one's head low and to mouth the platitudes of the day, and yet this is a stance that has within recent German memory led to the most horrendous atrocities in human history. Is withdrawal from society morally tenable? And does a departure from common sense necessarily mean a descent into madness? Whatever the answer to these questions, it is clear that Schlötel's problems are outgrowths of the actual social and economic conditions in the GDR, where people neither feared for their jobs nor needed to work very hard at them. Social security was bought at the price of economic inefficiency, while an ideology of social justice could be preserved only through forced conformity and the death of open debate. These contradictions were endemic, irresolvable, and (in hindsight) fatal, and thus scarcely "non-antagonistic."

Schlötel was originally produced by the East Berlin Volksbühne, where Hein was working as a dramaturge. Following his dismissal from the Volksbühne and the political turmoil of the mid to late 1970s, Hein turned his attention to the dynamics of revolution and the psychology of the revolutionary hero. The plays that resulted — *Cromwell, Lassalle,* and *Ah Q* — deal with revolutionary figures far removed from the GDR, but the analogies were clear enough so that the first two could initially be produced only on West German stages. Hein shows the reason why in his notes to the seemingly remote subject matter of *Cromwell*:

> Our interest in the English revolution is an interest in ourselves. Historical consciousness is egocentric: people desire to know their fathers so that they can understand themselves. As Hegel says, we pay attention to past events only insofar as they concern *us*, as they constitute and entangle us. ("Anmerkungen zu *Cromwell*" 173–174)

With this clear signal, Hein was announcing an exploration of what had gone awry in the socialist revolutions of the twentieth century, an inquiry that would yield an accurate prognosis for the regime of the GDR. His dramatic vehicle would no longer be subverted Socialist Realism, but instead an eclectic appropriation of Shakespeare's histories, Brecht's epic theater, absurdist farce, and other resources put at his disposal by European theatrical history. These plays, written at the same time that Hein was fashioning his early fiction, share with them the device of addressing questions of contemporary political relevance through the experiences of individuals, while differing in their degree of directness; many of the stories, for example, are actually set in the contemporary GDR. The trade-off is that the plays tend to demonstrate their thematic concerns more pointedly than the detached, serene, and hyper-realistic fiction, which relies on omission and understatement for its most important effects.

Cromwell, written in a style that is by turns Shakespearean and Brechtian, riddled with anachronisms that invoke the jargon of other, later revolutions, portrays the moral collapse of an idealist (or rather, an ideologue) into an enfeebled tyrant amid the machinations of merchants and bankers, the ultimate power brokers. The anachronisms reinforce Hein's point that dramatized history is necessarily "an interest in ourselves": in seventeenth-century England, we are presented with "Red Brothers" (90), a "commissar" (97), and "compañeros" (103), as well as technological oddities such as "cigarettes" (103), "loudspeakers" (124), and "machine gun fire" (167). Given the claim that the English Civil War has contemporary significance, it quickly becomes apparent that Oliver Cromwell's career frequently parallels the careers of Lenin, Stalin, the East German leadership, and perhaps even Hitler. Hein imagines Cromwell as both a fanatical ideologue and a tragic figure; his devotion to a pious dream of England replete with singing larks, ringing church bells, and happy, free peasants (99), in short, a dream of prelapsarian paradise, is what finally severs Cromwell from the reality he is creating around him. Ideology proves to be intoxicating and deadly so far as practical politics is concerned.

Cromwell's revolution is betrayed not through treachery or failure of nerve, but through unchecked delusions of self-righteousness. Whatever the public may think of him in the short term, Cromwell determines early on to "compel" England's love (100); he later remarks that it is the task of leaders to determine (that is, invent and impose) the "will of the people" (136). He initially promises not to harm the king (99), but moves by degrees to harsher and harsher actions that lead to Charles's patently illegal arrest (121) and execution (137). Cromwell's characteristic moral rectitude, which initially manifests itself in orders regarding the suppression of womanizing and the promotion of Bible study among the troops (99–100), turns into something more frightening when he orders the execution of an officer for stealing seven sheep to celebrate a victory (106–108). Cromwell the simple farmer begins to take on kingly airs, announcing that his "audience" with rival parliamentary leader Manchester is over (123), and his wife is drawn to the comfortable life of upper-class London (she ends up a drunk [144–145]). With the king dead and Cromwell firmly in control, the resources of the military are applied to maintaining power in the face of popular discontent: Cromwell launches a war against the Irish peasants solely to promote domestic solidarity, and lets the war double as an occasion for purging (and slaughtering) his erstwhile allies, the leftist-populist Levelers, a move he justifies by accusing them of conspiring with the Royalists (153–154) — an unlikely scenario. When such abuses provoke a real conspiracy, it leaders and troops are executed in the play's culminating atrocity (160–161).

Like Schlötel, Cromwell is a man of ideals who loses his sanity, or at least his moral standing, by succumbing to the seductions of ideological absolutism. Both characters embody a phenomenon that Hein will turn to again repeatedly: the reemergence of Don Quixote in modern garb, the divine fool who is *right* but who falls victim to a world of cynical opportunists. These latter figures, the pragmatic manipulators who seldom lose their grip on power, are never admirable. The fool-like Ladybird (the play's most overtly Shakespearean character) speaks for them after witnessing the murder of Lilburne (the leader of the Levelers), uttering cynical commonplaces reminiscent of things that were said about Schlötel:

> Wer beständig mit seinem Schädel gegen eine Betonmauer rennt, muß entweder Blind wie eine junge Ratte sein oder lebensmüde. Der Mann [Lilburne] war beides. (168)
>
> [Someone that constantly runs his head into a concrete wall must be blind as a young rat or else tired of living. This man (Lilburne) was both.]

This dismissive attitude, following the extremely pathetic demise of one of the play's more sympathetically drawn characters, clearly is meant ironically despite any approach it makes to the truth (and no one in a German audience would have failed to note the allusion to a concrete wall). The cynics have won, and the merchant Spidernach is able to predict with confidence that "progress" (that is, exploitation) will proceed unimpeded, thanks to Cromwell's upsetting of the old aristocratic order, his destruction of radical leftist elements, and his own timely departure: "Seine Revolution befreite uns gründlich von allen Wirrköpfen. Der Weg für einen geordneten Fortschritt liegt offen. Für die nächsten fünfhundert Jahre haben wir die Revolutionäre vom Hals" [His revolution freed us completely from all the nuts. The way for orderly progress now lies open. For the next 500 years we'll have the revolutionaries off our backs: 163].

Also premiering in 1980, along with *Cromwell*, was another experiment in a somewhat dated genre, *Lassalle fragt Herrn Herbert nach Sonja. Die Szene ein Salon.* Hein observes that his *Boulevardstück* "plays with the artistic forms of the nineteenth century and mistrusts them" ("Anmerkung zu *Lassalle*" 76), pointing to the dichotomy between the farcical mood of the play, with its stock, even stereotypical figures and action, and the implications of its subject matter for subsequent German history. In his notes to the play, Hein draws a seemingly farfetched parallel between himself (remembered as an 18-year-old, in Poland, observing the anniversary of the Warsaw Uprising) confronting for the first time the enormities of twentieth-century German history, and the figure of labor leader Ferdinand Lassalle in the previous century. Standing on either side of the Holocaust, each bears an obscure responsibility for it. Hein recalls himself searching for words to express his mixed sense of guilt and innocence, an exercise that reveals how his own selfhood is conceivable only as a historical phenomenon:

> As a German, in Poland, standing at the always-open grave of that Diaspora. A few phrases in the back of my head: Know thyself, learned in Greek study at the (still) humanist *Gymnasium*. The repeated refusal

to carry a cross that is not mine — and I yearn not to be guilty of this —, the slow dawning of the original entanglement, long before birth, without possibility of correction. Not to accept, but to assume a state of guilt as possibility for the future. The utopia of crime: What was, can no longer be. To grasp the relation of language to history: What I say, I am, but my language is a level of a level of a level.
("Anmerkung zu *Lassalle*" 77–78)

Hein's cryptic remarks are an attempt to position himself as a thinking German within twentieth century history — not as an outsider, but *within* it, potentially an agent of change. Lassalle, for his part, likewise struggled to bring about social change, though his ability to do so was constricted by limitations in his outlook and imagination, which were themselves conditioned by history. In his note on the play, Hein describes Lassalle as one

> naming a few endpoints after a great beginning, and too possessed by hope to survive its collapse; incapable of being satisfied with small steps forward — the only possibility in periods of restoration. The painful awareness of failure and the nonsensical, extraordinary gesture of linking his own "I" to the world. ("Anmerkung zu *Lassalle*" 79)

Two impossibilities mirror one another: the private individual's desire to affect world history at least as much as it affects him, and the public man's struggle to attain satisfaction in private life without damaging the effectiveness of his work. Hein's plays (and later his fiction) are filled with characters thus losing themselves between the Scylla of inaction or withdrawal and the Charybdis of wrongheaded, self-defeating activism.

Lassalle's relationship with the working class whose interests he supposedly champions is a study in idealism emptied by hypocrisy and self-indulgence. The setting of the play, a "salon" reeking of bourgeois social climbing, "as comfortable as it is banal" (8), marks Lassalle from the start as an outsider and *arriviste*, parading and exaggerating his newly-acquired social status by means of lavish spending (which is somewhat mysteriously funded by, of course, a woman friend). His quasi-aristocratic airs combine with condescension toward the workers (such as Vahlteich, his secretary) to create a figure whose absurdity is scarcely tempered by being mirrored in other, even more compromised labor "leaders" in the play. Lassalle's pederast friend von Schweitzer, for example, heaps scorn on Vahlteich (who has been uncharacteristically invited to a social event staged by Lassalle) for admiring a working-class novel he had written:

> Hörn Sie zu. Was sie da gelesen haben, das war Dreck, verstehen Sie, billigster Schund, abgeschmackt, banal, eben Dreck.... Das ist Agi-

tation, mein Lieber, und Agitation muß nur eins sein: erfolgreich. Etwas Rührung, Liebe, eine mittelmäßige Moral, gängige Poesie, eine seichte Tiefe, das erwärmt das Herz und belebt die dünne Fantasie der Leute. Dazu die Parteithesen, hübsch garniert, das ist alles. Um Himmels willen keine Kunst, das macht keinen Effekt. (54)

[Now listen. That thing you read is trash, do you understand? The cheapest junk, tasteless, banal, trash in a word . . . . That's agitation, my dear man, and agitation has only one purpose: to be successful. A little sentimentality, some love, a mediocre moral point, some serviceable poetry, a superficial profundity, that's what warms the heart and enlivens the feeble imagination of the people. Throw in the Party theses, nicely sugar-coated, and that's it. For heaven's sake, no art. That ruins the effect.]

This is Schweitzer's mode of addressing one of the workers successfully touched by his "agitation." Lassalle's own lifestyle, that of a luxury-loving, syphilitic libertine (20–21), is an insult to everything that actual workers have to suffer on a daily basis, as when he repeatedly misses a meeting with a delegation of Berlin workers, first because he sleeps until noon after a night of debauchery, and subsequently because of his intrigues surrounding another woman, the Sonja of the title (26–27). In his defense he makes remarks like: "Um fünf Uhr früh aufzustehen, das ist unmenschlich. Das macht das Vieh, aber kein Mann, der mit Verstand arbeitet" [To get up at five in the morning is inhuman. A cow might do that, but not a man with any sense: 19]. Similarly, when his brother-in-law asks, "Wem willst du mit Luxus imponieren? Deiner lächerlichen Arbeiterpartei? Weißt du, wie deine Plebejer leben?" [Whom are you trying to impress with all this luxury? Your ridiculous workers' party? Do you know how your plebeians live?], Lassalle answers, "Ja. Darum habe ich die Partei gegründet" [Yes. That's why I founded the party: 38]. No East German reader of Hein's play would fail to draw an analogy between such attitudes and the arrogance of the GDR leadership, which preached working class solidarity while sequestering itself in a heavily guarded compound, tooling about in chauffeured Volvos, and sparing itself no Western-made consumer delight. The degradation of a communist martyr like Erich Honecker, the roofer who spent more than a decade in Nazi jails for his beliefs yet ended up a petty tyrant making gifts of bananas at Christmas time to an unhappy citizenry, presents the most extreme case imaginable of perverted ideals and resurgent class distinctions.

Lassalle's Jewishness contributes to his status in the play as a person in history rather than a "historical figure." Just as the comic surface of the play is belied by the seriousness of the subject matter (the fateful grounding of a workers' party, and German paternalism, as represented by Bismarck, who hovers in the background of the play), so the function of Lassalle's Jewishness and of Jews in general appears at first glance to be comic, yet when viewed through the lens of the Holocaust, the stereotypes and bigotry of the play's nineteenth-century milieu create considerable audience discomfort, the more so for being offered as innocent raw material for comedy. Lassalle's discomfort with his class origins (his shaky position as a nouveau riche) overlaps with and even partakes of his society's rampant anti-Semitism. Hein is careful (and historically accurate) to maintain a distinction between how Lassalle's mother spells her name ("Lassal") and the Gallicized way he spells it. The mother, moreover, is a mindless, piety-spouting figure — a social liability, obviously — whom Lassalle keeps hidden from public view as much as possible. Her appearance on stage usually involves comic abuse from Herr Herbert, Lassalle's manservant, whose conduct Lassalle tolerates and even encourages. Lassalle's brother-in-law Friedland conforms closely to familiar Jewish stereotype: he is a comically Yiddish-speaking businessman obsessed with Lassalle's spending habits. He and Herbert collaborate in the last lines to cheat Lassalle's proper heirs and creditors out of as much money as possible.

Herbert is a figure of particular interest. He exemplifies, of course, the crafty servant of classical comedy — he typically makes acerbic observations on the action, such as to point out that Lassalle's workers' party lacks workers (11). More importantly, he stands for a rising, truculent proletariat that embraces authoritarianism as a model for social relations. The authorities themselves will ultimately discover a political tool in the anti-Semitism manifested in his treatment of Frau Lassal and in his remarks after Lassalle's death: "Meine Freunde hatten mich gewarnt, das bringt nichts ein bei so nem neureichen Juden. Nun sitz ich im Schlamassel" [My friends warned me that working for a nouveau riche Jew would be a dead end. Now I'm screwed: 66]. Thus far, Herbert and his "friends" have been content to follow whatever leader they thought would benefit them most, whether a Bismarck (Herbert's previous employer) or a Lassalle. But with these words blaming the Jew Lassalle for his troubles barely out of his mouth, Herbert imagines a different solution:

> Wissen Sie, Vahlteich, ich habe schon manches Mal gedacht, ich sollte vielleicht auch ne Partei gründen. Lächeln sie ruhig. Ich hab so ein paar Ideen. — Na, es mag zu früh sein, darüber zu sprechen. Jedenfalls meine ich, unsereins sollte auch mal auf den Putz haun, wir müssen nicht immer die Dummen sein. (66)

[You know, Vahlteich, I've thought now and then that I should start up a party myself. Go ahead and smile. I have some ideas. — Well, it may be too early to talk about them. Anyway, I think that someday our type ought to take a crack at cleaning things up, we don't always have to play dumb.]

Coming from an arrogant, ambitious, anti-Semitic bully, this promise of a new political party obviously evokes National Socialism. Vahlteich and Herbert, as the play's two representatives of the working class, thus represent two possible political directions for it: Vahlteich is the proto-socialist, Herbert the proto-Nazi. Unfortunately for European history, Vahlteich is naive and idealistic where Herbert is crafty and unscrupulous. The position of Lassalle respecting this dualism is doubly odd. He has nothing but impatience and contempt for his honest, uncouth, and ignorant secretary, yet a sort of admiration for Herbert's boldness and emulation of the aristocracy (not to mention for his former intimacy, so to speak, with the arch-aristocrat Bismarck). This is because Lassalle, too, like Herbert, is a social climber, not a genuine member of the working class and not even a sincere defender of the workers' viewpoint, and scarcely could he be: he is an intellectual, perfectly aware of how much more cultivated he is than the average uneducated worker. At home in no class and self-deceived about his relation both to the power structure and to the powerless, Lassalle embodies the plight of the intellectual in every period, and his despair near the end of the play (62–63), though trivialized as the result of failure in love according to the play's dominant conventions, is that of the intellectual discovering his simultaneous distance from and guilt for reality.

The pinnacle of Hein's theatrical achievement to date may have been reached with the 1983 play *Die wahre Geschichte des Ah Q*, which received a brilliantly funny staging under the artistic director of the Deutsches Theater, Alexander Lang, creating a sensation in East Berlin and probably hastening Lang's departure for the West. The play openly challenged every socialist piety about revolution, progressive political thought, the working class, the leadership role of the Party, and the role of intellectuals — all of this displaced, of course, far from the GDR or from any other socialist country. Set in China at the time of the Revolution of 1911–12, the play depicts a political transformation in name only, with the preexisting oppressive power structure remaining largely intact. The play's most cynical observations have to do with the pretensions of intellectuals who think they are laying the groundwork for revolution, but who have no more influence on the actual revolutionaries than they had on the *ancien régime*. It should be recalled that at the same moment Hein was writing *Ah Q*, he was putting into practice his dictum about the East German stage being a great encouragement to fiction-writing. The play, then, represents a culminating moment in Hein's career, completing the critique of revolutionary ideology that dominated the earlier plays, and drawing the conclusions implicit in the critique: that no revolutionary can long guide the revolution, that reason never escapes its historical entanglements, that individuals are the playthings of historical disaster. And it discovers a new theme: the attractiveness of anarchy as the antithesis of the "administered world" (to borrow Adorno's term) of totalitarianism, and the concomitant sterility of the anarchist position, a position outside of society and thus incapable of influencing its course.[8] And it announces in relatively unambiguous terms Hein's artistic credo: "Ich habe keine Botschaft für sie.... Sie sollen sich selber was denken" [I have no message for them.... They should think of something themselves: 107].

The play is first and foremost a satire on intellectuals and revolutionaries who fancy themselves the engines of social change, when they are at best impotent fools, or at worst self-absorbed, anti-social parasites. Thus, in a sense, the play is about the ordinary tendency of people to imagine themselves better, and better off, than they really are. Progressive politics and the study of political philosophy merely serve to cloak the drunkenness of Wang, the humbug intellectual, while enthusiasm for "anarchy" substitutes for an ordered, meaningful life for Ah Q, the petty criminal. The homeless pair are being given shelter in a temple, supposedly in return for maintaining it, but they do nothing as snow falls through a hole in the roof. When the temple watchman reminds him of his duties, Wang, who is simply lazy, dresses up his behavior as an ideologically sophisticated resistance to exploitation:

> Ich werde ein Kirchendach ausbessern. Für wen hältst du mich? Bin ich ein Pfaffenknecht? Soll doch dein Priester auf die Leiter, soll er sich den Hals brechen.... Von der Erde werden wir euch fegen. Ertränken im heiligen Blut der Revolution. (88)
>
> [Me repair a church roof. What do you take me for? Am I some kind of clerical lackey? Let your priest go up a ladder and break his neck.... We will sweep all of you off the face of the earth. Drown you in the revolution's holy blood.][9]

Ah Q's foray into political thought involves an idiotic attraction to the word "anarchy," which he hears Wang hurl at the temple watchman. When they are alone again, Ah Q expresses his admiration for Wang's rhetorical flourish:

AH Q	Ein schönes Wort. Scharf und kräftig. Und es klingt. Anarchie. Was meinst du damit?
WANG	Mit Anarchie?
AH Q	Ja.
WANG	Das heißt, daß ich gegen alles bin. Gegen alles, verstehst du? Ein Anarchist ist gegen alles.
AH Q	Sind wir Anarchisten?
WANG	Wir haben keine andere Wahl.
AH Q	Wie schön. — Ich bin gern Anarchist. Ich habe soviel Haß in mir. Gegen alles. — Es lebe die Anarchie. (90)
[AH Q	A beautiful word. Sharp and powerful. And it has a nice ring to it. Anarchy. What do you mean by it?
WANG	By anarchy?
AH Q	Yes.
WANG	It means that I am against everything. Against everything, do you see? An anarchist is against everything.
AH Q	Are we anarchists?
WANG	We have no other choice.
AH Q	How beautiful. — I like being an anarchist. I have so much hate in me. Against everything. — Long live anarchy!]

Hein takes care not simply to cast Wang and Ah Q as wholly unsympathetic characters by juxtaposing them with the temple watchman, whose excruciating fatuousness contrasts unfavorably with their sarcasm and occasional slyness, and with Mask, the policeman, an unquestioning servant of power. As a champion of law and order in the best German tradition, Mask explains how easily people adjust to new regimes and new forms of legal violence (117). And even Mask is not to be dismissed altogether — he earns some sympathy by being the most traumatized person in the play, his face disfigured by the master he serves (118). In a police state even the police are victims.

All in all, the audience thus finds itself in the position of having more in common with Wang and Ah Q than with the nominally respectable characters, and appropriately so: the audience members, too, know how to play the hypocrite and put the best face on their compromises with authority. Yet sympathy between audience and characters, especially a sympathy founded on shared hypocrisy, is not what the play aims at. Instead, in the best tradition of the epic theater, Hein wants his audience to reflect on its situation.[10] In the two most startling scenes in the play, stage illusion is violated as Ah Q and Wang offer unflattering appraisals of the audience itself (taking the Brechtian, not to mention Shakespearean, technique of directly addressing the audience a surprising step further). The first example contains Ah Q's much-quoted attempt to find an earth-shaking "message" to give to the audience, and a meaning for his own life:

AH Q	Ich möchte ihnen etwas sagen. Ein überwältigendes Gefühl mitteilen. Einen Satz, der alles sagt. — Fast alles.
WANG	Gib nicht auf.
AH Q	Wie ein Schrei. Wie eine Naturkatastrophe. *Geht an die Bühnenrampe*: Menschen, oh Menschen — *Geht zurück*. Ich habe keine Botschaft für sie.
WANG	Es war ein guter Anfang.
AH Q	Ich wollte ihnen etwas über den Tod sagen. Über das Leben. Aber was?
WANG	Der Ansatz war nicht schlecht.
AH Q	Es ist doch schon alles gesagt.
WANG	Sie sollen sich selber was denken. Muß man ihnen alles vorkauen. — Es war ein ausgezeichneter Anfang. (106–107)
[AH Q	I want to tell them something, to share an overwhelming feeling. One sentence that says everything. — Almost everything.
WANG	Don't stop now.
AH Q	Like a shriek. Like a natural catastrophe. *Goes downstage*. People! Oh, people! *Goes back*. I have no message for them.
WANG	You made a good start.
AH Q	I wanted to tell them something about death, about life. But what?
WANG	The beginning wasn't bad.
AH Q	It's all been said already.
WANG	They should think of something themselves. Do they always have to be spoon fed? — It was an outstanding start.]

Despite the jarring shifts of register between Wang's laconic banality and Ah Q's histrionic posturing, this passage promising no message succeeds in making Hein's message quite clear: fools though the characters on stage may be, the biggest fools are those sitting in the audience waiting for enlightenment to shower down on them. Hein borrows a move from Baudelaire's "Au lecteur" by enticing an audience to think itself superior, and then springing on it its share in corruption.

The same counter-realistic gesture recurs toward the end of the play, when Ah Q and Wang have woken up clueless in a putatively post-revolutionary world. The pair attempts hilariously to rationalize their evident irrelevance and to figure out their next move, when suddenly the audience is again implicated in the same sort of self-serving obliviousness to their own venality:

WANG   Wen interessiert schon ein Blick ins Getriebe der Welt.
AH Q   Wen interessierts nicht?
WANG   Alle. Sie habens ohnehin schwer genug.
AH Q   Jeder hat sein Kreuz.
WANG   Sieh dir ihre Gesichter an. Es interessiert sie nicht.
AH Q   Warum nicht? Es ist ihr Leben. Wir spielen schließlich Szenen aus der Welt der Angestellten. Das sollte sie interessieren.
WANG   Sind das Angestellte?
AH Q   Schau sie dir an.
WANG   Alle?
AH Q   Alle. Irgendwie.   (126–127)

[WANG   Who really wants a glimpse into the world's machinery, anyway.
AH Q   Who doesn't?
WANG   Everyone. They have it hard enough already.
AH Q   Everyone has a cross to bear.
WANG   Just look at their faces. They aren't interested.
AH Q   Why aren't they? It's their life. The fact is that we are portraying scene from the world of employees. That ought to interest them.
WANG   Are those employees?
AH Q   Just look at them.
WANG   All of them?
AH Q   All of them. One way or another.]

Ah Q proceeds to list the accouterments of employees: a key to the men's room, a set of rubber stamps, a pension, a female colleague, a potted plant, a card file, a personalized coffee cup, an office illness, a hand in the till, and so on. This passage shares with the previous one a comic aesthetic of banality that approximates in dramatic form, though with very different emotional force, the flatness of Hein's typical narrative voice, which similarly confines itself to the quotidian. The scene attains a peak of absurdity as Ah Q describes himself as an "employee" (126) — a word which, no matter how reified here, can scarcely be applied to either main character. The resemblance of this scene to the earlier one lies in its brief but disconcerting violation of the play's otherwise prevailing stage conventions as a means of chastising the audience for its complacency. As "employees," the members of the audience care only about their own job security, their professional advancement, the perquisites of rank, incidental opportunities for self-enrichment, and so on — all cast in the most contemptuous light possible by being associated with random office bric-a-brac worthy of Bouvard and Pecuchet. Busy feathering their nests, the "employees" — that is, everyone in society *except* the socially marginal Wang and Ah Q — pay no attention to politics or other manifestations of historicity, except those (such as revolution) directly affecting their personal lives. Even then, as Mask had foreseen, quick and advantageous collaboration would be their goal. Only social parasites like Wang and Ah Q are in a position to view the normal world of workers and bureaucrats with such sovereign disdain, yet the premise of the whole passage is that they, too, are hoping for a niche in the system. Turning this around, the "employees" of the audience can be seen now merely as more successful parasites than Wang and Ah Q, and perhaps, in a special sense of the term, as more perfect anarchists, since they have actually succeeded in pursuing self-interest while being against "everything." The meaning of "anarchist" has likewise undergone a reversal, so that instead of meaning a radically autonomous individual outside of society, its epitome now is the orderly, convention-bound clerk, an entirely subordinate and alienated atom struggling against every other atom in a delusive quest for "advancement." This latter sense of "anarchy" reappears in *Der fremde Freund* where it designates a major consequence of modern social organization, especially that of Germany, whether East, West, or Nazi.[11] It is no accident that Ah Q's mouthing of clichés in the name of anarchy includes a motto that once greeted concentration camp prisoners: "Jedem das Seine, wie die Philosophen sagen" [To each his own, in the words of the philosophers: 113]. The ultimate expression of this darker (and much more familiar) version of anarchy is barbarism.

As the pseudo-revolution unfolds, the concluding scenes of the play reinforce the criticisms implicit in the self-reflexive moments of audience-bashing: nothing changes, people adapt, life goes on, misery remains. Revolution, as in the case of *Cromwell*, changes the dramatis personae (and maybe not even them) without necessarily changing the system. This time, the revolution takes place while Ah Q, Wang, and Mask are getting drunk in celebration of Ah Q's return from the city with the fruits of his thievery. Wang is chagrined the next morning to find that the revolution, or some revolution, has taken place without anybody bothering to consult *him*, the resident revolutionary ideologist. He expresses skepticism about any revolutionary Party to which he hasn't been invited: "Wer kennt sie schon, diese Revolutionspartei. Sind es wahrhafte Revolutionäre, Anarchisten wie wir? Oder sind es Opportunisten?" [What does anybody know about this revolutionary party? Are they real revolutionaries, like us? Or are they opportunists?: 124]. The temple guard insists that he has it directly from His Lordship, the local ruler, that the revolution was genuine. Wang remarks with contempt:

> WANG Hör dir das an. Es ist Revolution, aber für diesen Kleinbürger ändert sich nichts. Macht seinen Bückling vor dem Herrn. Es gibt keinen gnädigen Herrn mehr.
> TEMPELWACHTER Ich weiß. Er heißt jetzt revolutionärer Herr.
> WANG Wer?
> TEMPELWACHTER Der gnädige Herr. (124–125)

> [WANG Just listen to that. A revolution takes place, but nothing changes for these petty bourgeois. Still bowing before His Lordship. His Lordship doesn't exist anymore.
> TEMPLE GUARD I know. Now he's called His Revolutionary Lordship.
> WANG Who?
> TEMPLE GUARD His Lordship.]

And in post-1989 East Germany, presumably, His Revolutionary Lordship became His Capitalist Lordship with similarly little fuss. In Hein's world, the intellectuals are self-important outsiders with plenty of ready analysis, but no impact on society, while the common people, represented by the temple guard, passively endure every change in the political weather. The ideology of the regime changes, but the underlying power relations remain constant: Wang is exasperated by everyone else's unreflective, matter-of-fact references to the "revolution" that has occurred, as the people take their cues, as before, from the powers that be. The major problem with Wang's ideology is that it has no rational connection with political and social reality.

This play's absurdist (anarchic?) resolution is capped by Ah Q's arrest and execution for minor crimes he did not commit — this not long after he rapes and kills a nun, for which he goes unpunished — and by the ludicrous maunderings of the temple guard, who represents the stupid conventionality of the common folk. Hein puts a lapidary summation of the play's political message into the mouths of his principle characters as Ah Q is being led away:

WANG	Halt dich tapfer, Ah Q. Denke daran, wir sind das Salz der Erde. Wir sind Verdammte, ohne Gefühl, ohne Eigentum, ohne Namen. Die Anarchisten kennen nur ein Gesetz, nur eine Leidenschaft, nur einen Gedanken: die Zerstörung.
MASKE	Und die Gesetze?
WANG	Gesetze sind Gewalt.
MASKE	Natürlich, Gewalt muß sein. Das Volk gehorcht nicht.
WANG	Auch Gesetze sind Anarchie. Alles Anarchie, mit Gesetz oder ohne. Alles Gewalt. Der Unterschied ist, wir sind ehrlicher, betrügen das Volk nicht.
AH Q	Es lebe die Anarchie. Nicht wahr, Krätzebart?
WANG	Sie wird leben, Ah Q. (132–133)

[WANG	Be brave, Ah Q. Remember that we are the salt of the earth. We are the damned, without feelings, without possessions, without a name. Anarchists know only one law, one passion, one thought: destruction.
MASK	And what about the laws?
WANG	Laws are violence.
MASK	Of course, there has to be violence. Otherwise the people won't obey.
WANG	Laws are anarchy, too. Everything is anarchy, with the law or without it. Everything is violence. The difference is that we are more honest, we don't deceive the people.
AH Q	Long live anarchy. Right, Scratchbeard?
WANG	It will live, Ah Q.]

One hears resonances of Jesus and Frantz Fanon in this deconstruction of reason as a disguised form or outgrowth of coercion, an anti-Enlightenment theme famously prominent in the plays of Heiner Müller.[12] Hein also employs the violence at the heart of the civilized order (law, social relations, intimate relations) as the organizing principle of *Der fremde Freund*, where covert and overt violence distorts the personality of a "normal" East German citizen. (That book's central image is a Soviet occupation tank preserving a social order that, in 1989, would disintegrate once the threat of Soviet arms vanished.) In *Ah Q*, however, these ideas are couched more ironically, coming from the mouth of a charlatan intellectual, while the "salt of the earth" (shorn of revolutionary romanticism) seems best represented by the temple guard in his lines that conclude the play:

Welcher Teufel hat mir gesagt, die zwei Galgenvögel aufzunehmen. Das Dach wollten sie reparieren. Und was haben die angestellt. Unsere kleine Nonne umgebracht. Heilige Jungfrau, bitt für uns, jetzt und in der Stunde meines Todes. Die Hinrichtungen waren früher prächtiger. Nicht einmal dafür hat man heute Zeit. (135)

[What devil told me to take in those two jail birds? They were supposed to fix the roof, and look what they did. Killed our little nun. Holy Virgin, pray for us now and in the hour of my death. Executions used to be more festive. Now people don't even have time for that.]

The temple guard's last complaint parodies the standard Romantic/modernist dissatisfaction with the pace of modern life and is intended primarily to be funny. Yet the gesture of giving the play's preeminent conformist/petty bourgeois/anti-intellectual the last word reproduces in a subtle way the gestures at the end of each of the earlier plays *Schlötel, Lasalle,* and *Cromwell*: after a brief period of disruption, business goes on as usual — extraordinary individuals come to ruinous ends, the common people keep their heads down, and the holders of economic and political power proceed with their projects as though nothing had happened. The social satire of all these early plays yields a rather bleak picture of humanity in the grip of ideology and economic exploitation. Yet in the culminating play of this series, and in the fiction that begins to appear after 1980, this mode of almost desperate satire begins to yield before the cool detachment of what Hein chooses to term "chronicling." In *Ah Q* more than in any previous play, Hein seeks to position himself equidistantly from all of the characters, and to allow each to present a whole, if deluded, worldview. In the fiction, freed from the imperative of dramatic plot development, Hein depicts individuals who have accommodated themselves at horrible cost, though sometimes with extraordinary bravery, to the realities they confront. Their adjustments to reality occur at a pace and with an open-endedness more suited to the uncertainty of lives caught up in historical catastrophes of the twentieth century, and infinitely more expressive of the tragic dimension of those lives, than had been possible before. The plays of the seventies and early eighties require heroes, however flawed, while the fiction and plays that followed require only human beings. Hein's project, transformed but by no means new (in fact, hearkening back to his roots in the Socialist Realist tradition), will be to define what "being human" can possibly mean in the modern age.

Notes

[1] For an introduction to and overview of the so-called *Kritiker-* or *Literaturstreit*, see Katrin Sieg's article "The Poets and the Power: Heiner Müller, Christa Wolf and the German *Literaturstreit*." For a retrospective assessment of its early Christa Wolf phase, see Karl Deiritz and Hannes Krauss (eds.), *Der deutsch-deutsche Literaturstreit oder "Freunde, es spricht sich schlecht mit gebundener Zunge*. See also Gertrude Postl, "The Silencing of a Voice: Christa Wolf, Cassandra, and the German Unification"; Thomas Anz (ed.), *"Es geht nicht um Christa Wolf": Der Literaturstreit im vereinten Deutschland*; and David Bathrick, *The Powers of Speech: The Politics of Culture in the GDR*.

[2] Challenges to the Socialist Realist concept of the positive role model (*Vorbild*) in fiction and other genres gained influence in the early to mid-1960s when sanctioned authors such as Christa Wolf, Erwin Strittmatter, and Hermann Kant, along with banned authors such as Uwe Johnson, began experimenting with failed or otherwise deeply problematic heroes in their novels. After a period of sharp resistance from conservative Stalinist critics, this looser definition of the requisite New Socialist Man, and the significance of his failure in some cases, became the new orthodoxy among academics, if not among cultural functionaries. See Haase, *Literatur der DDR*, 495–501, for the official account of the early-1960s period when a characteristic socialist national literature arose that had as its special interest the representation of "creative socialist personalities" (495). Even more radical reassessments of Socialist Realist principles followed in the wake of Ulrich Plenzdorf's socially critical 1973 novel *Die neuen Leiden des jungen W.* [*The New Sorrows of Young W.*] and its stage version, filling the pages of academic journals like *Weimarer Beiträge* for month after month. After the 1970s the term and the dogma largely fell out of use without ever being replaced by another comprehensive literary theory.

[3] This approach to art, giving free rein to utopian aspirations while criticizing the current reality for its relative backwardness, turned out to be a two-edged sword. Hein and most other critical and dissident writers of the GDR had great success taking the GDR to task for its failure to live up to its own ideals. Such overtly critical writing could thus with some justice be termed Socialist Realist, despite the anti-governmental slant, and such a designation would have the virtue of emphasizing the heightened political engagement (not to mention the wholly foreign cultural-political background) that still distinguishes writers from the East from many of their Western counterparts.

[4] See, for example, the definition of "Konflikt" in the *Wörterbuch der marxistischen-leninistischen Philosophie* 294.

[5] For a full-scale dystopian exploration of the breakup of the extended family and the GDR's treatment of the aged, see Günter de Bruyn's 1984 novel *Neue Herrlichkeit* [New Glory].

[6] Hein's other early- and middle-period plays include *Vom hungrigen Hennecke* [Hungry Hennecke] (1974), "a short piece written in a variety of verse forms for children's theater . . . that ironically treats the heroization of the legendary GDR coal miner Adolf Hennecke" (McKnight 136), *Die Geschäfte des Herrn John D.* [The Business Deals of Mr. John D.] (1979), "a satirical variety show about Rockefeller's unscrupulous monopolization of the oil industry" (McKnight 140), and *Der neue Menoza oder Geschichte des kumbanischen Prinzen Tandi: Komödie nach Jakob Michael Reinhold Lenz* [The New Menoza, or The Story of the Kumbanian Prince Tandi. A Comedy based on Jakob Michael Reinhold Lenz] (1982), which subjects the *Sturm-und-Drang* critique of Enlightenment Europe to a Brechtian historical concretization (Roßmann 12). Hein also undertook translations for the Volksbühne, most notably of Racine's *Britannicus*.

[7] The high-water mark for the *Produktionsstück* was Heiner Müller's 1957 play *Der Lohndrücker* [The Wage Shark], which depicts the kind of workplace struggles, situated against a fascist past and socialist present, that were the background to the Berlin workers' uprising of 17 June 1953. Provoked by an increase in the mandated "production norms," this genuine workers' revolt nearly toppled the government before being put down with the help of Soviet tanks.

[8] Hein regards his contemporaneous novelistic treatment of social and personal alienation, *Der fremde Freund*, as a companion piece to this play about ineffectual anarchists. The novella's narrator, Claudia, is a more banal and hence more disturbing case of social withdrawal and paralysis than the comic, Beckett-like figures of the play. In the interview accompanying the original publication of the play in *Theater der Zeit*, Hein acknowledges that most readers fail to see a connection, but insists that it is there: the play is a loose, ambiguous treatment of themes presented more rigorously and unambiguously in *Der fremde Freund*. Of special importance is rape: both works contain rape scenes, and in both cases rape serves as a metaphor of a broader exploitation endured by all the characters, including the rapists. In *Ah Q*, "all five characters have been raped in some sense," including Mask, the mutilated and brutal policeman, "who wishes to do nothing more than perform his duties well. Perhaps he is the most violated of all; in any case, his is the grimmest outcome" ("Ansonsten" 56). Hein characteristically emphasizes the common nature of external and internal violence, and of victims and victimizers. See also the interview "Mut ist keine literarische Kategorie."

[9] The translations from *Ah Q* are my own, but I have consulted Anthony Meech's unpublished rendering of the play into English as *The True Story of Ah Q*.

[10] Hein harbored similar intentions for the readers of *Der fremde Freund*. The reader is forced to deal with the question of how to be happy and fulfilled in modern society, and Hein's emphasis is on the individual's struggle to find an answer: "I believe . . . that the pressure to ask oneself this question is really what makes the whole book. That the reader is very strongly compelled to answer this question of possibility, or in any case not to evade it" ("Ich kann mein Publikum nicht belehren" 70).

[11] See *DFF* 100–101 / *TDL* 85–86 for Claudia's description of the wedding picture anarchists.

[12] For example, see Müller's *Der Auftrag* and *Leben Gundlings Friedrich von Preußen Lessings Schlaf Traum Schrei* for direct assaults on Enlightenment values and intellectual achievements.

2: Individuals in the Slough of History: Hein's Early Short Stories and *Passage*

The Task of the Chronicler

AS THE 1970S DREW TO A CLOSE, THE CHILLY political climate in the GDR led to Hein's departure from the Volksbühne for a freelance career, first as a playwright, then increasingly as a fiction writer. In 1980, Hein's work became available to the East German reading public through a collection of short fiction entitled *Einladung zum Lever Bourgeois*. (The book, minus one story and differently arranged, appeared in West Germany under the title *Nachtfahrt und früher Morgen* in 1982.)[1] These early stories map out directions that Hein would pursue in the middle phase of his career, exemplifying in particular the procedure and attitude he calls "chronicling."[2]

The stories, especially the brief sketches Hein groups under the title "Aus: Ein Album Berliner Stadtansichten," depart from Hein's earlier dramatic device of portraying heroic figures as human beings trapped by historical forces, focusing instead on *ordinary* people in those same overwhelming circumstances. Except for the relatively long frame stories "Einladung zum Lever Bourgeois" (Invitation to the Lever Bourgeois) and "Die russischen Briefe des Jägers Johann Seifert" (The Russian Letters of the Huntsman Johann Seifert), which are set respectively in seventeenth-century France and nineteenth-century Russia, all of the stories depict individuals living through the past hundred years of German history, a nightmare culminating in the Nazi Holocaust, but reaching well back into European history and forward into the German experiment with socialism. Through detached, almost clinical accounts of entirely plausible (but often horrifying) events, the stories explore possibilities for villainy, resignation, resourcefulness, and heroism of people facing inexorable forces of political repression, poverty, bigotry, war, and private betrayal. In a century that provided ample incentives for beastly behavior, Hein preserves a belief in the efficacy of free will. The razor's-edge balance between powerlessness and self-determination was Hein's *own* as a critical writer in the GDR, and he continually forces his primarily German readership to face its moral culpability and potential. Out of such explorations came not only the longer fiction of the mid-1980s, but also, after a prolonged dramatic hiatus, the late-eighties play *Passage*, which will be discussed in this chapter as a particularly clear summation of — and prescription for — the predicament illustrated by Hein's early snapshots of German history. *Passage* marks the point at which Hein reintegrates his dramatic work, which emphasizes extraordinary situations and heroic (or ignoble) actions, with the more pedestrian themes of human endurance and responsibility that repeatedly manifest themselves in the stories of social chronicling.

Hein's assumption of the title "chronicler" has a concrete basis in East German political experience. Like Heiner Müller and many other writers once forced to adjust themselves to a Socialist Realist cultural policy, Hein refuses to play the role of didact in his fiction, at least in the sense of someone claiming to have final answers to major questions. Hein notes that the narrow precepts of Party-line criticism rest upon a patronizing attitude toward the public and end by compelling the writer to feign superior knowledge that he does not possess:

> What the [East German] critics demand is always solely a moral stance; the writer is supposed to be a moral authority. I reject that, because behind this role as moral authority, which it might be possible for a writer to play, lurks the role of the prophet. That was a role for writers in the nineteenth century, when the author was thought of as a great, wise figure who was able to tell the people which way it needed to go. I am more modest than that, I think. I am not smarter than my public, I can't show them the way. I am as clueless as my public. All I can do is say something about the way we have come. About the future path I can say nothing. I would regard that as much too arrogant. To be a moral authority would cast me in the role of prophet. That is why I prefer to enlighten, let us say — to provide unambiguous and precise analysis of the actual. I think that the analysis of the actual can itself be explosive enough to reveal a future path. If I am able to contemplate my present situation mercilessly, with distance, free of pity, free of passion or prejudice [*ohne Haß und Eifer*], then I think that this provides a chance to find a future path.
>
>   ("Wir werden es lernen müssen," 52)

Needless to say, the prophetic stance is not merely a nineteenth-century phenomenon; the most important object of Hein's criticism is the prophetic afflatus of Marx, Lenin, Stalin, and their literary executors. The chronicler, by contrast, renounces all passion and prejudice, that is, insofar as narrative technique is concerned, for it would be absurd to claim that Hein or any other author lacks moral, philosophical or political views, least of all in the politically supersaturated East Bloc. Hein himself admits to a kind of moralistic intention:

> In a certain sense I am a moralist: not aiming necessarily at changing things, but perhaps at provoking thought so vigorously that people will simply not be able to go on as before. I have no formulas for how people ought to live. (Hein, "Gespräch," 122–123)

Hein's objection to playing the "moral authority" is ultimately a challenge to state authority, which so often dons the mask of morality to further its aims. The dilemma for any politically engaged East German writer was to embody artistically the social contradictions of the day without resorting to authoritarian means of persuasion, such as stereotyping, moral hectoring, and the concealment of contradiction or ambiguity.[3] The chronicler, on the other hand, cultivates *Gelassenheit* — composure, calm — in the face of even the most painful facts:

> This is the composure, I believe, with which writers like Kleist or Hebel point out the most monstrous things without hysteria: Here is the how the world is, we have to recognize it, we can't evade it, if we are to develop tools, a vocabulary, that enables us to live in it. Because literature is in part an aid to living. It can move an individual to comprehend experiences, to process his own experiences with a little more knowledge, to make them more productive. In this connection, the quiet, worldly-wise stance of Kleist, Hebel, Kafka, Garcia Marquez, or Borges is simply very agreeable to me. ("Gespräch," 126)

The divergent reactions among East German critics to Hein's short stories illustrate what was really at stake in his use of a detached, anti-ideological stance. On the negative side, Marianne Krumrey argued that in "Die russischen Briefe" Hein errs in being too ironic, and should reflect reality directly; that he deals ahistorically with historical materials; that he is an essentialist trafficking in eternal configurations like *Geist* (intellect) and *Macht* (power), revealing a non-Marxist belief in a transhistorical human nature; and that he implies that people are only objects, never agents, of history. Krumrey condemned Hein's subtlety and allusiveness as a "crippled form of communication" compared to what socialist culture has made possible (145–146). On the positive side, Frank Hörnigk insisted on the need to respect Hein's narrative gesture of detached objectivity instead of rendering a quick judgment; otherwise Hein's "Nachricht" [message] is lost ("Christoph Hein" 110). This message is what some found difficult to swallow. What really bothered Krumrey and other critics is precisely Hein's success at historicizing and de-reifying the GDR, in effect deconstructing the central assumption of East German ideology: that communism was the unambiguous victor of history. Hein had committed the mortal sin of seeing continuities between the GDR and the old Germany.

When Hein listed his literary mentors in 1982, the stories had already demonstrated signs of influence by at least some of them; here were prose fiction models equivalent to the Socialist Realist, Shakespearean, and Brechtian models informing the plays, sharing, as Hein reads them, precision of description coupled with cool detachment from the human realities being described. Kleist and Hebel in particular provide examples of "chronicling" that find their more or less precise counterparts in the early stories.[4] Kleist is specifically alluded to in the title of one story, "Der neuere (glücklichere) Kohlhaas" (The newer [luckier/happier] Kohlhaas), which actually imitates the distinctive idiom of Kleist's novellas, and many others have a novella-like character. Most importantly, Hein is attracted to the narrative stance and tone of Kleist's great novellas — their terrifying detachment from the horrendous events that they depict, and the flat, uninflected style that puts banalities and atrocities on the same level of readerly experience. In Kleist's short anecdotes and, even more, in the *Kalendergeschichten* of Johann Peter Hebel, Hein found models of narrative economy, precision, colloquial simplicity, and humor. *Einladung*'s "Berliner Stadtansichten" are fairly close imitations of Hebel's brief and suggestive sketches, but infused with a historical sense that is entirely modern. The other authors mentioned — Kafka, Borges, Garcia Marquez — seem, as practitioners of what might broadly be called surrealism and its postmodern variants, quite distant from Hein's fascination with the real, the political, the historical, even the mundane, but in no case (except in some of his more recent work) the fantastic. Here again, as with Kleist, considerations of content or genre are less important to Hein's work than the narrative and stylistic trick of describing the bizarre as though it were the most ordinary thing in the world. Hein differs from these writers principally in his choice of sources for the bizarre: everyday lives led by average people in the familiar, waking, working, modern world — in all its brutality. In his fiction, Hein regards his sole duty to be the articulation of the empirically real, or at least the representative, especially where ideological fantasy usually obscures the truth. Engaged in this project of chronicling, the writer may touch on politics or morality, but not by any other route than fictionalized concreteness. Otherwise one fails either to describe *or* convince.

Einladung zum Lever Bourgeois:
Plan and Frame

Hein organizes the highly disparate voices and stances of the narrative experiments in the volume *Einladung* by arranging them in approximately chronological order, at least in the original version, where the title story "Einladung zum Lever Bourgeois" appears first.[5] The story (discussed at length below in chapter 4) is a fictitious monologue by Jean Baptiste Racine, the French dramatist and court historian, whose accommodations with political reality (such as averting his chronicling gaze from atrocities committed in the name of the king he serves) have secured his place at court, but left him wracked with self-loathing.[6] The figure of the dramatist and failed chronicler is no doubt an ironic, cautionary mask for Hein himself.[7] The book thus opens with the complex theme of the historian's moral responsibility to report what he sees, and historiography as a discipline is established as a prime resource for those wishing to resist arbitrary power. Historiography exposes the intellectual's relation to the state, so that Racine's experiences and reflections touch on the nature of the discipline, the impact of history and politics on the individual, the pressure to accommodate oneself to the powers that be, the possibility or impossibility of individual action or choice, and the potential of historiography as ideological critique. "Einladung," together with the final story of the collection, "Die russischen Briefe," frames the other narratives and helps to situate the book with respect to the historical circumstances of Hein's writing.

"Die russischen Briefe" reprises most of the themes addressed in "Einladung," but now from the perspective of an uneducated man, Johann Seifert, a servant of the German sage Alexander von Humboldt. Perhaps in a nod to Goethe, Hein copies the procedure used in constructing "Die Leiden des jungen Werther": he fabricates a set of letters and assembles them into an epistolary novel, then fabricates an editor to explain the origin of the letters and their significance. Unlike Goethe, Hein identifies himself ("C.H.") as the editor/historian of the fictitious letters, yielding a symmetry between himself and that other historian and playwright, Racine, whose narrative concludes the volume. The humorous editorial preface leaves little doubt that the difficulties encountered in Russia by Seifert and Humboldt, and the subsequent fate of these letters addressed to Seifert's wife, constitute a thinly veiled allegory of the East German struggle between intellect and power, in accordance with Hein's dictum that our interest in the past always means interest in ourselves. According to C.H., Seifert's letters (precious historical documents shedding light on Humboldt's travels) had been preserved through the fortuitous intervention of a chain of secret police organizations:

> Auf der Rückseite des jeweils letzten Bogens finden sich der vollständige Name des Schreibers und sein Aufenthaltsort sowie der Name der Adressatin und ihre Berliner Adresse. Neben den amtlichen Poststempeln tragen sämtliche Bogen die Stempel der Petersburger Geheimpolizei sowie verschiedene Dienstsiegel Preußens und des Deutschen Reiches. Nach den Aufdrucken zu schließen, müssen die Seifertschen Briefe in Rußland abgefangen und drei Jahre später von der Petersburger Geheimpolizei an ihre preußischen Kollegen übergeben worden sein. Für die Annahme, daß Ludmilla bzw. Mila Seifert die Briefe ihres Gatten je zu Gesicht bekam, gibt es keinen Anlaß.
> (*NUFM* 9)

> On the back of each final sheet can be found the full name of the writer and his current place of residence, along with the name of the addressee and her Berlin address. Alongside the official postmark, each letter bears the stamped emblem of the Petersburg secret police, with various additional stamps and seals of Prussia and the German Empire. Based on this evidence, it appears that the Seifert letters were intercepted in Russia by the Petersburg secret police and three years later passed along to their Prussian colleagues. There is no reason to believe that Ludmilla ("Mila") Seifert ever saw her husband's letters.

Though it may stretch credulity to imagine the czarist security apparatus collegially handing over material of this sort to a rival organization, Hein's cynical implication is clear: two rival oppressive governments, even though hostile to each other, share more interests in common than either does with its respective citizenry. And since "Prussia" always functioned for East German writers as code for their own state, Hein was making a scarcely-veiled reference to the contemporary hand-in-glove relations between the KGB and the East German Stasi. He tactfully stops short of explicitly including the Stasi in company that includes the Nazi Gestapo, which in its turn had assumed custody of the Seifert letters. C.H. relates that after Germany's defeat in 1945, the Gestapo files were ransacked and the Seifert letters used as wallpaper backing, leading to their eventual rediscovery during an apartment renovation. Hein's account grows increasingly ludicrous with its description of a consequent rash of wallpaper removal in the interest of historical research. The sober and pretentious language of German science typified by C.H. contrasts archly with the absurdity and banality of the events.

The story proper also deals with state surveillance. The delicate subject of the secret police is central to Hein's examination of how state power infiltrates the private lives of citizens, and recurs in works like *Horns Ende* and *Der Tangospieler*. In "Die russischen Briefe," the narrative impetus is provided equally by Seifert's homesickness, Humboldt's travels and frustrations, and the persistent efforts of a Russian agent, Menschenin, to frighten Seifert into informing on his master. The irony is that, unknowingly, Seifert does write the desired report — in the form of his letters. A further irony, and one of more personal importance to Hein, involves the stupidity of the state apparatus represented by Menschenin: Humboldt is interested only in science, while the paranoid Russian security apparatus, unable to imagine such disinterestedness regarding political affairs, regards him from the start as a Prussian agent.

In truth, Humboldt's range of progressive and critical views is beyond the Russians' comprehension as anything other than a different kind of threat — that of the free-thinking intellectual. Seifert's letters contain frequent asides or mini-lectures taken down verbatim from Humboldt, so that this story contains the first example of Hein's favored device of scattering essayistic meditations through his narratives (a predilection shared by Milan Kundera and many other writers lumped together as "postmodernists," but which is as old as the novel). An admiring but frequently uncomprehending Seifert recounts Humboldt's views on the debasement of language (*NUFM* 12); the falseness and shallowness of high society (14–15); the omnipresence of state security operations (16, 19–21); the humiliation of having to pretend one is a partisan of the power structure (28–30); discrimination and bigotry, especially against Jews and homosexuals (33–35); the artificiality of marriage and the thoughtlessness that usually accompanies child-rearing (40–42); Prussia's reactionary and destructive system of education (50–52); the impotence of liberal or radical politics, and disappointment and pessimism concerning government, culture, and progress (58–60); and finally the danger from minor functionaries who align themselves with the state to satisfy grudges (65–66).Unlike the essayistic passages in *Der fremde Freund*, in which the protagonist Claudia constructs a coherent, if wholly false, representation of her life, Humboldt's lectures scarcely add up to a complex psychological portrait.[8] Rather, in this early exercise of the device, Hein is content to follow the common East German practice of placing criticism of the contemporary scene in the mouths of historical or even mythological figures (as one also observes in plays like *Cromwell* and *Lassalle*).[9] As Hein's fiction evolves, it ultimately abandons the direct use of the non-narrative, preferring instead to integrate such elements into a realistic, psychologically compelling worldview. Yet the effect remains the same:

instead of taking a political and moral position, Hein *represents* characters who do so, opening the possibility of an oblique ideological critique which, at its best, is too fine-grained and ambiguous to trouble the censors.[10] Hein's readers are obliged to think for themselves when all viewpoints are given equal weight, as in Humboldt's lectures and Seifert's comments on them. No abstraction is allowed to divert attention from a concrete realism that counters ideological fossilizations. Thus Seifert carries on a stream of anti-Semitic commentary while reporting accurately, if incredulously, his master's more enlightened views, and embodying the pervasiveness and stubbornness of German anti-Semitism in an otherwise sympathetically drawn character.

The narrow viewpoints and moral imperfections of Hein's two frame-narrators paradoxically qualify them as representative chroniclers. The worst threat to historically accurate writing is the programmatic blindness of ideology, not simple prejudice, ignorance, or bias. All chroniclers suffer from personal and social handicaps that prevent them from grasping the world objectively, yet so long as they grasp it concretely at least in part, rather than merely reciting a political, religious, or other ideological script, they become the mediators of truth even in spite of themselves. The practical conclusion that Hein draws from this — that a multiplicity of viewpoints is more congenial to truth than any single one can ever hope to be — lies behind his call in the 1980s for *Öffentlichkeit* ("openness" — uncontrolled public discourse, a free market of ideas, *glasnost*) and an end to censorship.[11] The same notion of history as an assemblage of fragments informs *Horns Ende*, discussed in chapter 4.

In the stories that lie between "Einladung" and "Die russischen Briefe," chronicling as a *theme* drops from view as the *act* of chronicling begins in earnest. Most of the pieces are grouped under the general heading "Berliner Stadtansichten," thus promising brevity, illustrative intent, limitation of viewpoint, and, in their totality, an overview of recent German history from the vantage point of its true capital. The remaining stories, "Leb wohl, mein Freund, es ist schwer zu sterben," and "Der neuere (glücklichere) Kohlhaas," abandon the detached authorial stance of the "Berliner Stadtansichten" to attempt, respectively, a more sentimental voice, and a more satirical, mocking one. It is the "Berliner Stadtansichten," however, that constitute the book's most completely realized achievement.

Postcards from Berlin

Although a number of narrative stances are tried out in the "Berliner Stadtansichten" — nearly-invisible omniscient narrators as well as first-person recollections — the stories or sketches uniformly exhibit an arresting emotional detachment, even when terrible events are being described or personal pain recollected. This demonstration of the chronicler-like, Kleist/Hebel/Kafka-like equanimity that Hein praises in various interviews has now been applied to the depiction of ordinary, unremarkable, and certainly unheroic figures — workers, petty officials, an actor, an adolescent boy, a widow, and so on. None of the characters exhibit any significant degree of insight into the historical circumstances with which they contend; instead, they try simply to cope.[12] The interpretive role played in the frame stories by Racine and Seifert now falls to the reader, who confronts the experiences of an individual or a family with almost no mediating commentary. The relation between the frame and the "Berliner Stadtansichten" is thus highly suggestive, even pedagogical — the reader him- or herself must, to a degree, learn the disciplined but sympathetic detachment of the chronicler, and then must exceed it. Hein's authorial gesture in these stories makes perfect sense when seen in its GDR context, where political engagement had been straitjacketed by ideology and human sympathy by revolutionary romanticism. Indeed, all of Hein's fiction demands that the reader confront the depicted reality coolly, rationally, and with an eye toward social criticism and moral assessment — precisely the aims of Brecht's epic theater, of course, though seldom applied so rigorously to fiction.[13] Hein's signature technique in these short stories and in much of his subsequent fiction is to depict characters so even-handedly, so dispassionately, that the reader cannot help but revolt against the characters' self-delusion, or cruelty, or weakness, or pettiness. We know (or at least we hope) that we could do better than these confused, powerless, spiritless people.

All set in Berlin, the "Stadtansichten" form a historical continuum beginning with Wilhelminian Germany and ending in the contemporary GDR. One of the most provocative facts about the stories to East German critics was, as mentioned above, Hein's assumption of a cultural and social continuity between these two endpoints, even in the GDR. Nothing changes all that much during this 100 years of history, there is no "Year Zero" in 1945 that offers a clean start, power simply passes from one group to another while the people remain powerless always. The careful historical balance of the "Berliner Stadtansichten," like that of the book as a whole, provides background and implicit commentary on what clearly is the main topic of interest: Hein's own GDR. Arranged roughly chronologically, the stories fall into four groups, "Friederike, Martha, Hilde" and "Die Witwe eines Maurers" providing a historic overview spanning Wilhelminian Germany and the GDR, "Die Familiengruft" representing the Nazi period with chilling conciseness, "Charlottenburger Chaussee, 11. August" encapsulating the *Aufbau* period in a single anecdote, and "Nachtfahrt und früher Morgen," "Frank, eine Kindheit mit Vätern," and "Der Sohn" investigating several aspects of the GDR.

It should be noted that the omission of "Der Sohn" in the West German edition significantly alters the overall impact of the stories, and obscures their function within the book. This is the most "critical" of the stories, dealing with the ineffectual resistance of a high-ranking GDR official's son to his comfortable fate as a member of the ruling class, and it is the most extensive of any of the "Stadtansichten" in its examination of contemporary East German social relations. In its raising of the taboo subject of socialist class inequality, "Der Sohn" also serves as a transition to the story that follows it, "Leb wohl, mein Freund, es ist schwer zu sterben," which is similarly concerned with the failure of a classless society to materialize in the GDR.

"Friederike, Martha, Hilde" follows a fairly unremarkable Berlin family through three generations. History is presented as a random collection of individuals' experiences, not the working out of transcendent laws, which is not to say that no assessment of its meaning can be made. The personal is the political, and vice versa: petty betrayals between husband and wife grade seamlessly into crimes against humanity. Hein uses mundane details and clichéd encapsulations of his characters' lives to emphasize the extremity of contradiction between what ordinarily happens and what can be called ordinary, or what people can bear to call ordinary. Thus while the story concludes with the journalistic summation "Ungewöhnliches sei nicht zu berichten" [There was nothing unusual to report: *NUFM* 77], the claim flies in the face of the ordinary atrociousness that has led up to it, which is only accentuated by Hein's flat, unemotional narrative voice. The family history begins with Friederike's marriage to a Christianized Jewish lace manufacturer, allowing Hein to introduce the theme of anti-Semitism, which infects the air breathed by all of the pre-First-World-War characters. The story is built of ironies large and small, as wayward history and inscrutable human individuality intervene in rational plans. For example, Martha, Friederike's daughter, is apparently the issue of her mother's affair with an adolescent boy, yet her nominal father (who knows of the affair) dotes on the girl, and later, as she matures, she begins to exhibit a pronounced resemblance to him. History, at least at this microscopic level, is wholly irrational and inscrutable. Hein's chronicling also permits itself ironies of a more writerly sort, such as the characterization of Martha's "sehr glückliche Ehe" [very happy marriage: *NUFM* 72], followed by a litany of problems that begins:

> Martha war in ihren gutaussehenden und gewandt auftretenden Mann mit dem kleinen Menjou-Bärtchen vernarrt; den vielfältigen Gerüchten, daß er sie häufig betrog, schenkte sie keinen Glauben oder nahm diese nicht wahr aus Furcht, ihn zu verlieren. Seine krankhafte, grundlose Eifersucht schmeichelte ihr anfangs, wurde ihr aber mit den Jahren lästig und stimmte sie ängstlich. (*NUFM* 72)
>
> [Martha was mad about her good-looking and smartly turned-out husband with the little Menjou-beard; she put no stock in the many rumors that he frequently betrayed her, or else refused to believe them out of fear of losing him. His pathological and groundless jealousy flattered her at first, but over the years it became oppressive and made her fearful.]

Like so many other suspicious goings-on in these stories, the husband's culpability remains unconfirmed despite its strong likelihood, and it is wise to remember that the truth may be other than what is expected. Indeed, these expectations lead most often to ironic outcomes. Every rise is followed inevitably by a fall, whether because of history (war, the Nazi period, anti-Semitism), or more mundane hazards (ignorance, jealousy, lust, greed, love, commonplace bigotry, biology), or both. A general structure of good news / bad news thus emerges in the story: Friederike marries, but the couple is childless; she has a child, but it is the issue of an affair with a boy; the husband loves the child despite suspecting its parentage, but then dies; Friederike inherits the factory, but she ruins it with mismanagement; she remarries, but her husband dies in the First World War; Friederike's daughter Martha marries happily, but the husband is both jealous and unfaithful; she bears several children, but dies after giving birth to the last one because of her husband's ignorance and jealousy; the youngest child, Hilde, is adopted by a childless aunt and uncle, but they are strict disciplinarians and ardent Nazis; Hilde does well at school, but she is expelled for being one-quarter Jewish; she has a true love, but her uncle thwarts the relationship out of anti-Semitic bigotry and the boy is killed on the Russian front; Hilde finally marries and has a child, but he is sickly and mentally deficient, and the husband leaves on account of it. Hein's sardonic concluding reflection on social progress in the GDR consists of Hilde, the end of her family line (the son having died at 26), being commended by the state for being a hard worker (77). The superficiality of the commendation, symbolizing the GDR's claim to have annulled the German past, contrasts with the story's three generations of mundane, irremediable tragedy. History has not been overcome in the German workers' state, it has merely been repressed.

The next several "Berliner Stadtansichten" range in tone and content from the absurd to the horrible, applying the detached narrative stance of "Friederike, Martha, Hilde" to more circumscribed but no less telling incidents. "Die Witwe eines Maurers" (The Bricklayer's Widow) makes fun of an apparently German propensity to dress up past events in the politically convenient garb of the day. Strictly following the *Novelle* form, the story opens with the (tongue-in-cheek) *unerhörtes Ereignis* of a 78-year-old woman who becomes caught up in the political events of her day despite having never wished to participate in its "Parteiungen, Kämpfen und Verbrechen" [factions, struggles, and crimes: *NUFM 77*]. Her husband, a returned soldier and Communist Party member, had been killed in the civil unrest of 1919. A coworker (and secret comrade) arranges a veteran's pension for the destitute woman by attesting to the authorities that her husband had been an innocent bystander. The Nazi regime continues to pay the pension and frightens the widow by listing her husband as a victim of the "Reds." After the war, her husband's comrade sees to it that the widow is registered with the new socialist government as a victim of Fascism, making her eligible for a pension. She tries in vain to refuse it, moves to a different location, finds new friends, and in general struggles to escape her — or her husband's — past. In the end, she almost succeeds in concealing herself from history:

> Als sie starb, konnten sich mehrere Nachbarn ihrer nur erinnern als einer scheuen, verängstigten Frau, die mit eingezogenem Kopf über die Straße huschte, um ihre kleinen Besorgungen zu erledigen. (78)
>
> [Upon her death, several neighbors were able to remember her only as a shy, fearful woman darting across the street on minor errands with her head bowed.]

The shortest and funniest of the "Berliner Stadtansichten," this story is really quite sad (only the comic extremity of the woman's flight from history prevents it from seeming pitiful), yet it contrasts with the muted pathos of "Friederike, Martha, Hilde," which is only intensified by that story's "happy" ending. "Die Witwe eines Maurers" strengthens the reader's sense (not shared by the women in "Friederike") that history — that is, life — is monstrously uncertain, random, and irrational. The widow is aware of this craziness and it makes *her* crazy.[14]

As is often the case, Hein seems to be attacking the rationalistic bias of Marxist historical thought, especially in the petrified form it had assumed in the East Bloc by 1980. He indulges in the Stalinist sin of "subjectivism" by privileging individual experience over doctrinal certainties about the laws and goal of history. The twentieth-century German experience of history emerges in such stories as "Die Witwe eines Maurers" as equal parts irrationality and inexorability, hence as a matter of power in its most arbitrary form. This, rather than messianic revolutionary hope, defines the experience of the "Berliner Stadtansichten" characters, and as philosophical content it complements the detached "chronicling" of Hein's fiction.

No doubt paired with "Die Witwe eines Maurers" for maximum effect, "Die Familiengruft" (The Family Tomb) is as horrifying as the preceding story is amusing. It is also the only story in the collection dealing directly with Nazi thuggery, and the first of the "Berliner Stadtansichten" to adopt a first-person narrative stance, with the narrator recounting events experienced by his uncle, an actor, and his family. The first-person stance of this and the next two stories valorizes individual subjective experience even more directly than in the earlier pieces, which is not to say, however, that every, or any, subjective viewpoint is "correct." Rather, Hein is formulating his idea, refined in *Horns Ende*, that historical "truth" must emerge from a welter of fragmentary viewpoints, whose veracity, taken singly, may be far from reliable. In this example, the narrator's account of his uncle's fate at the hands of the Nazis is partly speculative, leaving certain questions unanswered as the story ends.

The known facts are sufficiently arresting. The actor-uncle, a member of a Jewish theater company in Berlin, was arrested in 1938 and sent to a concentration camp, only to be released just as suddenly and arbitrarily two weeks later. Still allowed to perform, yet facing a highly uncertain future in Germany, Uncle Eugen applies to emigrate, but, in a further example of governmental inscrutability, receives no answer. After suffering through a period of declining circumstances, we are told that the uncle and his family simply disappeared one day in 1941, only to be found dead a month later in another family's tomb in the vast Jewish cemetery in Berlin-Weißensee. The narrator uses the testimony of neighbors and acquaintances in reconstructing the events leading up to this bizarre end, and learns that the uncle, fearing deportation, had taken his family and gone into hiding in the tomb. Not long after, they were discovered there by the Gestapo (evidently on a tip). Once again, however, the authorities behave capriciously: the Gestapo detachment allows the family to remain in the tomb, and begins visiting them, schnaps bottles in hand, demanding to be entertained from the actor's repertoire of operetta tunes. After several such visits, Uncle Eugen poisons himself and his family.

The narrator is fascinated by the gaps in the story, unanswered questions like: Why did Uncle Eugen choose such an unlikely place to hide? Why didn't he find another hiding place after the Gestapo found him? And oddest of all: Why did Uncle Eugen carry with him a bundle of "schmuddligen Bühnentexte" [soiled play scripts: *NUFM* 82]? The narrator remarks:

> Es waren zumeist kokette, nichtssagende Stücke, allein für das Amüsement gedacht und insofern ungeeignet, ja vielleicht sogar unpassend für den Aufenthalt in der Gruft. (*NUFM* 82)
>
> [They were mostly coquettish, insignificant plays, meant only for amusement and hence unsuited, even perhaps inappropriate, for a sojourn in a tomb.]

The bizarreness of the narrator's prim concern about burial-vault etiquette marks an abrupt lurch into allegory: for Jews, all of Germany was a tomb in 1941, and it was no less incongruous or "inappropriate" to be performing light opera on a stage tolerated (for the moment, inexplicably) by the authorities, than to be doing it in the Weißensee cemetery. Without contradicting the shift in symbolic register, the narrator offers a psychological explanation that itself veers once more into the allegorical:

> Ich denke, er hat die abgegriffenen Hefte in sein Versteck mitgenommen, weil sie zu seinem Leben gehörten wie Tante Rosa und die drei Kinder.
>
> Und vielleicht vergaß er in der Gruft die Angst, wenn er mit seiner zarten und doch sicheren Stimme die dummen Texte sang. Vielleicht haben ihm die Hefte geholfen bei dem Versuch, in einem Grab zu überleben, bei diesem Versuch, der sich so bald als Irrtum erwieß. Denn sein Leben und das seiner Familie konnten auch die Toten nicht retten. (*NUFM* 82)
>
> I think that he took these well-thumbed scripts with him into hiding because they were as much a part of his life as Aunt Rosa and the three children.
>
> And perhaps, in the tomb, he forgot his fear when he sang the stupid lyrics with his soft but steady voice. Perhaps the scripts helped him in his attempt to survive in a grave, an attempt that would so soon turn out to be a mistake. For not even the dead could save him and his family.

In light of this passage, Hein's occasional remarks about the function of East German literature as a form of *Lebenshilfe*, or aid to living, appear suspended over an abyss of irony.

Similarly distant from the third-person, Kleist-like narrative-nowhere of "Friederike," "Charlottenburger Chaussee" is a mediated personal testimony, and the first and most openly ironic of the four concluding "Berliner Stadtansichten" set in the GDR. The story is essentially a send-up of the Marxist notion of *Klassenkampf*, or class conflict, put mischievously into the mouth of a philosophy professor at East Berlin's Humboldt University, where "philosophy" would have been understood as code for Marxism-Leninism. (Hein, it should be remembered, earned a degree in philosophy from Humboldt.) Like *Lassalle* and the novels, "Charlottenburger Chaussee" links history and ideology to the most intimately personal realms, in particular sexuality; call it class struggle if you like, Hein appears to be saying, but it can be better understood in other terms. The professor tells of his experience in 1951 as a member of the Freie Deutsche Jugend (the Communist youth group) assigned with several others to distribute leaflets in the Western sector of Berlin. The real center of interest for the boys in the group is not politics, however, but Karla, a beautiful girl with large breasts under her blue FDJ shirt. In the West they encounter a policeman who orders them to return to the Soviet sector:

> Er war nicht älter als wir . . . . Wir umringten ihn und redeten auf ihn ein. Keinem von uns entging, daß der junge Polizist immer wieder zu Karla sah, auf ihre von uns allen bewunderten Brüste. Dies verbitterte uns nicht weniger als seine abfälligen Bemerkungen und die Anordnung, den Westsektor zu verlassen. Mit den Worten, daß sich Deutsche schämen sollten, die blauen Russenkittel zu tragen, griff er plötzlich nach Karlas Bluse und riß sie ihr herunter. Wir standen wie gelähmt, starrten auf zwei schutzlose Brüste, sahen das verwunderte und doch lächelnde Gesicht Karlas und den jungen Polizisten, der nun verlegen vor ihr stand. Für Sekunden war es still. Dann schlugen wir zu. Das war Klassenkampf, begriffen wir augenblicklich . . . .
> (*NUFM* 83–84)

> [He was no older than we . . . . We surrounded him and began badgering him. It escaped no one that the young policeman repeatedly cast glances in Karla's direction and could not help staring at the breasts we all admired so much. This embittered us no less than the disparaging remarks and the order to leave the West-Sector. Suddenly, saying that Germans should be ashamed to wear that blue Russian get-up, he reached out and ripped open Karla's blouse. We stood there paralyzed, staring at the two undefended breasts, seeing Karla's aston-

ished but still smiling face, and that of the young policeman, who now stood embarrassed before her. For a few seconds it was quiet. Then we attacked him. In the blink of an eye we grasped that *this* was class struggle . . . .]

They leave the policeman dead (with the leaflets next to his body) and flee back to the East. Hein allows no pause to fall between the extremely funny line concerning the nature of class struggle and the fatal beating that follows, so that potential irony remains ours only, and cannot be imputed to the philosophy professor, who ends his account with a wistful memory of Karla: "Dieses Mädchen, sagte der Philosoph, liebten wir alle" [We all loved this girl, the philosopher said: *NUFM* 84]. The real focus of the story, or at least the recollection of the event, is Karla, and the professor's seemingly unreflective burlesque of Marxist categories throws an ironic light over the whole story and, especially, over the official keepers of Marxist doctrine, of whom the professor is one.

Although it is arguably not the most interesting of the stories, the next "Stadtansicht," "Nachtfahrt und früher Morgen" (Night Journey and early Morning), served as title story in the West German edition, no doubt because of its subject matter: an attempted illegal border crossing.[15] In the GDR the story was probably publishable at all only due to the unappealing characterization of the principal would-be defector. Hein's selection of narrative stance — the story is told by an adolescent literally along for the ride — anticipates his creation of Thomas in *Horns Ende*, where, as here, an adolescent boy on the fringe of the adult world becomes aware of the real relations shaping that world, for instance, sex and power. Hence the story exhibits the public/private conflation at the center of *Lassalle* and *Der fremde Freund*. The nameless boy narrator accepts an invitation from his friend Max to make an all-night trip, with the aim, as it turns out, of transporting a teacher, his wife, and his daughter to Berlin, where they plan to escape to the West through the sewer system. The teacher is nervous and garrulous, overbearing with his wife and irritating to Max. In Berlin, the agreed-upon rendezvous with a guide fails to materialize, and there is no choice but to drive back where they had come from. In the morning, the boy discovers that something is up between Max and the teacher's wife as they discuss her husband:

> Max haute wütend mit der Faust auf den Tisch und sagte: "Scheiße. Das ganze Abhauen ist Scheiße."
> . . .
> Max saß wortloß am Tisch.
> Unvermittelt fragte die Frau: "Warum hassen Sie meinen Mann?"

Ich war überrascht, als Max erwiderte: "Weil er ein Versager ist. Weil er Sie nicht in Frieden läßt. Er taugt nur dazu, davonzulaufen."
(*NUFM* 89)
[Max slammed his fist angrily on the table and said: "Shit. This whole escape business is shit."
. . .
Max sat in silence at the table.
All at once the woman said: "Why do you hate my husband? "
I was surprised when Max answered: "Because he's a failure. Because he won't leave you in peace. The only thing he's good for is running away."]

While Max's denunciation of the disloyal teacher must have placated the government censors, Hein's purpose is to create an emotionally-charged atmosphere that the boy is not equipped to understand. After the passage above, the wife undoes her bathrobe and, ignoring the boy, exposes herself provocatively to Max. "Plötzlich verstand ich, weshalb Max mit solchem Haß zu ihr sprach, und ich erschrak über seine heftige, unbeherrschte Liebe" [Suddenly I realized why Max spoke to her with such hatred, and I was shocked by his violent, uncontrolled love: *NUFM* 90]. The boy concludes by attesting to a new and acute awareness of how little he understands about the world: "Ich versuchte zu begreifen, warum ich es nicht verstand" [I tried to grasp why I did not understand it: 90].

"Frank, eine Kindheit mit Vätern" (Frank, a Childhood with Fathers), a male version of the "Friederike" story with the same multi-generational serial organization, bears a more explicit organizing theme: all the parents in the story want their children to do better than they have done, and all the children try their best not to disappoint their parents. However, with almost Zola-esque inevitability and considerable pathos, stupidity always intervenes, producing circumstances that will burden the subsequent generation. The peculiar title, faintly evocative of a still-life painting, suggests the static condition in which the characters find themselves, the eternal return of the same human weaknesses as history keeps repeating itself for these people. The story begins in Wilhelminian Germany with the eponymous Frank's great-grandfather, a tenant farmer and son of a day laborer, whose only goal in life is to see his son educated, "damit dieser ein leichteres Leben führen könne als sein Vater" [so that the boy could have an easier life than his father: 90]. The first cycle of catastrophe completes itself when the father falls in France in 1916, and the son has to drop out of the expensive *Gymnasium* he attends. The next begins as the son wurde Postbote, Volontär einer Berliner Tageszeitung und später Makler an der Börse. Wegen Unterschlagungen kam er für vier Jahre ins Zuchthaus. (91)

[became a mailman, a trainee at a Berlin daily, and later a broker in the stock exchange. Convicted of embezzlement, he spent four years in prison.]

Frank's grandfather marries after being released from prison, opens a cellar drug store jointly with his wife, and conceives an updated version of his father's dream:

Sein Traum war es, den Sohn in Amerika ausbilden zu lassen, um aus ihm einen jener sagenumwobenen Pioniere der Technik zu machen, von denen die Zeitschriften und Magazine achtungsvoll berichteten, sie seien sensibel wie alten, europäischen Poeten, und ihre Gehirne arbeiteten mit der Exaktheit großer Rechenmaschinen. (*NUFM* 91)

[His dream was to have his son educated in America, in order to make of him one of those legendary pioneers of technology that the newspapers and magazines credited with sensibilities rivaling the old European poets and brains functioning with the precision of mighty calculating machines.]

The dream of personal betterment and the exaggerated vision of America lead, unsurprisingly, to another downfall. After the partition of Germany by the Allies, the son is sent to study in West Berlin, where he meets an American con man who claims to be a Harvard physics professor, and who promises to train the boy to succeed him in exchange for a large sum of money. When the American disappears with the family's life savings and with a government loan meant for improvements to the drugstore, the druggist and his wife flee to the West to avoid prosecution, and the boy (who is denied entry to America when the papers provided by the con man prove false) ends up wandering the world as a deck hand. He eventually returns to East Berlin and, going to night classes, earns an engineering degree, but then meets with difficulty in his new career, prompting a renewed version of the family dream:

Seine geringen beruflichen Erfolg führte er auf die unterbrochene und zu spät beendete Ausbildung zurück, ein Nachteil, den er seinen beiden Kinder ersparen wollte. (*NUFM* 92)

[He blamed his meager professional success on the interruptions and late completion of his education, a disadvantage that he wished to spare his two children.]

But catastrophe again intervenes, this time in the form of his son Frank's learning disability. Though advised to send him to a special school, the parents decide that such a move would endanger his future success, and they instead provide him with extensive tutoring. The boy does poorly nonetheless, and eventually tries to kill himself out of shame for the disappointment he causes his parents. Though well-intentioned, they are too blinded by the story's ever-present dream to take any appropriate action to save Frank: "Die erschrockenen Eltern saßen fassungslos am Krankenbett ihres Sohnes; seine Tat wie die Erklärungen und Ratschläge des Arztes blieben ihnen unverständlich" [The shocked parents sat uncomprehendingly at their son's bedside; they could make no sense of their son's action, nor of the doctor's explanations and advice: 92]. Frank later succeeds in killing himself. The story remains the least political of the "Berliner Stadtansichten," despite its setting, with neither history nor political oppression being necessary to account for the delusions that plague Frank's family and position him at the end of a long tradition of doomed aspirations. Only in a rather abstractly Marxist sense can this striving be connected with the political and economic circumstances of its characters. Hein seems rather to be pushing the limits of depicted subjectivity, moving as far as possible from the programmatic, didactic plots demanded by Socialist Realism, or even the relatively socially-charged plots to be found in stories like "Friederike" or "Die Familiengruft." On the other hand, the pathos in such a story can easily verge on sentimentality, a danger avoided here but certainly courted in "Leb wohl, mein Freund, es ist schwer zu sterben" (Have a Good Life, My Friend, It Is Hard to Die), discussed below, which also limits its focus to purely personal aspirations and illusions.

One of the most interesting stories in the entire *Einladung* collection is the last of the "Berliner Stadtansichten," "Der Sohn" (The Son). Though the story was dropped from the Western edition of the book, it is one of the most critical of Hein's early narratives in its treatment of the supposedly classless society fostered by *Realsozialismus*. This story of a Party functionary's son can be readily generalized into a paradigm of the GDR itself: we are presented with a privileged but dysfunctional family that suffers from all of the ills endemic to the East German social fabric. Pavel is born (like the GDR, and like Hein himself) amid the rubble of a defeated Germany at the end of the Second World War, named by his father for the Red Army officer who liberated him from a concentration camp, where he had no doubt been imprisoned for his Communist affiliation. Hein's narrative emphasizes the triumphalist political atmosphere of the early GDR, presenting Pavel's boyhood talent and promise as inextricably bound up with his youthful fanaticism and with the self-righteousness and sense of earned privilege enjoyed by his well-connected father, an attitude that many victims of Nazi persecution, among them the GDR's leaders, carried to their graves. But heartfelt political convictions soon mingle with less altruistic feelings:

> [Pawels] Bestreben, dem geliebten Vater zu gleichen, dessen Unerschütterlichkeit und entschlossenes Auftreten in den sich überstürzenden Ereignissen der Nachkriegsjahre von ihm bewundert wurden, er übersah auch nicht das respektvolle Verhalten der Lehrer im Umgang mit seinem Vater, führte ihn gelegentlich zu eigenwilligen Handlungen, deren seine Erzieher nicht Herr werden konnten oder wollten.
> (*Einladung* 62)
>
> [(Pavel's) efforts to emulate his beloved father, whose imperturbable and resolute manner amid the chaotic rush of the post-war events he admired — and he did not fail to notice his teachers' respectful demeanor in dealing with his father — led him occasionally to independent acts which his teachers were neither able nor willing to curb.]

It is clear that a major part of the father's appeal is his power, and Pavel is quick to become arrogant as he starts exercising power himself. Pavel's "independent acts" are deadly serious; for example, he denounces the father of a classmate (a toolmaker and war cripple) for making anti-Soviet statements, and calls on the man to explain himself before a student assembly. The man takes his family and flees to the West, "nicht willens, sich vor Zehnjährigen zu verantworten oder Repressalien befürchtend" [unwilling to answer to a bunch of ten-year-olds, or fearing reprisals: *Einladung* 63]. Although Pavel is no less critical of himself (ascetically refusing luxuries when he feels guilty of a weakness or failing) and thus worthy, perhaps, of a certain respect, his teachers suppress their unease over his behavior primarily out of fear of his father.

Pavel's fervor predictably turns against its source and model as he enters adolescence, when increasing conflicts with his father bring to the surface the latter's violent nature and, by implication, the power relations prevailing (or failing to prevail) between Pavel's (and Hein's) generation and the generation of wartime saints and criminals preceding them. Hein presents Pavel's sudden interest in Western literature and other ideas inimical to Communist orthodoxy as an entirely generational phenomenon, again undermining the apparent genuineness of Pavel's self-discovery:

> Man begann sich für Literatur zu interessieren, stürzte sich über die neuesten amerikanischen Bücher, las französische Surrealisten und stritt bis in die Nacht über die Philosophien eines Kierkegaard, Nietzsche und Sartre. Pawel saugte mit der gleichen Inbrunst wie

seine Altersgenossen die widersprüchlichsten Gedanken in sich hinein.... (*Einladung* 65)

[Everyone became interested in literature, plunging into the newest American books, reading French Surrealists, and arguing over the philosophies of Kierkegaard, Nietzsche, and Sartre late into the night. Pavel absorbed the most contradictory ideas with the same ardor as the rest of his generation....]

Pavel begins introducing ideas gleaned from this reading into classroom discussions, and when his teachers are tolerant until he anonymously posts a collage of defamatory articles from Western newspapers. He confesses his guilt when another student is blamed and threatened with expulsion, but his privileged status saves him from serious repercussions (just as it gave him access, through his father, to the forbidden newspapers in the first place — even his rebellion is rooted very close to home). His relationship with his father assumes what seems to be a new character, as first revealed during a meeting of Pavel, his father, and the school director:

[Sein Vater] ließ Pawel in sein Zimmer rufen, befragte ihn eindringlich, schrie ihn an und wurde, da Pawel ihm nur verstockt und widerwillig antwortete, so wütend, daß er den Sechzehnjährigen vor den Augen des Schuldirektors schlug. (*Einladung* 66)

[(His father) called Pavel into the room and began interrogating and shouting at him. When Pavel showed himself stubborn and reluctant to answer, he grew so enraged that he struck the 16-year-old before the eyes of the school director.]

This is a crucial moment in the story, revealing the coerciveness and violence binding this family, and marking the beginning of a rapid deterioration of relations between Pavel and his father.[16] Father and son begin arguing constantly over politics, and after further physical abuse, Pavel moves out, leaving his none-too-insightful father baffled:

Der Vater suchte verzweifelt zu ergründen, weshalb sich sein Sohn ihm entfremde, warum er die Ideale seiner Kindheit vergessen oder verraten habe und wieso er ihm gegenüber geradezu als politischer Gegner auftrat. (*Einladung* 67)

[In despair the father tried to understand why his son had become alienated from him, why he had forgotten or betrayed the ideals of his childhood, and why he now confronted him virtually as a political enemy.]

The reasons are evident enough as he continues to try to control his son at a distance. He uses his influence to stop a friend of Pavel's with Western connections (and hence presumably a bad influence) from attending college with his son, even though he is aware at the time that this will have no effect on his son's behavior, while it will wreck the other boy's career. (*Einladung* 68).[17] Clearly, the man has a very limited repertoire of human-relations skills, all of them learned from Stalin. Relations with his son reach their nadir when Pavel makes two attempts to flee the country, the second of which, even with his father's intervention, lands him in prison, where he must endure forced labor.

In a story less satiric than this one turns out to be, the likely conclusion would now be Pavel's expulsion from the GDR; but instead Pavel's fortunes begin to mend. The cause, tellingly, is his father's threat to leave him to his fate if he should commit any more ill-considered acts. Unexpectedly, instead of prodding a proud and rebellious son into a culminating act of self-assertion, the result is submission by what begins to look like a cynically calculating son. Pavel begins university study, and persists, at first, in rebelliousness by annoying his neighbors with noise and the comings and goings of women. Summoned by the police, he resolves (in his very last act of resistance) not to invoke his father's name in his defense. Hein narrates with measured understatement:

> Seine Befürchtungen waren grundlos. Das Gespräch mit dem Polizeioffizier, der Pawels Vater als Politiker kannte und schätzte, verlief freundschaftlich und endete mit dem Rat des Offiziers, künftig die Lautsprecheranlage leiser einzustellen.... (*Einladung* 69)
>
> [His fears were groundless. The police officer knew and esteemed Pavel's father as a politician. The interview proceeded genially and ended with the officer advising Pavel to turn down the volume in the future....]

From this point on, Pavel settles ever more comfortably into the social niche that he had so long affected to spurn. He is aided in this by the tact of people who — like the police officer — studiously avoid mentioning the real reason for their forbearance. He finishes his studies and embarks on the illustrious career his parents had foreseen:

> Bei den Kollegen war er beliebt, und seine Meinungen waren stets geachtet als die des Sohnes eines verdienten, hohen Funktionärs.
>   Pawel selbst aber fügte sich in den zuverlässigen Lauf der Welt. Er begriff, daß sein Aufbegehren gegen eine abgeleitete Existenz und die wilde Suche nach seinem wirklichen und eigenen Leben schon ein Teil desselben war und gab sich zufrieden mit den unaufhörlichen Erfolgen. (*Einladung* 70)
>
> [He was beloved by his colleagues, and his opinions were always respected as those of the son of a high-ranking functionary.

> As for Pavel himself, he submitted to the reliable way of the world. He came to realize that his rebellion against a pre-planned existence and his frantic search for a genuine, autonomous life were in fact a part of the plan, and he contented himself with unbroken successes.]

Pavel has finally achieved a level of cynical self-knowledge that enables him to fit perfectly into the role his society has prepared for him.

Tragedies of ruined careers and exile, of Pavel's alienation from his parents, of his mother's alcoholism and terminal cancer, and of his father's verbal and physical abusiveness are all examples, on the one hand, of the random cruelty of everyday life, but on the other they are superimposed over and ramified by cruelties more specific to the GDR. Rather than broadly condemning life in the GDR, Hein specifies the particularity of its misery, including political and ideological aspects, while avoiding comparisons with other social systems, or predictions, or recommendations, or side-taking. True to his vocation as chronicler, Hein's first order of business is to delineate the facts as he sees them, for even without tendentious commentary, "the analysis of the actual can itself be explosive enough" ("Wir werden es lernen müssen" 52). Sympathy is extended neither to Pavel nor his father. Pavel is trapped, but he takes advantage of his privileges and learns to like being trapped. His success, like his independence, is a sham; nothing but privilege underlies it. His feeble attempts at rebellion end in the acceptance of privilege, but it is evident that there was never really any alternative. The conclusion of the story bears a family resemblance to accounts throughout Hein's work of characters at once resilient and craven who manage to find an accommodation with atrocious circumstance. The irony of the "happy ending" in this case is more biting than usual because it involves a member of the ruling class: Pavel overcomes all obstacles on the way to becoming what there was no question of not becoming.

As the last story of the "Berliner Stadtansichten," "Der Sohn" is an indictment of East German society, showing what it had become (an aristocracy built around a nomenklatura) and why (over-confidence in ideological rectitude, leading to abuse of power), and in effect portraying the death of genuine idealism or progressive politics in this country founded so optimistically on the ruins of Nazi Germany. The historical, generational, and class-related details concerning Pavel seem to indicate that such factors are as determining here as in Hein's earlier narratives. From the individual's perspective, little has changed since Wilhelminian times: a ruling class still rules, and the oppressed are still oppressed, though now they are ideological deviants, not Jews.

The persistence of social inequality links "Der Sohn" with the subsequent story, "Leb wohl, mein Freund, es ist schwer zu sterben," which again concerns itself with class differences in *Realsozialismus*.[18] In the story, an overweight woman visits a male friend from her youth, a veterinarian married to a very young woman, "fast noch ein Mädchen" [hardly more than a girl: *NUFM* 96], and with a young son. The visitor plainly suffers both from embarrassment about her own appearance and from lingering romantic feelings toward her old friend. Fischer regards the story as one of Hein's most daring forays into the precise delineation of trivial, even banal, subjectivity (*Christoph Hein* 58), yet the story invites a more socially oriented reading as well. The woman, Katrin, and the veterinarian, Peter, nostalgically recall their old circle of friends:

> Sie sprachen über Berlin, über die unzertrennlichen vier Freunde, die beiden Studenten Peter und Jens, die Laborantin Elvira und die Pelznäherin Karin. Man erinnerte sich an Jazzkonzerte, an die gemeinsame Harzreise, an eine Lehrveranstaltung in der Tieranatomie, zu der man die beiden Mädchen mitgenommen hatte und wo ihnen übel geworden war. Sie sprachen über das Café in der Friedrichstraße, wo eine Kellnerin sie mit Handschlag begrüßte, und über den Besuch der Synagoge, über die Schallplattenabende mit Kerzen und Wein in der Einzimmerwohnung Elviras und über die Berliner Museen, die man hier in der Provinz am meisten vermisse.
> "Sie haben auch studiert?" fragte Karin plötzlich.
> Die Frau des Arztes nickte, sie sei Lehrerin, genauer, sie sei Lehrerin gewesen. Der Haushalt, das Kind und ein schwieriger Mann beschäftigen sie vollauf. Dabei lächelte sie den Arzt an.
> "Und wie geht es dir?" fragte er.
> "Gut," erwiderte sie, "ich habe viel Arbeit." (*NUFM* 97–98)
>
> [They talked about Berlin, about the four inseparable friends, the two students Peter and Jens, the lab technician Elvira, and the furseamstress Karin. They recalled jazz concerts, a group trip to the Harz Mountains, a lecture demonstration on animal anatomy the students took the girls to, where they became ill. The talked about the cafe on Friedrichstraße where the waitress greeted them by name, and about the visit to the synagogue, about evenings spent listening to records with candle light and wine in Elvira's studio apartment, and about the Berlin museums, which one missed most of all in the provinces.
> "Did you also attend college?" Karin asked suddenly.
> The doctor's wife nodded and said she was a teacher, or more precisely, had been a teacher. The house, the child, and a difficult husband kept her completely busy. With this she smiled at the doctor.
> "And how are things going with you?" he asked.
> "Fine," she replied. "I have lots of work."]

Hein contrasts the freedom and mild Bohemianism of the friends' youth, which briefly overrode class differences among the future professionals, the technician, and the seamstress, with the respectable, stodgy, smugly bourgeois lifestyle adopted by the doctor, whose name is not Peter *Burger* for nothing. With a young wife who stays at home, Dr. Burger correspondingly plays the role of proud but benevolent paterfamilias, fulsomely bragging about his ill-behaved child (*NUFM* 98) and patronizing the women on the subject of "diese kleinen Geschichten voller Herz und Schmerz" [these little stories full of passion and pain: *NUFM* 99]. He is referring to the recent marriage of Jens and Elvira, which he had not deigned to attend; indeed, he seems inclined to cut off all contact with his pre-bourgeois life — he has never bothered to tell his former friends that he is married and a father (99). This vaguely embarrassing past life is dismissed as merely "sentimental" by both the doctor and his wife, who laughs openly at Karin when she betrays real emotion (100). The story thus is not merely a commentary on the plight of fat people nor a comparison of youth and maturity — the clammily stereotypical family scene and the counter-example of the other two friends guarantees that. Of course, it would also be inaccurate to say that the story is solely about class, as can be seen in light of "The Son." In both stories, we are shown what happens when young people in the GDR come to maturity: early promise (individuality, rebelliousness, idealism) is either diverted into more conventional channels, or it proves itself to have been a mere illusion of freedom, or both. The veterinarian and his wife are more like stereotypical West German yuppies than a stereotypical East German couple — they are embarrassed by the pretense of intimacy by someone who is neither cool nor refined. Thus the problem is not simply class, but could be viewed also as a conflict between conformist and individualistic styles of behavior.

Michael Kohlhaas in the GDR

The last of the central stories in the collection is Hein's adaptation of Kleist's "Michael Kohlhaas," titled "Der neuere (glücklichere) Kohlhaas" [The newer (luckier) Kohlhaas], and relocated to Thuringia, during the years 1972–73. Hubert K., the hero, lodges a complaint with the authorities when his several-hundred-mark salary bonus is reduced by 40 marks (Hein picks a trivial sum) because of work missed due to illness. His complaint is rebuffed administratively, and then judicially, before he is finally awarded the 40 marks through intervention at the highest levels of the government. Meanwhile, because of his all-consuming obsession with his "rights," Hubert K.'s wife takes the children and divorces him. Like "Die russichen Briefe," the story is a stylistic tour de force, imitating the language of Kleist's novellas, but this time, the pretense of authenticity is replaced by a anachronistic disjunction between Kleistian style and contemporary East German content. Much as the play *Cromwell* employs anachronistic terms and technology — "compañeros," "petit bourgeoisie," "machine guns" — to force a comparison between the English Civil War and the revolutions of the twentieth century (directing critical attention, it should be stressed, toward the latter), so "Kohlhaas" forces a comparison between the issues raised in Kleist's novella and what might be the analogous issues in the modern German socialist state. Hence the story is not just an imitation or parody of Kleist's "Kohlhaas," as some critics have tried to view it, but a satire in which the achievements of *Realsozialismus* are measured against the Romantic roots of revolutionary idealism.[19]

One of Kleist's central themes in "Michael Kohlhaas" is the incapacity of human communities to act in accordance with reason, even as embodied in their own laws and ideals; one consequence of this is that the truly idealistic man or woman will come to grief among the venal and confused majority — and equally, that the majority will come to grief at the hands of its idealists. Under such circumstances, virtue itself becomes a source of social disorder; it is precisely Kohlhaas's virtues (piety, hard work, charity, rectitude) that lead, under the circumstances, to disaster. Hence Kohlhaas was "one of the most righteous and at the same time most horrifying men of his time.... The sense of justice... turned him into a thief and a murderer" (Kleist 2: 9).

The fate of the untimely, unwelcome idealist in a pragmatic world is a familiar theme in Hein's work. It was most directly treated in the play *Schlötel oder Was solls*, and is indeed a common topos in GDR literature. In *Schlötel* (which was discussed at greater length in chapter 1), an academic is sent into "production" because of his uncompromising idealism, which has made him an uncomfortable colleague at his institute. He attempts to improve the efficiency of the factory through a grassroots campaign to institute a pay-reform scheme, but he encounters resistance equally from his fellow workers, their supervisors, and the local party officials, all of whom have arrived at reasonably comfortable — if cynical — accommodations with the status quo. Schlötel ultimately goes insane and throws himself into the Baltic. Manfred Behn notes that in Hein's original version of *Schlötel*, the hero was an idealistic Westerner gone East, and the play was a much more typical *Produktionsstück* in the manner of Heiner Müller; but in the revision, the concept has been radicalized, making the theme purely intra-GDR (Behn 2). An increasingly prominent theme starts to emerge: the disparity between ideals and the private, trivial circumstances of people's lives — in short, their comfortable accommodations with reality. Schlötel cannot accept such disparities between public and private, and is therefore doomed; his behavior earns only scorn and he is finally diagnosed as "hirnwütig" [demented], that is, unbending in the face of realities everyone else tacitly acknowledges (Fischer, *Christoph Hein* 47). Yet all Schlötel has done is to take Marx at his word concerning the non-alienated conditions of labor in a communist society, and to point out the discrepancy between communist ideals and institutionalized holdovers from the capitalist past (Funke, "Spiel" 151). In a similar sense, Hein takes Kleist at *his* word, transposing the human values that motivate Kohlhaas to the context of the GDR, where they appear to have little relevance. A Kohlhaas in the GDR can only be represented as an object of derision, because the very possibility of independent thought and action has been neutralized by the prevailing ideology.

The exact nature of Hein's use of Kleist can be inferred from a comparison of the openings of the two stories. Hein's "Kohlhaas" begins with the description of Hubert K. as "das Muster eines *Rechnungführers*" [a model accountant: *NUFM* 102]. This recalls Kleist's opening description of Kohlhaas as "das Muster eines guten Staatsbürger" [a model citizen: Kleist 2: 9], with a telling difference: Kohlhaas is respected as a human being, while Hubert K. is respected as a human adding machine — no New Socialist Man, but the very picture of an alienated laborer, and the parodic representative of a fully rationalized society. The machine-like characterization of Hubert K. puts in an ironic light the original Kohlhaas's delicate sense of justice, said to have been as sensitive as a gold balance (Kleist 2: 14). Hein replaces sensitivity to injustice with the meticulousness of book-keeping, a mechanical operation which, lacking any moral dimension, is equally serviceable within any social system. Reinforcing this degraded parallelism, Hein is careful to emulate Kleist's identification of Kohlhaas's essential virtue — the love of justice — as the ultimate cause of his brigandage. The analogous situation for Hubert K., the essential characteristic that leads to farcical domestic tragedy instead of tragic death, will necessarily be ludicrous. Hein describes that characteristic with Kleistian precision:

> Nach allgemeiner Ansicht der unterrichteten Bürger war auch das spätere Geschehen selbst eine Folge allzu genauer Lebensführung unseres Mannes, und sein häufig zur Erklärung seiner Handlung erfolgter — und ebensogern, wenn auch zumeist ironisch zitierter — Ausspruch, er habe nichts wollen, als sich *sein Recht schaffen*, wurde von den gleichen Bürgern kurz und bündig als Kleinkrämerei abgetan.
> (*NUFM* 102)

[According to the general view of well-informed citizens, later events were themselves a consequence of our man's all-too-precise manner of conducting his life; his frequent assertion, offered as explanation of his conduct, that he desired nothing more than *his rights under the law*, was curtly and irrevocably dismissed by these same citizens, who nonetheless enjoyed quoting it mostly in an ironic vein, as a trivial obsession.]

As a moral agent, Hubert K. promises to be a shriveled nitpicker in comparison with Kohlhaas, whose abused horses were less the issue than an outraged respect for the rule of law and his own "angeborene Macht" [native sovereignty: Kleist 2: 31]. And as a moral environment, the GDR emerges as a place where profound questions of justice can never even be raised, but where petty self-absorption consumes people's lives. Without being explicit (and unpublishable), Hein casts scorn on the GDR's enshrined self-image as a just, equitable, and utopian society of *Realsozialismus*; the great moral and political aspirations of the Enlightenment and Romanticism have been forgotten, not fulfilled, buried under a mountain of factitious legalism and empty political rhetoric.

The opening characterization of Hubert K. indicates how Kleist's novella is being used as a standard of moral and political gravity. Kleist's paradoxical vision of the human condition scarcely reappears in Hein's story, because the point of the latter is to show the shallowness of the GDR's "vision" of what is human. The titanic collisions between law and morality, order and anarchy, equality and privilege never materialize in Hein's GDR, because the GDR rested on a political philosophy that claimed to have abolished the possibility of such conflict. It is tempting to view the story as a send-up of the GDR's canonical notion of "non-antagonistic contradictions" in socialist society, as opposed to the class-based "antagonistic" ones plaguing society in Kleist's day. Hein allows that the GDR may indeed be free of the old class conflicts that motivated Kleist's story, but the problem for *Realsozialismus* (or for any industrial, urbanized society, Hein will later argue) is that new, equally real conflicts have arisen — for example, between the prerogatives of family life and those of the workplace, or between the autonomy of the individual and obligations to the social whole. "Der neuere (glücklichere) Kohlhaas" gives East German ideologues the benefit of the doubt, assuming that socialism's non-antagonistic contradictions can ultimately be resolved to everybody's satisfaction, but in order to believe this, we have to agree that the ideal human condition is an ideal banality. The Hubert K. proceeding is a meager, silly affair with none of the revolutionary romance or moral gravity of the Kleist story; human existence has not simply lost its meaning in socialism, it has lost its seriousness amid all the surplus absurdity and contradiction.

Hubert K.'s struggle with authority for his "rights" differs in another significant respect from Kohlhaas's struggle: Kohlhaas is ruthless and unswerving in the pursuit of his aims, whereas Hubert K. is much more weakly and intermittently motivated (as befits the lesser gravity of his predicament). And though Hubert K.'s behavior derives from his his accountant-like turn of mind, the subsequent development of the story shows that pride and social censure have a bigger influence than strength of conviction. Hubert K. at first merely complains about the missing 40 marks to his coworkers, all of whom, even those whose pay was similarly docked, prefer to celebrate the large windfall that the pay bonus nonetheless represents. Hubert K.'s sour attitude briefly makes him the object of ridicule in his office, of the "bald verebbenden Spott seiner beide Kolleginnen" [quickly ebbing scorn of his two female colleagues: *NUFM* 104], whose amusement Hubert K. finds especially galling. His irritation has no further effect, however, than to cause him to be brusque with his wife, who, like his female colleagues, is delighted about the pay bonus. It is only at the prodding of an acquaintance whom Hubert K. meets on vacation (an engineer who is actually more interested in Elvira K. than in the money question) that he decides to pursue his complaint further. The resultant ridicule increases his resolve, as does the levity at the eventual hearing of the conflict commission. Deciding to seek redress in court after his complaint is again dismissed as unfounded (109), Hubert K. again appears to be driven more by his coworkers' scorn than by any abstract principle: his plan appears to him "die überhaupt einzig mögliche Antwort auf die für ihn so erniedrigende Veranstaltung des Vortags" [the only possible answer to the personally humiliating proceedings of the previous day: *NUFM* 110]. When the court, too, decides against him, Hubert K. bitterly renounces any further effort toward redress (114), but by now the case has become a public matter no longer fully under his control. He stands by passively "mit unsicherer Freude und dankbarer Verwirrung" [with uncertain joy and grateful confusion: *NUFM* 115] as a young, ambitious union official takes the initiative in obtaining a review of Hubert K.'s case in Berlin. The higher authorities are moved to examine the case by Hubert K.'s alleged words, "Ich habe kein Vertrauen mehr in die sozialistische Gesetzlichkeit" [I no longer have any faith in socialist rule of law: *NUFM* 115] — words which the union official has apparently put into Hubert K.'s mouth. When Hubert K. finally wins his case, his earlier passivity is stressed a final time:

> Hubert K. . . . feierte an dem Abend dieses für ihn so denkwürdigen und freudigen Tages . . . , in dem er, so rasch ermüdet nach ersten Versuchen, sich in der Welt sein Recht zu verschaffen, auf die außerordentlichste Weise von dieser Welt darin unterstützt wurde.
> (*NUFM* 117)
>
> [Hubert K. . . . celebrated at the end of this day, so remarkable and joyous for him, on which he, once so prematurely despairing in his first attempts to defend his rights before the world, now found himself supported in the most extraordinary manner by that world.]

The contrast with Kleist's Kohlhaas could not be more bluntly drawn. Kohlhaas's fascination derives from his implacable courage and lack of concern for his own material well-being; when his wife asks him why he is preparing to sell his house in Kohlhasenbrück, he replies, "weil ich in einem Lande . . . in welchem man mich, in meinen Rechten, nicht schützen will, nicht bleiben mag. Lieber ein Hund sein, wenn ich von Füßen getreten werden soll, als ein Mensch!" [because I do not wish to remain in a country that will not protect my rights. Better to be a dog than a man if I am to be trampled on: Kleist 2: 27]. Hubert K., on the other hand, is vacillating, confused, peevish, with no higher purposes than pride and 40 marks. The story seems to suggest that the individual in the modern world, having seemingly benefited from the revolutionary idealism motivating the first Kohlhaas, is a figure only for comedy, not tragedy. The state is always the state, but the individual seems to have been diminished (perhaps not by socialism, but by other changes of modern life — industrialization, bureaucratization, standardization of all sorts — life in the administered world). When material well-being is guaranteed and courage means standing up to office banter, great heroism and great criminality both become inconceivable.

As a novella, the outcome of Hein's story should violate expectation; this implies that the expected outcome in the modern GDR would be Hubert K.'s failure to achieve redress at the hands of a corrupt bureaucracy — the same cynical assumption that underlies much of the action in Kleist's novella. But in the GDR version, the range of moral issues has shrunk ludicrously: Kohlhaas staked his life and his family's material well-being on his quest for justice, and was executed for his efforts; Hubert K.'s great cause is the recovery of 40 marks, and he loses nothing but his reputation and his marriage. Correspondingly, the abstract moral satisfaction that comforts Kohlhaas on the scaffold has been reduced in Hubert K.'s case to the monetary reward and his continued job security in the *Realsozialismus* of the GDR, which for its part, in the persons of the tribunal that decides in Hubert K.'s favor, views this proceeding as a successful confrontation with "schwere Konflikte in unserer Gesellschaft" [serious conflict in our society: *NUFM* 117]. These conflicts are neatly solvable because socialist society allows only non-antagonistic conflicts to arise, not antagonistic ones. This is the theory, at least, and Hubert K. seems to be satisfied with it. Hein replaces Kleist's vision of inscrutable, inhuman fate with a shabby earthly utopia governed by "scientific socialism." As Ursula Heukenkamp points out, Hubert K.'s struggle never has anything to do with justice — it is a shallow matter of forms and rules (629). Hein implies that the socialism of the GDR succeeded most spectacularly where it most lowered its expectations. Hubert K. emerges as the star of a propaganda piece illustrating the wonders of socialist justice, where disputes are resolvable and everyone lives happily ever after. The story's parodic flourishes prevent this position from seeming even remotely plausible, reminiscent though it may be of official rhetoric.

There is another clue to how we should evaluate the events of Hein's "Der neuere (glücklichere) Kohlhaas": the title of the story is modeled on Kleist's anecdote "Der neuere (glücklichere) Werther" (The newer [luckier] Werther, 1811). The anecdote concerns a young Frenchman, Charles C., who has fallen in love with the wife of his much older master, Herr D., a merchant. Although Charles C. makes no attempt to seduce her, the wife notices his distress, takes pity on him, and tries (using various excuses) to convince her husband to send Charles C. away on a business trip. Herr D. refuses, claiming that his employee is indispensable. While the merchant and his wife are visiting a friend in the country, Charles C., who was left behind to tend the business, creeps into Frau D.'s bedroom, undresses, climbs into her bed, and falls asleep. He is awakened in the night by the unexpected return of the married couple, who discover Charles C. in bed, to the consternation of all. After the couple retreats to a neighboring room, Charles C. obtains a pistol and shoots himself through the chest. Remarkably enough, the bullet passes relatively harmlessly through his lung, passes through the wall, and kills the merchant. Charles C. soon recovers, and after a year he marries the merchant's widow, who eventually bears him 15 children. Luckier, indeed! (Kleist 2: 276–277).

Kleist's "Werther" grotesquely twists the end of Goethe's *Werther* by removing all of its pathos and substituting a precise fulfillment of the young lover's desires. In a way this is a parody of the older story, but it is also a commentary on the difference between literary convention and reality: literary conventions, by their nature, do not surprise, but reality often does. A narrative that follows historical fact will seldom be purely tragic, comic, or even farcical; it will more likely be a chaotic mixture of these. Thus with Kleist's anecdote, the reader doesn't know whether to laugh or cry, whether to draw a lesson or not. The anecdote, like many others of Kleist's and, indeed, like the genre of the novella, creates perplexity by abandoning the Aristotelian dictum that a plot must seem *likely* even in its impossibility. Achieving his effects by defying all expectations of plot, Kleist justifies his procedure in the anecdote by pretending to historical veracity, which suggests that history is a source of randomness, freedom, monstrosity, always capable of exceeding the bounds of the expected, including the expectations created by literary convention (or political ideology). Thus in Goethe's *Werther*, classical norms of aesthetic completeness are conserved despite the introduction of characters and values foreign to a classical sensibility, whereas in Kleist's "Der neuere (glücklichere) Werther," the inscrutability of real human experience, its capacity to elude rational expectations, sweeps aside the classical fantasies of reason, causality, morality, and mastery.

Hein's "Der neue (glücklichere) Kohlhaas" alters the themes of Kleist's "Michael Kohlhaas" in much the same way that Kleist altered Goethe's *Werther*. Kleist demonstrated in the "Werther" anecdote (and, of course, much more forcefully in his novellas and plays) that reality was much more mysterious than the rationalistic worldview of classicism would allow. Goethe's proto-Romantic dualism and its attendant psychological discomforts appear quite conservative next to Kleist's discovery of a world in which nothing can be trusted, where everything, not just the corruptions of human society, is founded on illusion. In Kleist's "Michael Kohlhaas," the illusory stability of conventional social structures and religious faith is probed by a pure, shining abstraction: justice; not divine justice, but concrete adherence to human law. Kohlhaas's simple demand that his society enforce its laws exposes the chasm between the abstract notion of justice and venal society of influence, connections, and class privilege out of which it paradoxically grew. Such an abstraction, if imposed on social reality, can only appear as a monstrosity, a portent from another world. Hein parodies Kleist by presenting a world free from this abstract and terrifying uncertainty — a world where everything is planned and everything works out, and where crass materialism is the only heroic ideal left.

Passage and Walter Benjamin

Hein's early stories and plays pose questions of social and moral responsibility, seeking to define the problem of the individual's place within mass society. The trajectory of his thinking proceeds from an initial rupture with the stereotypes of Socialist Realism (as in *Schlötel*, where the idealized New Man becomes a mere ideological shadow, finding no place of contact with the world of political fact, and ending in madness), and moves toward a more general critique of personal autonomy (as in *Cromwell*, where the pragmatic revolutionary hardens into a murderous ideologue and thereby loses control of both himself and history) and of political engagement (as seen in the travails of the intelligentsia in *Lassalle* and *Ah Q*, where the theory and practice of revolution prove to be ludicrously at odds with one another). Meanwhile, the short fiction begins with nearly plotless scenarios about quite ordinary characters. In their attention to concrete, visually-imagined detail, these pieces can be recognized (as Hein himself joked) as the work of a stage-writer pursuing his craft in the guise of prose; however, it would be a mistake to overlook the thematic suggestiveness of this style. Hein so completely defines the historical and material circumstances of his characters that they can scarcely move — their individuality is hidden by their more evident helplessness amid the flow of historic events, flashing briefly into view in moments of resistance, or endurance, or grief. The schematic quality of the "Berliner Stadtansichten" is itself a new and provocative way to formulate the same problems raised by the plays: how to act, whether action is possible, whether and how action is free. In effect, Hein makes it seem as unlikely as possible that autonomy can exist, and then looks for ways to reintroduce it against all hope and reason.

Hein's play *Passage* (1987) addresses the same predicament and the same kinds of characters as the early stories, presenting apparently helpless people tossed up on the shore of violent European history. *Passage* and the stories in particular stand out in Hein's oeuvre as stories about innocents rather than collaborators in historical injustice. And while much of Hein's work before and after the play details the pathologies of history's victims, *Passage*, like the stories, tries to imagine those victims' hidden reserves of strength.

This three-act *Kammerspiel* concerns a group of refugees — communists, Jews, and others of indeterminate origin — who are waiting in 1940 in a town in the non-occupied south of France for a chance to cross the nearby border into Spain. Until the German invasion of France, German nationals had merely been interned; now, they are subject to direct German authority in the occupied portion of France, and elsewhere to indirect pressure from the Gestapo. Non-occupied Vichy France has become at best a way station for refugees waiting for passage elsewhere, and at worst a cul-de-sac; Spain, meanwhile, opens and closes its border unpredictably. All of the characters are shown in a positive light; there is no villain, apart from the cardboard Gestapo men who briefly appear.

Act 1 opens with Dr. Frankfurther, a Jewish Sinologist, and Kurt, a young Communist, playing a desultory game of chess until Kurt disrupts things, establishing him as impetuous and angry in contrast to Frankfurther's passive intellectualism. Kurt is a fiery, sometimes stupid character — a little Schlötel, a little Ah Q (though less self-serving), a little Cromwell's lieutenant Ireton (in his ruthless aspect); he is admirable, though, for his straightforwardness, his refusal to be patient and stoic like Frankfurther (who eventually kills himself, after all — his emotions are turned inward and this is the result). As the landlady, Rosa Grenier, serves them breakfast, tensions become apparent: she is illegally harboring refugees, and it is costing her money and sleep. To emphasize the precarious tolerance of the refugees by the community at large, as well as its curiosity and silent watchfulness, Hein departs from realism early in the play by having the windows to the room periodically opened and closed, signifying surveillance.[20]

The leader of the refugee group, Lisa, is introduced, and then Hauptmann Hirschburg, a German officer of Jewish heritage, who had been sent to join the others against Lisa's express orders. Kurt, disliking German army officers on principle, accuses him of being with the Gestapo. But in fact, Hirschburg is merely a fool; his self-proclaimed identity is wholly German, and he insists doggedly that he has been hounded out of the army because of some mistake. The others resign themselves to his presence, and Joly, the mayor of the town and an accomplice in protecting the refugees, suggests that Hirschburg dress the part of a tourist more convincingly (his dandyish yellow shoes remain a reminder of his lost status throughout the play).

Act 2 opens with the refugees sitting idly waiting for news. Kurt and Frankfurther now are somewhat reconciled; Frankfurther explains his Sinological research, and Kurt is both impressed and scornful to learn that so many interpretations can be derived from a single ideogram such as the one Frankfurther has studied. Hirschburg airs the view (to be encountered again later in *Die Ritter der Tafelrunde*) that all art should be useful. Bad news arrives from the train station — the arrival of two men calling themselves representatives of the German Red Cross. They are on their way to inspect the town to make sure, ostensibly, that no Germans are being detained against their will (an absurd thought anyway). The refugees try to make themselves look like tourists, rearranging and prettying up the room and so forth. They all have false papers: Otto/Phillipe, for example, dresses like and pretends to be a Frenchman, and Hirschburg has what he claims is a visa to China, but which, when read by Frankfurther, turns out to be a pledge never to set foot on Chinese soil (but no matter, European border guards don't read Chinese). The Red Cross men show up, obviously Gestapo, and confiscate everyone's papers. The refugees are ordered to wait where they are while the papers are examined in town. Frankfurther abruptly falls over dead, having taken cyanide. After the Gestapo men leave, the refugees hastily pack up and prepare to flee, except for Lenka, a refugee from Prague, who is waiting for her husband. The act ends giving the impression that everyone, including Rosa Grenier's daughter Marie, who is in love with Kurt, is really about to cross into Spain, though it is unclear how they will do so without papers.

The opening of Act 3 demonstrates the depth of the character's paralysis anew: the refugees are all still here, after having tried and failed to leave. (Again abandoning realism, Hein blithely ignores the fact that everybody should have been arrested by now.)[21] A dinner table is set, and the refugees enter one by one, dispelling the impression created in the last act that they were all leaving — of course they have not left; there is no place to go. Bad news arrives again from the town: a large party of extremely obvious Jews, Polish Hasidim in kaftans, have shown up, and must be hidden somewhere or disposed of. The mayor is exasperated and angry: the Jews are here, apparently, because Hirschburg gave his destination in this town to a friend in Marseilles, the name of the place was passed along to someone else, and this is the result. (Earlier, in act 1, Lisa was very angry when she found out that Hirschburg had left this trail behind him, and accused him of destroying all her work). Hirschburg hears all this, and hears that these Jews (all old men) have managed so far to travel from Auschwitz all the way across Germany and France, and that they wish to pass into Spain. He takes responsibility for having brought them here, and announces that he will personally lead them across the border, through the Pyrenees by night. The others scoff at this, but render what help they can. After Hirschburg departs, the claustrophobic atmosphere of the play is disrupted by surreal stage effects, as a wall of the little room opens upstage, the sky becomes visible, and all of the players gaze out into the night. They are all planning to leave now, so they say (again). Hein avoids any hint of realism or reasonable plausibility, there being no more guarantee than at the end of act 2 that they are really going anywhere. Only the possibility, and that an absurd one, remains, as the curtain descends.

The play deals directly with the problem of the individual in history, investigating whether individual action is possible or not in the face of crushing state power and great historical events, and insists (against all evidence to the contrary, against reason) that choice is possible.[22] The realistic level of the play makes it clear that these refugees have no power, no choice, that they must passively wait, and that the stoic virtue of patience is the highest one a refugee can possess. Frankfurther is patient, and an advocate of patience, but he ultimately gives up and chooses death. Lenka is patient, but she refuses to go over the border before getting word from her husband, whom we may assume to be dead or imprisoned. Kurt, on the other hand, is impatient and mercurial, and a somewhat problematic character in part because of this; however, he is also the most dynamic, least paralyzed character in the play. Hirschburg is the most surprising figure, when he turns from stoicism to the most visionary kind of action at the end, redeeming all his military foibles (associated by Kurt especially with the Nazis) in a single stroke. But the escape from this regime of stoic waiting is accomplished in the play by non-realistic, wildly adventurous means — the impossible story of the old men is concocted, and another old man (Hirschburg, who even walks with a cane because of a limp) is to lead them into Spain and thence to Lisbon. Clearly Hein has made the Jews so *obviously* Jews not merely for some dramatic, plot-based effect (the obviousness of the Jews makes it necessary, in cause and effect terms, to get rid of them quickly), but more importantly as a call for *un*-reasonableness, a rejection of the logic that dictates caution, patience, waiting.[23] Hirschburg articulates the play's final position on reason versus unreason for the incredulous mayor:

BÜRGERMEISTER Sie wollen mit diesen alten Männern über die Pyrenäen?
HIRSCHBURG Ja.
BÜRGERMEISTER Das ist, entschuldigen Sie, das Dümmste, was ich in meinem Leben je hörte.
HIRSCHBURG Sie haben gewiß recht, Herr Bürgermeister. Aber kann uns Vernünftiges helfen? Sagen Sie. Dann muß uns etwas Dummes helfen. (71)

[MAYOR You plan to conduct these old men over the Pyrenees?
HIRSCHBURG Yes.
MAYOR Forgive me, but that is the stupidest idea I ever heard in my life.
HIRSCHBURG Of course you are right, Mr. Mayor. But can reasonable behavior help us? Tell me. Otherwise, something stupid will have to help us.]

According to the mayor's logic, which does after all reign through most of the play, the escape party under Hirschburg is suicidally stupid.

However, what course of action does that imply — handing the old men over to the Gestapo? Logic, self-serving and otherwise, cannot co-exist, past some point, with morality. Logic, patience, stoicism, under these circumstances, amount to suicide (Frankfurther) — an abdication of responsibility, a fall into despair. Either the morality goes, or the reason goes, to be replaced with Hirschburg's courage. And perhaps with Kurt's impetuosity? This remains uncertain at the end.

Of no small moment in the play is Hein's invocation of Walter Benjamin in the character of Frankfurther. The circumstances of Benjamin's suicide in 1940 in Port-Bou, France, while waiting to pass into Spain, supply the plot and setting of the play; Frankfurther's on-stage death when confronted by the Gestapo is modeled closely on Benjamin's death in the face of imminent arrest and deportation to a concentration camp. Frankfurther's life work, the book manuscript that he entrusts to the other refugees, mirrors the papers left behind by Benjamin which would later be published as the *Passagen-Werk*, his materialist study of the origins of the modern urban world. Benjamin's reflections in the *Passagen-Werk* and elsewhere on questions of historiography and the social role of intellectuals parallel Hein's treatment of the same problems, and, of course, the title of the play alludes to Benjamin. However, as the fate of Frankfurther suggests, to say nothing of those other suicidal intellectuals Schlötel and Horn, Hein's assessment of Benjamin's ideas is highly ambivalent.

Benjamin's thinking on the notion of progress, on the delusion of teleological historiography, and on the possibility of revolutionary action within history touches on issues that were urgently important to Hein and other writers living in the GDR. Benjamin calls on materialist historiography to "build the great construction out of the smallest, sharpest, most minutely detailed parts. Indeed the crystal of the total event is to be found in the analysis of the small, discrete moments" (*Das Passagen-Werk* 1: 575). The ambition concealed in this seemingly modest project (which, as is apparent, closely resembles Hein's determination to be a dispassionate, painstaking chronicler of concrete historic situations) is to elude the nets of narrative continuity that have little relation to historical truth, and still less to the possibility of political intervention. Tendentious histories of the usual sort exhibit an orderly, calculated, superficial coherence (for example, Nazi racialist explanations of Germany's plight after the First World War), while true historical insight lacks any such narrative order. It appears unbidden, in a flash: "It is not as if the past throws its light on the present or the present on the past; rather, a picture is produced when the past and present meet to form, as in a flash of lightning [*blitzhaft*], a constellation"

(*Das Passagen-Werk* 1: 576). Thus history is more than a science, Benjamin insists; it is also a form of *Eingedenken,* of mindfulness or realization, in which the pressure of the past momentarily halts the consciousness-numbing, headlong rush of contemporary events, and opens a space for the redemption of all past calamities (1: 589). A truly materialist historiography must arrest history in order understand it.

Hein gives shape to the notion of *Eingedenken* in the ghostly dialogues that serve as a framework in his novel *Horns Ende,* where the dead historian Horn exhorts the living boy/man Thomas to *remember* what he would rather forget. The book's insights emerge not from the accuracy of the stories the narrators tell, but from a constellation their differing views create, and from the forced juxtaposition of past and present. A close thematic relation between *Horns Ende* and *Passage* is evidenced by the *Programmheft* for the original Dresden production of 1987. Alongside an account of Benjamin's flight and suicide, reflections by Heinrich Mann on exile, a description of a French refugee camp by Louis Aragon, and other literary reference points, there are two pages reprinting the ghost dialogues from *Horns Ende,* a book largely unavailable in the GDR in the late 1980s. That novel's message and demand — "Remember!" — finally reaches its audience through a play set on the eve of the Holocaust. Hope may still be entertained, because the worst has not yet occurred. The question, then, is what to do.

The problem with Benjamin's non-teleological history and with his favored metaphor of the synchronic lightning flash (replacing the diachronic, progressivist locomotive of history) is their static form: a scarcely bridgeable gulf opens between thought and action. Benjamin succeeds in imagining a moment of clear insight into material historical reality, but it relies upon an escape from history *as process,* and he never succeeds in explaining how insight is to contribute to action. Fischer argues that the figures of Frankfurther and Kurt represent Hein's attempt to dramatize Benjamin's failure as an intellectual to master present reality (disclosed by the parallel suicides of Benjamin and Frankfurther), while examining the opposite alternative of pure action without reflection, as personified by Kurt:

> The drama directly presents (in the character of Kurt) the question of the praxis of scientific theory in the moment of danger, which demands reactive behavior rather than analysis and planning. Benjamin himself was fascinated by this tension, and attempted to incorporate it as the central possibility of understanding in his materialist historiography. (*Christoph Hein* 122)

But Benjamin's vision of unified theory and action proved to be a failure not just in his personal life, but also in the subsequent course of history (*Christoph Hein* 125, 131). Fischer sees in such figures as Ah Q, Wang, and Claudia the same paralyzed, benumbed waiting that characterizes *Passage*, all of them riding "in the train of history, paralyzed, benumbed, behind curtained windows, unable to find the emergency brake, and indifferent as to the direction they are moving" (115). Hein repeatedly borrows Benjamin's characterization of passive indifference as a "basic existential pressure during modernity's decline" (129), finally identifying Benjamin himself as one of its most notable victims, frozen by history, passively waiting for death.[24]

Hein's deconstruction of this history-induced paralysis builds on Benjamin even as it criticizes him. In this, Hein closely resembles Heiner Müller, who similarly attempts to transform the notion of involuntary or compelled historical *Eingedenken* into a renewed possibility of social engagement. Benjamin's most developed metaphor concerning the nature of historical consciousness, the "angel of history," was central to East German reflection on history and the possibility of changing it:

> A Klee painting named "Angelus Novus" shows an angel looking as though he is about to move away from something he is fixedly contemplating. His eyes are staring, his mouth is open, his wings are spread. This is how one pictures the angel of history. His face is turned toward the past. Where we perceive a chain of events, he sees one single catastrophe which keeps piling wreckage upon wreckage and hurls it in front of his feet. The angel would like to stay, awaken the dead, and make whole what has been smashed. But a storm is blowing from Paradise; it has got caught in his wings with such violence that the angel can no longer close them. This storm irresistibly propels him into the future to which his back is turned, while the pile of debris before him grows skyward. This storm is what we call progress. (Benjamin, "Theses on the Philosophy of History" 259–60)

This vision of history as the totality of catastrophe rather than a progressive narrative, as a moment of *Eingedenken*, with historical insight detached from the power to act within history, agrees with the ideas developed in the *Passagen-Werk* and is much more uncompromising in its denial of an escape from paralysis. Heiner Müller, seeking an escape back into action, into a revolutionary engagement that is theoretical without being impotent, rewrites Benjamin's metaphor in his "Glückloser Engel" fragment, turning the Angel's gaze toward the future. Though frozen in place, the angel awaits release through the delayed, renewed force of history:

THE HAPLESS [*glückloser*] ANGEL. Behind him the past washes up, scattering pebbles on wings and shoulders, with a noise like buried drums, while before him the future is blocked, his eyes pressed in, the pupils exploded like stars, his wrenched words a noisy gagging, his breathing choked. For a time his wings can still be seen beating, the sound of stones striking over behind him heard amid their rush, which grows the louder the more vigorous their vain movement, sporadic, slowing. Then the moment closes over him; rapidly buried alive where he stands, the hapless angel comes to rest, flight gaze breath petrified waiting for history, until the renewed rushing of mighty wingbeats propagates in waves through the stone and announces his flight.
(Müller, "Der glücklose Engel" 18)

In the reading of this text offered by Frank Hörnigk, an important East German critic of both Hein and Müller, Müller's image of the frozen angel is a representation of the "petrified hope" for the "only possible version of utopia." This hope

> arrests history by naming and confronting it, by working to overcome it, steadfastly, without illusions, repeatedly and necessarily pointing to the historically available examples of social emancipation, formulating Communism not as an escape, but as a "real movement." ... For Heiner Müller, [this petrified hope] is imposed by the continuous experiential pressure of one's own history and of the past, the horror of confronting the "slaughterhouse" of fascism, embedded in the "ice age" of a "centuries-long capitalist world war . . . ." ("Texte" 127)

How to escape the paralyzing pressure of history? Hörnigk sees a possible answer in the latent potential of Benjamin's insistence on viewing history not as a science but as a process or form of *Eingedenken*, of remembering and reflecting on the past in its totality while acting in the present with hope for the future for, as Benjamin proclaimed, "What science 'demonstrates,' mindfulness [*Eingedenken*] can modify..." (*Das Passagen-Werk* 1: 589). Hörnigk regards sustained mindfulness as the only possibility for effecting a "rupture of the continuum of the historical process." The revolution must be carried out

> in the name of all the dead, all the generations of the murdered — or not at all. This must apply first and foremost to the proletarian revolution, which expressly bases its legitimacy on the claim that the self-liberation of the working class is meant to be part of a larger struggle toward liberation from the past altogether, and hence a redemption of a general human desire for happiness. (Hörnigk, "Texte" 128)

Hörnigk adduces the example of Müller's *Der Auftrag*, with its report by the dead of a betrayed revolution, as an example of how the aborted revolutions of the past can be revived: "History can begin. Its place is now called Africa, Asia, Latin America, the Third World" ("Texte" 130–131). A related aspect of *Eingedenken*, of remembering the dead while consciously acting in the interest of the future, is the necessity of maintaining an awareness of the contradictions of history, of both sides of the story, to avoid telling the history of the winners only, to avoid triumphalism and the specious teleological thinking that goes with it. Müller directly addresses the need for this contradictory awareness in his play *Der Horatier*, and Hein addresses it indirectly through a deconstruction of East German ideology (a narrative spun by the putative victors of history) enabled by the tactic of dispassionate chronicling.

In Hein's novels, and in many of the plays, the reader's main problem is how to assess the viewpoint and actions of an individual who is enmeshed in a particular historical and social situation. *Passage* is the work where Hein poses the question of reason and action most starkly. The inaction of the characters in this play could be viewed as a lack of engagement, while the apparently hopeless actions at the end bespeak a willingness to persevere in the face of all reasonable (and inhuman) objections. What makes the play particularly challenging, though, is the implausibility of the example offered as inspiration — the successful flight of the bearded, hatted, kaftaned, aged Jews across Nazi Europe. The example itself is hard to credit, so what of the moral reasoning deriving from it? Here the judgment of character is replaced by a more abstract problem of judging logically contradictory moral positions and courses of moral action. The play also does more than simply put imperfect characters in historical situations, as happens in *Cromwell*, where the actions of the characters can be traced largely to the contradictions they inherit from history, both in their personal makeup and in the current pressure from society. Here, there is much less of a guiding ideological yardstick for measuring the moral strength of the characters' actions or lack thereof. Certainly the situation is more complex in its rendering than anything in *Cromwell*, where Cromwell deconstructs along fairly clear lines, being a contradictory product of contradictory social conditions, and not an intellectualizing revolutionary like the ideologues of the Leveler faction. He is destroyed by the same social contradictions that create him as a leader. In *Passage*, however, society does not seem principally to be composed of "contradictions" — it is absolutely evil, and the only contradictions in such a situation derive from the mutually contradictory possible responses to that monolithic evil. It is remarkable that Hein states the problem in terms of possibility/impossibility, and, still in a context of real historical events, seems to valorize impossibility, and to view rationales governed by what is merely possible as intellectualized, inwardly-turned oppression.

Notes

[1] "Der Sohn," the last of the short narrative sketches grouped as "Berliner Stadtansichten," charts the development of a Party functionary's son; this GDR-specificity may have been the cause for its being dropped from the Western edition. The latter nonetheless touts itself as an "unexpurgated edition." The title and arrangement of stories in the Western edition also hint at a political agenda: the title story "Nachtfahrt und früher Morgen" earns top billing evidently by virtue of its subject matter, *Republikflucht*, or "fleeing the Republic," the official term for defection to the West.

[2] Fischer points out that the early stories, in their detachment and terseness, still show the hand of a dramatist. Hein's aim is to represent the social by depicting the minute particulars of everyday life in a multilayered, non-reductive way (*Christoph Hein*, 51).

[3] Hein's understanding of this dilemma follows in a long GDR tradition first defined by Christa Wolf in *Nachdenken über Christa T.* (1968, translated into English as *The Search for Christa T.*, 1970), which dramatizes the difficulty encountered by any person (and perforce any artist) who wishes to escape a pre-fabricated, over-simplified vision of social reality. Christa T. is a character who eludes artistic or political categorization, and is therefore a refutation of the intellectual hegemony of such categories.

[4] Drommer's essay accompanying the East German edition of the short story collection notes the resemblance of some of the pieces to "tape recorder fiction" or Hebel-like *Kalendergeschichten* (189). Fischer has pointed out the resemblance of the "*Berliner Stadtansichten*" group to Kleist's anecdotes (*Christoph Hein*, 57).

[5] The partial exception to this is the final story, "Die russischen Briefe des Jägers Johann Seifert," which nominally takes place in 1829; but "Seifert" might also be regarded as part of the group set in the contemporary GDR, since Hein prefaces the story with a faked scholarly note describing the putative discovery of the letters. In any case, the Western edition moves the story to the beginning of the book, with unfortunate consequences. The revised arrangement obscures the centrality of the historiographic concerns suggested by the prominence of "Einladung" in the East German edition, and effectively decontextualizes "Die russischen Briefe," making it difficult to gauge the level of irony with which we should read either this story or the ones that follow.

[6] Fischer sees the central theme of the book as the predicament of the court poet, hence the original positioning of "Einladung" at the beginning (*Christoph Hein* 51–52). In this view, Hein's writing of these stories constitutes a performative embodiment of the themes that Racine is forced to address. Grünenberg similarly construes the theme of "Einladung" as "intellectuals and power" (247). Heiner Müller undertakes a more extended (and no less

self-lacerating) treatment of the indignities endured by court poets in his play *Leben Gundlings Friedrich von Preußen Lessings Schlaf Traum Schrei*.

[7] Further attesting to a fascination with his French forebear, Hein also has translated Racine's *Britannicus* (*Die Ritter*, 195–263).

[8] Heukenkamp, indeed, regards the whole Seifert story as nothing but a transparent mask for Hein, its historic dimension an unconvincing pretense (630). Funke, on the other hand, argues that Hein is not simply using history as a device, but is serious about grasping the essence of history. Hein expects his reader to make comparisons between past and present, and to be surprised by contradictions (149).

[9] According to Behn, Seifert and Humboldt may be grouped with Cromwell, Lassalle, and Racine, among others, the provocative question for the reader being in all cases: How does an intellectual avoid ending up like these people? (7).

[10] The multi-layered system of complex vetting procedures imposed on and carried out by East German publishing houses tended, by the 1980s, to focus on certain forbidden topics and buzzwords. There might be no mention allowed, for instance, of the term "ecology." This still left a great deal of room for more ambiguous or oblique social criticisms. See Darnton 204–205.

[11] See "Öffentlich arbeiten" and "Die Zensur."

[12] Hörnigk suggests that by sandwiching ordinary people between prominent figures like Racine and Humboldt, Hein is lifting the former out of anonymity (111). This is correct as far as it goes, but I think that the comparison cuts both ways. As Fischer has it, the stories deal with spiritless people who conform to their time and place without having the *illusory* (and corrupting) higher motivations of a Racine or Humboldt ("*Einladung*," 133).

[13] Heukenkamp contends, on the other hand, that the "Berliner Stadtansichten" are not especially innovative, being influenced by Anna Seghers, and through her, Kleist. She acknowledges, though, that Hein's characters are far less aware of the forces behind their troubles than are Seghers' or Kleist's characters (630). I believe that this is a crucial difference, since the fostering of the *reader's* "awareness" (*Bewusstsein*, a Marxist buzz-word) is Hein's ultimate purpose. Unlike Seghers, Hein refuses to weigh in on what even he regards as the side of right; this the reader must do for him or herself. The flatness, the lack of decoration in the stories leaves gaps and tears in the narrative which the reader must fill in (Funke, 150).

[14] Linsel compares the story to *Der fremde Freund*, noting that both have a heroine who is superficially fortunate, un-damaged, a survivor of difficult historical circumstances, but on whom history has left a defining deformity.

[15] In a representative Western review, the *Süddeutsche Zeitung* named this the *best* of the "Berliner Stadtansichten" (Franke), perhaps demonstrating the western appetite for East German escape yarns.

[16] The theme of intergenerational violence and betrayal, as manifested in East German society as a whole, is nowhere better depicted than in Reiner Kunze's short story collection *Die wunderbaren Jahre* (The Wonder Years, 1976).

[17] McKnight states that "The Son" is based in part on Hein's experience trying and failing to enroll in the Babelsberg film school in 1966 (*Understanding Christoph Hein* 12). The relevant section of the story is presumably this account of the classmate whose educational plans are thwarted by Pavel's influential father.

[18] The story's title alludes to the English title of a sentimental popular song (*NUFM* 99).

[19] The *Frankfurter Allgemeine Zeitung* reviewer Uwe Wittstock's completely misses the point of the story when he pompously criticizes Hein for failing to match Kleist's moral seriousness, having instead provided his hero with such a trivial cause to fight for that murder and arson would be absurd. As if modern authors were obliged to use classical models only in an unironic, respectful manner! At least one other reviewer, Konrad Franke for the *Süddeutsche Zeitung*, was perspicacious enough to note the suggestiveness of supplying irony where Kleist had lacked it. Fischer also provides a better reading, despite a certain annoyance with the preciousness of Hein's stylistic imitation of Kleist, when he points out the alienating effect produced by using Kleistian language to describe the GDR, highlighting its thoughtless conformism ("*Einladung*," 131).

[20] In the Dresden production, the local villagers were themselves seen standing at the window, peering in at the refugees like visitors at a zoo. Even more startlingly surreal, Kurt at one point performed a soft-shoe minstrel routine in front of the open window. This director-added spectacle had nothing to do with Kurt's development as a character, but served to temper Kurt's strident individualism with a reminder of his common and degrading lot as a refugee. It also underscored the role-playing motif that runs through the play and which is exemplified by the following statement by Otto: "Das Ganze ist ein Spiel. Wir spielen Sommerfrische, das Dorf spielt den Ahnungslosen. Solange sich alle daran halten, geht es uns gut" [The whole thing is an act. We play vacationers, the town plays dumb. As long as everyone sticks to his role, we'll be fine: 23]. Erika Stephan links this motif to the characters' concluding embrace of irrational hope: ultimately, the playing of imaginary roles is the only productive activity possible in the state of paralysis prevailing in the play (220).

[21] Stephan notes the number of "astonishing loose ends" in the play, among them "the unexplained disappearance of the Gestapo delegation, Otto's missing biography, the fairy-tale-like phenomenon of the group of old Jews traveling unopposed across Europe" (214). I would group these with the many anti-realistic staging effects, both Hein's and the director's. As for the Jews, though, it is interesting that Hein himself, in a 1989 conversation with the author, defended the story as based on fact.

[22] "In *Passage*, Hein again uses the existential theme of waiting in a closed room, hoping to take a step into being, fearing to step into nothingness, with both alternatives dependent upon one's mustering the resolve to exercise a choice" (McKnight, *Understanding Christoph Hein* 153).

[23] Klaus Dieter Kirst, the director of the Dresden production, characterized the effect of the old Jews as "a staggering challenge to everyone to contemplate the limits of the possible" (quoted in McKnight, *Understanding Christoph Hein* 153).

[24] Janssen-Zimmermann takes a considerably softer view of Frankfurther's putative failure, suggesting that Hein admires his principled rejection of the extermination awaiting him at the hands of the Nazis, while at the same time criticizing the viability of his intellectual stance as a model for personal identity and social engagement (*Gegenwürfe* 132).

3: Power and Repression in *Der fremde Freund*

Displaced Persons

IN HIS PLAYS AND SHORT STORIES, CHRISTOPH HEIN displays a keen interest in the inexorable pressure of historical events on relatively helpless individuals, paradoxically emphasizing their responsibilities in the face of, and in spite of, history. Set in the urban, anonymous, industrial GDR, these narratives identify the individual's temptation to withdraw from society and from history as the most insidious threat to individual happiness. To "withdraw" from history is really to submit absolutely to the role of victim (or victimizer) within a given historical reality. That the withdrawal can only be illusory — there is no "outside" to history — provides the field of conflict in Hein's narratives. Social alienation and historical amnesia are closely linked, so that detachment from one's surroundings becomes explainable (though not excusable) as a logical consequence of the experience of history.

In *Der fremde Freund*, Claudia, an East Berlin doctor, recounts the events of her year-long relationship with Henry, an architect who has died in an apparently random act of violence. Claudia icily describes her self-sufficient detachment from everyone around her, including Henry, and prides herself on not letting the problems of others overwhelm her (she has enough of her own, she notes). Ostensibly, the plot revolves around the death of Henry, but the novella's real concern is the destruction of Claudia as a fully living person. The bulk of the narrative is Claudia's account of her sterile day-to-day life, culminating in an autobiographical excursus that circles round again to her present condition as a thick skin with nothing inside. The skills of self-control and conformity that Claudia learned as a child in the Stalinist 1950s linger in adulthood in the form of a thoroughgoing repression (*Verdrängung*) of memories of the past, or more precisely, of a past Claudia who had the capacity for love. Taking into account Hein's ambiguous handling of Claudia's identity, she may be thought of as a displaced person (*verdrängte Person*), a refugee from history and from herself, who has exited the narrative prior to its opening, which, unsurprisingly, is a repressed dream.[1] Her life, and her world as we see it, is filled with moments of violence that recall and repeat the initial violence wrought on her by state power, and compounded by her complicity with it.

Because of its subject matter and tone, some East German critics charged that *Der fremde Freund* was an anti-social or even anti-socialist work, and complained that Hein had at any rate not stated his own position with sufficient clarity. Other critics perceived a profound political engagement. Following the book's critical and commercial success, Hein was often asked by interviewers to account for the contradictory responses he evoked. He used these occasions to articulate his view that the proper relation of the writer to the reader is not that of a prophet, but is instead collaborative, a mutual struggle to understand the past: "About the future path I can say nothing," he writes in "Wir werden es lernen müssen" (52). Hein takes care to distinguish himself from writers and critics who, in line with socialist cultural policy, regarded it as their duty to educate and guide the public. A basic tenet of Leninist centralism was the role of the Party, understood to be the most ideologically advanced segment of the proletariat, in shaping the beliefs of the masses through education and art. But if the public has no guides, it consequently must take responsibility for itself, which is what Hein sees happening in the responses to his novella:

> I believe (and I have had this confirmed by discussions and by letters from readers) that what really counts in this book is the compulsion to pose this question. That the reader is very strongly pressed to answer this question, or at least not to evade it.
> ("Ich kann mein Publikum nicht belehren" 70)

The reader's central duty to *think* means not only that authors should avoid didacticism or condescension, but also that interpretation tells as much, maybe more, about the interpreters as about the book interpreted. "All criticism is self-criticism.... People's accusing fingers always point at themselves..." (Hein, "Lorbeerwald" 18). Hein contends that the disagreements about his book ultimately result less from the book's structure than from the dissimilar experiences of its readers:

> Books are not in fact read the same way they are written; every reader reads them differently, depending on the sort of dialogue that opens up. *Der fremde Freund* proves this point dramatically: there was vigorous criticism for and against it, there were readers who said it was a pessimistic book, and readers who said it was a profoundly optimistic book. ("Wir werden es lernen müssen" 54)

For Hein, a mark of his novella's success is its ability to be read in many different ways, but what this meant in practice was an ambiguity not readily enlisted for the purposes of any one ideological camp. In the same interviews, Hein objects to certain readings of his book, indicating that he does regard some as wrong or simplistic, while endorsing others.[2] Elsewhere he condemns cavalier critical practice as a manifestation of totalitarianism through language, so his interview remarks need not be taken at face value.[3] Rather, they reflect the peculiar situation of the GDR in the 1980s, where state-sanctioned publishers released books that were virtually manifestos against Stalinist cultural policy, and establishment critics fell into one of two camps: those who continued to enforce old norms at the expense of innovative literature, and those who tried to more or less assimilate the challenging new literature into norms alien to it. Hein's novella is clearly a response to this critical mix of explicit censorship and circumspect rationalization. The sheer bulk of commentary that grew up around the book provides a fine example of how the GDR's public organs of culture went about their business, and its diversity gives the lie to over-simple expectations of ideological conformity. (Western reviews, by comparison, were much more predictable.[4]) Because the novel depicts mechanisms of psychological repression in the GDR, the responses of East German reviewers and critics often provide double-edged insight into the book's structure and effects.

Critics and ideology

Der fremde Freund appeared to initially positive reviews in the GDR press, which departed from the frequently carping tone it had used to greet Hein's plays. Although not reviewed in *Neues Deutschland*, the flagship Party newspaper, the book received notices in several prominent local and special-constituency dailies and weeklies. After a lag allowing for the publication of the book in West Germany (under the title *Drachenblut*), Hein's newest work also received mostly glowing reviews from numerous western newspapers and magazines. As criticism of the book unfolded in the East, critics eventually began questioning its ideological soundness, a problem that would be carried into the academic journals before reaching a de facto resolution in Hein's favor. (The book would eventually be reprinted in East Germany in large paperback editions.) In the East, the critics' identification of the important formal questions, their judgments of Hein's stylistic success or failure, and their assumptions about reader response followed from political and critical commitments that often fit poorly with Hein's recalcitrant text.

Helmut H. Schulz, writing for East Berlin's *Berliner Zeitung*, excuses the book's openness to controversial and widely divergent readings by viewing it as exhibiting an extreme, and hence rare, degree of realism; Hein's is a book that "trusts to its material and succeeds without symbolism." In apparent contradiction to this, however, Schulz reads the bleak picture of "reality" that emerges as a provocation to the reader, who must not succumb to hopelessness even though the first-person narrator Claudia herself may be beyond hope: "For me, though, this depiction signals a whole series of alternatives, and only a new and sharp-sighted generation will succeed in approaching these intimate aspects of experience and making new discoveries there." The book provides detailed and believable descriptions of life, which, by virtue of their faithfulness to reality, should educate readers to find better strategies for their own lives. Paradoxically, the book is both negative and positive, critical yet Socialist Realist, describing reality faithfully, yet in such a way that real readers will reject it. The question might be raised (and it later would be) as to who the critical yet idealistic readership of the book really could be, since the assumption that it is a younger generation seems more piously optimistic than anything in Hein's novella warrants. Schulz concludes more cautiously: "The character in the book never gains understanding, but some readers will arrive at insights."

In much the same vein, Christoph Funke (in *Der Morgen*) and Ingrid Feix (in *Junge Welt*) see the book as a cautionary tale whose readers will be forced to find ways out of the dilemmas it poses. Funke argues that although Claudia is a thoroughly negative, fearful, and socially isolated character, she may serve as a provocation to readers in their own adjustment to society:

> The virtuoso storyteller Christoph Hein in fact turns this fear of knowing one's self and coexisting with other people into a means of compelling the reader to respond critically to [Claudia].

Feix expresses nicely the distress one feels while trapped within Claudia's narrative:

> Christoph Hein depicted a figure whom one follows intently, but with the utmost reluctance, who seems aloof and indifferent, who simply lives contrary to the way one expects and wishes.

Even though the social and personal realities of the book never come into question, readers are expected to reject Claudia's perception of them.

The reviews mentioned so far avoid mention of the historical and social causes for Claudia's condition, a matter of obvious sensitivity in a novel that blatantly depicts the inhumanity of Stalinist authoritarianism. The question of how far toward the present day this critique may be taken lies behind Sybille Eberlein's complaint (in the *Tribüne*) that Hein provides no adequate and socially generalizable motivation for Claudia's antisocial behavior:

> I regretted greatly that Christoph Hein provided no sufficient motivation for his heroine's ever more complete flight from social responsibility, and that I have to be satisfied with Henry's death. Hein shows how fearful parents and societal failures provide the basis for the destruction of a childhood friendship. Later, individual confrontations, no longer necessarily connected with social development, have an influence on the woman's view of herself as outside all social bonds. Increasingly, they make of the doctor a being alienated from her humanity in a social "somewhere" that exists nowhere.

The objection that Claudia's early experiences are unrelated to her later ones and that the society in which she grew up has nothing in common with the present-day GDR was possible only if one refused to draw the obvious conclusion: that vestiges (or worse, more than vestiges) of Stalinism still persisted into the 1980s, not just as institutions, but in damaged individuals. Henry's death results from his own active self-destructiveness, which complements Claudia's more passive withdrawal from life; the two fates are not bound merely by coincidence, or by an arbitrary authorial decision. Eberlein finds it hard to accept the appropriateness of Henry's death precisely because it reveals the general social applicability which she claims the book lacks.

Eberlein's review nonetheless anticipates the more thorough attempts to analyze the structure of *Der fremde Freund* that would follow, replacing a simplistic notion of Socialist Realist utility with an inquiry into the mechanisms of social causality as they are reflected in the novella. A cannier effort in this direction is Klaus Hammer's article for *Sonntag*. Agreeing with the other reviewers, Hammer regards Claudia as a provocation to East German readers, whose ideological orientation should cause them to reject Claudia's paralysis and to reflect on their own lives: "The author does not intervene in his story; the blindness of his speaker, which is never directly analyzed, should provoke the awareness of the reader, leading him to reexamine his own attitude toward life and to consider the need for change." Hammer identifies Claudia's specific failure as a refusal to seek her individuality within a social context, which indeed is the only way that individuality can mean anything: "The question of identity: To what extent can I be I? Is the way cleared socially for me to discover my 'I'? Hein's speaker refuses to pose these questions at all." Claudia's alienated individuality runs counter to the ideological norms of her society, and like a disease it destroys what humanity she still possesses. Hein's minute depiction of a depressing, non-idealized reality through the eyes of one of its victims aims at rallying support for the neglected potential of socialism, revealing "a sense of quite contemporary responsibility" (that is, *Parteilichkeit*) on the part of the author. The narrator, according to this reading, is ultimately responsible for her own "damaged diminished humanity," having failed to appropriate the possibilities offered her by her (socialist) society. Hammer paints her as a wholly negative character as a means of rehabilitating the book's most troubling aspect: Claudia's compelling, intelligent observations about that society, which clearly hit home regardless of her psychological problems. (Of course, Claudia's sociological critique applies equally well to the West, as many Western critics noted.) Whereas Hammer claims that "Hein aims at eliciting neither horror nor sympathy," I would contend that Hein means to arouse *both*. Claudia's defense of personal autonomy is not so easily dismissed. The most devastating passages of the book, touching on the 17 June 1953 Berlin workers' revolt and the persecution of religious believers, concern precisely the opposite problem: history's effacement of the individual.[5] Yet Hammer's response illustrates the determination with which many critics sought an officially acceptable rationale for praising a book which so clearly invites condemnation on political grounds, a vulnerability exploited later by more doctrinaire commentators.

By the time discussions of Hein's novella began appearing in the GDR's scholarly journals, hostile critics had marshaled their forces. The principal objection raised was that readers would be easily misled because of the high degree of authorial detachment. Another charge was that Hein had misrepresented his society, or, in a variation on this, that his main character's behavior was not satisfactorily motivated. Finally, some critics questioned Hein's political commitment. These objections were voiced in late 1983, when *Der fremde Freund* was treated to that peculiar GDR institution, a "Für und Wider" [Pro and Con] discussion in *Weimarer Beiträge*, with three of the six critics attacking the novel, and the final word going to an ideologue who tells Hein that he needs to develop a "more mature worldview" (Wilke 1655). Although some of these objections, particularly the problem of motivation, find their echoes among Western critics, in the GDR they were always colored by Socialist Realist assumptions: politically engaged novels ought to make clear the author's political stance, they ought to contain positive heroes who can serve as models for social action, and they ought to depict reality in light of the advance of socialism. Only when such views are known to be unstated assumptions do the hostile critiques make any sense. And given their assumptions, the hardliners were quite justified in taking offense at Hein, judging from his later remarks about the social value of diverse interpretations and the uselessness of didacticism in "Wir werden es lernen müssen" (53).

In the mildest objection among the *Weimarer Beiträge* essays to Hein's ambiguous relation to his characters, Klaus Kändler worries that the novella never even suggests what the alternative to life-as-Claudia might actually be: "Not a single character appears in the novella whose strengths might be opposed to such an attitude and such a mode of living" (1640). We are left, Kändler assumes, with the need to connect the dread felt in the opening dream to the coolness of the narrative, although this critical approach is nowhere explicitly endorsed by the text itself. Rüdiger Bernhardt questions much more sharply whether such a uniformly negative set of characters, requiring a great deal of critical distance, should be set before the reading public: "It remains uncertain whether this critical distance is possible in view of the public's current level of experience with literature" (1637). Bernhardt is particularly distressed that his students often identify with Claudia, finding confirmation of their own experiences (1635). Drawing facile conclusions about Hein's degree of social commitment from the authorial distance of his narrative — and this after admitting that *Der fremde Freund* could be read in various ways — Bernhardt rejects the novella outright and accuses its author of showing "insufficient ability . . . to keep in view the opportunities for development in [East German] society" (1638).[6] Ursula Wilke best expresses the complaint that Hein fails to portray accurately the advanced socialist society of the GDR. Wilke echoes more sensible critics when she complains that the book is too uniformly grim to be realistic, but her definition of reality turns out to be thoroughly partisan: the novella fails by not delivering the approved view of East German society as a place where disaffected individuals could always avail themselves of rich opportunities for personal fulfillment:

> Oddly, nobody ever requires more of her . . . . The doctor never encounters situations that would expose her to maturer ideas, kindlier people, better behavior, that would make her reflect on herself . . . There is a discrepancy in this false way of identifying personality with society. Society in its multiplicity is more than just personality, which is precisely why so many opportunities for personal development exist here and now [in the GDR]. The novella is obligated to convey this.
> (1653–1654)

In short, Claudias *do* exist in socialist society, but only because some individuals reject socialist values and opportunities. Hein's own position differs from this in its willingness to admit that the GDR must be blamed or credited, after 40 years, for the people it has created.[7]

The scholarly defenders of *Der fremde Freund* responded to these attacks with a strategy dating back to the literary breakthroughs of the early 1960s. Instead of letting Socialist Realism define literature, they used literature to redefine Socialist Realism (although by this time, few critics were interested in defending that doctrine by name). This meant that a new literary current had to be identified and defined as organically socialist, so that Hein and other troubling writers could henceforth be viewed as interesting new contributors to a longstanding tradition. In a profound sense, these critics were in league with Hein in a constellation of social projects — liberalization of cultural policy, surely, but also the leftist dream of social reform that had been perverted by Stalinism. Fundamental to that dream is the proper assimilation of history (the main burden of *Horns Ende*) and a constructive response to the dehumanizing forces of industrial society, concerns Hein regards as central to *Der fremde Freund* ("Ich kann mein Publikum nicht belehren" 69). If the critical response seems only concerned with establishing literary categories which now, after the dissolution of the GDR, have little importance, the intention behind the categorizations should not be forgotten, nor its consonance with Hein's own project.

No clearer moment of critical revisionism is to be found than in the 1984 round-table discussion on the shape of GDR literary history that appeared in *Weimarer Beiträge*. The discussion pitted relatively conservative conceptions of GDR literature (for instance, the central importance of the anti-fascist tradition) against more innovative views critical of the cultural-political assumptions prevailing since the 1950s. All of the participants piously endorse the official view that the GDR had advanced to a high level of socialism, and that the country's new literature could be understood as a reflection of that unique social condition. Even though one perhaps cannot link literary developments with specific actions of a state, the question remains of how "the fact of the formation of new social structures, of new relations between people, new qualities of personality" had affected literature ("DDR-Literaturentwicklung" 1589). While this appears to have set the stage for a programmatically Marxist criticism, the emphasis was on *newness*, implying a distinction not just from capitalist literature, but also from what many critics had expected socialist literature to look like. Whether or not the ideological shell surrounding this emphasis on the new was anything more than a Trojan horse, the effect of the argument was to smooth the way for almost any rationalization in favor of heterodox literary forms. For example, Dieter Schlenstedt argues that even in the 1960s the principal mark of East German literature was to exploit the "field of possibilities" (a Marxist cliché) introduced by the socialist order (1591). What this means in practice is that literature typically engages in constructive collaboration with and criticism of its society, in contrast to the didactic model of Socialist Realism (1592). Schlenstedt accordingly designates the recent works of Hein and others as "socialist critical realism":

> Critical realism — I understand that to mean a procedure of artistic representation that never positively states its values, but instead draws attention to them by exposing deficiencies, illustrations that conceal what is wished or hoped for, mobilizing the imagination, but open to the unambiguous substitution of an affirmative content.... But at the same time I see that this kind of literature is accepted in some members of our literary establishment only with the greatest hesitation. I fear nonetheless that inequalities between literary process and literary evaluation cannot by resolved in favor of the latter. In the introduction to his *Outline of the Critique of Political Economy*, Marx gives a pertinent piece of advice. He speaks there of the connection between the capability of gaining insight into history, of overcoming outdated mythologies, and the capability of a society "to criticize itself," which, as he says, occurs seldom and only under specific conditions.... Therefore the ability to engage in self-criticism could be seen as progress, as an achievement. The criticism in "socialist critical realism" is self-criticism. (1605)

With Marx as his authority, Schlenstedt takes the existence of a critical bent in recent literature as an argument for the maturity of East German society, reasoning from the evidence of the works themselves rather than from a theoretical abstraction. Meanwhile, it is obvious that the problem is not with the production of critical literature (which had never been in short supply), but in the willingness of the powers that be to reconcile themselves to it. Hein surely agrees with Schlenstedt's vision of a socially critical — hence engaged — literature, for his novella is highly critical of the aspects of East German history and policy that led to the deadening of real engagement. Central among these is Stalinist literary censorship, with its denial of lived reality and contempt for historical fact. All of this suggests that Schlenstedt is trying provisionally to de-fang the novella in order to mollify its most vehement detractors, who rightly sense a threat to themselves. For his part, Hein has expressed satisfaction with both positive and negative evaluations of his heroine Claudia, preferring *genuine* reader participation to sanctioned formulas in literature and life; but for Schlenstedt, it is finally necessary to play down the book's ambiguity, to recover it as politically unthreatening, that is, as having one orthodox meaning: "I think that when Hein's book is read with attention, one finds that the character is constructed critically, right down to her forms of speech" (1608).

Schlenstedt's approach was to become the accepted one, so that several years later Dietrich Löffler is able to summarize the reception history of *Der fremde Freund* as a gradual liberation from the narrowness of Claudia's worldview to an understanding of the suggestiveness of her self-contradictions and silences. Yet the suggestiveness is not without its limits, and Löffler sets them when he claims that the novella is principally a response to the legacy of fascism. His apology for the novella's historical rigor is ambivalent:

> I know of no other work in the present-day literature of the GDR in which the existential difficulty of a person must be so strictly understood as the consequence of a political phenomenon, namely fascism. Of course, Claudia does grow up in the post-war era and, though this is not narrated, was presumably taught how to correctly appraise German fascism. What she failed to learn, however, was how to assess the guilt, the experience, of the people around her. She remains trapped in a silence that suppresses her questions, represses her feelings, and ultimately flattens her vitality. (Löffler 1485)

To understand the bleakness of *Der fremde Freund* as an indictment of fascism made good political but dubious critical sense, as Löffler almost acknowledges here. It seems fairly obvious that the book's first historical concern is the early 1950s, not the years before Claudia's birth, and that Nazism is, at most, a secondary or contributing cause for her silence and alienation. Her behavior is fully explainable by the experiences she undergoes in the Stalinist GDR, and Löffler's silence on this subject can be likewise explained by the persistence, even as he wrote in 1987, of that same political order. Yet after establishing his credentials in this manner, Löffler turns around and attacks the ideology to which he must otherwise still submit:

> Hein's fiction has been repeatedly criticized for lacking a historical dimension. I regard this accusation as completely spurious. To put it bluntly: Claudia's problems can only be understood as problems of the post-war generation. Her character is a serious treatment of history as a dynamic process, as a series of events with definite consequences. Hein's fiction offers resistance not to historical insight, but to ideological constructs, to the longing for an absolute transforma-

tion of human behavior consequent upon the end of fascist rule and the beginning of socialist relations. (Löffler 1485–1486)

This complaint against unnamed critics accuses them, conventionally enough, of un-dialectical thinking, but to dismiss ideology itself as un-dialectical is rather more provocative. Löffler hints at a far more liberated critical practice than he actually undertakes.

Frank Hörnigk's remarks about *Der fremde Freund* more successfully escape the critical traps set by dogmatic ideology, while remaining within a tradition of dialectical criticism. In so doing, he approximates Hein's stated views about his work and his readership. Hörnigk stresses the role of the reader's "co-production" of literary works, exploding any critical model that sees good art as mere illustration of "scientific" social analyses, and requiring that readers or theater-goers engage in "back-translation" of his work into the terms of their own life experience (Hörnigk, "Christoph Hein" 109). Sidestepping earlier objections to Hein's portrayal of historical events (in particular complaints implying insufficient ideological conformity), Hörnigk stresses the fictiveness of Hein's facade of historical authenticity. Hein is unwilling to grind his own ideological ax, and avoids using analysis of historical fact as a way *out* of history, or a way into an ideal future; it is the readers who must decide what to do about the social contradictions thus exposed. In *Der fremde Freund*, the special case of Claudia is provided not simply to provoke judgment of her, but to move beyond and behind such a moment to the objective analysis of the social relations that make her existence possible (111). Hein's approach to his materials does more than throw his social criticisms into high relief: through the indeterminacy of the authorial and narrative stance of this text, in which the prescribed role of pedant has been self-consciously renounced, even the author himself is implicated in the critique of detachment and objectivity which is the novella's subject. If the readers are exposed by their interpretations, so the text critiques the author's stance more trenchantly than do its merely ideological detractors, as Hörnigk explains:

> The goal of communication [between writer and reader] can only be to establish a dialogue between equals about questions both sides find significant — in no case a lecture, but an attempt at collective self-discovery, in which the reader is required to interpret the particular literary situation. This does not exempt the opinion and standpoint of the author. He is sublated here in the textually immanent distance from the narrator; he betrays his presence both in the consciously alienating narrative device (in which a man tells the story of a woman and thereby reveals what he thinks a woman would say) and in the manner in which this narrative device (speaking) more and more be-

comes a masking device, at the end of which stands a warning of final paralysis: the mask which the narrator has carved into her flesh has become a second skin to her. (113)

The author and readers betray themselves respectively in the acts of producing or interpreting a text; but in this text, they betray particularly those aspects of themselves that resemble Claudia, with her pretense of detached objectivity. To treat Claudia objectively, with detachment, is to imitate her, even to the point of pathological disassociation from reality. The East German critics who acknowledged no resemblance between the gray world of *Der fremde Freund* and the everyday reality of East Berlin were substituting socialist dogma for personal experience; it really makes little difference whether they were sincere or not, because the mechanisms of repression — of self-censorship — are identical in either case. The novella itself comprehends every possible gradation of just this kind of good-to-bad faith spectrum. But a "proper reading" surely cannot consist of total identification with Claudia, either, precisely because her personality is a dense network of repressions that complicate identification of any sort. Taking into account Hörnigk's observation that the novella compels its readers to be aware of relations underlying the action (not merely to sympathize with or to abhor Claudia), it is appropriate now to turn to the structures of textual repression whose practical effectiveness has already been hinted at.

The Repression of Dreams

The dream with which *Der fremde Freund* opens is no sooner experienced than repressed. This collision between compulsive remembering and willed forgetting presents in miniature the basic movement of the entire book, where reluctant recollections of a dead lover and painful memories of childhood constantly break through Claudia's defenses. Since Hein clearly invites interpretation of dream and narrative in light of each other, close attention to the dream seems to be in order. On the other hand, caution should be used in trying to find keys to the narrative in the dream, which functions less as a table of contents than as an overture that establishes main themes and poses questions whose significance only later becomes apparent. Claudia's peculiarly disjointed identity, her fear of contact with other people, her use of daily routine to anesthetize herself against memory, and her endless rationalizations are all introduced in these opening pages.

"Am Anfang war eine Landschaft" [In the beginning was a landscape] (*DFF* 5; *TDL* 1), the narrator begins, and the landscape is one that will recur many times through the book:

> Der Hintergrund ein Zypressengrün, ein schmaler Streifen vor kristallen-leuchtender Leere. Dann eine Brücke ... über eine Schlucht ... sie ist brüchig, eine Ruine. Zwei Balken über einem grundlosen Boden. (*DFF* 5)
>
> [A background, cypress-green, a narrow line of gleaming crystalline emptiness. Then a bridge spanning an abyss.... broken down, a ruin. Two beams spanning a bottomless deep: *TDL* 1–2].

Claudia's photographs will capture the same kind of scene numberless times, always of "Bäume, Wege, Steine, zerfallene Häuser, lebloses Holz" [trees, paths, rocks, tumbledown houses, lifeless wood: 101–102; 86], expressions of an interest only in "Linien, Horizonte, Fluchten" [lines, horizons, perspective: 102; 87], never in people. At the book's end, Claudia revises this, seeing her photographs as ruins themselves, "Ausschnitte, die nichts begriffen haben. Ihnen fehlt Horizont, ihnen fehlt das Verwelken, Vergehen und damit die Hoffnung" [fragments that don't capture anything. They lack a horizon, they can't wilt or decay, and thus they also lack hope: 210; 178]. The dream-vision of this landscape even takes on photographic aspects, as the bridge is approached "wie eine Kamarafahrt" [like a camera zooming in: 5; 1], which perhaps makes this dream the one exception to all of Claudia's other "creations" — here there *are* people, there *is* hope, or at least terror. The dream-landscape can also be linked to at least one narrated incident, the visit to a ruined mill that immediately precedes Claudia's humiliating discovery that Henry is married:

> Von der Mühle waren nur noch Mauerreste und verfaulte Balken zu sehen.... Wir mußten vorsichtig laufen, um nicht ... zu stolpern.... Ich bewegte mich tastend auf die dünne, buschhohe Birke zu, deren verkrümmter Wipfel sich nach außen bog, nach dem freien Feld. Sehnsucht nach dem Wald. Der Spiegel der Kamera erfaßte den Baum, einen freigelegten Eisenträger, den Horizont. Dann kam ein radloser Kinderwagen ins Objektiv. Ich versuchte, weiterzugehen. Ein Stein bröckelte, etwas fiel hinunter. Plötzlich bekam ich einen Schweißausbruch. Ich faßte nach der Mauer und tastete mich zurück. Ich wagte nicht, aufzublicken und verwünschte meine Waghalsigkeit.
>
> (*DFF* 65–66)
>
> [All that was left of the mill were fragments of walls and rotting beams.... We had to make our way carefully so as not to stumble.... I groped my way along a crumbling wall toward the skinny birch, no taller than a shrub, its twisted crown bent toward the out-

side, toward the open field, longing for the forest. My viewfinder captured the tree, a naked girder, the horizon. Then a baby carriage without wheels. I tried to edge further along. A stone gave way, something rolled down. Suddenly I broke out in a sweat. I reached for the wall and groped my way back. I didn't dare look around; I cursed my recklessness.] (*TDL* 55–56)

This is strongly reminiscent of the dream pair as they edge forward over the bridge, afraid to look down, a similarity that has prompted critics to see the mill scene as the main turning point in the novella.[8] But the climax of the novella actually occurs in the lengthy reminiscence that occupies the ninth chapter, which is followed by various gestures of closure (autumn grades into winter, Claudia's neighbor Frau Rupprecht dies, Henry dies, etc.) as Claudia's life settles back into a routine of day-to-day obliviousness. The dream, like the ninth chapter, reveals a significant event (or memory of an event) which, at the end of the dream as at the end of the novella, sinks back into a background of willed amnesia. The dream's opening allusion to Claudia's habit of photographing dead landscapes links it to the transformation the photographs undergo in the last chapter, where they become harbingers of Claudia's own death. Her approaching death is paralleled by the conclusion of the dream, which for the first time presents Claudia in the act of forgetting her dreams and memories, and thus forgetting and annihilating herself.

An essential attribute of the dream sequence, especially in view of its function as introduction to the narrative, is the ambiguity of the narrator's identity. Uncertainty on the reader's part is less important here than the narrator's lack of, or rejection of, self-knowledge: even she does not know who she is, or if she does know, she is unwilling to acknowledge the fact. "Ich oder die Person, die vielleicht ich selbst bin, zögert. Ich — behaupten wir es — sehe mich um" [I, or this person who may be me, hesitate. I — let's say it is me — look around: 5; 2]. The identity of the narrator's companion — "sein Gesicht bleibt traumverschwommen, ein Mann, sicher ein Bekannter, ein Freund" [his face remains dream-blurred, a man, definitely someone I know, a friend: 5; 2] — is also obscured, looking forward to the blurring between Claudia's "distant lover" Henry and the briefly mentioned new "Freund" [boyfriend: 211; 179] who succeeds him in an apparently endless chain of repetitions. Anticipating Claudia's coolness toward Henry and the other interchangeable people in her life, the dream narrator resists being helped across the bridge while thinking: "Er soll mich loslassen.... Jeder für sich" [He should let go of me.... Each for himself: 5; 2]. This facade of self-sufficiency seems related to the uncertainty as to who precisely these "selves" are; as with Claudia's subsequent behavior, the roots of present emotional deadness can be traced to a past, and a past self or selves, that have been repressed. It will remain for the main narrative to show the structure and meaning of this causal linkage, which in the dream appears arbitrary.

Together with the novella's urgent concern with identity, Claudia's remarks about psychological repression in the eighth chapter and elsewhere contain clues to interpreting the landscape and situation of the dream. We are presented with a romantic landscape, in whose center opens a gorge with a river at its bottom. A ruined bridge precariously spans the abyss. The principal characters in the dream, under an unspecified compulsion, must cross the bridge in spite of the danger. As they do so, five athletes appear and run effortlessly across, past the narrator and her companion, who stand paralyzed and despairing. Hein invites a straightforward reading of the ravine and the crossing as metaphors of life, or more precisely, of life as Claudia conceives it. The abyss itself stands for the portions of her psyche that Claudia has hidden from herself and from others:

> Offenbar erfordert das Zusammenleben von Individuen einige Gitterstäbe in eben diesen Individuen. Die dunklen Kerker unserer Seelen, in die wir einschließen, was die dünne Schale unseres Menschseins bedroht.... Wie erst würden uns die sichtbar gemachten Ablagerungen auf dem Grund unserer Existenz schrecken.... Ein radioaktiver Müll des Individuums, der unendlich wirksam bleibt, dessen fast unhörbares Grollen uns ängstigt und mit dem wir nur zu leben verstehen, indem wir ihn in unsere tiefsten Tiefen einsargen, verschließen, versenken. Ins uneinholbare Vergessen getaucht. (*DFF* 116–17)
>
> [To live in society at all, individuals apparently have to set up barriers inside themselves. The deep dark dungeons of our souls, where we incarcerate anything that threatens the thin layer of our humanity.... Think how terrified we'd be if we had to look at all the layers of sediment at the bottom of our existence.... Our personal radioactive waste, which remains potent indefinitely, whose almost inaudible rumblings alarm us, and with which we can live only if we entomb it, seal it, and sink it in our deepest depths. In inaccessible oblivion.]
>
> (*TDL* 99)

Hence the dream narrator's emphasis on the depth and danger of the gorge she must cross; the bridge consists merely of "Zwei Balken über einem grundlosen Boden.... Ich starre zum Waldstreifen hinüber, unverwandt, um nicht hinunterzublicken. Der Blick in die Tiefe. Ich weiß, wenn ich hinuntersehe, falle ich" [Two beams spanning a bottomless deep.... I keep my eyes fixed on the line of trees opposite, so as not to look down. Down into the abyss. I know if I look, I will fall: 5–6; 2]. To look down is to remember, and to remember is to die, to lose one's "surface" identity. The ambiguity of the dream-narrator's identity exposes this belief as untenable — it is in fact the repression of the "deep" self, of memory, that results in personal oblivion. Marking the start of the novella's descent into what underlies Claudia's surface existence, Hein lets his heroine think of her elevator ride in the opening scene as "Eine schweigende Fahrt in die Tiefe" [A silent descent into the depths: 9; 6], an elegant description of the verbose voicelessness to follow.

Claudia's views, with their references to repression, to unconscious depths of the personality, and so on, appear to bear at least a superficial relation to the ideas of Freud, though he is never mentioned by name. Freud is assuredly an influence on Claudia's arguments for the social utility of her brand of willed amnesia, yet they are a gross distortion of what Freud actually wrote. In *Civilization and its Discontents*, Freud contends that society originates through a repression or displacement of the two fundamental human instincts of Love (eros, libido) and Death:

> Civilization is a process in the service of Eros, whose purpose is to combine single human individuals, and after that families, then races, peoples and nations, into one great unity, the unity of mankind. Why this has to happen, we do not know; the work of Eros is precisely this. These collections of men are to be libidinally bound to one another. Necessity alone, the advantages of work in common, will not hold them together. But man's natural aggressive instinct, the hostility of each against all and of all against each, opposes this programme of civilization. This aggressive instinct is the derivative and the main representative of the death instinct which we have found alongside of Eros and which shares world-dominion with it. And now, I think, the meaning of the evolution of civilization is no longer obscure to us. It must present the struggle between Eros and Death, between the instinct of life and the instinct of destruction, as it works itself out in the human species. This struggle is what all life essentially consists of, and the evolution of civilization may therefore be simply described as the struggle for life of the human species. (21: 122)

Through repression of these instincts, libido is sublimated into useful, socially integrative activities beyond sex itself, and the instincts of aggression are redirected against the Ego itself, forming the Super-Ego, which guards against aggressive ("unethical") behavior in its agency as "conscience." This process of sublimation and the harnessing of guilt as a mechanism of social control leads to the "discontents" of the essay's title:

> Sublimation of instinct is an especially conspicuous feature of cultural development; it is what makes it possible for higher psychical activities, scientific, artistic or ideological, to play such an important part in civilized life. If one were to yield to a first impression, one would say that sublimation is a vicissitude which has been forced upon the instincts entirely by civilization . . . . It is impossible to overlook the extent to which civilization is built up upon a renunciation of instinct, how much it presupposes precisely the non-satisfaction (by suppression, repression or some other means?) of powerful instincts. This "cultural frustration" dominates the large field of social relationships between human beings. (21: 97)

All of this contrasts starkly with Claudia's remarks about repression and society:

> Die Generation meiner Großeltern hatte dafür Sprüche parat: Wenn man einem Übel ins Gesicht sieht, hört es auf, ein Übel zu sein. Ich habe andere Erfahrungen. Was man fürchtet, bringt einen um, wozu sich also damit beschäftigen . . . . Was soll es helfen, Verdrängungen bewußt zu machen. Verdrängungen sind das Ergebnis einer Abwehr, das Sichwehren gegen eine Gefahr. Sie sollen dem Organismus helfen zu existieren. Ein Lebewesen versucht zu überstehen, indem es verschiedene Dinge, die es umbringen könnten, nicht wahrnimmt. Ein heilsamer, natürlicher Mechanismus. Wozu diese Leichen ausgraben, mit denen man ohnehin nicht leben kann. Schließlich, die gesamte Zivilisation ist eine Verdrängung. Das Zusammenleben von Menschen war nur zu erreichen, indem bestimmte Gefühle und Triebe unterdrückt wurden. (*DFF* 115–116)

> [My grandparents' generation had folk sayings like: Fear will disappear if you look it in the eye. My experience has been different. The thing you fear most can do you in, so why focus on it? . . . . What good does it do to make people aware of their inhibitions? Repression is self-defense, defense against danger. Designed to help the organism exist. A living being tries to survive by not perceiving the various things that could destroy it. A healthy natural mechanism. Why exhume these corpses that no one can live with anyway? In the final analysis, all of civilization is one big repression. Human beings discovered they could live in society provided they repressed certain feelings and drives.]
> (*TDL* 98)

Only the last sentence resembles anything Freud could have agreed with. Missing from Claudia's discourse on repression is a notion of economy: whereas Freud would have required that the energy of the repressed drive be redirected elsewhere, Claudia believes that the thing repressed is simply annihilated, erased, never to be heard from again. Claudia's type of "repression," which involves a different target (memories instead of drives), also aims at a different purpose, self-defense against threats from the social world, or in other words, the direct opposite of what Freud conceived of as the integration into that world through redirected libido. In short, Claudia merely tries to dignify her argument for self-unconsciousness (so to speak) by appending a Freudian cliché to it.

Yet Freud's relevance here goes beyond Claudia's specious use of him. *Civilization and its Discontents* opens with a discussion of the strategies used by the psyche to maximize happiness in accordance with the pleasure principle. According to Freud, individuals face three kinds of threats to happiness: "from our own body . . . from the external world . . and finally from our relations with men." Two broad categories of response to these threats are possible for the individual, who can attempt actively to maximize pleasure, or to avoid pain. Freud notes that

> Against the suffering which may come upon one from human relationships the readiest safeguard is voluntary isolation, keeping oneself aloof from other people. The happiness which can be achieved along this path is, as we see, the happiness of quietness. Against the dreaded external world one can only defend oneself by some kind of turning away from it, if one intends to solve the task by oneself. There is, indeed, another and better path: that of becoming a member of the human community . . . . (21: 77)

The parallels to Claudia's behavior are obvious. Her withdrawal from society is motivated by the pain brought by relationships, and those that we see in the novella confirm the urgency of the need for some kind of defense. The political attacks on Claudia (and Hein) stemming from this rejection of social involvement end up unintentionally parodying Freud's apolitical remark that, despite its dangers, membership in the human community is preferable to isolation. Claudia is a chilling example of the contrary view. She has chosen "the happiness of quietness," or silence, learned from her parents as a defense against a special kind of social danger associated with totalitarianism. Of Freud's enumerated methods of compensating for life's discomforts — "powerful deflections, which cause us to make light of our misery; substitutive satisfactions, which diminish it; and intoxicating substances, which make us insensitive to it" (21:75) — all three are manifested in Claudia. Deflection: she throws herself into her work; substitution: she makes photographs; intoxication: she continually medicates herself with alcohol, tranquilizers, and sleeping pills. Perhaps even her compulsive cleanliness (a shower after any experience that demeans her) can be traced to Freud's identification of cleanliness as one of the hallmarks of civilized (but only partly rational) behavior (21: 93–94). Without succumbing to the ever-present temptation to psychoanalyze her every action, to read Claudia in such a way is to confirm how much she is a product of her social environment even though she thinks she is a rational observer and manipulator of it. Further observations by Freud about the social role of aggression will prove enlightening in the discussion below of the novella's violence.

The dream-preface ends in a confusing flurry of distancing and appropriation: the dream events fracture into asynchronous pictures and sounds (again as though this were film), and the dream narrator (awake now?) attempts to remember the dream, but finally repression wins out:

> Später, viel später, der Versuch einer Rekonstruktion. Wiederherstellung eines Vorgangs. Erhoffte Annäherung. Um zu greifen, um zu begreifen. Ungewiß bleibt seine Beschaffenheit. Ein Traum. Oder ein fernes Erinnern. Ein Bild, mir unerreichbar, letztlich unverständlich. Dennoch vorhanden und beruhigend in dem Namenlosen, Unerklärlichen, das ich auch bin. Schließlich vergeht der Wunsch. Vorbei. Die überwirkliche Realität, meine alltäglichen Abziehbilder schieben sich darüber, bunt, laut, vergeßlich. Heilsam. Und nur der Schrecken, die ausgestandene Hilflosigkeit bleibt in mir, unfaßbar, unauslöschlich.
>
> (*DFF* 7)

> [Later, much later, attempts at reconstruction. Re-creation of an event. Hoped-for approximation. To grasp, to comprehend. Its precise nature remains uncertain. A dream. Or a distant remembering. An image I cannot reach, nor ultimately understand. Nonetheless a reassuring presence within the nameless, inexplicable entity that is also me. Finally the desire passes. Finished. Buried beneath my over-real reality, beneath images of my daily life, gaudy, loud, insignificant. Healing. And only the terror, the experience of utter helplessness, remains inside me, elusive, ineradicable.] (*TDL* 4)

The most striking thing about this conclusion to the dream-preface is its near-incoherence. The narrator (or "nameless, inexplicable entity") variously describes the dream (or memory) as "reassuring" and as something that wounds her, that calls for "healing," yielding a sensation of ineradicable terror. She wishes both to remember and to forget what the dream/memory was about, and in neither case is the reader certain why. And what is the temporal relation of the dream-preface to the main narrative? Despite all the thematic and verbal links between the two parts of the novella, we are given no clue, except perhaps the negative one near the end: "Ich habe keine Alpträume" [I don't have nightmares: 211; 179]. Indeed, if the preface is less a dream than a "distant remembering," why shouldn't the "main" narrative be reclassified as a dream, a complex fantasy organized by psychological trauma, a depiction of the narrator's unsteady "surface" existence? The preface's conclusion does clearly provide the return of what is so resolutely repressed throughout the remainder of the book, namely, the abject misery underlying all of Claudia's declarations of "I'm fine." Yet none of this explains how the dream/memory can be a comfort, unless we view it as an expression of the longing occasionally hinted at in the narrative: to return to infancy, and thus to a non-alienated relation to the world. "Ich will kein großes Mädchen werden" [I don't want to be a big girl], thinks a drugged and drunken Claudia, "Ich will nicht, Mama, ich will nicht" [I don't want to, Mama, I don't want to: 71; 60]. Similarly, the much-quoted litany of invulnerability and longing for love that occurs near the end of the novella:

> Ich bin auf alles eingerichtet, ich bin gegen alles gewappnet, mich wird nichts mehr verletzen. Ich bin unverletzlich geworden. Ich habe in Drachenblut gebadet, und kein Lindenblatt ließ mich irgendwo schutzlos. Aus dieser Haut komme ich nicht mehr heraus. In meiner unverletzbaren Hülle werde ich krepieren an Sehnsucht nach Katharina.
>
> Ich will wieder mit Katharina befreundet sein. Ich möchte aus diesem dicken Fell meiner Ängste und meines Mißtrauens heraus. Ich will sie sehen. Ich will Katharina wiederhaben.
>
> Meine undurchlässige Haut ist meine feste Burg. (*DFF* 209)

> [I'm prepared for everything, I'm armed against everything, nothing will hurt me anymore. I've become invulnerable. Like Siegfried, I have bathed in dragon's blood, and no linden leaf has left a single spot of me unprotected. I'm inside this skin for the duration. I will die inside my invulnerable shell, I'll suffocate with longing for Katharina.
>
> I want to be friends with Katharina again. I want to get out of the thick hide of my fears and mistrusts. I want to see her. I want Katharina back.
>
> My impenetrable skin is my mighty fortress.] (*TDL* 177)

Here the contradictions are tinged with an irony that does nothing to allay the despair.

The narrator's assertion that "Finally the desire passes" may offer a fulcrum for understanding the significance of the dream by directing us once again to Freud. The passing of the desire is clearly a repression of that desire, not its benign atrophy. The content of the dream, as seen above, can be linked with Claudia's muffled desire for love and companionship, just as Freud would lead us to expect. What is puzzling, however, is the mechanism or force that motivates the repression that here takes place, leaving behind only a vague "terror" and (in the main narrative) the occasional relapse into conscious longing for Katharina. The narrator — Claudia — is not merely being perverse; as Hein is at pains to demonstrate, her actions and her thoughts are plausible responses to her private and public experiences. Although Hein contends, justly, that his book depicts a social condition common to all industrial societies, the development of the narrative and the construction of its main character follow unerringly from the specificity of Stalinist totalitarianism in the German Democratic Republic. The psychological violence that Freud discerns at the basis of all civilized life takes on the substantiality of steel in *Der fremde Freund* when social control, and social violence, manifest themselves physically. While the book is not exclusively a denunciation of Stalinism, its figuration of Stalinist repression must be recognized before the force of its broader social critique can emerge.

Varieties of violence

The psychological repression exhibited in the dream-preface of *Der fremde Freund* initially has no clear object — repression and its consequent malaise are merely presented, not explained. The main narrative, which provides many objects of repression and ultimately hints at the reasons for it, is constructed as a series of reminiscences punctuated by discursive sections on philosophical issues. These brief "essays" retard rather than advance the plot, while they assist in forming our sense of Claudia's character: she appears to be at her most rational, cynical, unsentimental, and practical when she generalizes about her experiences instead of simply describing them.[9] Thus the narration is balanced between remembering (Claudia recounts, in fits and starts, her year with Henry) and rationalization (she discourses on the anarchy lurking behind the institution of marriage [*DFF* 100–101 / *TDL* 85–86], the proprietary male view of sex [104–107; 89–90], the need for psychological repression [114–117; 97–99], male violence against women [159–161; 133–135], and more on the dangers of self-knowledge [178–179; 149–150]). Yet as the word "rationalization" suggests, these essays are not really objective or disinterested; they invariably follow from troubling personal recollections. These discursive episodes, which catch Claudia in the act of fashioning and maintaining her surface persona, are depictions of the act of repression itself as it is reflected at a conscious level. The essays culminate in the anomalous ninth chapter, where Claudia's reminiscences about her childhood break through her usual defenses, at the same time that her matter-of-fact tone and tendency toward generalization mark this as another exercise in rationalization and repression. Claudia's memories surface only to be thrust permanently back into oblivion, but not before the reader is able to pick out the defining thread running through all of the novella's rememberings and forgettings — the fact of socially organized violence, and its logical outcome in a personality like Claudia's, avowedly "invulnerable" within an "impenetrable skin." All of Claudia's essays concern varieties of violence, whether of men against women, or of the ego against itself. By locating Claudia's childhood within a specific historical context — the founding years of the GDR, seen not as an idealistic "building" of socialism but as a period of brutal social oppression — Hein invites comparisons between historical brutality and the violence evident in Claudia's everyday life.

Hein has resisted critical attempts to use the ninth chapter, with its stories of Claudia's gym classes, of her handsome teacher Herr Gerschke, of Fräulein Nitschke and the Russian tank, of Uncle Gerhard, and of course of her friend Katharina, as a political key to the novella. Yet McKnight argues, and I would agree, that these events constitute a "turning point" in Claudia's development (*"Alltag*, Apathy, Anarchy" 182), despite Hein's tendency to play down their importance during workshops at the University of Kentucky in 1987 (McKnight, "*Alltag oder Anarchie*" 8). Granted, Hein is not merely grinding a political ax; as in *Horns Ende*, the Stalinist backgrounds to *Der fremde Freund* coexist with other historical factors. What counts in both books is the real character of German society: the continuities, in fact not limited to Germany, that have manifested themselves under every political system. Krzysztof Jachimczak, interviewing Hein, cites as main themes in all Hein's works the oppositions individual vs. society, spirit vs. power, present vs. past, reality vs. reasons of state (Hein, "Wir werden es lernen müssen" 55), all of which amounts to one thing: the subordination of human needs and moral values to the exigencies of power. In another interview, Hein protested against a reading that saw alienation and violence as his main themes, insisting rather that these are derivative ones, and that the real theme in *Der fremde Freund* is the present condition of civilization, including the trade-offs that have been made for the sake of technological progress and economic efficiency ("Ich kann mein Publikum nicht belehren" 68–69). This supports McKnight's view that the novella's real focus is on the effect of history at the level of the individual, the same concern evident in Hein's earlier short story collection. The episodes of violence, especially political violence, are crucial to an interpretation of the novella, but only because they reappear, disguised, in Claudia's personality and in her present-day surroundings.

With all of these qualifications in mind, it is possible to assess the structure of the ninth chapter as a vortex of violent experiences culminating in Claudia's break with Katharina, but formally centered on the novella's most concrete symbol of violent state oppression: the Russian tank that briefly appears in the square of Claudia's hometown following the Berlin workers' revolt of 17 June 1953.[10] Soviet tanks occupy a privileged place in the history of the GDR, having intervened in its history in 1945 at the de facto founding of the socialist state, and again in 1953 to avert that state's collapse. Heiner Müller captures the ambiguity of these tanks as symbols of both *Befreiung*, or liberation, as official GDR parlance designated the fall of the Nazi regime on 7 May 1945, and symbols of foreign occupation. In *Wolokolamsker Chaussee III: Das Duel*, Müller catches the irony attendant on any political assessment, positive or negative, of this brutal symbol of state power. The scene takes place near the end of the workers' revolt, as a factory director faces his striking deputy and wonders when the Soviets will intervene to rescue the revolution:

> And What is taking the tanks so long I thought
> They must come and they will come
> Those that bore us in '45
> A second time the smell of oil
> And steel dust and the sweat of soldiers My
> Memory knew When the air tastes like smoke
> The tanks are coming What's delaying them now
> They must come and they will come
> The tank our argument of last resort . . . .
> Then they came. He heard them first
> I could tell by his eyes
> We are taken to the breast once more
> The nurse is already coming She rides
> A T-34 and has milk for all
> Some like her and some don't
> But she soothes them all . . . . (242–243)

Evident in this monologue is the mismatch between the Communist Party's rhetoric about the historic mission of the first socialist state on German soil, and the political reality that the GDR existed only because of its importance to Soviet security. Thus the ghost of Stalin rides atop the tank turrets while "Under the tracks Red Rosa rots / As wide as Berlin" (243). To Müller, the second coming of the tanks is a second murder of Rosa Luxemburg, the ideologist of the general strike and spontaneous workers' action, and the critic of Lenin's centralist party structure, which would fulfill itself in Stalinist totalitarianism. The tank suggests inevitably the failure and perversion of the German Left and the consequences for the entire society and for the world: war, repression, the subordination of the individual to the state. Claudia, a child of the Second World War, has been nourished/soothed (*gestillt*) by the midwife of the difficult German revolution — the tank — and the power it represents.

Claudia's tank is a pale reflection of the Soviet armor rolling into Berlin; in her provincial town, it has mainly a symbolic function. The children of the town are drawn to it out of curiosity:

> Wir rannten zum Marktplatz. Es war nur ein einziger Panzer nach G. gekommen. Er stand mitten auf dem Platz. Das Rohr des Geschützes war mit einem Futteral überzogen und gegen das alte, verwitterte Kriegerdenkmal gerichtet, das wir in diesen Tagen zum ersten Mal zu Gesicht bekamen. Am Vortag hatten Unbekannte das Holzgerüst mit der großen, ausgesägten Friedenstaube und dem Fahnenschmuck zusammengeschlagen, unter dem das alte Monument verborgen war.
>
> Wir standen mit anderen Leuten auf dem Bürgersteig und betrachteten den Panzer. Es tat sich nichts. Die Leute flüsterten nur miteinander. Später ging die obere Panzerklappe auf, und ein junger, russischer Soldat sah heraus. Er schien keine Angst zu haben. Er nickte zu uns herüber. Dann stieg er aus. Ein Polizist trat zu ihm. Der Soldat sagte etwas und gestikulierte. Dann trat er mit dem Stiefel gegen die Panzerkette. Der Polizist nickte und gestikulierte gleichfalls erklärend mit den Händen. Dann trat auch er gegen die Panzerkette. Sie kauerte sich hin und sahen beide unter den Panzer. Offenbar erklärte der Soldat etwas. Dann stieg er wieder ein. Die Klappe wurde geschlossen. Es blieb ruhig, und ich langweilte mich. Wir gingen nach Hause. (*DFF* 144–45)

> [We ran to the marketplace. Only a single tank had come to G. It was parked in the middle of the square. The gun, covered with a tarpaulin, was pointed toward the weathered old First World War monument, which we were seeing for the first time. The day before, unknown persons had torn down the wooden structure with the large plywood peace dove and the decorative flag arrangement, and exposed the old monument underneath.
>
> We stood with the crowd on the sidewalk and looked at the tank. Nothing was happening. People whispered to one another. Later the tank's upper hatch opened and a young Russian soldier looked out. He didn't seem to be afraid. He nodded to us. Then he climbed out. A policeman went up to him. The soldier said something and gestured, then kicked the tank's track with his boot. The policeman nod-

ded and also gestured, explaining something with his hands. Then he too kicked the track. Both of them crouched and looked underneath the tank. Apparently the soldier was explaining something. Then he climbed back inside. The hatch closed. Things remained quiet, and I was getting bored. We went home. (*TDL* 122–123)

The aspect of straightforward political allegory in this passage is similar to that of the Müller passage just quoted. The tank arrives to preserve a political order whose disruption is indicated by the unveiling of an old symbol of German militarism, the war monument, yet the method of preservation is equally militaristic. Thus the destruction of the peace dove cuts two ways, as suggested by the spectacle of the tank aiming its gun at the monument, as though to forestall further misuse of this potent symbol. The tank is greeted casually, even with boredom — its presence seems not to surprise anyone. The policeman who converses with the Russian soldier serves in a chain of command running all the way down to the curious children, giving social materiality to an abstract power which we now see concretely revealed.

The tank's meaning is both expressed and hidden by the "peace" that it restores:

> An jenem Tag stürzten die Jungen mitten im Unterricht an die Fenster und schrien: Die Panzer kommen, die Panzer kommen.
> Wir hörten das mahlende klirrende Geräusch der Panzerketten. Dann wurde es still. (*DFF* 144)
>
> [On the day of the tanks, the boys jumped up in the middle of class and ran to the window, shouting, The tanks are coming, the tanks are coming.
> We heard the grinding, clanking sound of the tank tracks. Then it became quiet.] (*TDL* 122)

The town's tank-imposed silence speaks clearly of the impact of political violence on each citizen's communal and private life. This happens first and most obviously in the case of Fräulein Nitschke, the teacher traumatized by her experiences in the Second World War. When the tank rolls into G.,

> Sie wirkte wie gelähmt. Wir umstanden sie und versuchten, ihr zu helfen. Sie war nicht ansprechbar. . . . Nach ein paar Minuten beruhigte sie sich. Sie schwitzte und wirkte erschöpft. (*DFF* 143)
>
> [She seemed paralyzed. We gathered around and tried to soothe her. She didn't respond to anything we said . . . . After a few minutes she calmed down. She was sweating and seemed exhausted.] (*TDL* 121)

For Fräulein Nitschke, a tank is a tank, and violence is violence. Her paralyzed silence typifies the townspeople's response to the military intervention, a response that Claudia will emulate in the short term and turn into a way of life later on. Silence, the inability or unwillingness to communicate, becomes isolation when transposed to a social context. This etiology of Claudia's social and self-alienation emerges from the aftermath of the tank episode, when she discovers that the adults are pretending — out of fear — that nothing has happened:

> In der Fabrik, in der Vater als Meister arbeitete, blieb alles ruhig. Trotzdem war Vater erregt und schrie mit meiner Mutter herum. Ich verstand nichts davon. Vater sagte mir, ich solle in der Schule keine Fragen stellen und nicht darüber diskutieren. Es sei jetzt nicht der Zeitpunkt. Im Unterricht wurde aber ohnehin nicht darüber gesprochen. Keiner der Schüler fragte nach etwas, und die Lehrer sagten gleichfalls nichts. Ich begriff nicht, warum darüber nicht gesprochen werden durfte. Aber da tatsächlich keiner der Erwachsenen über den Panzer sprach, spürte ich, daß auch ein Gespräch etwas Bedrohliches sein konnte. Ich fühlte die Angst der Erwachsenen, miteinander zu reden. Und ich schwieg, damit sie nicht reden mußten. Ich fürchtete, daß nach einem ihnen aufgenötigten, quälenden Gespräch über eins ihrer Tabus mich wiederum sieche, widerliche, geschlechtskranke Leute bis in meine Träume hinein verfolgen würden. Ich lernte zu schweigen. (*DFF* 145–46)

> [In the factory where Father worked as a foreman, everything remained quiet. Nevertheless he was agitated and kept screaming at my mother. I didn't understand any of it. Father told me I shouldn't ask questions in school or talk about what had happened. This wasn't the time. But in class nothing was said anyway. The children didn't ask and the teachers didn't explain. I didn't understand why, but since none of the grown-ups mentioned the tank, I sensed that even a conversation could be dangerous. I felt their fear of talking to each other. And I kept quiet so they wouldn't have to speak. I was afraid that if I forced them into a painful, reluctant discussion of one of their taboos, I would again be followed, all the way into my dreams, by wasted, disgusting people with venereal diseases. I learned to keep quiet.]
> (*TDL* 123)

At no other place in the novella do the forces of state power cross so visibly into social and private behavior. As a child, Claudia was surprised that nothing was said about the tank (or what it meant) in public, for instance, in school, and she correctly sensed a danger. However, she misinterprets the nature of the danger, seeing it as another taboo of the sort that her mother had passed along to her during a discussion of sexual matters. What began as a pragmatic response to political oppression (silence, caution — particularly for a communist factory foreman intent on keeping his job) appears indistinguishable, to a child, from the various other tabooed subjects underpinning her social relations. Silent, cautious, she imitates the form of her adult models' behavior, knowing nothing of its substance; for the pragmatic advisability, even charity, of not forcing another to speak and thereby risk exposure, Claudia substitutes the categorical avoidance of communication. Political events give rise to psychological ones, but the relation, mediated by effects that supersede causes (the silence becoming an end in itself) is not homologous. Yet violence recurs at the level of psychology, suggesting some underlying homology after all. Before her breakdown, Fräulein Nitschke had infuriated the children by not simply punishing them for their aversion to learning: "sie zeigte, daß unsere Dummheit und unser Unverständnis sie schmerzten..... Sie hoffte, daß ihre Betroffenheit uns beschämen würde. Das haben wir ihr nie verziehen" [she let us see that our stupidity and lack of understanding pained her.... She hoped that her dismay would shame us. We never forgave her for that: 143; 121]. After the tank episode, she briefly turns into an object of sympathy:

> Wir waren einige Tage befangen und zuvorkommend. Doch bald war es vergessen, und wir rächten uns — ausgeliefert der herrischen, unentrinnbaren Autorität unserer Lehrer — für alle uns angetane Gewalt an jener Lehrerin, die sich als einzige bereit zeigte, uns als kleine, komplizierte und eigenständige Persönlichkeiten zu akzeptieren.
>
> (*DFF* 143–44)
>
> [For a few days we were chastened and obliging. But we soon forgot, and — at the mercy of the overweening authority of our teachers — we took revenge on that one teacher for all the violence perpetrated against us. On the only teacher who'd been willing to accept us as complicated little beings in our own right.] (*TDL* 121–122)

By locating this account of Fräulein Nitschke's fate in the middle of the tank narrative (which, moreover, is told in a slightly confusing, nonchronological manner, with the story of the teacher momentarily diverting attention), and by evoking and explicitly naming the social (and even physical) violence wrought upon the children by their teachers, Hein, or perhaps rather Claudia, appears to suggest an analogy between the political power symbolized by the tank and the psycho-social oppression of the children. Fräulein Nitschke's status as a victim of war and her relative innocence with respect to the children support this view, positioning her as a figuration of the children's own helplessness. More ominously, the children reenact and perpetuate the injustice they have experienced, taking on the role of oppressor when the teacher plays victim. The casual violence of everyday social life already constitutes a background of oppression before the tank ever arrives. The sources of this oppression are outside the purview of the novella, but they may be hinted at in the etiology of alienation described above, in which violence and fear lead to a social indifference that expects and accommodates violence in social relations. By explicitly juxtaposing history, society, and individual experience, the tank episode specifies ways to relate Claudia's brittle self-sufficiency to the novella's other incidents of violence.

The degree to which *Der fremde Freund* is a catalogue of violent acts has not been sufficiently discussed by critics, not even by those East German commentators who were scandalized by the text's overall lack of human warmth. The most extreme case of violence, and the event that precipitates the narrative, is of course Henry's murder, even though the details are supplied only at the end of the novella. Besides this example, Hein has crammed his novella with rape, assault, theft, and drunken brawling, along with less physically explicit but no less brutalizing acts of deceit, marital infidelity, dysfunctional sexuality, and generalized psychological cruelty. The prevalence of force in the novella's world reflects both Claudia's own personality (she apparently chooses to associate with violent people, perhaps because they threaten less intimacy) and the social circumstances that foster violence. Claudia's philosophical digressions (such as the discussion of repression remarked on above) more frequently than not concern just this problem of the sources of violence, her usual procedure being to blame society, human biology, history, and so on. These discussions invariably rationalize her own behavior and exonerate her from any blame for what she construes to be the plight of humanity and her own fated place within it. A different story emerges when the moments of social and personal violence are scrutinized more disinterestedly. To list and discuss all of these moments would mean recounting virtually the whole book; what follows is a selection of significant incidents grouped around three characters.

Anne

One of the first incidents narrated is Claudia's coffee break with her colleague Anne, who is described (with equal parts aversion and pretended indifference) as a periodic victim of marital rape:

> Sie hat vier Kinder und einen Mann, der sie alle zwei Wochen einmal vergewaltigt. Sie schlafen sonst regelmäßig und gut miteinander, wie sie sagt, aber ab und zu vergewaltigt er sie. Er brauche das, sagt sie. Scheiden will sie sich nicht lassen, wegen der Kinder und aus Angst, allein zu bleiben. So nimmt sie es halt hin. Wenn sie Alkohol trinkt,

> heult sie und beschimpft ihren Mann. Aber sie bleibt bei ihm. Ich halte Distanz zu ihr. Es ist anstrengend mit einer Frau befreundet zu sein, die sich mit ihren Demütigungen abgefunden hat. (*DFF* 14)
>
> [She has four children and a husband who rapes her every two weeks or so. Apart from that they enjoy their sex life, which is pretty regular, she says, but now and then he rapes her. She says he needs it. She doesn't want a divorce because of the children and because she's afraid of being alone. So she puts up with it. Whenever she's had a drink or two she starts to bitch and moan about her husband. But she stays with him. I keep my distance. It's a strain being friends with a woman who's resigned to her own degradation.] (*TDL* 10–11)

This passage introduces several important motifs: the characterization of sex as violent and dangerous, a violation of personal integrity; Claudia's belief in the danger of sympathizing with the problems of others and her valorization of personal and social detachment; and her sense of the "strain" upon her own emotional stability. The last of these is especially ironic in this opening example, since Claudia's own life is *full* of resigned degradation, as soon becomes apparent. Anne may even be read as a distorted reflection of Claudia. They are both physicians; further, they wear the same clothing size, and Claudia imagines asking Anne to switch clothes (and roles) with her:

> Sie präsentierte ihr neues Kostüm, schwarz mit einem lila Schal. Ihr Mann hat es ihr gestern gekauft. Sie erzählte mir, daß es furchtbar teuer war, ihr Mann es aber anstandslos bezahlt habe. Das Geschenk danach. Arme Anne. Vielleicht sollte ich mir das Kostüm ausborgen. Es wäre geeigneter für den Friedhof als der dicke Mantel. Andrerseits, was habe ich mit ihren Vergewaltigungen zu schaffen. (*DFF* 15)
>
> [She shows off her new suit, black with a lilac scarf. Her husband bought it for her yesterday. She says it was terribly expensive, but he paid for it without a word. The present after. Poor Anne. Maybe I should borrow the suit. It would be more appropriate for the cemetery than my heavy coat. On the other hand, what do I want with her rapes?] (*TDL* 11)

As though a literalized version of Claudia, Anne is an anesthesiologist, a specialist in the deadening of pain. The odd description of her sex life, an alternation of rape and "pretty regular" sex which she tolerates resignedly, parallels Claudia's reaction to the abuse she endures in the course of the narrative, which includes a quasi-rape by Henry. And finally, Anne's husband is also a doctor, like Claudia's ex-husband Hinner. All of this suggests that Anne, in her overt degradation, differs from Claudia only in degree, not in kind, that she represents a different but not necessarily worse response to the violent abuse that both women suffer, that Claudia's rather contemptuous attitude toward Anne attempts to ease the nausea of self-recognition. "I keep my distance," Claudia says, from Anne and from herself. A victim masquerading as a contented wife, Anne appears again in the penultimate chapter, more overtly than before threatening Claudia with self-recognition:

> Ich bin kein Mülleimer, in dem andere ihre unentwirrbar verzwickten Geschichten abladen können. Ich fühle mich dazu nicht stabil genug. Ich vermeide es, mit Anne, einer Kollegin, die von ihrem Mann regelmäßig vergewaltigt wird, länger als eine Stunde zusammenzusitzen. Ich vermeide es, mich mit ihr irgendwo anders zu treffen als in Gaststätten und Cafés, in aller Öffentlichkeit also. Sie ist dadurch gezwungen, ein Mindestmaß an Disziplin zu halten. Sie kann sich dort nicht gehenlassen und mich mit den Schäbigkeiten und dem verkrötzten Gefühlshaushalt ihres Mannes überschwemmen. (*DFF* 198–199)
>
> [I'm not a garbage pail for people's hopelessly tangled stories. I don't feel stable enough. I avoid spending more than an hour with Anne, the colleague who's regularly raped by her husband. I avoid meeting her anywhere but in public, in restaurants and cafés. That forces her to preserve at least a semblance of decorum. She can't let herself go and shower me with the details of her husband's shabbiness and messed-up psyche.] (*TDL* 168)

Only by fending off such intimate revelations can Claudia maintain the illusion that she is "fine."

Henry

Henry's violent death is prefigured by various incidents of violence or near-violence, but it is already deducible from his philosophy of life, a more articulated and resolute version of Claudia's. Externalizing and concretizing the violence that in Claudia's case remains mostly emotional, Henry says or does virtually nothing that doesn't point directly to violence or the potential for violence. His behavior and views remind Claudia of herself from the start, and just as she avoids analyzing herself, she refuses to analyze Henry. Yet for the reader, it is evident that Henry carries many of Claudia's own beliefs to their logical conclusion — death. We are given no information about his background or childhood, because we will already learn enough about Claudia, and the lessons appear to be transferable. In the first exposition of his philosophy of life, Henry responds with Hollywood existentialism when asked to explain his aversion to heights:

Ich fürchte ganz einfach, davonzufliegen, sagte er sehr heiter, oder wenn du es prosaischer haben willst, herunterzustürzen. Etwas sollte doch passieren: Ich lebe, aber wozu. Der ungeheuerliche Witz, daß ich auf der Welt bin, wird doch eine Pointe haben. Also warte ich.
(*DFF* 30)

[I'm just afraid of flying away, he said happily. Or, to be more prosaic, of falling. Something's got to happen: I'm alive, but what for? This incredible joke, the fact that I'm here in the world must have some point. So I keep waiting to find out.] (*TDL* 24–25)

Henry's vision of life, this passive "waiting," is filled with an aimless motion seen best in his plainly self-destructive love of dangerous driving. He tells Claudia early in their relationship, "Wenn ich fahre, spüre ich, daß ich lebe" [When I'm driving, I feel alive: 37; 31]. Lest there be any doubt about the sterility of Henry's "philosophy" and its origins, he shortly adds that his dream is to be a "Rennfahrer oder Stuntman. Stuntman für Verfolgungsjagden" [race car driver or a stunt man. A stunt man for high-speed chases: 38; 32]. Claudia responds:

Etwas gefährlich, meinte ich.
Er lächelte: Ja, etwas lebendiger.
Hast du keine Angst vor Unfällen? fragte ich.
Es gibt Ärzte, entgegnete er und sah mich an.
Ja, sagte ich, es gibt aber auch tödliche Unfälle.
Er schwieg und zog die Mundwinkel nach unten. Nach einiger Zeit sagte er: Ich fürchte mich nicht davor zu sterben. Schlimmer ist es für mich, nicht zu leben. Nicht wirklich zu leben. (*DFF* 38)

[Wouldn't that be rather dangerous?
He smiled. Of course, and rather alive.
Aren't you afraid of accidents? I asked.
There are doctors, he said, and looked at me.
Yes, I said, but there are also fatal accidents.
He said nothing, just pulled his mouth down at the corners. After some time he said, I'm not afraid of dying. It's worse for me not to be alive. Not to really live.] (*DFF* 32)

Henry's goal in life is to court a violent death; the belated revelation that he had been a boxer merely confirms his overall stance toward society — one of active aggression, bespeaking a self-alienation which, like Claudia's, excludes large chunks of his own life from consciousness, substituting non-reflective, semi-conscious sensations in the here-and-now, everyday world that Claudia, too, embraces. A more perfect practitioner of self-alienation than Claudia, he advises her to "Gib es endlich auf" [Forget it: 137; 116] as she struggles — unsuccessfully — to reappropriate her past. Claudia marvels at his coolness and asks what Henry remembers of his childhood:

> Er erwiderte, er denke nie daran.
> Manchmal, sagte ich, manchmal aber überfällt uns unsere eigene Vergangenheit wie ein unerwünschter Schatten. Wir können sie nicht aus unserem späteren Leben heraushalten.
> Ich lasse es nicht zu, erwiderte er.
> Und warum? fragte ich ihn.
> Er beugte sich über mich und sah mich in die Augen.
> Weil es zwecklos ist, sagte er dann, weil es uns unfähig macht zu leben. Und ich brauche es nicht, fügte er hinzu, ich habe da keine Schwierigkeiten mit mir.
> Das kann ich nicht glauben, sagte ich. (*DFF* 157)

> [He replied that he never thought of it.
> But sometimes, I said, sometimes our own past comes over us like an unwanted shadow. We can't keep it out of our later life.
> I don't let it near me, he replied.
> Why not? I asked.
> He bent over me and looked into my eyes.
> Because it's pointless, he said. Because it makes us incapable of living. And I don't need it, he added. I don't have any problems with myself.
> That's hard to believe, I said.] (*TDL* 132)

Indeed it is, as Henry's death proves.

This notion of an intrusive shadow from the past could be an allusion to Walter Benjamin's theory of artistic "aura," which has similarities to the Derridean understanding of "presence." A key illustration of aura (which involves the illusory intuition or appropriation of otherness across an artistically mediated gulf of time or space, constituting the cult-value of the artwork) uses the image of the shadow:

> What exactly is aura? A peculiar interweaving of space and time: a singular manifestation of distance, however close it may be. To follow in repose on a summer afternoon a chain of mountains on the horizon, or a branch, which casts its shadow on the observer, until the moment or the hour plays a part in these things' appearance — that is what it means to breathe the aura of this mountain or of this branch.
> ("Kleine Geschichte der Photographie" 57)

McKnight cites this passage as a source for the description of Claudia's rape and draws connections between it and her landscape photography, which avoids heavily "auratic" or "cultic" subjects such as human portraiture ("*Alltag*, Apathy, Anarchy" 187–188). In Hein's usage, the term aura can designate a non-rational sense of coherent selfhood and social integration. In his essay on Benjamin, Hein seems to be meditating on Claudia when he speaks of aura in connection with the psychological mechanisms that shield the psyche from the overwhelming deluge of experience and change:

> We traditionally rescue ourselves from the discontent caused by technological evolution by invoking modes of thought relatively inaccessible to Reason. "Le coeur a sa raison, que la raison ne connait pas," says Pascal: The heart has its Reason, which Reason does not know. The discontent seduces and leads us to this Reason of the heart, over which we have scant control, and where, surrounded by the aura of humanity, traditional human values, abilities, and functions seem to allow us approach closer to ourselves, to come to ourselves. The missing contentedness we seek is to be found at the place where we are identical with ourselves. And whenever social, political, technological, or artistic evolution unnerves us, arouses discontent, we save ourselves by returning to received values, that is, values that are accepted and respected, and which people have ceased to question.
> ("Maelzel's Chess Player" 166–167)

Claudia's experience of social and political change has left her profoundly non-identical with herself, but she deviates from Hein's coping formula by trying to integrate herself through disintegration, repressing everything that doesn't accord with her present life, and always succumbing to the malaise caused by the return of the repressed. In his essay Hein cites three realms of human endeavor that embody this coping function — religion, philosophy, and art (168) — yet none of these help Claudia, because she relies exclusively on practical reason, which, like Henry, can only prescribe amnesia. Claudia obeys the dictates of reason in shunning the auratic, but this leads to incomprehension of her own life: "The absence of aura . . . may allow clarity of vision, but a perplexed, helpless vision" ("Maelzel's Chess Player," 172).

Although Henry reveals nothing about his youth, his desires (for instance, to be a race car driver or stunt man) connect him with two passages that depict young people waiting aimlessly, and sometimes violently, for their lives to take shape. Not accidentally, Henry's behavior in each case is a mixture of curiosity and hostility. In the fifth chapter, Henry irritates a group of teenagers when he refuses to give them a ride to a destination they cannot specify: "Das kommt darauf an, wo Sie hinfahren" [Depends on where you're going: *DFF* 60–61; *TDL* 52]. In return he suffers verbal abuse and mock violence:

> Wir stiegen ins Auto. Ein Junge rief uns etwas zu, und die anderen lachten. Als Henry losfuhr, warf einer eine Handvoll Kiesel und Sand

gegen die Scheiben. Henry stoppte sofort, aber ich bat ihn weiterzufahren. (*DFF* 61)

[We got into the car. A boy yelled something at us, and the others laughed. He threw a handful of pebbles and sand at the windshield as Henry pulled away. Henry stopped the car instantly, but I begged him to drive on.] (*TDL* 52)

When Claudia dismisses them as merely bored, Henry replies, "Ja . . . sie langweilen sich. Sie werden sich ihr ganzes Leben langweilen" [Yes . . . they're bored. They'll be bored all their lives: 61; 52]. The same constellation of social isolation, aimlessness, boredom, and incipient violence emerges during the ambulance visit Claudia and Henry make to a dance at a factory cafeteria. Violence permeates the account of the dance, making it sound more like a war zone than an entertainment:

Im Erdgeschoß hatte man die Garderobe eingerichtet. Dort saßen auch die Verletzten. Ein Kollege untersuchte sie. Zwei Polizisten und mehrere junge Männer standen herum. Die Verletzten wirkten apathisch. Sie waren angetrunken und stierten vor sich hin. Das meiste waren oberflächliche Verletzungen, die bereits vernarbten. Zum Klammern der Platzwunden war es zu spät . . . . Einer schien ein gebrochenes Nasenbein zu haben. Es sollte geröntgt werden. Der andere hatte offensichtlich zwei Finger gebrochen. Die übrigen bekamen Mull und Heftpflaster aufgeklebt. Es gab wenig Arbeit. Ein zweiter Rettungswagen war nicht notwendig gewesen. Die jungen Männer, die um die Blessierten herumstanden, zogen sie von den Stühlen hoch und brachten sie mit unsanften Griffen zum Werkstor. (*DFF* 123)

[The coat-check area had been set up on the ground floor. That was where the injured were sitting. A doctor from the other ambulance was examining them while two policemen and several young men were standing around. The injured seemed apathetic. They were a little drunk and stared listlessly ahead. Most of them had superficial lacerations that were already scabbing over, so it was too late to stitch them up . . . . One seemed to have a broken nose. It would need to be X-rayed. The other apparently had two broken fingers. The rest of the injured were patched up with gauze and adhesive tape. There wasn't much work; a second ambulance hadn't been necessary. The young men who were standing around pulled the injured up from their chairs and escorted them roughly to the factory gate.] (*TDL* 104)

Something odd is going on; the police and bouncers seem not to be preventing or stopping the violence, but merely supervising it, containing it within tacitly accepted social bounds. The text resonates with loaded terms (like ***die Verletzten***, the injured, also translatable as "the wounded") that reinforce the identification of the bouncers with more general networks of social and even military violence:

> Die jungen Männer, die bei den Verletzten gestanden hatten, kamen die Treppe hoch. Einer von ihnen, er war vielleicht achtzehn Jahre, kam zu uns.
> Was nicht in Ordnung? fragte er und antwortete dann gleich selbst: Alles im Griff.
> Er zwinkerte selbstgefällig und ging mit seinen Freunden in den Saal. (*DFF* 125)
>
> [The young men who had hustled out the injured came up the stairs. One of them, who was maybe eighteen, approached us.
> Any problems? he asked, and immediately answered himself: Everything's under control.
> He gave us a self-satisfied wink and went into the ballroom with his friends.] (*TDL* 106)

After throwing out a sleeping drunk, the same "young man" winks again and declares, "Rationelles Arbeiten hier" [We run a tight ship here: *126;* 106], an expression, brutally ironic here, with overtones of socialist central planning. The singer with the band refers to the bouncers as the *Ordnungstruppe* [order patrol] adding, "ohne sie sähs hier bunter aus" [Without them this place would be a lot wilder: 126; 106]. Yet amid all of this imperfectly suppressed violence, the majority of the young people merely sit and drink silently, with almost nobody dancing, and the music too loud for conversation. It would be rash to deduce any general social significance from such a scene, yet there is no doubt that the scene holds up a mirror to Henry's life. In conversation with the policemen waiting outside the building, comes Henry close to reversing his earlier condemnation of "bored" young people; now he empathizes with them:

> Henry fragte sie: Auf was warten die da oben? Sie kommen her und warten.
> Ach was, sagte ein Polizist, die wollen nur saufen.
> Saufen und Krawall machen, bestätigte der andere.
> Dann lachten sie beide.
> Nein, widersprach Henry, sie warten, daß irgend etwas passiert. Sie hoffen, das etwas geschieht. Irgend etwas, vielleicht ihr Leben.
> (*DFF* 126)
>
> [Henry asked them, What are those kids up there waiting for? They come here and then sit around waiting?
> Hell, one of the policemen said, they just want to booze it up.
> Booze it up and cause trouble, the other agreed.
> They both laughed.

No, Henry said, they're waiting for something to happen. They're hoping something will happen. Anything, maybe their lives.]
(*TDL* 107)

Henry is describing himself, and echoing his earlier assertion, "I'm not afraid of dying. It's worse for me not to be alive. Not to really live." The text offers no examples of life "happening" except violent or potentially violent ones — the young people's boozing and brawling, Henry's reckless driving — and what happens in between such moments is best exemplified by Claudia, who, trying to avoid such "happenings," adopts a stance of detachment with respect to society which is, finally, a stance of complete submission to power. In the world of organized violence revealed at the dance, Claudia plays the role prescribed for her by Henry in their early conversation: as a doctor, she is there to patch up people like Henry, or like these young people, when their propensity for violence gets out of hand. Like most of the people at the dance, Henry goes away "irgendwie enttäuscht" [somehow disappointed: 127; 107].

Henry's encounter with a tractor driver and his own violent death can now be placed in their appropriate context. The two events parallel one another just as the encounters with the young people do, and all of the subliminally violent episodes already discussed contribute to the rationale and structure of these two explicit ones. Henry's attempt to overtake the turning tractor immediately follows the encounter with the "bored" teenagers and, as though in reaction to it, enacts (not for the first time) the fantasies of stunts and race cars Henry had confessed to Claudia. At rest in a potato field after running off the road, he is proud of this latest stunt: "Noch einmal gut gegangen, sagte Henry und lächelte mich beruhigend an" [Another narrow escape, Henry said, and smiled at me reassuringly: 62; 53]. The essence of a "stunt" is to risk death but not to die, or more broadly, to engage in dangerous behavior without suffering harm. Since a stunt remains a stunt only if the level of danger is raised after each survival, the inevitability of Henry's violent death looms over this scene: he will be killed by a teenaged boy with a single blow in an utterly senseless barroom brawl.

Following Henry's death, his friend Herr Kramer (who witnessed the killing and narrates it to Claudia) reveals that Henry had been a boxer, a fact Claudia was unaware of. Boxing is akin to the other daredevil feats that populate Henry's fantasies and determine his actions, sharing (and literalizing) their suggestion of physical violence. Throughout this discussion it has been argued that the manifestations of psychological violence in *Der fremde Freund* parallel and evidently follow from state power and its argument of last resort, physical coercion. Henry, then, represents one strategy of survival within a violent society, a strategy complementary to Claudia's: instead of withdrawing into a rationally organized denial or repression of social oppression, he withdraws into fantasies of prepotency. It has already become clear enough that when these fantasies are realized, they paradoxically result in forms of self-directed violence, replicating rather than negating the violence from without. Yet Henry's final experience of violence looks less like the outcome of this ominous play of reality and fantasy than an arbitrary stroke from outside the novella's narrative logic. Hein's approach to the event displays a high degree of authorial sarcasm as power wins the decision over repression at Henry's expense. Herr Kramer tells Claudia:

> Er war früher Boxer, wußten Sie das?
> Ich wußte es nicht.
> Henry tänzelte professionell, und die Jungen lachten über ihn. Er machte ein paar Schläge in die Luft, als ob er sich warm machen wollte. Dann schlug der Junge zu. Henry fiel um. Er fiel steif wie ein Stock nach hinten. Der Junge mußte etwas wie einen Schlagring benutzt haben. (*DFF* 203)

> [He used to be a boxer, did you know that?
> I hadn't known.
> Henry danced like a pro, and the boys laughed at him. He feinted into the air, as if he were warming up. Then the boy struck. Henry fell over. He fell backwards, stiff as a board. The boy must have had something like brass knuckles.] (*TDL* 171)

Henry's shaky illusion of freedom, a clichéd love of adventure that corresponds to Claudia's claims of autonomy, collapses when confronted with real violence. A slightly ridiculous amateur boxer cannot stand up to brass knuckles any more than unarmed citizens can stand up to Soviet tanks. Henry's death ends up being symbolic of nothing at all, except perhaps the farcical inadequacy of his relations with society. The fact that it is a seventeen-year-old boy that kills him obviously invites consideration of Henry's two previous encounters with teenagers. These have shown how much he shares with them: nihilism, boredom, veiled or open hostility. Like him, the teenagers are reacting and adapting to a society which is at best indifferent to their individual existence, at worst opposed to it.

The destruction of Henry's fantasy of freedom, equated in the novella with Henry's physical destruction, is also a comment on the situation of Claudia, whose fantasies are similarly motivated. The central belief — or delusion — to which Claudia clings is that of her mental health. The same woman who admits in other contexts that she isn't "stable enough" to listen to other people's problems, that her life since childhood has been filled with the vague fear that was reflected in the dream preface, who welcomes the arrival of Daylight Savings Time because it offers a break from the monotony of her existence (*DFF* 197; *TDL* 166–167), declares that her nerves are "vollkommen in Ordnung" [in fine shape: 208; 176] and that she has become invulnerable to life's disappointments. Claudia's stridently positive concluding litany ("I'm prepared for everything, I'm armed against everything," etc.) merely charts a collapse back into despair that lends added resonance to the last word of the text: *Ende*. This "end" refers conventionally to the novella, but it also marks the end of Claudia, not as a biological entity, but as a human capable of hope, the visualization of freedom in spite of its objective absence. The only freedom Claudia visualizes now is negative, a hermetic social isolation. Claudia's lifelong attempt to escape from her vulnerability to other people (and to society, and to history) was symbolized early on by her photography, consisting of lifeless landscapes, resembling the way the dream preface's "überwirkliche Realität" [over-real reality] must be quickly obscured by what she calls "meine alltäglichen Abziehbilder ... bunt, laut, vergeßlich" [images of my daily life, gaudy, loud, insignificant: 7; 4].[11] The photographs that begin to oppress Claudia with their lifelessness and bulk were originally meant to help her forget and repress what frightened her (human contact, epitomized for her by the hand striking a blow, or by the ravages of venereal disease); now they become, like Henry's fantasies of vigorous immortality, agents of what they were meant to replace. Whether covering unpleasant realities with sterile photographs or herself in a Siegfried-skin of emotional isolation, Claudia has only redirected the violence directed at her, delaying but not escaping its impact on her. Dying within and because of her illusory self-sufficiency, she is little different from Henry, or like the novella's aimless and alienated young people, now violent, now passive, waiting for "life" to happen. Upon turning forty, Claudia thinks, "Es war belanglos, es veränderte sich nichts. Ich wünschte mir, daß etwas geschehe, daß irgend etwas mit mir passieren würde, aber ich konnte nicht sagen, was es sein sollte" [It was insignificant, nothing had changed. I wished that something would happen, that something would change, but I couldn't say what it should be: 197; 166] .

Fre(u)d and Maria

Both Anne and Henry have exhibited a veiled kinship to Claudia by virtue of their victimization and powerlessness, their self-defeating struggles to manage and repress the unbearable realities of their lives. It remains to be shown how Hein constructs characters who are the necessary counterpart to these victims, namely, the wielders of power. Relatively abstract manifestations of power — such as the tank, or the policemen at the factory dance — though suggestive, do little to illustrate the mechanisms by which power oppresses and *inhabits* Claudia. To observe this social dissemination of power in its pure aspect, rather than through its victims in an inverted form (as seen already in Henry and Claudia) as self-directed violence, it is necessary to turn to the novella's depiction of sexual politics. Under this rubric can be grouped the themes and events in the text that might be labeled feminist in spirit, as well as the account Claudia gives of her own initiation into sexuality, which will bring the discussion back to the lengthy and somber epiphany of chapter 9.

Claudia's vacation hosts Fred and Maria offer a strategic entry point for this final category of violence. Claudia's relationship with Fred is typical in that they both live in Berlin yet never make any effort to see each other there, thus maintaining a mutually-desired emotional distance. The visit to Fred's house is unrelievedly awful; he subjects his wife Maria to various sorts of abuse, and makes sexual advances toward Claudia. Despite her refusal to characterize Fred and Maria as "friends" (82; 70), Claudia unaccountably continues to visit them each year:

> Ich fragte mich, wozu ich hergekommen war. Ihre Streitereien kannte ich den vergangenen Besuchen. Warum mir jedes Jahr seine Tiraden anhören und ihre Verzweiflung erleben, all das, was sie so aussichtslos miteinander verbindet. (*DFF* 80)
>
> [I asked myself why I'd come. From my earlier visits I knew all about their fighting. Why did I subject myself year after year to his tirades and her despair, these mutual bonds which kept them hopelessly enfettered.] (*TDL* 68)

It would seem that nobody is more enfettered than Claudia, who keeps coming back despite her better judgment. Hein stresses that even the visit depicted in the novella is not the last one — at the end of her narrative, Claudia confirms, in one of several evocations of paralyzed cyclicity, that she will go again the subsequent year (*DFF* 211 / *TDL* 178). Her relationship with Fred combines in one character most of the varieties of inescapable oppression (by family, friends, colleagues, and society in general) that she describes elsewhere in her narrative. These coalesce in the figure of a domineering and abusive man, introducing a thread of feminist analysis that will resurface several more times. Yet in a manner typical of this text, the external force of oppression is only one moment in a dialectic of compulsion and complicity; the feminist arguments ring hollow when they merely rationalize Claudia's fear of personal contact. Even more telling is Fred's warped version of psychoanalysis, a rationalization and method for objective violence that parallels Claudia's distortion of Freudianism as a rationalization of and method for psychological violence — her will to forget, be silent, conform. Nowhere is the fatal subversion of spirit by power more succinctly displayed.

Claudia's co-optation by an ideology of violence in the guise of psychoanalysis is betrayed by her initial sympathy for Fred's cruel treatment of Maria, which turns into a mock-psychoanalysis. Elsewhere Claudia may be a victim, but here she emulates, however superficially, the role of oppressor. When Fred insults Maria the first time as "eine dumme Gans, jedenfalls so ziemlich" [pretty silly — more or less], the text signals that Claudia doesn't even fully recognize her own complicity: "Ich lachte, wußte aber nicht warum" [I laughed, but didn't know why: 78; 66]. She subsequently recalls her cruel childhood game of judging people by their fingernails and earlobes, and suppresses an impulse to rate Maria by these criteria. In a clear parallel to this game of childish authoritarianism, Fred notices Claudia's scrutiny of Maria and launches into a tirade of psycho-babble:

> Fred bemerkte, daß ich sie ansah. Er ging zu ihr, drückte einen Finger auf ihr rechtes Wangenbein und zog das Augenlid nach unten. Er lächelte mich an: Schau, eine gut ausgebildete narzistische Hypochondrie. Ich möchte sie klassisch nennen . . . . Dazu eine Anlage zur Hysterie, als Ergebnis verdrängter Triebe und unverarbeiteter Außenreize. Du mußt wissen, sie leidet. Sie ist unverstanden, unterdrückt, kastriert. Sie hat irgendwo gelesen, daß die moderne, selbstbewußte Frau unglücklich zu sein hat, und sie will auch eine moderne, selbstbewußte Frau sein. Also sie hat Depressionen. Ach, Gott, wie depressiv sie ist. Und der Schuldige an dem ganzen Elend bin ich, der Mann, das Ungeheuer, der Patriarch. Der ihr beständig seinen Willen und seinen Penis aufdrängt. (*DFF* 79–80)

> [Fred noticed I was looking at her. He went over to her, pressed his middle finger against her right cheekbone, and with his index finger pulled down her eyelid. He smiled at me and said: See, a well-developed narcissistic hypochondria. I would call it almost classic . . . . In addition, a tendency toward hysteria, as a result of repressed instincts and unassimilated outside stimuli. You have to understand that she's suffering. She's misunderstood, oppressed, castrated. She read somewhere that the modern, self-aware woman has to be unhappy, and she wants to be a modern, self-aware woman too. So she suffers

from depression. My God, how depressive she is. And of course I'm the one who's to blame for the whole misery: the man, the monster, the patriarchal tyrant. Constantly forcing his will and his penis on her.] (*TDL* 67–68)

Unlike the previously discussed essay on the social benefits of repression, Fred's "diagnosis" is no more than nonsense organized by a desire to injure Maria, yet many of its particulars can be linked to Claudia. Fred's mention of "repressed instincts" needs no elaboration. The problem of "unassimilated outside stimuli," aside from its bearing on Claudia's theory of defensive repression, surely looks ahead to the female patient who takes offense when Claudia traces her heart problems to "gestörten Beziehungen zur Umwelt" [a troubled relationship with the outside world: 120; 102]. Similarly, the accusation that Maria has picked up her malady from reading books corresponds to the joke about the psychiatric patient who "die einschlägige Literatur kennt und der Therapie seine selbstgebastelte Eigenanalyse entgegensetzt" [read all the pertinent literature and blocked his therapy with his home-grown self-diagnosis: 117; 100]. The theme of patriarchal tyranny will be taken up below.

Claudia retreats before Fred's onslaught only to be cornered, naked, by him in her room, again the object rather than the subject of abuse. Her analysis of his games of sexual humiliation further exposes his (and her) psychoanalytic jargon as a tool of control, a manipulation of sexuality in the interest of conformity: private, social, political; it makes no difference. Fred merely enjoys exercising power:

Es sollte eins seiner Gesellschaftsspiele werden. Ich glaube, er nennt sie angewandte Psychoanalyse. Der von allen Zwängen und Hüllen dessen, was wir Kultur nennen, befreite Mensch sei, wie er sagt, ein höchst einfach funktionierender Genitalapparat, der, endlich freigelegt, allen anderen menschlichen Bedürfnissen eine orgiastische Abfuhr erteilt, um sich als unabweisbarer, übermächtiger Trieb zu behaupten. Gelegentlich benennt ers einfacher: eine Reise in das Innere des Menschen, ein Besuch bei der wilden Bestie, dem Schwein. Sein Spiel kannte viele Variationen. Seine trüben Einfälle und die so provozierten Tränen oder kräftigen Worte, all die kleinen Demütigungen sollten ihm helfen, seine Langeweile zu vertreiben.

(*DFF* 81–82)

[It was another of his parlor games. I think he calls them "applied psychoanalysis." As he says, a human being stripped of all the compulsions and concealments that we call civilized behavior is simply a set of well-functioning genitalia, which, when finally liberated, provides an orgiastic release for all other human needs, and so asserts its own force as irrefutable, all-powerful. Occasionally he gives this game a simpler label: a journey into the human interior, or a visit to the wild beast, the swine within. The game has many variations. And his horrible whims and the tears or outbursts he provoked, all the little humiliations, were merely devices to keep his boredom at bay.] (*TDL* 69)

The intimate connection between sexuality, violence, and social control grows into a major motif after its introduction here, in this chilling description of "force as irrefutable, all-powerful." As Fred's behavior makes clear, the application of these adjectives to sexual instinct hides a more fundamental motive, whether instinctive or not: the will to power. As has been previously seen, Freud's notion of civilization as a deployment of libido against destructiveness has been twisted into its opposite: civilization in Hein's novella means the subjugation of libido *to* destructiveness. Like any ideology, Fred's ramblings obscure an actual structure of power, elaborating a vulgarized Freudianism that sets civilization in simple opposition to sexuality, and pointing toward an illusory "liberation" from civilized constraints.

The violence that shapes Claudia can be tracked through all the devious permutations of her sexual life, which is taken here in Freud's broadest sense as both aim-inhibited and non-aim-inhibited libido, that is, the totality of Claudia's sexual, emotional, and social relations. When the bizarre episode with Fred is briefly interrupted by Henry's arrival, Claudia's thoughts turn immediately to the matter of whether she has any friends, and if not, why. She is certain that Fred and Maria aren't her friends, but no more than that. She alludes vaguely to her friendship with Katharina, but dismisses it as "wohl auch alles kindlich und unerfahren" [probably too childish to mention: 83; 70] — a typical and reflexive act of repression. Clearly rationalizing, she tries to explain herself to Henry:

> Wahrscheinlich brauche ich keine Freunde. Ich habe Bekannte, gute Bekannte, ich sehe sie gelegentlich und freue mich dann. Eigentlich aber wären sie austauschbar, also nicht zwingend notwendig für mich. Ich bin gern mit Menschen zusammen, viele interessieren mich, und es ist mir angenehm, mit ihnen zu reden. Aber das sei auch alles. Manchmal habe ich ein unbestimmtes Bedürfnis nach etwas wie einem Freund, einer kleinen, blassen Schulfreundin, aber das sei selten und mehr so wie die Tränen, die ich wider Willen im Kino weine bei irgendeinem Rührstück. Wirklich traurig sei ich da ja nicht. Ja, so ist das, sagte ich. (*DFF* 83)

> [I probably didn't need friends. I had acquaintances, good acquaintances; I saw them occasionally, and I enjoyed their company. But in reality they were interchangeable, and therefore not essential to me. I

liked being with people; I found many of them interesting, and it gave me pleasure to talk to them. But that was about it. Sometimes I felt a vague yearning for something like a friend, a pale little school friend, but it didn't come very often; it was like crying, in spite of myself, over some sentimental movie. It wasn't real sadness. Yes, that's how it is, I said.] (*TDL* 70–71)

The narrative contains no more poignant denial of reality. Yet Claudia has not yet perfected her isolation and repression, and at Henry's prompting she wonders if she had been truly different as a child, pointing forward to her more profound self-examination in the ninth chapter. What emerges makes little sense in terms of the immediate context, but a great deal of sense in view of the novella's overall construction:

> Ich glaube, sagte ich, ich war damals anders.
> Sicherlich hatte ich Hoffnungen und gewiß so etwas wie Absichten und genaue Vorstellungen über das Leben. Aber Angst hatte ich auch damals schon. Und vielleicht war ich nie eine andere gewesen, und es war damals nur der Anfang von allem. (*DFF* 84)

> [I think I was different then, I said.
> I certainly had hopes, and must have had something like plans and a clear notion of what life should be like. But even in those days I was afraid. And maybe I never was any different, and maybe that was just the beginning of all this.] (*TDL* 71)

In one sweep, Claudia characterizes her entire current life ("all this") as the stuff of despair. Underlying this, apparently, is a lifelong fear, presumably the same diffuse fear that persists after the dream, a "terror" that consists of the "ausgestandene Hilflosigkeit" [experience of utter helplessness: 7; 4], a reaction, in short, to power.

The tank episode of the ninth chapter, which has been viewed here as pivotal to an understanding of the novella's dialectic of power and repression, has little to do directly with questions of libido, but it is framed by episodes that do deal directly with the question. The story of Herr Gerschke (with the attendant explanation by Claudia's mother as to the dark side of sexuality), and the story of Katharina, explore respectively the relation of power to non-aim-inhibited and aim-inhibited libido, or in other words, sex and friendship, Freud's cornerstones of social coexistence. The narrative structure foregrounds the Katharina story so blatantly, and it has elicited so much critical commentary, that a detailed discussion of it here is unnecessary. It should be remembered that this ruined friendship is not presented as the cause of Claudia's later withdrawal, but as part of a complex historical situation dominated by the political situation of the 1950s, an effect rather than a cause. Of more suggestiveness for the novella as a whole is Claudia's initiation into sexual knowledge in the aftermath of the scandal surrounding Herr Gerschke. The history teacher who had been the object of every school girl's fantasy disappears amid reports that he had "vergriffen" [laid hands on: 140; 119] one of them, and Claudia's ignorance of what this means is dispelled by a classmate, yet she still doesn't understand "warum es so schlimm war, daß er eine Liebschaft mit einer Schülerin hatte" [why it was so bad that he'd had an affair with a student: 141; 119], since, after all, this was everyone's fantasy. Her mother "enlightens" her with a grim account of sex:

> Mit den Illusionen [of love] zerstörte sie in mir meine schönste Hoffnung, den Wunsch, schnell erwachsen zu werden. Ich wollte nicht mehr heiraten oder wenn doch, dann sehr spät. Ich wußte nun, daß man sich keinesfalls zu früh mit einem Mann einlassen durfte, daß man sich seiner Liebe durch jahrelanges Warten versichern mußte, daß jede Frau nur einen einzigen Mann lieben durfte, für den sie sich bewahren mußte. Schreckliche Krankheiten, sieche Gestalten voller Auswüchse und Eiter, ein Leben, das nur noch den Tod erhoffte, waren mahnende, eindringliche Gespenster, die mich für Jahre verfolgten.
>
> (*DFF* 141)
>
> [Along with my illusions she destroyed my loveliest dream, the hope of growing up quickly. I didn't want to marry any more, or at least, I wanted to marry very late. I knew now you absolutely had to avoid getting involved with a man too soon, that it took years to be sure of his love, that every woman was allowed to love only one single man, for whom she had to save herself. Terrible diseases, wasted figures covered with scabs and pus, a life whose only desire was death — these were the stern, insistent ghosts that pursued me for years.] (*TDL* 120)

The discovery later on that Herr Gerschke is innocent cannot undo the mother's wholesale assault on Claudia's sexuality. Its covert violence (which can be readily analyzed as an instrument of patriarchal control) inflicts damage — and compels conformity — more subtly than the crude sexual taunts of the gym teacher, Herr Ebert (134–35; 115–116). As the seemingly random sequence of narrated topics proceeds from the slander against Herr Gerschke, to Fräulein Nitschke, to the tank, to the betrayal of Katharina, and finally to imprisonment of traitorous Uncle Gerhard, the text elaborates how historical circumstances (the Nazi past, the horror of war, the Russian occupation, Ulbricht's anti-religion campaign) systematically undermine personal bonds and aspirations, replacing them with fear, silence, isolation, and, often enough, active collaboration with the wielders of power (demonstrated equally in Uncle Gerhard's betrayal of his SPD comrades to the

Nazis and Claudia's father's objections to her involvement with the religious Katherina).

As the examples above suggest, the area of human conduct where power propagates itself most insidiously, atomizing organic social groupings and replacing them with replications of its own hierarchical abstractions, is sexuality. All of Claudia's thinking about sex is colored by its assumed and accepted connection with violence. The most striking example of this occurs during Claudia's "essay" on marriage and male domination, where human reproduction is cast as an assault on female autonomy carried out by manipulative men. Whereas she feels a sense of involvement when bringing her photographs into existence, Claudia reflects that it was "Anders als bei meinen Kindern, meinen ungeborenen Kindern. Ich hatte nie das Gefühl, beteiligt zu sein" [Different with my children, my unborn children. I never had the feeling of being involved: 103; 88]. But Claudia is clearly rationalizing when she muffles these overtones of regret and portrays her pregnancies with her husband Hinner as invasions by an outside force:

> Mit den Kindern hatte ich nichts zu tun. Ich war nicht daran beteiligt. Es geschah nur mit mir. Ich hatte sie nicht gewollt und bekam sie gegen meinen Willen. Ich fühlte mich von ihm benutzt. Eine austragende Höhle, die Amme seiner Embryos. Ich hatte kein Kind gewollt, und er konnte es dennoch in mir entstehen lassen. Ich blieb ungefragt, ich zählte nicht, ich war nicht beteiligt, ich war das Objekt. Während er mir ins Ohr flüsterte, stöhnte, Liebesbeteuerungen wiederholte, entschied er über mich, meinen Körper, mein weiteres Leben. Ein monströser Eingriff, der meine ganze Zukunft bestimmen sollte, ein Eingriff in meine Freiheit. (*DFF* 104–105)
>
> [I had nothing to do with these children, I wasn't involved. It was just something that happened to me. I hadn't wanted them, they were there against my will. I felt used by him. An incubating vessel, the caretaker for his embryos. I hadn't wanted a child, yet he could make one start growing inside me. I wasn't consulted, I didn't count, I wasn't involved, I was just an object. While he whispered in my ear, moaned, repeated endearments, he was deciding for me, for my body, for my future. A monstrous intervention that would determine my entire life, an intervention in my freedom.] (*TDL* 88–89)

All sex, then, is essentially rape, and abortion is a radical assertion of personal freedom.[12] Of course, the ominous sterility of her photography undercuts, in her particular case, the valorization of artistic creativity over her biological functioning as a woman. Her turn inward, her purported rejection of any outside control, ceases to be distinguishable from a complete abdication of freedom. At most, as in Henry's case, her resistance to power has made her merely suicidal; at worst, it has turned her into a willing accomplice to the social domination she thinks she is resisting. Moreover, in another example of the reversibility of passive and active roles, Claudia's memory of an abortion confuses it precisely with sex and rape, inverting her reasoned categories. She remembers herself treated by the doctors as "Ein Objekt anderer. Ich lag auf einem Bett, einem Stuhl, die Beine angeschnallt, die Scham rasiert, wegrasiert" [Somebody else's property. I lay on a bed, a table, my legs strapped down, my pubic hair shaved, shaved off completely: 106–107; 90]. During the procedure through a haze of anesthesia she feels herself being yet again raped:

> Zwischen meinen Beinen ihre Stimmen, das leise Klirren des Operationsbestecks, und wieder sein Atmen, sein Flüstern, seine Beteuerungen. Hinter den geschlossenen Lidern eine riesige, gleißende Sonne, die sich mir nähert. Ich will allein sein, nur noch allein. Laßt mich, ich will nicht, ich will nicht mehr. Ich flüstere.... Dann sind da Wälder, ein kühler verhangener Himmel, der Weg, der zu einer Brücke führt, brüchigen Resten. Ich verkrieche mich im Gras, unter den Bäumen. Ich spüre kratzende Zweige, die Kälte des Erdbodens, feuchte Blätter.
>
> Nein, die auf das Bett, den Stuhl Hingestreckte war nicht ich, bin nicht ich. Ich hatte nichts damit zu tun. (*DFF* 107–108)

> [Between my legs their voices, the gentle clinking of instruments, and again his breathing, his whispering, his endearments. Behind my eyelids a huge, glaring sun, coming closer. I want to be alone, just alone. Leave me alone, I don't want to, I don't want to anymore, I whisper.... Then the woods are there, a cool overcast sky, the path that leads to a bridge, broken remains. I crawl into the grass, under the trees. I feel branches scratching me, the coolness of earth, wet leaves.
>
> No, the woman stretched out on the table wasn't me, isn't me. I had nothing to do with that.] (*TDL* 90–91)

The return to the dream preface indicates that "the woman stretched out on the table" is indeed Claudia, the objective, externally determined Claudia who has been systematically repressed since the initial decision to forget the past and forsake the future, to become immersed in everyday triviality. This passage also echoes (anachronistically) the other evocation of the dream, the rape scene with Henry in the forest, with its "Schatten und Licht, Hell Dunkel, Vordergrund Hintergrund, die Kühle der Erde, die Baumwurzel, die meinen Rücken wund rieb. Nein, dachte ich, nein" [Shadows and light, brightness, darkness, foreground, background, the coolness of the earth, the tree root scraping away at my spine. No, I thought, no: 70; 59]. And, of course, Claudia echoes Schlötel's weird claim that he has nothing to do with himself.

To avoid being implicated as a collaborator in her subjugation, Claudia offers an analysis of sexual politics that is both reasonable and a rationalization, since it neatly absolves her from guilt. When Hinner found out that something was amiss in their marriage, she says, he immediately looked to the sexual dimension of it for the cause:

> Seine Reaktion war wohl die übliche männliche. Ein Produkt der jahrhundertealten Männergesellschaft: Verlust an Menschlichem durch Ausüben von Herrschaft. Eine Herrschaft, die das Geschlecht als das primär Unterscheidende und Dominierende ansieht, muß ihm übermäßige Bedeutung beimessen. (*DFF* 105)
>
> [His reaction was probably the typical masculine response. A product of hundreds of years of patriarchal society: the more power men wield, the less human they become. And since this power is based on gender as the primary differentiating and dominating factor, naturally those who wield it attach excessive importance to sex.] (*TDL* 89)

The truth of this assessment cannot hide the fact that Claudia herself evidently attaches too little importance to sex; she remains unaware of the degree to which power has lodged itself within her own sexuality, not just as a foreign agent but as the internal locus of personal negation. Though accurate as far as it goes, her historical analysis of patriarchy stops short of articulating the full ramifications (and introjections, as Freud would add) of this and other exercises in domination. The more power men wield, the less human they and *women* become.

At the end of the chapter 9, Claudia brings out the same arguments when Henry strikes her — the appropriate culmination of a chapter that catalogs the entanglements of love and violence, and perhaps the bleakest but most commanding spot from which to survey the novella in its entirety. Henry slaps Claudia when she tries to seize control of the steering wheel, fearful of another mishap. He doesn't apologize, and she is glad.

> Ich wußte, daß er nicht zu den Männern gehört, die ihre Frauen oder Freundinnen schlagen, aber ich weiß auch, daß irgendwann, in irgendeiner besonders komplizierten und nervösen Situation jeder Mann schlagen wird.... Sie fühlen sich zumindest unbewußt uns überlegen, und ihr Zuschlagen, sosehr es sie auch selber erschreckt, ist erzieherisch, ein Akt göttlicher Pädagogik. Intellektuell sind sie fähig und bereit, die Frau als ebenbürtig, gleichrangig anzusehen. In ihren tieferen Schichten beherrscht sie uneingestanden ihr männliches Selbstwertgefühl, ein Mischmasch aus Verklemmungen und Hochmut. (*DFF* 159–161)
>
> [I knew he wasn't one of those men who beat their wives or girlfriends, but I also know that at some time, in some particularly com-

plicated or upsetting situation, every man will hit.... At least unconsciously they feel superior to us, and their hitting, no matter how much it startles them, has a pedagogical intent, it's an act of divine pedagogy. Intellectually they're capable of recognizing women as equals, as beings of the same rank, and they're willing to do so. But in their deeper selves they're still dominated by their masculine sense of self-worth, a weird mixture of inhibitions and arrogance.]
(*TDL* 133, 134–135)

Claudia, meanwhile, considering herself above such self-deceptions and resolved to accept human relations as cruel, violent, unreliable, and temporary, precariously maintains her equilibrium by beating down a moment of panic and despair, and by denying finally that the slap had been anything objectionable:

> Wenn der Regen fällt, werden wir naß, ich bin kein kleines Mädchen mehr, damit muß ich mich abgefunden haben. Es läuft alles in seiner gewohnten Ordnung, alles normal. Kein Anlaß für einen Schrei. Nur nicht hysterisch werden. Ich will bleiben, was ich bin, eine nette, sehr normale Frau. Es ist nichts geschehen. (*DFF* 162)
>
> [When it rains, we get wet; I'm not a young girl anymore and I should get used to it. Everything runs on its usual course, perfectly normal. No reason to scream. Don't get hysterical. I want to remain what I am, a nice, very normal woman. Nothing happened.]
(*TDL* 135–136)

In the context of this chapter, what she says appears to be true. Violence is universal, and any analysis of why violence occurs is strictly a matter of intellectual curiosity, not remediation. Nonetheless, Claudia's response of perfect acquiescence strikes most readers as unsatisfactory. The novella rigorously exposes every superior stance, every attempt to escape historical determinacy, as another masked form of submission, while its narrative logic implies no such determinism. Claudia's behavior can be understood both deterministically and contingently: even though her actions do make perfect sense, and satisfactory explanations for them are ready to hand, she doesn't *have* to act the way she does. Claudia's narrative is a failed effort to escape her history, a nonnarrative that denies the very need for its telling, that hollows itself out by means of a series of deliberate repressions.

Notes

[1] Freud uses the terms *Unterdrückung* (meaning oppression or suppression) and *Verdrängung* (meaning displacement, as of emotions or memories from consciousness) interchangeably in his essay "Civilization and its Discontents," and both can be translated as "repression." Thus my punning on the sense of "verdrängte Personen" (displaced persons, that is, refugees) has some warrant in Freud's own usage.

[2] For instance, Hein has stated that violence and alienation are not the book's main themes, that it is really about the price paid for having achieved our level of civilization. ("Ich kann mein Publikum nicht belehren" 69.) This is of course a generalization, not a contradiction.

[3] See "Waldbruder Lenz" 70–71.

[4] Western reviewers had first to deal with the problem of audience — was the book as meaningful to West Germans as to East Germans? Although most agreed that it was (for instance, Rolf Michaelis for *Die Zeit* and Uwe Wittstock for the *Frankfurter Allgemeine Zeitung*, among many others), a few adopted a patronizing tone and saw the book only as a report from the hellish East (for instance, Stephan Reinhardt for the *Frankfurter Rundschau* and Heinz Mudrich for the *Saarbrücker Zeitung*). Aside from this question, Western reviewers concerned themselves mainly with arguments about the book's historic verisimilitude and psychological plausibility, the question of the author's attitude toward Claudia being much less urgent than in the East.

[5] On the other hand, one Western reviewer, Karl Corin, writing in the Stuttgarter Zeitung, was obtuse enough to complain that Hein "rather placating[ly] . . . recites the Party's cast-iron Official Version [of 17 June 1953]: that nothing much had really taken place on that date" — this in spite of the fact that Hein describes these events from the perspective of a small Thuringian town, not as seen along the Stalinallee in Berlin.

[6] The most scandalous criticism stays on the level of insinuation, however, when Bernhardt worries aloud about the "problematic" meaning of the runners in the dream, who wear jerseys bearing "rune-like symbols" (1638). It appears that Hein is suspected of fascist sympathies because he evokes swastikas in the mind of a critic.

[7] Among the "Für" critics in the "Für and Wider" collection, Bernd Leistner complained that Hein's stance respecting Claudia was altogether *too* clearly critical; the piquancy of the book comes from the sympathy Hein preserves for a character who is doomed from the start in her search for completeness. In an apt choice of words, Leistner praises the book as "honest [*unverlogen*] — and idealistic at the same time" (1645). Gabriele Lindner dismisses the question of Hein's own views as outside the purview of the book, and as-

serts that for her own part the book moved her to wonder what could be done to correct a society where people like Claudia are possible (1645–1648).

[8] Brigitte Böttcher, for example, treats the mill scene as "the key passage in the novella: The dream finds its real analogy in chapter five, which marks the climax, the turning point of the novella. All of the significant motifs are concentrated here, and from this chapter on Claudia's self-portrayal changes from a nerve-racking inventory to a search for the roots of her problematic existence" (147).

[9] Claudia's reasonableness is crucial to her appeal and her frightfulness as a character. Her reasoning is essentially sound, yet it has not saved her. Confronted with a situation in life, Hein has remarked, Claudia arrived at a solution that is obviously wrong [offenbar falsch], but this is not the same as saying she made an error at some point or points. She "has actually made no error" [eigentlich hat sie keinen Fehler gemacht]. Yet she has been trapped in her life as it is: "I suspect it was unavoidable" [Ich vermute es war unvermeidbar] (Personal interview by author, 9 May 1988).

[10] Hein once joked that since the tank must be viewed as a fairly normal means of transportation in the twentieth century, like the Mercedes, Volkswagen, or Trabant, critics shouldn't make too much of it in his books. While acknowledging that the tank has historically been the clearest emblem of state power for East Europeans, he warns against interpreting that emblem in *Der fremde Freund* and *The Tango Player* the same way one interprets the crucifix in the middle of a church (Personal interview by author, 4 May 1989).

[11] McKnight points out that the "*Abziehbilder* are like stickers or decals that cover over unpleasant memories and longings ("*Alltag*, Apathy, Anarchy" 180) They resemble the photographs that eventually threaten to drown Claudia (*DFF* 210; *TDL* 177–178).

[12] For a detailed discussion of Hein's idiosyncratic handling of abortion as a symbol, see Robinson, "Abortion as Repression in Christoph Hein's *The Distant Lover*."

4: Hein's Historians: Fictions of Social Memory

Ideology and History

WHILE ALL OF CHRISTOPH HEIN'S WORK REVEALS A fascination with the impact of history on individual experience, several of his most ambitious texts deal explicitly with history as an intellectual discipline and space for social engagement. The early story "Einladung zum Lever Bourgeois" (1980)[1] and the novels *Horns Ende* (1985) and *Der Tangospieler* (1989; translated into English as *The Tango Player*, 1992) explore the significance of history as material fact and social memory through fictive portrayals of historians: Racine is court historian to Louis XIV, Horn (along with Bürgermeister Kruschkatz and, in a different sense, Dr. Spodeck) is a professional historian whose career has been diverted by political circumstance, and Hans-Peter Dallow is a once and future professor of history at Karl Marx University in Leipzig. The narratives themselves and Hein's published essays and interviews leave little doubt that the professional activity (or inactivity) of these writers of history may be understood in relation to Hein's own sense of responsibility as a writer of fiction, of *histoire* or *Geschichte* in all senses. As Hein frequently stresses, history is anything but the dusting-off of neglected tomes:

> History interests us for the sake of the present. Historical contemplation is always a naming [*Benennen*] of the immediate time and place. The judgments of history are never free from current interests and they exert an influence on contemporary society.
> ("Die fünfte Grundrechenart" 61)[2]

Accordingly, the approaches taken by Hein's professional historians to their subject matter provide a scale of values and methods suited for judging the engagement of ordinary people with the social realities confronting them. Though historians bear a special social responsibility, their pursuit of truth amid rampant falsehood epitomizes a practical and moral necessity shared by every member of society.

In keeping with the non-partisan stance Hein advocates, a chronicle consists not of ready-made generalizations but of hard, individual facts and experiences, the traces of the real that make possible the construction as well as the deconstruction of ideological fiction. Yet this implies that objectivity with respect to the facts must coexist with intense subjectivity, since all chronicles of any value amount to personal reports, eyewitness accounts of events experienced by a real human observer. The writing of history therefore has a dual character: it is both social chronicle and autobiography. Hein regards all art, including his own, as "social autobiography":

> My subject matter is located in my eyes and ears, it sits under my skin, because it very much gets under my skin. As always it is the beam in my own eye, the stake in my own flesh. Literature in the future will also speak of what concerns individuals, of what affects them. It will be autobiography, not private, yet nonetheless personal, not representative, yet nonetheless social autobiography. Reports by individuals about these individuals in the world, a world which I assimilate according to my understanding, abilities, and attitudes — the world which I am. ("Öffentlich arbeiten" 34)

While history is the ultimate subject matter of art (a point on which Hein and his Party-line critics would have agreed), history itself is to be understood as personal experience, as social autobiography rather than the unfolding of impersonal laws. Hein's books on history address simultaneously questions of historical reality, ideological distortion, personal/political responsibility, and the nature of art, but Hein sees himself principally as a chronicler (or historian) of the real, the mundane, the ordinary. Art and history describe relations of individuals to these social and political conditions. Thus in *Horns Ende*, a succession of "historians" (amateur or professional, it makes no difference) chronicle a relatively insignificant moment in the history of a relatively insignificant town, each from his or her idiosyncratic point of view. To attempt a more general history, Hein seems to suggest, would involve falsifications of reality more insidious than anything these individuals can be accused of. The novel is constructed according to principles already worked out in the early collection of short stories, combining the representative banality of the "Berliner Stadtansichten" with the self-conscious reflection (and first-person viewpoint) of "Einladung zum Lever Bourgeois." Yet these limitations of ordinariness do not prevent the narrated facts from having political meaning. Speculating as to how much we can really know about history, Hein remarked in 1982 that "Every event manifests itself to us merely as the tip of an iceberg: a self-concealing network of causes and interests hides behind the face of the obvious facts" ("Gespräch" 128). The chronicler, unlike the ideologue, presents facts, opinions, and even falsifications of fact to the reader without overtly or covertly dictating the appropriate conclusions to be drawn from them.

The question arises as to what may be the ultimate purpose of these exercises in "social autobiography." Hein has above all characterized his art as *Lebenshilfe*, an aid to living, meaning that it helps people to assimilate confusing or painful experiences and respond to them productively. Hein's subversion of East German cultural orthodoxy consists in the production of texts that portray individuals in the toils of historical, social, and political events much larger than they — subversion, because to respond to political events productively is to respond politically. Taking seriously the Marxist goal of building political consciousness among the masses, Hein relies on the notion of chronicling as a way of counteracting the government's pervasive *Bevormündung* (tutelage, patronage) of its citizens. The reader is required, perhaps for the first time, to bring an independent evaluation to bear on the facts of recent, even contemporary history, without any obvious ideological meddling on the part of the author or the state. (Clearly, the didactic import of this procedure discloses Hein's kinship with his Socialist Realist colleagues — he, too, has an ax to grind after all. Yet a genuine difference can be seen in the kind of effect desired: Hein enjoys watching the Rorschach-like effect of his shrewd narrative strategies on readers, remarking blandly that criticism tends to reveal more about critics than authors ["Wir werden es lernen müssen" 53–54].) Hein believes adamantly that political change can only come about when individuals take responsibility for their actions, or better, when they conceive of themselves as capable of acting. In bringing about this kind of political self-awareness, "Literatur ist machtlos, aber sie ist nicht ohnmächtig" [Literature lacks power, but it isn't powerless: "Worüber man nicht reden kann" 49]; that is, literature cannot claim to exert direct political power — Creon need not listen — but it can alter the way people think about historical facts and the facts of their lives. Thus the real efficacy of chronicling lies not so much in the unearthing of new facts, but in naming things known but never articulated, in dragging formerly inert realities onto the field of political action. Not the facts chronicled, but the chronicle itself achieves this:

> It hasn't been the reported event, the specified state of affairs, but the report itself, the chronicle, the description that caused a sensation, created excitement, and led to action being taken. Not the *condition* of our beautiful and terrible world, but the *report* about that condition constitutes a happening. Still more: The condition, the state of affairs, the incident may be generally known and seemingly tolerated, while the naming of it, the simple literary or non-literary description, in

which nothing is said that wasn't already known, leads to an uproar of joy or horror and to effective action.
("Worüber man nicht reden kann" 47–48)

The power of historical writing seems to derive from its capacity to inspire personal recognition and acknowledgment of a reported state of affairs, not from its proximity to timeless, abstract truth. The concrete experience of socialist countries over seventy years was that abstract, "scientific" accounts of history amounted to what Hein calls "die fünfte Grundrechenart" — the fifth basic arithmetical operation — a calculation whose desired outcome is preordained, with the data selected or manipulated so as to yield it ("Die fünfte Grundrechenart" 60). For Hein, history cannot be described by formulas, but is particular and subjective, in other words, literary.

The key concept in Hein's view of the social functions of literature and historical chronicling is *Öffentlichtkeit*, "publicness," or, to borrow Gorbachev's related and contemporary concept of *glasnost*, "openness." Hein repeatedly cites the GDR's lack of *Öffentlichkeit* as the most glaring and dangerous failure of East German culture, and hints at an even broader, political significance:

> Openness [Öffentlichkeit] is not a means by which culture is propagated, rather it is culture's precondition. This does not mean "limited openness" (a self-contradictory notion), nor does it mean "openness for an elite."
>
> Selected culture is the opposite of culture. When disagreements are lacking, or take place only behind closed doors, when conclusions are reached in isolation from society, then not only this aspect of culture but culture as a whole withers, and becomes impoverished.
>
> Culture is more comprehensive than that which appears useful, or comfortable, or agreeable, and it dies with each restriction. For culture is not just the admired and successful work of the individual, but the total spiritual work of the whole people, including the work of specialists, of artists. Only insofar as this total work is carried out openly do we have culture. ("Öffentlich arbeiten" 36)

When applied to the writing of history, Hein's conception of *Öffentlichkeit* underscores the importance of allowing disparate voices and viewpoints to flourish and compete, this being the only way to compensate for the essential fragmentation, distortion, and outright lying that all discourse exhibits. Though no friend of what capitalist ideologues call the "free market," Hein fiercely champions a free market of ideas, whether in history or art; not surprisingly, this position culminates in Hein's denunciation of the GDR's practice of literary censorship in his essay "Die Zensur." Yet Hein's artistic practice itself provides the strongest protest against intellectual conformity, nowhere more so than in these meditations on history. The monologic narratives *Der fremde Freund*, "Einladung zum Lever Bourgeois," and *Der Tangospieler* ultimately prove to be depictions of intellectual and spiritual bankruptcy, while the polyphony of *Horns Ende* enacts a genuinely dialectical discourse, pitting contradictory worldviews against one another without hiding the extremity of the contradictions. Nothing less can save historical discourse from dogmatic Marxism's shockingly undialectical special pleading and self-justification.[3]

Racine's Public and Private Histories

Hein's characterization of the French playwright and courtier Racine, the focus of the short story "Einladung zum Lever Bourgeois," assembles many of the traits of other characters inhabiting the later, more ambitious narratives. The story, which describes Racine's morning routine on an ordinary day, is set in early 1699, shortly before the 59-year-old writer's death due to a liver ailment, possibly cancer. Sitting in agony atop a chamber pot, unable to void his excrement, Racine thinks about his roles as court historiographer, reigning playwright, husband, lover, and superannuated Versailles functionary, dwelling unhappily on the conflicts between official duty and private desire, on the need to suppress historical truth out of political expediency, and on the personal price he has paid for his enviable status at the court of Louis XIV. In his willing repression of his past experiences, his renunciation of personal desire, and his capacity to rationalize his self-destructive actions, Hein's Racine anticipates Claudia in *Der fremde Freund*; in his remarks about the nature of history and its writing, he points the way toward Horn, Kruschkatz, and Spodeck in *Horns Ende*. The story's straightforward linkage of public expediency to personal devastation marks it as an early effort to capture in narrative form the conflicts Hein had expressed dramatically in *Schlötel* and especially in *Cromwell*. Its discovery of history per se as a central theme had momentous importance for Hein's subsequent work.

The contradictory and tendentious record of Racine's life provided Hein with a great deal of freedom in constructing a complex character and inferring motivations for his sometimes enigmatic actions.[4] Among the most puzzling of these was Racine's sudden renunciation of stage writing in 1677 — soon after the production of *Phèdre*, and at the height of his 13-year dramatic career. After a life of mild libertinage (two of his leading actresses became mistresses), he reconciled himself with his Jansenist upbringing and married a wealthy, respectable wife, and soon after, with Boileau, was appointed royal historiographer, which, according to Saintsbury, in practice amounted to being named the king's "chief flatterer": "Very little came of this historiography. The joint incumbents of the office made some campaigns with the king, sketched plans of histories, and left a certain number of materials and memoirs; but they executed no substantive work" (Saintsbury 207). In contrast to Racine's biographer Mary Duclaux, for instance, Hein has no interest in explaining away the royal historian's inactivity (Duclaux 144), nor does he follow the tradition, founded by son Louis Racine and copied by subsequent hagiographers (for instance, Duclaux 129), of ascribing the playwright's transformation primarily to religious motives. Instead, Hein's story proposes that the common root of these perplexing facts lay in the failure of Racine's relationship with his second mistress, the actress Marie de Champmeslé, whom Hein elevates on rather thin biographical warrant to the central passion of Racine's life. (Brereton, by contrast, dismisses her as "an episode, though a long and important one, in his life . . . [which] left him somewhat bitterly inclined towards her" [154].) Hein explains Racine's behavior as playwright and historian as a complex response to the contradictions between those public and private roles.

Hein's Racine is trapped between the pressure of state power and his altogether stifled desire for a fulfilling private existence, which here amounts to a desire for love and free expression. At the time of the story, he has been a successful courtier for twenty years, yet he remains preoccupied with the personal price paid for this position of prestige and power.[5] His reminiscences, like Claudia's, circle around their main point before revealing it; thus the first memory to surface while Racine sits on his chamber pot is of the campaign in Holland 20 years earlier, when the newly appointed court historian had accompanied Louis XIV into the field as a chronicler of the war. He remembers his experiences in the village of Neerwinden as the last time he was fully in possession of his health, and the implication is clear that the atrocities he witnessed there — and helped to hush up — had something to do with his physical deterioration. Racine's physician has informed him that "Letzte Gewißheit über Ihren Zustand, Verehrter, . . . werden außer Gott wir alle erst nach der letzten Eröffnung unseres geschätzten Hofhistoriographen haben" [Final certainty as to your condition, Excellency, will be granted to any apart from God only after the esteemed court historian's final disclosure: *NUFM* 121] — a macabre pun on the senses of *Eröffnung* as "disclosure" or "revelation" (such as a court historian might be expected to deliver) and "autopsy" (*Leichenöffnung*). Hein transforms the illness into a metaphor: Racine's internal disorder is a physical analog to his undisclosed knowledge of a specific historical fact, the brutality at Neerwinden. Hein portrays the younger Racine as an innocent, exposed for the first time to the realities of warfare and, more broadly, to absolutist power. As an old man, he still vividly recalls the savagery of the crime and its handling by the military authorities:

> Das Verfahren gegen die drei Offiziere. Eine holländische Bäuerin war vergewaltigt worden, man fand sie dann zusammen mit ihrem Kind in der Stallung tot auf. Die Untersuchung wurde eingestellt, um höhere Interessen nicht zu inkommodieren. Alltag der Armee. Der Bauer, der die drei Offiziere angezeigt hatte, ein Nachbar jener Frau, verübte später — wie der französische Kommandant im Dorf bekanntgeben ließ — Selbstmord. Schuldig des Diebstahls von Militäreigentum. Bemerkenswert daran, daß er sich in seiner Scheune mehr als zwanzigmal eine Forke in den Körper gestoßen haben mußte, so daß sein Leib in zwei Teile zerriß. (*NUFM* 122)
>
> [The proceeding against the three officers. A Dutch peasant woman had been raped; she and her child were found in the stable dead. The investigation was arranged so as to avoid inconveniencing higher interests. Standard operating procedure in the army. According to a statement issued by the French commandant of the village, the farmer who implicated the three officers, a neighbor of the woman, later committed suicide. Guilty of stealing military property. The remarkable thing was that he must have stabbed himself more than twenty times with a pitchfork, so that his body lay torn in two in his barn.]

Confronted with this compound atrocity, Racine did nothing and remained silent, not, he says, because of any lack of courage, but because of "Lebenserfahrung" [life experience: *NUFM* 123]. He claims to have no feelings of guilt mixed with his prudence, "weder damals noch heute" [neither then nor now: 123], yet his account of Neerwinden, filled with windy rationalizations, is a document in guilt. Racine casts himself as "ein kleiner Geschichtsschreiber, gegen die allmächtige, allgegenwärtige Armee" [a puny historian, against the omnipotent, omnipresent army: 123], before admitting that as one close to the king, he might have exerted influence. Then he tries vainly to play the cynic:

> Aber wozu. Was dann. Sollte er in die Scheune gehen, um dann Mord, Mord zu schreien? Die reinen Helden in der Literatur. Auf der Bühne ist es angebracht. Helden. Tat und Tod. Er ist kein Schauspieler. (*NUFM* 123)

[But for what. What then. Should he have gone into the barn and screamed Murder, Murder? Perfect literary heroism. Suited for the stage. Heroes. Deeds and death. He is not an actor.]

Such words from the former playwright have a desperately false ring (lying to himself here, he is surely an actor in spite of himself), and they point to the nature of what he has truly done in renouncing the stage: as later becomes clear, he has set aside any hope of a life undistorted by fealty to the state. That his post as historian supposedly obliges him to report the truth before bending to the interests of the state appears to him nothing but a cruel joke, since to tell the truth in this case would constitute "Staatsverleumdung" [defamation of the state: 123] — one of several instances in this story of crimes and state institutions as typical of the GDR as of France under Louis XIV.

The climax of Racine's guilty remembrance is a succinct statement of political pragmatism in the face of absolute power — a cynical position that Racine himself cannot espouse with any conviction. The resulting muddle of self-exculpation and *Realpolitik* clearly anticipates the confused half-truths Claudia will use in *Der fremde Freund* to numb herself to her misery:

> Nur Idioten und Kinder verwundern sich über die Welt. Die Bestialität der Polizei, der Armee ist abscheulich, ekelhaft, aber untauglich für Meditation. Allenfalls für ein Gespräch mit gleichermaßen Enttäuschten: eine Andeutung, eine ironische Bermerkung, ein verzweifeltes Lachen, Charakter en passant, man weiß. Vielleicht ist die Fähigkeit, ein Verbrechen verschweigen zu können, die Bedingung der menschlichen Rasse, in Gesellschaft zu leben. Das "höhere Interesse" eines Staates anzuerkennen, ist bestialisch, möglicherweise aber die Voraussetzung seiner weiteren Existenz. Der des Staates, des Individuums ohnehin. Und der verdiente Staatsbürger ist zu ehren um seiner schweigenden Mitwisserschaft willen. Da ist es süß, für das Vaterland zu sterben, um ihm nicht anderweitig dienen zu müssen.
>
> Die Scheunentor zu öffnen, um nie wieder schlafen zu können, um sich vor sich selbst zu ekeln, auszuspeien? Nein, es widerspricht der Vernunft, Kenntnisse zu erlangen, zu erzwingen, die uns unerträglich sind. (*NUFM* 123-4)
>
> [Only idiots and children are astonished by the world. The brutality of the police, of the army is abominable, sickening, but unsuited for meditation. Perhaps at most discussion with people equally disillusioned: an insinuation, an ironic remark, a despairing laugh, moral character *en passant* — one knows. The ability to say nothing about a crime may be a condition for the survival of the human race, for life in society. To acknowledge the "higher interest" of the state is brutal, yet perhaps the precondition for continued existence. Of the state,

certainly of the individual. And the loyal citizen is to be honored for his connivance. How sweet it is to die for the Fatherland, and thus escape serving it further.

To open the barn door, and then never again to sleep, to be sickened by oneself, to vomit? No, it goes against reason to obtain, to extort knowledge that would be unbearable.]

This passage is a mother lode of ideas and themes that dominate Hein's later work. There is the thinly-veiled criticism of the GDR's organs of repression, the police and army (the security police are mentioned elsewhere in this story and also in the first story of the collection, "Die russischen Briefe des Jägers Johann Seifert"); the clear allusion to that infamous silence of average German citizens who claimed afterward to know nothing of atrocities committed under their noses by the Nazi regime (the best example will be the story of the Gohl family in *Horns Ende*); the ironic espousal of a theory of adaptive repression in the face of political and personal unpleasantness (Claudia being the prime, but not sole, example — Kruschkatz, too, finds himself unable to sleep once he forgets to forget); the depiction of a deadly nihilism that relegates political idealism to "idiots and children" (Marlene Gohl and Thomas of *Horns Ende* inevitably come to mind, and also the hapless idealists of *Passage*, while the best portrait of a nihilist is Dallow in *Der Tangospieler*, who perfects the attitude that had been a mere pose for the protagonists of *Die wahre Geschichte des Ah Q*). In general, Racine is an early version of the recurring character who, under pressure from a crushing social reality, unwittingly loses control of his or her private life; the more vehemently these characters claim to evade or subvert their totalitarian milieus, the more inevitable their transformation into simulacra of the power structures that dominate them.[6] Hein's frequent use of history as a theme provides one way of manifesting the general phenomenon of individuals' social determination; as Hein has said, history (that abstraction of the social universe) is always personal: "One wishes to know one's fathers in order to know oneself" ("Anmerkungen zu *Cromwell*" 173).

Although Racine derides those who would lose sleep and make themselves ill by opening the "barn door" to the horrors around them, he is himself a victim of such a self-induced illness. The horrors from which he has averted his eyes are no less real to him for all his claims to the contrary. Hein leaves little doubt that Racine's terminal illness is an inward consequence of his outward actions, the effect, as it were, of a poison he has secretly consumed:

> Racine is presented as the type of the political conformist who frantically shuts his eyes to the cruelty and morbidity of the Sun King's ab-

solutist regime. Yet the repressed awareness of the real situation finds an outlet in horrible physical torments. Illness is a synonym here for the rape of one's own spirit. Hein wishes to say that uncompromising conformity of intellectuals to the prevailing power means absolute destruction of the personality. (Krumrey 143)

Racine, perched on his chamber pot, recalls the Neerwinden episode while pondering how long it was since he was last healthy. The recollection ends with another evocation of physical illness caused by repressed feelings:

> Die Übelkeit kam erst, als sein Blick auf eine Mistforke fiel, die an die Stallung seiner Gastgeber gelehnt war. Drei schmutzbedeckte iserne Zinken, fußlang, vierkantig, spitz auslaufend. Wieviel ist zwanzig mal drei. Er erbrach grünlichen Magensaft. (*NUFM* 124)

> [The nausea first came over him when his gaze fell on the dungfork leaning against his host's stable wall. Three foot-long iron prongs, filth-incrusted, square-angled, tapering to points. How much is twenty times three. He vomited green bile.]

Now, twenty years after the thought of the farmer's death made him vomit, Racine describes himself as "ein Kloß von Erinnerungen und Schmerzen" [A clump of memories and pain: *NUFM* 124]. He likens his stomach to a battlefield, like the Dutch ones he remembers: "Der Schauplatz der Schlacht. Schlachtplatz. Letztes Heldentum im Rückzug auf den Wanst. Verinnerlichter Lebenskampf" [The scene of battle. Battlefield. Retreat to the belly the supreme sacrifice. Internalized struggle for life: 126], a battlefield, moreover, without possibility of escape: "Flucht ist hier nicht einmal eine Denkmöglichkeit. Die Feindlichen sind miteinander verwachsen" [Escape is out of the question. The enemies have become one another: 128]. The internal and external, public and private have been entirely conflated. Racine has become the product of his society and of his accommodations with it, from which he is now dying.[7]

However, the root of Racine's illness consists of more than complicity in the cover-up of a specific war crime; there is also the whole complex of values and possibilities that was rejected when he decided to remain silent, to give up his artistic career, and to renounce a mistress. In his imagery and language, Hein conflates these values as aspects of an ambiguous hope whose loss is fatal. As Hein notes elsewhere, "There are hopes . . . to which there is no human alternative" ("Maelzel's Chess Player" 193). As the story draws to a close, the outline of this central tragedy emerges:

Trotz der Krankheit fühlt er sich kräftig. So kräftig und unbeugsam wie in jenem Jahr, als er Catherine heiratete, die er nicht liebte, und Marie verließ, deren Atem er noch heute zu verspüren meint. Er verließ sie an dem Tag, an dem er beschlossen hatte, eine Arbeit zu beenden, weil er nicht weiter imstande war, länger zu warten. Zu hoffen. Er schloß sie ab wie einen Brief, an dem man lange geschrieben und so viele neue Blätter hinzugefügt und so oft die einzelnen Worte und Buchstaben verbessert, ausgewechselt und nachgezogen hatte, bis man unversehens, aber nicht unerwartet erfuhr, daß es keinen Adressaten mehr gibt, keinen. Nicht für seinen Brief. Damals meinte er, mit Masken zu sprechen, mit freundlichen Masken, hinter deren Augenhöhlen der Wind des Vergessens längst seine gründliche Säuberung vollzogen hatte. Die Tränen, die er über die Masken laufen sah und die überdeutlich Spuren in der Schminke hinterließen, gaben ihm keine Antwort. Sie waren die Hinterlassenschaft eines versickerten Lebens, nur für wenige Momente noch sichtbar.

Er flieht blindlings. Was hat er schon einzutauschen! Am gleichen Tag, an dem er die für ihn lange unerklärliche Herkunft der Tränen begriff und er seine Zwiesprache mit den ausgestorbenen Augenhöhlen abbrach, verabschiedete er sich von Marie de Champmeslé und heiratet wenige Monate später Catherine, die er kaum kennt und nie geliebt hat. (*NUFM* 128-9)

[Despite his illness he feels strong. As strong and unbending as in the year when he married Catherine, whom he did not love, and left Marie, whose breath it seemed he could sense even today. He left her on the day he decided to finish an undertaking, because he was no longer capable of waiting. Of hoping. He closed it like a letter which one had long been writing, adding so many new pages and so often improving, rearranging, and revising words and spellings, before noticing unexpectedly, but without surprise, that there was no longer anyone to send it to, nobody. Not for his letter. He thought at the time that he was speaking to masks, friendly masks, behind the eyeholes of which a wind of forgetting had long since completed a thorough cleansing. The tears (which he saw run down the masks and leave exaggerated trails in the makeup) gave him no answer. They were the remnant of a life which had trickled away, still visible for a few moments.

He flees blindly. What does he have to lose! On the same day that he understood the cause of the tears, which had so long perplexed him, and broke off his dialogue with the extinguished eyeholes, he took his leave of Marie de Champmeslé, and marries Catherine a few months later, whom he hardly knows and has never loved.]

The characterization of his relationship with Marie de Champmeslé as a letter, along with the statement that his rupture with her coincided with a decision "to finish an undertaking," allude to a relationship which, according to some of Racine's biographers, was terminated by de Champmeslé, not by Racine (Duclaux 124; Brereton takes an opposing view [154]). Hein disregards this item of indeed dubious information and integrates the break-up with the turning point in Racine's career. Hein's Racine despairs, it would seem, of holding de Champmeslé's love, of ever finding a real woman beneath the actress's personas, the "friendly masks" to which he has been addressing himself. When he decides that the woman he had loved is no longer behind the mask, that he has been erased from her affections "thoroughly" by the "wind of forgetting," he gives up not only hope of de Champmeslé's love, but hope of any kind. In place of hope, he accepts security, respectability, and incidentally the death of his artistic and (as has become evident) moral imagination. Racine's disillusionment at Neerwinden was merely an epilogue to the deliberate self-disillusioning he had already imposed on himself out of impatience, timidity, and despair:

> Marie hat er verlassen, um sich loszureißen von dem, was er, er wußte es damals bereits, bald schmerzlich vermissen würde. So war er rücksichtslos gegen sich und andere geworden, nur, um nicht zu zögern. Um nicht an seiner für ihn ungeheuren und entsetzlichen Entscheidung zu zweifeln. (*NUFM* 129)

> [He left Marie in order to tear himself away from what he already knew he would soon painfully miss. He had been ruthless with himself and with others only to keep from hesitating. To keep from wavering in a decision that was monstrous and catastrophic for him.]

Racine's fatal decision will be the same one arrived at by Claudia, who is willing to sacrifice everything hopeful and hence unpredictable in her life to an unsuccessful attempt to avoid pain, and by Dr. Spodeck, who exaggerates his youthful experience of paternal despotism into a sterile destiny of lovelessness; its precise opposite would be worked out in the leap of faith taken by Hirschburg and the other refugees at the conclusion of *Passage*. Racine is an early example of an individual who surrenders unconditionally to state power; as a lapsed playwright and failed historiographer, he points toward Hein's subsequent meditations on the social functions of history and art.[8]

Theories of history in *Horns Ende*

Hein's most ambitious prose work, the novel *Horns Ende*, centers on two deaths in a small East German resort town, Bad Guldenberg. One, the murder of Gudrun Gohl, takes place in 1943, when she substitutes herself for her mentally retarded daughter Marlene, whom Nazi officials have assigned to a "special home" (*HE* 156) as part of their eugenics program to eliminate inferior individuals. News of her murder (officially, she died of pneumonia) soon follows. The other death is the suicide of Herr Horn in the summer of 1957. Horn, a historian and a Communist, had been unjustly purged from the Party years before; his refusal to forget the wrong done to him exposes him to further political attacks. Accused finally of being a Western spy, he hangs himself. No connection between these two deaths is ever explicitly drawn; instead, the narrators provide mostly factual accounts of the town's history since before the Nazi period, and of their own experiences up to 1957 (and beyond, in the case of Kruschkatz, the Bürgermeister of Bad Guldenberg at the time of Horn's death, who provides a postscript to the major events from his vantage point in a retirement home in the early 1980s). Structured as a cycle of subjective reports by various narrators, the novel is punctuated by surreal passages in which the voice or ghost of Horn interrogates Thomas, the youngest narrator (now a man in middle-age), enjoining him to overcome his reluctance to remember the circumstances of Horn's death. Thus Thomas, and by extension all of the narrators, are engaged in a struggle with their own memories, fervently wishing to forget the past but prevented from doing so by a moral imperative, the repetitions of Horn's (and Hein's) exhortation "Erinnere Dich" [Remember!: *HE* 5], a command aimed at people like Claudia in *Der fremde Freund* who have learned to keep their mouths shut and their memories short. Under this compulsion, the narrators detach themselves from the general amnesia of Bad Guldenberg, whose tranquillity comes to look less benign, more a "repression of the collective historical memory" (Schachtsiek-Freitag 540).

In the 1986 interview with Krzysztof Jachimczak (the February 1988 publication of which in *Sinn und Form* was one of the few and meager examples of East German *Öffentlichkeit* enjoyed by Hein's novel), Hein identifies the major themes of *Horns Ende* as history, conceptions of history, and the writing of history ("Wir werden es lernen müssen" 62). As an East German writer confronting these themes, Hein feels he must compensate for the years of official distortion about recent German history. The notion of a "Year Zero" from the ashes of which a new, uncontaminated East Germany arose has to be debunked:

> There was caesura *and* continuity. The accusation that I put too little emphasis on the caesura and see nothing but continuities can only stem from the fact that until now the caesura has been overemphasized, this Year Zero. Germany's treatment of history entered a very strange phase after 1945. In West Germany, the Nazi Period began to

> be repressed immediately, even as early as the Nuremberg war crime trials; the decisive factor here was the onset of the Cold War between the two Blocs. In the GDR, it was opposition: the antifascist tradition was celebrated, which was understandable and morally quite correct; but the GDR couldn't just proclaim opposition, either. Because the GDR wasn't born out of the antifascist resistance alone — it was born out of the collapse of the Third Reich, out of the Red Army's victory over Hitler, out of a war that the Germans lost. It is simply a falsification and distortion of history to lay claim to the oppositional stance, as though Hitler had been a usurper and not a legitimate head of state elected by the German people, or as though the whole populace, or the part of it now living in the GDR, had all been active in the resistance. ("Wir werden es lernen müssen" 60–61)

Hein's remedy to the unbalanced and all-too-convenient view of history promulgated by the Party is to restore fictively the corrective influence of dialogue — between, for example, Thomas and dead Herr Horn, or of the author or narrator with himself, or between the different historical periods represented in the novel ("Wir werden es lernen müssen" 59).

Hein's starting point in the novel is therefore this simple moral imperative, that individuals face up to the reality of their past deeds rather than covering them up and, so to speak, re-writing history:

> I can't show the GDR springing out of a Year Zero simply because the foregoing history is unpleasant. It's unpleasant to me, even me, but I have to acknowledge it, I have to endure it. And the GDR will have to endure it, too.... ("Wir werden es lernen müssen" 62)

In 1957 or 1980, in Bad Guldenberg or any other German town, East or West, this primarily means acknowledging complicity in the crimes of the Hitler era and admitting that no radical discontinuity insulates the totalitarian past from the putatively democratic, anti-fascist present. What remains to be carried out in the novel is the detailed exploration of *how* to remember, which is the problem also of how to represent history. The historian-narrators of *Horns Ende* — what Phillip McKnight calls the "triptych" of "philosophers of history" ("Ein Mosaik" 415, 418), Dr. Spodeck the physician, Bürgermeister Kruschkatz, and Herr Horn, to which I would add a fourth, the apothecary's son Thomas — tell their stories and the story of the town for different reasons and with different emphases. While weaving these fragmentary narratives together so as to maintain suspense and uncertainty, Hein also allows them to comment on one another, to come into conflict, and to illustrate opposing ways of coping with past and present life in Bad Guldenberg. In this way, the novel's diverse viewpoints and voices substitute for an *Öffentlichkeit* that never otherwise existed in the GDR, sustained by Hein's unswerving protest against socialist piety and complacency. Believing that reality is full of contradictions, not just tidy scientific laws, Hein allows the contradictions within his novel free play. Accordingly, none of the narrators speaks unequivocally as the author's mouthpiece: "Beliefs [Sätze] of my own occur in each of the characters" ("Wir werden es lernen müssen" 62). Hein's personal views are distributed across a variety of characters whom the reader may judge very differently. This deliberate dispersal of authority within the novel further illustrates Hein's anti-authoritarian model of historical truth: no one person, dogma, party, nation, or bloc has a monopoly on truth. In fact, all "truths" contain distortions, falsehoods, and it is only the differential relations among these competing untruths that allow us to approach the real.[9]

Spodeck

Unequaled in Hein's writing for his self-corroding cynicism, Dr. Spodeck gets the first and last word in the novel, setting the tone even if not representing a privileged moral position or historiographic methodology. Yet he is also the only *practicing* historian in the novel, apart from Horn himself. His approach to writing history is akin to his practice of maintaining a private collection of patient case histories dealing with psychological disorders (a youthful interest thwarted by his tyrannical father and by Spodeck's own weakness of will). His history of Bad Guldenberg is a compilation of the human folly he has witnessed there:

> Es ist keine Historie der Stadt, die ich schreibe, ich führe keine pathetische Heimatchronik, die den Eitelkeiten obskurer Stadtgrößen schmeicheln will. Was ich auf diesen Blättern notiere, sind lediglich die niederträchtigen Affären und bösartigen Handlungen, durch die sich meine ehrenwerten Mitbürger auszeichneten. Es sind die widerlichen Geschäfte der Einwohner meiner Stadt, die es nie versäumten, ihre eigennützige Boshaftigkeit mit salbungsvollen Reden und achtbaren Motiven zu maskieren. Es ist eine Geschichte der menschlichen Gemeinheit. Ich kann nicht darin lesen, ohne von heftigem Lachen geschüttelt zu werden, von einem Lachen der Menschenverachtung und des Mitleids über einen solchen Aufwand von Energie um ein paar schäbiger Vorteile willen. (113–14)
>
> [It is not a history of the town that I am writing, no pompous local chronicle designed to flatter the vanity of obscure local eminences. Rather, I am setting down on these pages merely the wretched affairs and vicious deeds in which my worthy fellow citizens distinguished

themselves. These are the repellent transactions of the residents of my town, who never fail to mask their self-serving viciousness with unctuous speeches and noble motives. It is a history of human baseness. I cannot read from it without being shaken by fierce laughter, laughter born of contempt for the human race and sympathy at its squandering of such energy in the pursuit of a few shabby advantages.]

The "pompous local chronicle" that Spodeck disdains to write is exactly the kind of sanitized history that Hein sees in the official East German accounts of the Nazi period and *Aufbau* (the period of the "building of socialism" in the late forties and fifties). Though Spodeck, like Hein, wishes to redress an imbalance in the official history, their reasons for doing so are quite different. The "history of baseness" is really a justification for Spodeck's failed life, a complicated effort (similar to Claudia's in *Der fremde Freund*) to prove that however degraded he may be, he really had no choice in the matter. At the same time that Spodeck admits to his own failures, he attempts to justify them by pointing out the background against which they occurred. This paradoxical stance (he thinks himself both better and worse than his fellow Guldenbergers) yields the complexity of viewpoint that makes Spodeck such an interesting character, one whose judgments may be narrow or incomplete, but never altogether wrong. Yet his account of GDR history, in its cynical as in its passionate moments, never approaches the merciless detachment Hein so admires. For this very reason he is a useful device for establishing a bleak, pessimistic mood which the novel will ultimately try to temper.

The most striking aspect of Spodeck's account is its alternation of self-loathing with righteous indignation. His cynicism might be expected to nourish resignation, but his actual response to the things he witnesses is outrage. Early in the book, Spodeck explains his decision to stay in his hated Bad Guldenberg and to carry out his hated father's wishes: he refuses to forget the wrongs and humiliations he has witnessed and suffered. His self-accusation and resentment merge imperceptibly with a strain of prophetic indignation, complete with biblical allusions:

> Den Auftrag, den mir mein Vater erteilt hat, werde ich ausführen. Ich werde ihn zu Ende bringen, um meiner selbst willen. Um der Demütigungen willen, die mir mein Vater bereitet hat, er soll nicht in Frieden ruhen, und um der Kränkungen willen, die ich von dieser Stadt erfuhr, der Freitische und Mildtätigkeiten, die ich genötigt war, dankend anzunehmen. Damals. Und wenn ich auch dieses verzeihen und vergeben könnte, ich kann es nicht vergessen. Ich kann die Feigheit nicht vergessen, mit der diese Stadt fortwährend neues Unrecht

geschehen läßt. Der Tod eines Mannes wie Horn sollte ausreichen, um diese Stadt wie ein biblisches Gomorrha auszutilgen. (7)[10]

[I will carry out the task assigned to me by my father. I will see it through to the end, for my own sake. For the sake of the humiliations prepared for me by my father, whom I will not allow to rest in peace, and for the insults that I endured at the hands of this town, the favors and acts of charity I had to gratefully accept. Back then. And while I might be able to forgive all of this, I can never forget it. I cannot forget the cravenness with which this town incessantly lets new injustices happen. The death of a man like Horn should be sufficient cause to annihilate this town like Gomorrah in the Bible.]

Similarly, Spodeck recounts his impressions of Guldenberg's complicity and opportunism as the Nazis rose and fell:

Ich habe in dieser Stadt gelebt, als die Braunhemden in ihr Hof hielten und umjubelt wurden. Ich habe gesehen, wie sich diese Stadt dem alltäglichen Verbrechen öffnete, bereit und willig, und der Heißhunger auf Verrat und Bestialität offenbarte den lange brach gelegenen Blutdurst. Die Denunzianten und Mörder kamen nicht von irgendwo, um dieser Stadt das Gesetz ihres Todes und der Verachtung aufzuzwingen, sie hatten mit uns gelebt, waren Bürger dieses verträumten, sanften Provinzfleckens gewesen, sie sind aus unseren Wohnungen hervorgekrochen, unter unserer Haut .... Die herzzerreißende Komik dieser Tage, die für mich vorauszuahnen war, wollte ich mir nicht entgehen lassen, die vielfältigen Wandlungen, die erwarteten wie die unvorhersehbaren. Es war beklemmend und schaurig, und es war schön. Und die Seiten meiner Geschichte der Gemeinheit füllten sich wie von selbst. Ich hatte in diesen Tagen das deutliche Empfinden, mit feurigen Lettern zu schreiben, wie ein alttestamentarischer Prophet seine Verwünschungen. (115–16)

[I was living in this town when the Brown Shirts held court and were enthusiastically cheered. I saw how ready and willing this town was to open itself to daily criminality, and how the craving for betrayal and brutality reawakened a long dormant thirst for blood. The denouncers and murderers didn't come from somewhere else, aiming to impose their law of death and contempt on this town; they had lived among us, they were the citizens of this sleepy, peaceful rural village, they had crept out of our own houses, out from under our own skins .... I had no desire to miss the heartrending comedy of those days, of which I already had an inkling — the multifaceted transformations, the expected as well as the unforeseeable. It was uncanny and horrifying, and it was beautiful. And the pages of my history of baseness filled up as though by themselves. I had in those days the distinct sensation of writing with fiery letters, like an Old Testament prophet setting down his curses.]

Yet Spodeck comes to identify himself with Guldenberg's grandest exemplar of commonplace evil: Dr. Konrad Böger, the "Wohltäter von Guldenberg" [benefactor of Guldenberg: *HE* 80] and developer of its medicinal spas, and in addition the abuser of various women and father of various illegitimate sons, among them Spodeck. After standing by while his mother is humiliated, renouncing his passion for psychology, and accepting his father's "gift" of the practice in Bad Guldenberg for the mandatory twenty-five years, all the while recording the moral degradation of Bad Guldenberg's other inhabitants, he realizes at last that he is in fact his father's son:

> Im Grunde bin ich wohl der gleiche eigensüchtige, herablassende Heuchler wie er.
> Ich hatte mich an alle Kränkungen gewöhnt, an mein Elend und mein Gejammer wie auch an die mich demütigenden Geschenke, und ich war nicht fähig, ohne sie auszukommen. Und was immer ich mir einredete, ich gehorchte meinem Vater nicht meiner Mutter zuliebe, sondern weil ich sein Sohn war, weil ich Fleisch von seinem Fleisch war. (80)
>
> [At bottom I am in fact as much a self-seeking, arrogant hypocrite as he.
> I became inured to all insults, to my misery and my sniveling, as well as to the humiliating gifts, and I was incapable of getting by without them. And whatever I may have insisted to myself, I obeyed my father not for my mother's sake, but because I was his son, because I was flesh of his flesh.]

Spodeck's belated identification with the corruption of his city (brought to perfection, in his view, by his affair with his ward Christine and his loveless marriage) may or may not be justified, but it certainly does not reduce the bite of his observations about the city's hypocrisy. It is Spodeck, after all, who observes and names the city's bigotry when confronted with the Gypsies (8–9), a matter of central importance for the novel since it connects the genocidal fascist past with the socialist present — then as now, the respectable citizens of Bad Guldenberg are eager to be rid of a nuisance. Such observations as this one remain valid, if one-sided, though in the context of the novel (as in all historiography) even a one-sided view is valuable, so long as it can be answered and disputed. Furthermore, Spodeck's indignant tone is not unfamiliar to readers of Hein's essays, in which Hein often allows himself a polemical and passionate stance that he never allows into his fictional works without elaborate distancing or irony.

There is certainly irony to be had in Spodeck's characterization, as well. Hein uses him startlingly as the spokesman for his personal credo of authorial detachment and social responsibility:

> Bis zum Tage meines Todes aber will ich die Geschichte der Gemeinheit mit dem klaren, unbestechlichen Blick der alten Chronisten ohne Haß und Eifer weiterführen, damit, was ich nicht abwehren konnte, nicht durch mein Schweigen bestärkt wird und ich mitschuldig werde an unser aller Niedertracht. (117)

> [Until the day of my death I will nonetheless persevere in my history of baseness with the clear, incorruptible gaze of the old chroniclers, without passion or prejudice, refusing to strengthen through my silence what I cannot avert, lest I become an accomplice in our general vileness.]

It is patently absurd for Spodeck to say any such thing; he is the novel's most passionate and most prejudiced character. Hein himself acknowledges that he has put his ideas in the mouth of a character who exemplifies their opposite:

> These are certainly my ideas [Sätze] that Dr. Spodeck is describing. But what he actually does is another matter entirely. Everything he says about the past has one function: to justify his wasted life, which even he knows to be a failure. For this he needs a chronicle that would be the opposite of what I have in mind. He is not in fact reporting *sine ira et studio*, but full of passion and full of prejudice [voll Haß und voll Eifer] . . . . Spodeck only wants a history of human baseness, a baseness which certainly has existed, but to see nothing else is also a distortion of history [Geschichtsklitterung].
> ("Wir werden es lernen müssen" 62–63)

Yet while Spodeck represents a perversion of what a true historian ought to be, he also exemplifies the norm of what real historians actually are — partisan, prejudiced, driven by obsessions that have nothing to do with their discipline. In the context of Hein's novel, Spodeck's cynicism serves the useful purpose of puncturing the dominant dogmas of the GDR, but he arrives at no definitive insights, whatever his pretensions. As evidenced by his paralyzed love affair and his plans to distribute copies of his history to the Bürgermeister, the museum director, and the priest, all of whom can reasonably be expected to burn theirs, his personality is virtually self-negating, a condition he shares with Claudia in *Der fremde Freund*.

Kruschkatz

The importance that Hein places on ideological or conceptual balance can be clearly seen in his handling of Kruschkatz, the Bürgermeister of Bad Guldenberg and, at first glance, a stereotypical Communist Party apparatchik. Early in the novel we see him spouting socialist platitudes and using his political weight to intimidate Spodeck (*HE* 35–36); using the language of Stalinist opprobrium, he dismisses Horn as an individualist (59) and humanist (86); he upholds the claims of historical necessity even when innocents must be sacrificed to it (63); and he displays throughout the novel the astute political skills of the successful Party functionary. Yet Hein has other plans for him:

> Kruschkatz was for me, during the writing, the most fascinating of the characters. He is a functionary, and before he even opens his mouth, he is already condemned by almost all of the other characters: the reader has a picture of a repulsive, corpulent, sweating, unpleasant, opportunistic functionary. And then I devote all my power and love to this figure, working against the prejudice, to make a human being out of him. ("Wir werden es lernen müssen" 63)

So Kruschkatz is given a beautiful and beloved wife whom he tragically loses, and a foil in the hateful figure of Bachofen, his deputy; he shows compassion for an old comrade ruined by intrigues; he attempts in good faith to appease Horn, though in vain; and he turns out to be fated to spend the remainder of his active life in a town he detests. Most significantly, he displays the most sensitive, intelligent, and reasonable mind of any of the other narrators. Though not without his obsessions, he apparently provides a trustworthy account of the events in Bad Guldenberg, emerging eventually as "the one man in this novel who acts with any self-awareness" (McKnight, "Ein Mosaik" 422). As a historian both in training and, reluctantly, in fact, his methodological convictions bear close scrutiny. Unsurprisingly, they turn out to be utterly paradoxical. Just as Spodeck, the ultimate partisan, can voice Hein's opinions while demonstrating wholly opposite behavior, so Kruschkatz, the Party hack, exhibits an ambivalent relation to the Party dogma he occasionally mouths. His interest as a character ultimately rests on the contradiction between dogma and disillusionment that Horn's death brings into sharp focus.[11]

Kruschkatz's ideas about history emerge in a seemingly haphazard way; as with Dallow in *Der Tangospieler*, the fact that he is a trained historian emerges only after the narrative is well under way. Kruschkatz must have the fact pried out of him by Spodeck:

"Sie sind, wie ich hörte, auch Historiker?"
"Ich wars, Doktor. Ich habe nicht den Kopf für die trockenen Wissenschaften. Ich bin ein praktischer Mensch." (*HE* 168)

["I understand that you, too, are a historian."
"I used to be, Doctor. I lack the temperament for dry scholarship. I am a practical man."]

History as an abstract, scholarly, theoretical concern versus practical politics: the distinction is false from the outset, and Kruschkatz's reliance on it stems from his unswerving commitment to a program of action that no longer commands his unquestioning faith. (This contradiction results in part from the novel's dual chronology, as the bitter, haunted 73-year-old narrator, confined to a retirement home circa 1980, remembers his actions in the 1950s and sees them to have been futile.) Kruschkatz begins narrating under an undisclosed compulsion that eventually appears to be a constitutional inability to forget — the opposite case to Claudia's refined amnesia in *Der fremde Freund*, where repression of memories is hailed as a prerequisite for survival — and indeed Kruschkatz wishes for death to come and relieve him of this burden (223–4). His narrative opens rather strangely for a Marxist-materialist-atheist:

> Es ist unsinnig und unwürdig, nach so vielen Jahren ausgerechnet über diesen Mann Horn zu sprechen. Es ist gotteslästerlich. Ich kann es nicht besser bezeichnen als mit diesem altväterlichen Wort (*HE* 20).

> [It is absurd and disgraceful to speak after so many years of this man Horn, of all people. It is blasphemous. I cannot find a better description for it than this archaic word.]

Kruschkatz's frequent use of religious expressions and imagery hints at his loss of a different kind of faith — in history as the manifestation of rational laws, and by extension in the Party's mastery of historical change. Kruschkatz says he is confident every detail of Horn's life and death could be reconstructed, "Möglicherweise so vollständig, daß die dazugehörenden nichtssagenden Einzelheiten wie abgelegte Büroordner, verstaubt und vergilbt, unsere Träume aufblähen und unser Gedächtnis quälen" [Probably with such precision that the associated insignificant details (like discarded office files, dusty and yellowed) would bloat our dreams and torment our memory: 20], but he fears that such an exercise would open an abyss of historical meaninglessness:

> Ich bezweifle also nicht den äußeren Erfolg, das nahezu vollständige Verzeichnis der Fakten. Vielmehr stelle ich das ganze Unternehmen in Frage. Die Entdeckung, daß es mehrere, zum Teil einander widersprechende Wahrheiten gibt, als endliches Ergebnis solcher Mühe wäre ein

niederschmetternder Witz. Noch mehr aber beunruhigt mich der Gedanke, daß die so gefundene Wahrheit beziehungsweise die verschiedenen, schlüssig, vollständig und widerspruchsfrei hergestellten Bilder keinen Adressaten haben. Das ist vorbei. (*HE* 20)

[I also have no doubt of outward success, the nearly complete cataloging of facts. Rather, it is the whole project that I am calling into question. The discovery that several mutually contradictory truths would be the final result of such exertions would be a devastating joke. Even more unsettling is the thought that the truth thus uncovered, or rather the variously, conclusively, comprehensively, and self-consistently manufactured pictures, would find no audience. That time is past.]

If alternative versions of historical reality are equally valid, Kruschkatz reasons, then they are equally meaningless and equally incommunicable. Something about Horn's story has evidently deprived Kruschkatz of any confidence in his grasp of history, with the result that he abandons the notion altogether:

Ich bin heute dreiundsiebzig Jahre alt, und wenn ich die Erfahrungen meines Lebens für eine daran uninteressierte Nachwelt in einem Satz formulieren müßte, würde ich sagen: Es gibt keine Geschichte. Geschichte ist hilfreiche Metaphysik, um mit der eigenen Sterblichkeit auszukommen, der schöne Schleier um den leeren Schädel des Todes. Es gibt keine Geschichte, denn soviel wir auch an Bausteinchen um eine vergangene Zeit ansammeln, wir ordnen und beleben diese kleinen Tonscherben und schwärzlichen Fotos allein mit unserem Atem, verfälschen sie durch die Unvernunft unserer dünnen Köpfe und mißverstehen daher gründlich. Der Mensch schuf sich die Götter, um mit der Unerträglichkeit des Todes leben zu können, und er schuf sich die Fiktion der Geschichte, um dem Verlust der Zeit einen Sinn zu geben, der ihm das Sinnlose verstehbar und erträglich macht. Hinter uns die Geschichte und vor uns Gott, das ist das Korsett, das uns den aufrechten Gang erlaubt. Und ich glaube, das Röcheln der Sterbenden ist die aufdämmernde Erkenntnis der Wirklichkeit. Die Toten brauchen kein Korsett.

Ich will mich mit diesen Bemerkungen meinen Erinnerungen nicht entziehen. Ich schicke sie voraus, weil ich meinen Erinnerungen mißtraue, weil ich allen Erinnerungen mißtraue. (*HE* 20–21)

[Today I turn 73, and if I had to formulate my life experience into one sentence for the benefit of a completely uninterested world, I would say: History does not exist. History is a kind of useful metaphysics good for helping one to cope with mortality, a beautiful veil wrapped around the empty skull of death. History does not exist, because whenever we collect the minute building blocks of a past age, we arrange and animate these little fragments and dim photographs solely with our own breath, falsifying them through our dim-witted irrationality, and thereby totally failing to understand them. Man created the gods in order to live with the unbearable fact of death, and he created the fiction of history to give vanished time a meaning, making it possible to bear and comprehend meaninglessness. Behind us history and before us God: that is the corset that enables us to walk erect. And I believe that the rattle of the dying is the dawning awareness of reality. The dead need no corsets.

I am not trying to evade my memories by making these remarks; I offer them as a preface because, distrusting all memories, I distrust my own.]

Kruschkatz turns out to be a disappointed metaphysician: without the comfort of Marxist historical teleology, history ceases to have any meaning for him, reverting to a random assemblage of facts organized by externally imposed, falsifying illusions. His predicament is that of the pious atheist, who must consciously reject what he subconsciously cannot live without. Thus it is important to note that disappointment over this falsification of dogmatic, teleological Marxism is only one of many possible reactions: it is specific to Kruschkatz, and certainly cannot to be generalized as a view shared by Hein, who disagrees with Kruschkatz's distaste for the present-day influence on what passes for history. (History is always a matter of present concerns, not past ones.) Despite his self-proclaimed practicality, Kruschkatz remains a metaphysician and an ideologue; Hein is the practical one, interested in bringing about changes in the here and now through the exercise of social autobiography. History as Hegel envisioned it may be an illusion, but history may still be understood as an active force in contemporary human affairs. Thus Kruschkatz is an unhappy nihilist, not a relativist. His detestation of a history that consists largely of distortions and fantasies by present-day, living people actually mirrors Horn's view, as expressed to Spodeck near the end of the novel; the two historians simply apply different value judgments to the same, commonly acknowledged situation. Horn accepts the inevitable fictionality of history and remains a historian, while Kruschkatz confuses fiction with reality and becomes a functionary (McKnight, "Ein Mosaik" 420–421).[12]

Kruschkatz's subsequent account of his second meeting with Horn betrays a more confused, and (as yet) less disillusioned attitude toward history, since most of the disillusionment emerges from thirty years of hindsight. In light of Hein's interview remarks, the earlier viewpoint is, like the later one, most likely neither wholly right nor wholly wrong. Kruschkatz's feelings toward Horn are complex and contradictory, as were Spodeck's. Like Spodeck, the Bürgermeister regards Horn as a coward, and for a similar reason: Horn's inability or unwillingness to adjust to reality in order to survive. Kruschkatz and Spodeck, experts at bending with prevailing winds, admire in Horn the same character traits that they disdain. The Bürgermeister elaborates:

> Horn war für diesen Tod bestimmt wie ein Ochse für den Schlachthof. Er war nicht lebenstüchtig. Er war für ein Leben unter Menschen nicht geeignet. Ich sage dies ohne jede Wertung oder Verachtung, ich habe ihn immer geschätzt. Und ich meine, es ist kein allzu hoher menschlicher Wert, auf dieser Erde lebenstüchtig zu sein. Es gab prächtige Menschen, die es nie waren. Aber da wir nun einmal genötigt sind, in menschlicher Gemeinschaft zu leben, ist ein gewisses Maß an Bereitschaft für dieses Leben, ob zu loben oder nicht, erforderlich und somit eine Tugend. (*HE* 61)
>
> [Horn was predestined for this death like an ox for the slaughterhouse. He was not competent at living. He was unsuited for a life among human beings. I say this without judgment or contempt, I always had a high opinion of him. And I think that competence at living on this earth is no very high human value. There have been splendid people who were never so gifted. But since we are, after all, required to live in human communities, a certain measure of readiness for this life is mandatory and to that extent a virtue, like it or not.]

Kruschkatz reveals the beginnings of his distrust of memory and rigid preference for ideological formulas when he criticizes Horn as one who never forgets: "Und nun stand er wieder vor mir, und ich erkannte an seinen kalten und reglosen Augen, daß er nichts vergessen hatte. Nichts vergessen und nichts hinzugelernt" [And now he stood again before me, and I knew from his cold and motionless eyes that he had forgotten nothing. Forgotten nothing and learned nothing: 26]. Learning, it would seem, involves more amnesia than anamnesis; what Horn actually has not learned to accept is his proper social role according to the Party's collectivist ethic.

> Er wollte Leipzig nicht vergessen, und verstehen konnte er es nicht.
> Ihm war dort Unrecht geschehen, gewiß, und an diesem Unrecht hatte ich meinen Anteil, ich habe es nie bestritten. Aber es gibt eine höhere Moral, vor der sich Recht und Unrecht die Waage halten oder gemeinsam zu fragwürdigen Werten schrumpfen. Es war ihm ein geschichtlich notwendiges Unrecht angetan worden im Namen eines höheren Rechts, im Namen der Geschichte. Ich war nur das ausführende Organ, die kleine Stimme dieses ehernen Gesetzes. Ich hoffte, ihm dies begreiflich machen zu können. Ich hoffte es, nicht weil ich mich entschuldigen, sondern weil ich ihm helfen wollte. Aber

Horn fühlte sich noch immer ungerecht behandelt. Er sah nur, daß ich ihm seine wissenschaftliche Karriere ruiniert hatte, und war nicht fähig oder willens, aus dem Winkel seiner gekränkten Ehre hervorzukommen. Er hatte sich in seinem Selbstmitleid eingerichtet und zog es vor, einsam zu bleiben, wenn er nur im Recht war. (*HE* 59)

[He would not forget Leipzig; he was incapable of understanding it.
  He had indeed been the victim of an injustice there, and I had played my part in this injustice, I have never denied it. But there is a higher morality, in respect to which justice and injustice balance one another, or dwindle equally into questionable values. A historically necessary injustice was done to him in the name of a higher law, in the name of history. I was only the executive organ, the tiny voice of this iron law. I hoped that I could make this clear to him, not in order to excuse myself, but because I wanted to help him. But Horn still felt himself unjustly used. He only saw that I had ruined his scholarly career, and wasn't able or willing to look beyond his wounded honor. He had settled into self-pity and preferred to remain alone as long as he was in the right.]

In all of this defensive self-justification reappears the familiar effort of a Hein character to rationalize his way out of responsibility. The effect is intensified by comparing this passage, together with the later one insisting (with the Nazis, as McKnight points out ["Ein Mosaik" 423]) that historical progress demands a "Blutzoll" [payment in blood: *HE* 63] from the innocent, with the Bürgermeister's earlier declaration that history, in the sense of rational laws unfolding through time, does not exist. The wording of the Bürgermeister's defense carries an insidious subtext — "I was only the executive organ" sounds suspiciously like "I was only following orders," the excuse preferred by war criminals everywhere, and similar to the one that will recur in *Der Tangospieler* as a rationale, once again, for irresponsibility. More directly related to theoretical questions about history is the observation that Horn would rather isolate himself and cling to the truth than acknowledge the "historical necessity" of the injustice done to him. From this it is possible to begin appreciating why so many of the novel's characters brand Horn a coward. The overriding theme of *Der fremde Freund*, namely, the possibility and necessity of political engagement in modern, urban, alienating society, might also be applied to Horn: to the extent that he sacrifices social ties on the altar of an absolute, he emulates not just Claudia (who has different reasons for isolating herself) but also Kruschkatz, his fellow ideologist. In spite of his disquisition on the fictions of history with Spodeck, Horn is as willing as Kruschkatz to subordinate the personal to the ideological, even if his ideology now is different (so will be Kruschkatz's in the end). On the other hand, when Kruschkatz pictures Horn as the bearer "mit nervös zitternden Händen die wehleidige Flagge eines fruchtlosen, erschöpften Humanismus" [with nervously trembling hands, of the melancholy banner of a fruitless, exhausted humanism: *HE* 86], his doctrinaire condemnation also happens to identify what Hein sees as the essence of historical writing or chronicling. Horn is criticized for indulging in a personal viewpoint, for keeping his observations on a human scale rather than appealing to theory, and this is precisely what Hein has recommended as an antidote to ideological conformism. Of course, such an orientation with respect to history also allows for distortions of an idiosyncratic but no less partisan kind — witness Dr. Spodeck — so Kruschkatz's objection may not be wholly off the mark in Horn's case.

Horn

For a central figure, Horn's appearances and statements in *Horns Ende* are remarkably sparse. The definitive ones are in the chapter prefaces, where Horn's ghostly voice browbeats the fully-grown Thomas into remembering the events of summer 1957. Thus the defining word for Horn is "Remember!" He stands for an uncompromising acknowledgment of historical fact: on this depends everything that may accurately be called history, and not ideology or polemic, written with "passion and prejudice." (In fact, the motif "Remember!" comes close to being an unequivocal moral imperative valid for all of Hein's writing.) Yet the forces of forgetting with which Horn struggles go deeper than mere partisanship — they are the rooted in the instinct of self-preservation that causes Claudia, for example, to censor her memories in order not to go mad. Horn's significance for the narrators, as for all the citizens of Bad Guldenberg, is that he disturbs the convenient, comfortable, falsified view of history that normal, sane individuals like to paint for themselves. Claudia likewise describes herself as "eine nette, sehr normale Frau" [a nice, very normal woman: *DFF*, 162; *TDL*, 136] immediately after she has been physically abused. The veiling of real history, barbaric and shabby, enables its endless repetition. Horn insists that, in a strict sense, historic events lack a real existence apart from living people's memory, which means that reflecting on society is a social act, a social memory, not limited exclusively to personal recollections, but an integral part of communal self-awareness: "Ich lebe nur in deinem Gedächtnis, Junge. Streng dich an. Bitte" [I live only in your memory, boy. Try. Please: *HE* 51].

As the representative of uncompromising memory, even Horn's physical appearance is suggestive of his burden and duty. Gertrude Fischlinger recalls his appearance when he first inquired with her about a room: "Er hatte eine merkwürdige graue Haut und breite, fast schwarze Augenringe. Ich dachte damals, daß er wohl lange krank gewesen sein müßte. Gelbsucht oder Tbc, vermutete ich" [He had weirdly gray skin and large, almost black circles around his eyes. I thought back then that he must have been ill for a long time. Jaundice or TB, I supposed: 17]. Horn's only disease, of course, has been his inability or unwillingness to forget what happened to him in Leipzig. Yet this is sufficiently fatal, and the black rings under his eyes may be understood as a telling symptom of sleeplessness, for as Kruschkatz explains, "es sind zwei sich ausschließende Dinge: gut zu schlafen und sich gut zu erinnern" [those are two mutually exclusive things: to sleep well and to remember well: 20]. No wonder Kruschkatz ends his own narrative wishing for death, the "sanftere[r] süße[r] Bruder" [gentle sweet brother: 224] of sleep, since his sleep is disturbed by "die Erinnerungen..., die sich Nacht für Nacht auf meine Brust hocken" [memories... that weigh down on my breast night after night: 223].

Horn is thus largely a symbolic figure, representative of a truly materialist, yet radically individual perception of history. This is the stuff of chronicling, Hein's avowed mode of narrative writing, so Horn's theoretical statements deserve special scrutiny when they do occur. Horn is also interesting, as noted above, for the condemnation that the other characters heap upon him. To one degree or another, and for varying reasons, all of the other narrators defend the utility of forgetting, or at least of distrusting memory, of subordinating it to some higher good, whether an ideology of social progress (Kruschkatz), the instinct of self-preservation (Spodeck), or the claims of the living as opposed to the claims of the dead (Thomas). Horn may also be viewed as an example of another recurring character type in Hein's writing: he is like Schlötel, the fanatical proponent of truth whose existence in a corrupt world drives him to madness and suicide, or Hubert K. in "Der neuere (glücklichere) Kohlhaas," whose adherence to a legal principle ruins his life, or Frankfurther, in *Passage*, who escapes capture by the Nazis by poisoning himself, and whose only concern *in extremis* is that his scientific treatise be preserved and published. In each of these cases, Hein raises the question of public versus private prerogatives, of abstract ideology versus concrete relations among people, of the fate of the intellectual amid the vicissitudes of history, and of the possibility of meaningful action in a historical context.

Like Kruschkatz, Horn speaks somewhat inconsistently about the nature of history, and should not be taken over-simply as a mouthpiece for Hein, although he certainly is this to a degree. As Kruschkatz understands him, he is simply someone who refuses to forget or forsake his personal viewpoint respecting history, who refuses to accept the ideological view that even the Bürgermeister loses faith in. At first, then, Horn's view of history seems to be almost naively positivistic, distinguishing simplistically between truth and falsehood. He explains the responsibilities of a historian to Thomas when the boy visits the museum:

> "Es ist nur ein kleines Museum, das wir haben, und doch schreiben auch wir die Geschichte. Wir sind es, die dafür einzustehen haben, ob die Wahrheit oder die Lüge berichtet wird. Verstehst du das, Thomas?"
> "Natürlich."
> "Nein, das verstehst du nicht. Die Wahrheit oder die Lüge, das ist eine entsetzliche Verantwortung. Wer das wirklich begriffen hätte, würde keinen Schlaf mehr finden." (*HE* 58)
>
> ["It's only a little museum that we have here, and yet we, too, are writing history. We are the ones responsible for telling truth or lies. Do you understand that, Thomas?"
> "Of course."
> "No, you don't understand. Truth or lies, that's a terrible responsibility. Anyone who really comprehended that would never be able to sleep again."]

What is this "terrible responsibility" to which Horn alludes? That sleep and historical awareness cannot coexist implies that sleep here may be taken as a metaphorical description of the common state of unconsciousness cultivated by the citizens of Bad Guldenberg, among others. The reason emerges now for the sleeplessness caused by memory — it is a consequence of an awakened conscience, or rather, of a consciousness confronted with its responsibility for creating and preserving historical meaning. If history exists only as an extension of contemporary needs and conditions, with living persons absolutely accountable for both the past and for the present, history ceases to be a discrete academic discipline and becomes instead the constitutive basis of society (as opposed to barbarity or anarchy).

The novel's culminating statement concerning the activity of history-making occurs in Horn's lengthy conversation with Spodeck about a new technique for the reconstitution of cinematic images. Spodeck believes that this has undermined a hitherto unimpeachable source of historical accuracy, the photograph:

Da haben ein paar Filmtechniker ein Verfahren ausgeklügelt, das es ihnen ermöglicht, dem Film jeden Wert eines Dokuments zu nehmen. Das ursprüngliche Bild wird auf einen in der Mitte gebrochenen Spiegel geworfen und erneut aufgenommen. Und je nachdem, in welchem Winkel die Spiegel zueinander stehen, kann man nun Teile des Bildes verschwinden lassen oder neue, nicht dazugehörige Bilder einspiegeln. Man kann somit nach Gutdünken Filmdokumente verändern und Mißliebiges gegen Beliebiges austauschen. Dem Betrachter bietet sich stets ein unverletzt scheinendes, originales Bild. Ihre Wissenschaft, Herr Horn, die Geschichtsschreibung, hat wieder einen Kronzeugen verloren. Ihnen stehen neue Fälschungen ins Haus.
(*HE* 197)

[It seems that a couple of film technicians have figured out a process that robs film of any documentary value. The original image is projected onto a broken mirror, and then photographed again. According to where the image falls, on which adjacent sections of the mirror, parts of it can now be made to disappear or new, unrelated images can be combined with it. The film maker can now alter film documents as he likes, replacing disagreeable things with agreeable ones. All the viewer ever sees is a seamless, apparently original picture. Your discipline of history, Herr Horn, has a lost another of its chief witnesses. You face new falsifications.]

Horn, on the other hand, has trouble understanding Spodeck's point, because for him, history is not a matter of simply collecting accurate facts or documents, but of reconstructing truth from a welter of inaccuracies and half-truths, of interpreting the distortions of truth in light of the present day:

Sie sehen zu schwarz, Dr. Spodeck. Was Sie als Fälschung bezeichnen, ist unser täglich Brot. Was ist denn Geschichte anderes als ein Teig von Überliefertem, von willkürlich oder absichtsvoll Erhaltenem, aus dem sich nachfolgende Generationen ein Bild nach ihrem Bilde kneten. Die Fälschungen und unsere Irrtümer sind der Kitt dieser Bilder, sie machen sie haltbar und griffig. Sie sind es, die unsere Weisheiten so einleuchtend machen. (*HE* 197)

[Your view is too bleak, Dr. Spodeck. What you call falsification is our daily bread. What else is history but a dough of hand-me-downs, of accidentally or deliberately preserved odds and ends, which succeeding generations will knead into an image of themselves. The falsifications and our errors are the binding material in these images, they make them durable and fit for use. This is why our sagacities appear so self-evident.]

Spodeck finds this Althusser-like position cynical, but it is merely realistic, Horn insists, the product of professional experience. As it turns out, Spodeck is merely trying to justify his own cynicism: he explains that he is actually pleased by the new technical advance in filmmaking, because it abolishes a false model for the operation of human memory, an ideal of verisimilitude, making it easier now to distrust or dismiss memories that are painful or unpleasant. Memories, Spodeck insists, record not the events, but the consciousness of the events, reflected and distorted by the biological equivalent of the filmmaker's broken mirrors. The lesson to be learned from this, he says, is that we should distrust our memories when they make life impossible, as has happened, he implies, in Horn's case. Horn refuses to be drawn over the brink of cynical but pragmatic skepticism:

> "Bedeutet das, Doktor, Sie raten mir, ohne Gedächtnis zu leben?"
>
> "Nein, das wäre unsinnig, weil es uns nicht möglich ist. Ich rate Ihnen nur, Ihren Erinnerungen zu mißtrauen. Wenn Ihr Gedächtnis Sie zum Leben unfähig macht, ist es vernünftiger, Sie bezweifeln einige gespeicherte Bilder in Ihrem Kopf und nicht das Leben. Es ist vernünftiger, denn, wie ich hoffe bewiesen zu haben, wir haben keine Gewißheit darüber, daß diese Erinnerungen uns nicht gründlich täuschen."
>
> "Vielleicht haben Sie recht, aber wir werden mit unserem Gedächtnis leben müssen. Welch ein entsetzlicher Gedanke, ohne Gedächtnis leben zu wollen. Wir würden ohne Erfahrungen leben müssen, ohne Wissen und ohne Werte. Löschen Sie das Gedächtnis eines Menschen, und Sie löschen die Menschheit." (*HE* 198-9)[13]
>
> ["Does this mean, Doctor, that you are advising me to live without memory?"
>
> "No, that would be absurd, because it isn't possible. I am just advising you not to trust your memory. If your memory renders life impossible, it is more reasonable to doubt a few stored images in your head than to doubt life. It is more reasonable because, as I hope I have shown, we have no guarantee that our memory isn't fundamentally misleading us."
>
> "Maybe you are right, but we must live with our memory. What a dreadful thought, to want to live without memory. We would have to live without prior experience, without knowledge, and without values. Take away memory from a human being and you take away his humanity."]

Spodeck's advice may have practical validity, but as Claudia's case proves, forgetting is not necessarily the most desirable condition of life, and as a strategy for survival it can backfire. Horn seems to be saying that the accuracy of one's memory may be flawed, but in order to remain human, one must operate under the assumption that, by and large, it is accurate. This is similar to his view about historical writing:

one does not simply give up in the face of unverifiability, but makes instead the best case possible for what the facts may have been. We are caught in a paradox of not having access to the truth, yet always needing to assert *something* as truth, lest we become total cynics like Spodeck and, lacking any firm conviction, fall absolutely under the sway of historical forces.[14]

Hein's meditation on film as a flawed analog of history-writing recalls his subsequent essay "Maelzel's Chess Player Goes to Hollywood," a reply to Walter Benjamin's famous essay, "The Work of Art in the Age of Mechanical Reproduction." In his essay, Hein elaborates a view of art and history that echoes aspects of both Spodeck's and Horn's historical views. Benjamin had argued that mass reproducibility of art works would abolish their mystified "cultic value" and reveal their articulation with politics:

> But the instant the criterion of authenticity ceases to be applicable to artistic production, the total function of art is reversed. Instead of being based on ritual, it begins to be based on another practice — politics. (226)

Having lost the "semblance of its autonomy" (228), art will call forth a new and critical attitude on the part of the public. In the case of film, the technically determined art *par excellence*, the viewer will become attentive to the technique rather than the presence of the actor, which remains so central to a stage production. "The audience's identification with the actor is really an identification with the camera. Consequently the audience takes the position of the camera; its approach is that of testing" (230–31). Benjamin sees in this new attentiveness to technical distortions of reality a revolution in perception similar to the discovery of the unconscious mind (239), so that art works now are viewed politically, as "evidence for historical occurrences, and acquire a hidden political significance" (228).

Hein, on the other hand, argues that Benjamin's political optimism caused him to overlook the effect of the marketplace on art: in capitalism, mass-produced art is always mass-marketed art, whose primary virtue is a calculable, guaranteed return on investment. This explains the formulaic, even algorithmic construction of most of what appears in movie houses and on television ("Maelzel's Chess Player" 179–80). The public, in its turn, learns to enjoy the predictability of such art:

> The mechanism has become visible to the audience. And this in no way impedes the consumption of these products, but has become a factor of their appeal. The audience is safe in the knowledge that nothing will frighten, confuse, or disturb it. Situations and plot devel-

opments, along with the construction of the characters, create in the audience a continual *déjà vu* experience. (181)

Instead of building historical consciousness, as Benjamin had hoped, mass-produced art tends to enmesh consciousness in a cycle of repetitive illusion. Hein argues that the "cultic value," Benjamin's "aura," returns in a new form: as the cult of celebrity and glamour surrounding entertainment figures. Insidiously, the emphasis on personality obscures the fact that the art industry is a machine driven not by individual human beings, but by market forces:

> The function of the human being is to provide the products of the machine with what the public traditionally regards as the *sine qua non* of art, namely, the aura of creativity and genius. He is there to give the machine product a human stamp, without which even the most one dimensional piece of artistic trash remains unacceptable to consumers. And the more plainly the machine dominates and its products betray an automatic, mass-produced quality, the more urgent the role played by the designated human. He must turn his person into a Potemkin village . . . . (186–7)

Art finally becomes nothing but an extension of the omnipresent market, or, in bureaucratic socialism, the omnipresent state. And yet, at the end of his essay, Hein endorses Benjamin's optimistic vision of the future:

> I nonetheless share Benjamin's hopes. These are hopes that run counter to experience, hopes for history that run counter to history. Because these are hopes to which there is no human alternative. (193)

Hein's argument here is characteristic: in the face of all historical entrapment and governmental oppression, people remain obligated to act as though they were autonomous. The Marxist critique of humanism, of which Hein largely approves, does not for him imply a lessening of individual human responsibility for imagining freedom, consciousness, and truth; indeed, these illusory and paradoxical values remain the very conditions of the "human."

Hein's essay clarifies certain issues that occupy the narrators of *Horns Ende*. Horn, responding to Spodeck's pragmatic advice to forget memories that make it impossible to live, offers a definition of "human" quite similar to the one implied in the essay. Horn replies that to live without knowledge or values means to cease to be human, an argument whose gravity is increased by Horn's impending death as a casualty of the contradiction between memory and present political reality. Benjamin's and Hein's shared "hopes" reappear as the insistence on "knowledge" and "values" that Horn upholds. Whereas Spodeck's "history of baseness" selectively depicts a Bad Guldenberg motivated solely by greed, hypocrisy, and love of power (reproducing on a grand scale the private experience of its author), Horn acknowledges the inevitability of factual distortion without using it to justify the skepticism or, ultimately, nihilism represented by Spodeck. Uncertain though the ultimate truth of fragmentary, historical "facts" may be, "people would always repeat the same mistakes if the potsherds were ignored. For this reason he tries to turn up and preserve as many sherds as possible" (McKnight, "Ein Mosaik" 421). Historical facts are always already distorted, selected, edited by a self-serving hand, but this merely means that history is a matter of interpretive rather than positive knowledge. By designing *Horns Ende* as a collection of subjective accounts, Hein points the way toward such an understanding of history, and no reader at this point in the book can escape noticing how well Spodeck's own writings bear out Horn's statements: it is precisely the distortions and exaggerations in the "history of baseness" that lead a careful reader to understand both Spodeck himself and the town he partially represents.[15] We never see, however, the other, different history that Horn might have written: it is up to posterity — Thomas — to reconstruct it, and to find the meaning of Horn's death.

Thomas

Thomas, the son of the respectable, stereotypically bourgeois pharmacist of Bad Guldenberg, acts as a counterbalance to the gloom of the Spodeck and Kruschkatz narratives. Thomas certainly takes himself as seriously as either of the other two narrators, but since his tragedies are mostly the standard ones for a child his age, he provokes as much amusement as sympathy. He manages almost incidentally to provide all of the key information about Horn's death, narrating it in Hein's flat, chronicling style, with little commentary. He qualifies as a theorist of history as well, partly by example (he wishes to forget everything about Bad Guldenberg as quickly as possible) and partly from his statements concerning Horn. Although Thomas seems to be the spokesman for a viewpoint opposite Hein's — he feels oppressed by history and tells his story only under extreme duress, confronted as a grown man by Horn's ghost — he exemplifies the least corrupted mode of narration in the novel (except perhaps for Gertrude Fischlinger, whom McKnight identifies as the novel's closest approximation to Hein's ideal historiographer, recounting the facts "without passion or prejudice"). For all his antipathy toward the town and its past, and his own past, Thomas displays a redeeming vigor that challenges the conformity and amnesia which, paradoxically, even he shares. Although no ideal figure of historical and political enlightenment, Thomas points toward a future somewhat brighter than that of mid-twentieth-century Bad Guldenberg, once, that is, he is prodded into remembering by the ghostly exhortations of Horn, which ensure that Hein's stubborn hope for human betterment will at least have a hearing in this somber novel.

Haunted by the ghost of memory, Thomas at one point tries to revolt:

> — Sie langweilen mich. Mich langweilen die Toten. Sie wollen nur Ihre Wahrheit sehen. Sie haben wenig begriffen. Sie sind ungerecht zu den Lebenden. Es ist alles schwer genug, und Sie können nur klagen.
> — Vielleicht, Junge, vielleicht hast du recht. Aber ich bin tot. Vergiß das nicht.
> — Auch ein Toter wiegt nicht mehr als die Wahrheit.
> — Ich bin tot.
> — Der Tod ist kein Beweis.
> — Ach, was du verstehst! Denk nicht nach. Erinnere dich. (186)

> — You bore me. The dead bore me. All they care about is their reality. They haven't understood much. They do an injustice to the living. Everything is hard enough, and all you can do is complain.
> — Maybe so, boy, maybe you're right. But I am dead. Don't forget that.
> — Not even a dead person counts more than the truth
> — I am dead.
> — Being dead doesn't prove anything.
> — Oh, what do you know! Don't try to think. Just remember.

Horn's ghost comes close to acknowledging that the living, too, have their claims, so the conflict between the two voices ends ambiguously. Thomas, who echoes Kruschkatz's remark that Horn "hatte ... nichts hinzugelernt" [never learned: 59] from his experiences, expresses a similar revulsion for what Horn represents when he recounts his first impressions of the museum, which looms over Bad Guldenberg like some ruined temple to Mnemosyne. The trip to the museum with his father comes to symbolize the whole experience of life in Bad Guldenberg, which to Thomas seems less like a place of forgetting than a place of suffocating remembrance, of traditions, conventions, and taboos that crowd out any possibility of freedom or pleasure. The museum, full of dead, stuffed animals and lifeless scenes, reflects the lifelessness of the town below. Thomas is especially perturbed by the stuffed animals with their insistent gaze:

> Ich erinnere mich an die gelblichen Glasaugen. In einer nachgebildeten Heidelandschaft standen ausgestopfte Füchse und Dachse. Sie

liefen, sprangen oder saßen in der immer gleichen Haltung, in einer angestrengten Bewegung, zu der sie für alle Ewigkeit verurteilt waren. Die eingesetzten Glasaugen waren alle von gleicher Farbe und Größe, der Iris war bernsteinhell. Die Glasaugen quollen hinter den Lidern hervor. Wohin ich auch ging, sie verfolgten mich, starrten mich nach. Diese von jedem Leben entleerten Augen zwangen mich, sie unablässig anzusehen. (*HE* 54)

[I remember the yellow glass eyes. In a reproduction of a heath there were stuffed foxes and badgers. They ran or jumped or crouched in one unvarying position, in the middle of a strained movement to which they were condemned for all eternity. The inserted glass eyes were all of one color and size, the iris bright like amber. The glass eyes bulged forward under their lids. They pursued me wherever I went, staring at me. I was forced to look incessantly at these eyes that were drained of all life.]

The dead animals demand Thomas's attention the same way that dead Herr Horn demands to be remembered. In both cases, Thomas senses that something hideous is being forced on him: death, or in the case of the chapter prologues, a past better left forgotten lest it overwhelm the present. Thomas later makes explicit the connections between Horn and his taxidermic kingdom (the eyes again), not to mention the oppressiveness of Guldenberg and the respectable life he is forced to lead. And like the other narrators, he diagnoses Horn's moral failure:

Herr Horn war mir unangenehm. Seine kühlen grauen Augen ängstigten mich. Er war wohl so alt wie mein Vater, dreiundvierzig Jahre, aber er wirkte viel älter, zerbrechlicher. Heute würde ich sagen, daß er verzagt und mutlos war, daß er seinem Leben nie die Kränkungen verzieh, die es ihm bereitete. Aber damals spürte ich nur die abwehrende Einsamkeit eines vergrämten Mannes. Schon als ich ihn das erstemal sah, an jenem Sonntag, an dem ich mit Vater und Bruder ins Heimatmuseum ging, empfand ich die alles zurückweisende Verschlossenheit dieses Mannes. (*HE* 190)

[I found Herr Horn unpleasant. His cool gray eyes frightened me. He was the same age as my father, 43, but he seemed much older, more fragile. Today I would say that he was utterly demoralized, that he never forgave his life for the injuries it had done him. But at the time I sensed only the defensive loneliness of a careworn man. From the very first time I saw him, on that Sunday when I went with my father and brother to the regional museum, I could feel how withdrawn and bitter he was.]

This critical assessment of Horn is more suggestive than Spodeck's or Kruschkatz's, and it suggests links to concerns that appear frequently in

Hein's work. The embittered historian has erred in withdrawing from society so completely, by remaining inflexibly willful at the expense of all else. Thus he resembles characters like Hubert K. or Schlötel, who sacrifice everything, including their connection with society and even their humanity, for an ideal. Though admirable to a degree, such uncompromising behavior is also anarchistically anti-social.[16] Thomas, himself naively prejudiced in favor of life and freedom regardless of the cost to memory, accurately perceives that Horn's motivations are principally negative: resentment, hatred, pride; they coincide in part with the passion for truth that Horn so eloquently describes, but he is also self-serving.[17] Both aspects of Horn's character must be kept in view before the nature of his tragedy can be understood.

In the flesh as in the ghost prologues, Horn acknowledges the taint of death that Thomas notices in the museum and wonders why he would willingly come there: "Warum willst du dich in einem Museum verkriechen, Junge? Was hast du mit den Toten zu schaffen?" [Why do you want bury yourself in a museum, boy? What business do you have with the dead?: 57]; and presumably the curator includes himself among these dead. In short, viewed from Thomas's standpoint, Horn belongs in the signifier chain Museum — History — Memory — Death — Truth — Enclosure. Thomas himself, longing to escape from Bad Guldenberg and forget about it, alternatively represents Forgetting — Life — Escape. Hein grants a partial validity to each viewpoint, and to the mutual distaste that Horn and Thomas must feel toward each other. The paradoxes in their characterizations and the contradictory symbolic matrices they inhabit forestall easy judgment by the reader, forcing instead an acceptance of the incommensurability of truths and viewpoints that so scandalizes Kruschkatz. McKnight notes as well the *agreement* between the boy and the Bürgermeister, both of whom wish to forget the past in order to live in the present. Kruschkatz was surely right, for example, to try to transcend the past enmity between Guldenberg and the Gypsies:

> Whose enemies are the gypsies, really? What have the Guldenbergers actually learned? Yet Kruschkatz is morally salvageable precisely by virtue of his desire to let go of the old stories that Horn and Gohl refuse to forget. What good is an antagonism carved in stone, eternal bitterness, eternal wallowing in the past? It is necessary to free oneself from the past and move forward. Such paradoxes remained unresolved, an open question, almost a vicious circle . . . .
> ("Ein Mosaik" 423–424)

Thomas emerges as the most contradictory figure of all, drawn unknowingly into the world of the historical museum which *is* Bad Guldenberg, and which contains not just recent acquisitions like Horn, but also older specimens like Herr Gohl, whose ghastly tragedy during the Nazi years makes him into a living monument to the past barbarity of his fellow citizens (one of whom had denounced him in writing to the Nazis, leading to his wife's murder in the stead of her retarded daughter [*HE* 156]). Even before Thomas is put to work helping Gohl paint the *trompe l'oeil* backdrops to the museum's exhibits, he has acquainted himself with Gohl's peculiar friends and fellow sufferers under the Nazis: the Gypsies, whom the Guldenbergers feel freer to abhor openly than they do Gohl. The pharmacist, for example, comments on the mysterious relationship between Gohl and the Gypsy king with smug condescension and unconscious irony: "Warum er ausgerechnet zu Gohl ging, wußte keiner. Vater sagt nur, da hätten sich die Richtigen gefunden" [Why he visited Gohl of all people nobody knew. Father merely said that they made a proper pair: 10]. Such attitudes support McKnight's view that the solidarity between the Gohl family and the Gypsies functions as the novel's "measure of humanity," which is destroyed (not for the first time) by the rape of Marlene. In spite of his avowed objectivity, Hein does provide certain "evaluative criteria" for his readers, as McKnight notes: "Bachofen's treason. Irene's death and unhappiness. Gertrude Fischlinger's sorrow. And, above all, the tragic fate of the Gohl family" ("Ein Mosaik" 418). Thomas, working for the Gypsies, working for Gohl, and listening to doomed Herr Horn describe the heavy responsibility for discovering truth, is one Guldenberger whose aversion to the past does not altogether blind him to its legacy and his own responsibility. He perhaps approximates the best that can be hoped for from Germany's first guiltless, postwar generation. Like Kruschkatz, Thomas gains in humanity by his contact with the Gypsies (McKnight, "Ein Mosaik" 425); it remains to be seen whether he can surpass the Bürgermeister in facing the responsibility bequeathed by Horn.

Unearthing anecdotes: *Der Tangospieler*'s Flight from History

Hein's books preceding *Der Tangospieler* examine history in its social, individual, and professional aspects; *Der Tangospieler*, while continuing in this vein, also satirizes conditions of life in the pre-*Wende* GDR by casting a special type of historian as Everyman. (The book, published in early 1989, was also the first — and last — critical treatment of the 1968 Warsaw Pact invasion of Czechoslovakia to appear inside the

GDR.)[18] In his other fiction, Hein generally refrains from the sort of direct, biting social commentary so evident in his plays, but in *Der Tangospieler* the social criticism is scathing. The book is less a meditation on history or a study of a historically defined character than a travesty of the old Socialist Realist convention of the New Man, that hoped-for product of life in a society where "the fulfillment of the individual is the precondition for the fulfillment of all" (Marx 53). If a society reveals something of its essence through the sorts of people who prosper in it, then the GDR of this book is a land of opportunism, cynicism, intellectual stagnation, and Orwellian historical revisionism. Yet Dallow, much like Claudia, in *Der fremde Freund*, is a normal person reacting in a reasonable way to the pressures and expectations of his society. His unselfconscious accommodation to his world points to the true delineations of power within it, giving the lie to public propaganda and private rationalization. Unlike Claudia, whose "I'm fine" becomes ever harder to believe, Dallow's ultimate apotheosis can hardly be denied, and therein lies the shock of the book: the perfect fit between his society's unstated rules and his self-serving disinterest in all things political or historical (a type of disinterest not limited to the East, of course). The most dreadful thing about Dallow is that he is *not* a monster — he is quite ordinary in ways that would have been apparent to any citizen of the GDR. This ordinariness, painstakingly detailed, is what enables Hein to maintain his vaunted stance of objective chronicling; the satiric sting at the end, despite its exaggerated neatness, relies on a long string of plausibilities.

The narrative itself may be briefly summarized as follows. After serving nineteen months for unintentionally ridiculing Party chief Walter Ulbricht (by playing the piano accompaniment to a student cabaret's satirical tango), Dallow is released from prison. He tries without success to reintegrate himself into society — his old academic institute turns him down, and he finds that no one will hire a politically compromised former university professor for menial jobs. Plagued by memories he wishes to forget (or, later, by resentments he will not let go of) and plagued by a pair of Stasi agents who try to enlist his services, he dissipates himself with drink and women before deciding to seek a job as waiter. A friend finds him a job on the Baltic coast at a summer resort, and he happily adjusts to a life without ambition and with plenty of young, nubile women. With the August 1968 Warsaw Pact invasion of Czechoslovakia, circumstances at his institute change after his successor Roessler commits a political error: he tells a full classroom that the reports of Warsaw Pact tanks in Prague are Western propaganda, the proof being that the GDR's sense of historical responsibility would prevent it from ever again invading a neighbor country. As a result, Dallow is invited to return to his old job. The book foregrounds two related metaphors: the paralysis Dallow suffers in his right hand in moments of stress, and the act of playing the piano. At the end, once Dallow has been reinstated, his paralysis departs, apparently for good, and he resumes playing. And in a scene reminiscent of the tank episode Claudia remembered in *Der fremde Freund*, Dallow is vouchsafed a vision of brutal political power and his relation to it.

One essential premise of the book may seem implausible — that Dallow, a Leipzig history professor, could have absolutely no interest in the historical events taking place in 1968 in the East Bloc. Yet Dallow is a not-unfamiliar type of academic. His scholarly work concerns an area of research approved by the Party and of no real importance to anyone else, nor of interest even to Dallow. He describes it to his girlfriend Elke:

> Sehr beeindruckend ist meine Wissenschaft nicht. Ich hatte mich mit Neuerer Geschichte zu befassen und unentwegt danach zu forschen, wie die illegalen sozialdemokratischen Zeitungen vor einhundert Jahren konspirativ gedruckt und über den Bodensee gerudert wurden. Und wie die tapferen Arbeiter und Handwerker der Prager Neustadt sich mit Besenstielen und Sandeimern des Bombardements von Windischgrätz erwehrten. Wenn von einer Wissenschaft nur noch Anekdoten übrigblieben, wird es ermüdend. (*DT* 99)

> [My scientific accomplishments are not very impressive. I was supposed to work in modern history, to burn the midnight oil discovering how illegal social-democratic parties managed secretly to print newspapers and row them across Lake Constance a hundred years ago. And how the brave workers and artisans of Prague defended themselves against Windischgrätz's cannons with broomsticks and buckets of sand. But it's tiresome when science has nothing more to do than unearth anecdotes.] (*TTP* 104)

Sarcasm is evident in this parody of public discourse in the GDR: the workers are always "brave" and the research that glorifies them continues endlessly. Dallow more than anyone is aware that his scholarly work is nothing but *rote Soße* (the red sauce that went with everything) — it was doubtless settled upon as a field promising sure advancement through the academic ranks. If Dallow's specialty has any relevance to the contemporary world (as it may well), Dallow has not troubled himself to discover it; all that matters is political correctness. Since he lacks any interest in the political events pressing around him, the term "Neuere Geschichte" seems ludicrously inappropriate as a description of what Dallow does, namely, accumulating dead facts and keeping them that way. As in the case of Kruschkatz in *Horns Ende,* and for similar reasons, Hein delays as long as possible the revelation that we are dealing with a professional historian, but as a comparison to any of the narrators in the earlier novel shows, Dallow is really the precise opposite of a historian, and equally a perfect servant of the state and his own interests. If to seek out historical truth inevitably means to deconstruct whatever partisan version of history the state may have decided to project, then the political meaning of "disinterest" in history becomes readily apparent.

Dallow's anti-historical attitude emerges first from his initial determination to forget his own most dramatic experience with state power: the nineteen months in jail for a trivial and unintentional political offense. He insists to his friend Harry that the time in jail was meaningless, wasted, and best forgotten:

> "Und wie war es?" fragte der Kellner zögernd. Es schien, als suche er dabei nach Worten.
> "Das ist alles schon vergessen," sagte Dallow und lächelte den Kellner an, "verlorene Zeit, nicht der Mühe wert, sich daran zu erinnern." (*DT* 16)
>
> ["And how was it?" asked the waiter after a moment's hesitation, during which he seemed to be searching for the right words.
> "I've already put it out of my mind," said Dallow and smiled at the waiter. "Lost time, not worth the trouble trying to remember."]
> (*TTP* 15)

He tells his parents the same thing: "Vergeßt einfach alles ... ich selbst kann mich an diese Zeit kaum noch erinnern" [Just forget the whole thing ... I barely remember it myself: 75; 78] and finds that he has been avoiding friends and family because

> Man würde ihm Mitgefühl bekunden wollen, und eben das zwänge ihn, jene Zeit, die er gründlich und rasch vergessen wollte, sich immer wieder ins Gedächtnis zu rufen, sich vor Augen zu führen, um sie zu beschreiben und schließlich auszumalen, wilder, farbiger und fürchterlicher, als sie tatsächlich gewesen war. (*DT* 58)
>
> [People wanted to show their sympathy, and yet that was precisely what kept sending him back to prison, back to the time he wanted to forget quickly and completely. But they kept forcing him to recollect it, to behold it, in order to describe and ultimately color events so that his life in prison seemed wilder, more picturesque and more frightening than it had really been.] (*TTP* 61)

His desire to forget the past is connected with a sense that the time in prison was meaningless, irrelevant to the rest of his life, and therefore irredeemably wasted. He accurately perceives that his friends expect from him not merely an account of the jail time, but an evaluation of it, and consequently an indication of his own future plans. Finding no meaning in it, he can form no plans. To now spend additional time thinking about something as pointless as his lost nineteen months looks like a further waste of time, an extension of his punishment; therefore, forgetting looks to him like freedom:

> Er wollte die Zeit aus seinem Gedächtnis löschen, um sich von ihr zu befreien. Die Inhaftierung hatte er nie als Strafe empfinden können, sondern allein als eine Kränkung und einen nicht wiedergutzumachenden Verlust von Zeit. Aber er hatte die beiden Jahre hinter sich gebracht, ohne verrückt zu werden, und er wollte künftig keine Minute mit einem nutzlosen Grübeln über die Haft und die unwürdigen Umstände, unter denen er im Gefängnis zu leben gezwungen war, verlieren. (*DT* 21)

> [He wanted to erase this time from his memory so he could free himself from it. He had never been able to view his imprisonment as a punishment, only as an annoyance, an irreplaceable loss of time. But he had managed to get through the two years without losing his mind, and from now on he refused to waste a single minute on senseless brooding over his imprisonment and the degrading conditions he had had to endure.] (*TTP* 20)

With the memory of *Horns Ende* freshly in mind, the reader of *Der Tangospieler* may be tempted to read Dallow's desire to forget as self-evidently misguided, as a rejection of historical reality and of responsibility similar to Thomas's complaints against the relentless voice of memory. Yet Thomas did have a valid point when he argued for the claims of the living, and he was not altogether wrong in trying to rid himself once and for all of ideological abstractions like "history." Dallow's case is even more enigmatic, because nothing intrinsic to the narrative directly contradicts his view, while the denouement even vindicates forgetting the past as quickly and as thoroughly as possible really *was* the best strategy for survival in the GDR in 1968. Adding to the difficulty of assessing Dallow is his abrupt decision to begin remembering after all. Specifically, he nurses a grudge against the prosecutor, judge, and defense lawyer who collaborated in jailing him. As might be expected, the desire to remember involves a new understanding and evaluation of the events.

The alleged meaninglessness of Dallow's time in jail turns out to be a starting point, not a conclusion. His belief that he had been imprisoned entirely by mistake succinctly expresses an ahistorical sensibility — events simply follow one another, or happen side by side without implying relations or patterns. This is the significance of Dallow's pseudo-philosophical description of existence as "ein Lichtspiel, ein Phänomen der Optik wie das Kino. Und was sind Lichtspiele und Wasserspiele, ein Zeitvertreib aus Nichts" [a light show, an optical phenomenon like the cinema. Or water dancing in a fountain. And what are light shows and electric fountains? Sheer follies, time-killers, made of nothing: 90; 95]; his jail term, likewise, as he tells his father, "ist auch nur eine Gelegenheit, um die Zeit totzuschlagen" [just another place to kill time: 67; 70]. His imprisonment, because it lacks necessary logical connections with anything else in his life, can only be regarded as absurd, a joke:

> Er war nicht ins Gefängnis gekommen, weil er kriminell, aufsässig oder mutig gewesen war; einer Dummheit wegen hatte man ihn verurteilt und in eine Zelle gesperrt, auch wenn das Urteil etwas anderes sagte und der Richter von etwas anderem überzeugt war. Das Gefängnis blieb ein Unfall innerhalb einer gleichmäßig dahinrinnenden Existenz. Nichts als ein Irrtum. Ein Versehen beider Seiten. Keine Veränderungen. Es gab nur eine Unterbrechung, von der er, nachdem sie nun einmal passiert war, gehofft hatte, sie würde noch eine letzte, wichtige Weichenstellung erlauben. Aber, und das ahnte er jetzt, er verstand nicht, die Chance zu nutzen, es war umsonst, es blieb ein bedauernswerter, nichtssagender Unfall. (*DT* 110)[19]

> [He hadn't landed in prison for being criminal, rebellious, or courageous; he had been convicted and jailed on account of a stupid trifle, even if the sentence said otherwise and the judge was convinced he was right. Prison remained an accident in the steady trickle of his existence. Just an error, nothing more. A mistake on both sides. Nothing new. It had only been an interruption, and now that it had happened he hoped it would lead to one more final, important change of course. But he realized he didn't know how to take advantage of this opportunity, all attempts were useless, the event remained a regrettable and insignificant accident.] (*TTP* 115)

Dallow denies the reality of his crime as it was understood by the judge — as a political act in violation of specific laws — but his claim of innocence (that he had never read the text accompanying the tango, etc.), though technically true, fails to satisfy either the judge (73–4; 76–77) or the reader. If nothing else, Dallow is surely guilty of a sort of criminal negligence with respect to politics. His remarkable stupidity recalls the deluded explanation Hauptmann Hirschburg, in *Passage*, gives for his persecution by the Nazi authorities: not that he has Jewish ancestry, but merely because of an "unglückselige[s] Mißverständnis" [unfortunate misunderstanding: *Passage* 29]. Before the play ends, however, Hirschburg sees his error and shoulders his historical burden by leading the fifteen elderly Jews through the Pyrenees. Dallow comes more gradually to an understanding that his conviction was more than an accident or error, as he looks at the aimlessness and isolation of his life as an ex-convict:

> Das Gefängnis, sagte er sich, war wohl doch mehr als nur ein Unfall in meinem Leben.
> ... Ihm war bewußt, daß ihn, tief versteckt und uneingestanden, Heimweh quälte, ein Heimweh nach der Zelle. Er vermißte jene sonderbare Geborgenheit, die vollständige, alles umfassende Vorsorge, das ausnahmslos geregelte Leben. In der Zelle hatte er nichts entscheiden müssen. (*DT 114*)

> [Prison must have been more than an accident in my life, he told himself.
> ... He realized he was homesick, deeply homesick in a way he would not admit, homesick for his cell. He missed that strange security, the comprehensive care, he missed the total regulation of his life. In his cell he never had to make a single decision.] (*TTP* 119–120)

This homesickness suggests even more than Dallow recognizes. His longing for confinement amounts to nostalgia for the lost security of his prior, conformist life. However inadvertent, his political infraction had been the act of a free man, and the state exacted its price for such freedom by treating him as a dissident. Dallow's plan of action once he realizes his homesickness for the cell is to look for work, that is, to rejoin the society from which he had been excluded; it is by no means a repudiation of his more profound longing for unfreedom.

Thus the meaning that Dallow extracts from his jail term is only partly valid. He thinks, correctly, that the smooth progress of his life has been disrupted and that he has lost sight of the future, but he never becomes conscious of the deeper relation between the conditions of life inside and outside of the cell. Having discovered significance in his past, he has a reason to remember, though in a limited way: he becomes like Horn, clinging to a conviction of personal injury at the hands of unscrupulous individuals — in Horn's case, his comrades, while in Dallow's, the judge, prosecutor, and lawyer. Both men suffered expulsion from a community, and both refuse to accept the ideological rationale for their suffering, insisting instead on complete exoneration. The difference between the two men, and the two books, is that *Der Tangospieler* is a satire: Dallow seeks to establish that he was truly, perfectly innocent of political motives, that he was a good, obedient, disengaged citizen despite appearances, and that he should never have been punished for the crime of independent thought. This is how his determination to remember the wrongs done to him should be read — in light of Horn's relatively (though not absolutely) selfless pursuit of truth in the face of ideological fantasy. Hein puts into Dallow's mouth a virtual parody of Horn's refusal, according to Kruschkatz, to forget or to learn anything from his fall:

> "Kannst du nicht vergessen?" fragte Elke unvermittelt.
> Dallow brauchte einen Moment, um zu begreifen, wovon sie sprach. "Ich will es nicht.... Ich will nichts vergessen, und ich will nichts verzeihen." (*DT* 181–2)
>
> ["Can't you forget? asked Elke abruptly.
> Dallow needed a moment to understand what she was getting at. "I don't want to.... I don't want to forget anything, and I don't want to forgive anything, either."] (*TTP* 191–192)

Dallow's primary argument for his innocence resonates with various associations he doesn't intend. Beginning with the prison official who processes his release, Dallow tells anyone who asks that he is a piano player by trade (6; 4). Close to a dozen times, he recites the same explanation for his misfortune and guiltlessness: "Ich war nur der Pianist" [I was only the piano player: 136, 142; 144, 150], "Ich war nur der Tangospieler" [I was only the tango player: three times 136–143; 144–151]), "Ich bin nur ein Kellner.... Und früher war ich ein Tangospieler" [I'm just a waiter... and once I was a tango player: 199; 213]. As he tries to explain at his trial, Dallow means by this that he had nothing to do with the words his piano playing accompanied, and that his role in the affair was incidental as well as accidental. Yet with so many repetitions, it is hard not to begin hearing "I was just the piano player" as "I was only following orders," in others words as a disingenuous profession of non-involvement and guiltlessness. This standard defense of concentration camp guards and other war criminals cannot be taken at face value; the implication seems to be that in some sense, he is indeed guilty of *something*, though Hein does not explicitly state what.

To grasp the nature of Dallow's actions, it is necessary to look at how piano-playing and paralysis operate in the book as metaphors. Dallow suffers from recurring paralysis in his right hand; meanwhile, he refuses to play the piano (or is incapable of it) until the final pages of the book. The paralysis strikes him whenever he is confronted directly by state power, as at the beginning while being discharged from prison, or during his dealings with the Stasi-men Müller and Schulze, or at the conclusion when he imagines being crushed by an armored vehicle. Twice he attempts to play the piano: unsuccessfully, after deciding that he must find a job and stop his aimless drifting, and successfully, at the conclusion, once he has his old job back. Paralysis is a clear enough symbol of helplessness in the face of superior power, but its significance for Dallow's politically-colored musicianship is subtler. He is quite right to regard his playing at the student cabaret as a minor, subordinate aspect of the whole production, and indeed the role of musical accompanist may be equated with Dallow's former (and future) role in his society: as a minor collaborator in his government's comprehensive program of ideological indoctrination, as a fully subservient "intellectual" committed to nothing except following the rules set by the state (whatever they may be — why bother reading the words before playing along?), in return for which he is guaranteed a comfortable life as an academic. In Hein's fictive universe, moreover, Dallow represents the worst possible subspecies of compromised intellectual: a compromised hack historian, someone who perverts the essential cultural work of history-writing into partisan drivel, while obscuring other, real historical truths.

When Dallow sits down to the piano in the final scene, after Warsaw Pact troops have invaded Czechoslovakia and Dallow has been restored to his former position at the university, he again plays an accompaniment:

> Dallow ... schaltete den Fernseher an und ging ins Bad, um sich lange zu duschen. Dann setzte er sich mit einer Flasche Vodka an das Klavier. Er hatte den Ton des Fernsehers abgedreht und sah auf die sich bewegenden Bilder. Er spielte laut und wild die kleinen, ihm geläufigen Klavierstücke von Chopin und sah dem stummen Film seines Fernsehgerätes zu, der Soldaten zeigte, die von der Bevölkerung begrüßt und offenbar von Armeegenerälen besucht wurden. Frauen mit kleinen Kindern auf dem Arm warfen Blumen zu den auf ihren Panzern sitzenden Soldaten, andere Bilder zeigten Prager Bürger in freundschaftlichen Gespräch mit den Soldaten. Dallow trank in kurzer Zeit die Flasche aus, stellte den Fernseher ab und ging ins Schlaffzimmer. Bevor er sich auszog, prüfte er die Klingel des Weckers und stellte ihn dann. Er wollte am nächsten Morgen pünktlich im Institut sein. (*DT* 205–206)

> [Dallow ... turned on the television, and went to the bathroom to take a long shower. Then he opened a bottle of vodka and sat down at the piano. He had turned down the volume on the television and was watching the pictures. He played the little Chopin he knew by heart, loudly and uncontrolled, as the silent film played on. It showed soldiers being greeted by the local population and reviewed by high-ranking generals. Women with small children were tossing flowers to the troops sitting on their tanks; in another scene citizens of Prague were making friendly conversation with the soldiers. Dallow soon fin-

ished the bottle, turned off the television, and went into the bedroom. Before he undressed he checked to make sure his alarm clock was working and then set it. He wanted to be at the Institute on time the next morning.] (*TTP* 219–220)

The fabricated history spewing out of the television finds in Dallow an able accompanist. Dutifully playing along, he prepares to go to work the next morning as a historian of forgetting. As in his performance with the student cabaret, Dallow ignores what is actually being said: the television sound is turned off, and Dallow is free to claim complete indifference to the contents of the broadcast, which Hein describes in a deadpan socialist-optimistic manner. In this parody of political disinterest, the uninvolved individual is really an active supporter of the prevailing powers, playing along, avoiding trouble, just following orders. Herr Dozent Dr. Dallow's utter disinterest in his chosen field of modern history presents a somewhat extreme example of how separated theory and practice can become in a repressive state, but the portrayal is not totally incredible. As someone who has learned to ignore, for personal advantage, even the most glaring contradictions in his life and society, Dallow is a travesty of the "really existing" Socialist New Man.

Hein thus leaves no doubt that Dallow should be understood as the opposite of a true historian. Though living in 1968 in the GDR, he lacks any interest in the social upheavals taking place in Czechoslovakia and Poland. Hein's flat, impersonal, yet highly concrete, almost Kleist-like narrative style allows him to draw his protagonist against a background of incidental news reports, overheard conversations, and other references to the political events that barely graze Dallow's consciousness. Thus newspapers, for example, play a large role in the book as a gauge of Dallow's interest in the world around him and a demonstration of his aversion to thinking about it. After his release, when he finds a number of old newspapers in his mailbox, he merely reflects that the news stories they contain must have been much less important than they pretended to be at the time (10; 9). Later he tries with little success (having paid no attention to such matters before) to decipher a newspaper's evasive reports about the socialist reform movements:

> Er las zwei kurze Artikel über Warschau und Prag, denen er nicht mehr entnehmen konnte, als daß die Zeitungsredaktion mit großer Anteilnahme und tiefer Sorge nicht näher benannte Vorgänge in diesen Städten beobachtete. (*DT* 106)

> [He read two short articles about Warsaw and Prague, from which he could only gather that the newspaper's editors were following certain events in these cities with great interest and deep concern, though what these events were remained unclear.] (*TTP* 111)

At this point he makes plans to subscribe to a newspaper, not in order to follow the news more closely, but to help kill time:

> In der Zelle waren es seine angenehmsten Stunden gewesen, die er mit dem Lesen der Zeitung verbracht hatte. Er hoffte, daß ihm die Tageszeitung auch jetzt, außerhalb der Gefängnismauern eine vergleichbare, interresselose Beschäftigung verschaffen könnte. Er hoffte, mit ihr die viele freie Zeit totzuschlagen. (*DT* 106)
>
> [In his cell he had spent his most pleasant hours that way. Now, on the outside, he hoped the newspaper would provide him with a similarly mindless activity. He hoped it would help him kill some of his abundant free time.] (*TTP* 111–112)

The notion that newspapers could serve the same purpose in or out of jail underscores the lack of any real difference between these two conditions for Dallow. Read psychologically, Dallow's desire to resume "killing time" is a sign of his latent yearning for the security of the prison cell; read as political allegory, it is a sign of his imprisonment within a totalitarian society whose most successful citizens are those who acquiesce fully in their own subjugation. The manner in which Dallow reads, with "teilnahmloser Aufmerksamkeit" [indifferent, detached attention: 105; 111], can be understood equally well as a description of his relation to society. As in Horn's single-minded commitment to the reality of the wrong done him, "indifferent, detached attention" is another botched approximation of what Hein sees as the ideal historiographic attitude, writing without "passion and prejudice." His distance from the ideal, however, is instructive: the chronicler remains dispassionate in order to make facts available for the construction of truth, whereas Dallow has no more complex motivations than self-interest and boredom. His attentiveness to events is wholly sterile, leading to no synthesis in his life or professional work, and his claim to political neutrality looks plausible only until his de facto involvement in history restores him unexpectedly to his university job. It is hard to escape the conclusion that this is a moment he has been waiting for, and in fact he is being rewarded for waiting rather than acting, for letting events control him rather than actively participating, which would mean overcoming his social alienation.

Dallow's bizarre detachment from the convulsions within the socialist world emerges most clearly from his encounters with people who exhibit a degree of political engagement. While he simply ignores the barrage of political commentary over Western radio (172; 181, and elsewhere) he displays condescension or puzzlement when confronted with other people's interest. Waiting for Harry at the bar on the first night after his release, Dallow sneers at the "junge, unreife Gesichter" [young, immature faces: 15; 14] of the students he hears discussing politics. (Evidently, a more mature attitude toward politics — such as Dallow's — would preclude having actual convictions, let alone loud public discussion of them.) Dallow's dismissal of student enthusiasm is redressed later, when the news of the invasion of Czechoslovakia brings Dallow's current bed partner to tears. She is horrified by Dallow's lack of concern:

> "Ich kann nicht verstehen, daß dich so etwas kalt läßt," sagte das Mädchen entsetzt.
> "Ich bin nur ein Kellner," gab Dallow zu bedenken.
> Das Mädchen protestierte. "Du bist ein lebendiger Mensch, du bist . . . "
> Dallow unterbrach sie und wandte freundlich ein: "Und früher war ich ein Tangospieler. Aber das ist lange her." (*DT* 199)
>
> ["I can't understand how you can be so indifferent," she said, somewhat horrified.
> "I'm just a waiter," Dallow answered her.
> The girl protested. "You're a living human being, you're a . . . "
> Dallow interrupted, objecting in a friendly voice, "Yes, and once I was a tango player. But that was a long time ago."] (*TTP* 213)

Dallow's standard demurral, "I was just the tango player," looks the more cynical for its juxtaposition with the student's unaffected grief over the crushing of the Prague Spring. Not even Müller and Schulze, the Stasi-men, can fathom Dallow's disengagement, especially in view of his profession and specialty. They are disappointed when they try to enlist Dallow as an ally in the current difficult political situation:

> [Schulze speaking.] "Sie sind Historiker. Sie kennen die tschechische und slowakische Geschichte. Sie sind für uns von Interesse, gerade in dieser Zeit."
> Dallow unterbrach ihn: "Ich beschäftigte mich mit dem 19. Jahrhundert. Die Gegenwart hat mich nie interessiert. Und Politiker fanden meine Aufmerksamkeit erst, wenn sie vermodert waren. Sie sind dann wesentlich aufrichtiger."
> Schulze lächelte.
> "Geben Sie sich keine Mühe," sagte Dallow grob, "was da in Prag passiert, kümmert mich so viel." Er schnipste mit den Fingern. "Und außerdem arbeite ich nicht mehr als Historiker. Schon lange nicht mehr. Zuletzt war ich Tangospieler . . . . " (*DT* 151)
>
> ["You're a historian, with a specialty in Czech and Slovak history. We're very interested in that, especially right now."

Dallow interrupted him. "My specialty is the nineteenth century. Current events have never interested me. And politicians only attract my attention once they've started to moulder in the grave. They're a lot more honest then."

Schulze smiled.

"Don't trouble yourselves," said Dallow curtly. "What's going on in Prague concerns me this much." He snapped his fingers. "And anyway, I'm not a historian anymore. I haven't been for a long time. My last job was as a tango player . . . .] (*TTP* 159–160)

The secret policemen leave immediately and promise not to return after Dallow assures them that he cares nothing for politics. This suggests that although the regime may genuinely have hoped to win Dallow over as an active co-worker, an equally acceptable outcome is for him to withdraw completely from political life. Hein virtually acknowledges the exaggeration of his protagonist's withdrawal by placing him among a group of more realistically drawn characters at a birthday party, some of whom try to involve him in a conversation about Czech politics. As so often in the book, Dallow responds with a seemingly ingenuous disinterest that bespeaks more satire than plausibility:

Einer der Männer erkundigte sich nach Dallows Ansichten und fragte, ob er Dubček Chancen einräume, politisch zu überleben.

"Ich habe keine Ahnung," antwortete ihm Dallow, "und es interessiert mich auch nicht."

Er sagte es freundlich und betont liebenswürdig, aber das Gespräch verstummte, und alle sahen zu ihm.

"Das kann nicht Ihr Ernst sein," sagte der Mann, der ihn angesprochen hatte. "In diesem Fall wären Sie der einzige Mensch in diesem Land, den die Ereignisse in Prag nicht beschäftigen. So oder so ist doch da jeder engagiert."

Dallow zuckte bedauernd mit den Schultern und erwiderte nichts.

"Aber Sie sind doch Historiker," sagte ein Mädchen, "das hat Elke mir erzählt. Ich dachte, gerade Sie müßte das dort interessieren."

Dallow lächelte sie freundlich an und korrigierte höflich: "Ich bin Pianist." Und erläuternd fügte er hinzu: "Tangospieler." (*DT* 158-9)

[One of the men wanted to know what Dallow thought and asked whether he thought Dubček had any chances of surviving politically.

"I have no idea," Dallow answered. "I'm really not interested."

He said it in a friendly manner, but it stopped the conversation and everyone looked his way.

"You can't really mean that," said the man who had put the question to him. "In that case you must be the only one in the whole country who isn't totally preoccupied with what's happening in Prague. One way or another we're all involved."

Dallow shrugged his shoulders to indicate his regret but did not respond.

"But you're a historian," said one woman, "Elke told me. I would think you'd be more interested than anybody."

Dallow gave her a friendly smile and corrected her politely: "I'm a piano player." And then he added, by way of explanation, "A tango player."] (*TTP* 167–168)

As justification for his uncommunicativeness, Dallow finally announces that he spent two years in prison. The man questioning him replies "Ja, und?" [Well, so what?: 160; 170], a laconic critique of the martyr-stance Dallow shares with Horn. In spite of their personal suffering, they face the same choices and responsibilities as all their fellow citizens; history has not halted for them or granted them a special dispensation.

As grim and absurd as his past experience may be, Dallow still must find a way to survive in society, either submitting uncritically to political power or finding some more or less critical relation to it (escape being virtually impossible, except perhaps in death). His choice is mirrored in the seaside *Windflüchter*, the deformed trees that survive by bowing and twisting before the wind. His admiration for the stubborn persistence of these trees, which have found a way "mit ihrer Bedrückung zu leben" [to live with their oppression: 192; 205], mirrors his desire to accommodate himself unquestioningly to the powers that be. Dallow even accepts this flight from history consciously: the *Windflüchter* symbolize for him the simple route out of his personal "Labyrinth" (192; 205–206). During his drive back to Leipzig and to his old job, he encounters a concrete manifestation of his historical circumstances and the choices open to him: a column of military vehicles returning from Czechoslovakia. In a scene reminiscent of the tank episode in *Der fremde Freund*, Dallow has a waking dream of being crushed by an armored vehicle:

> Ein Schützenpanzerfahrzeug blieb zehn Meter vor ihm stehen, er sah das blasse, übernächtigte Gesicht des jungen Soldaten. Halbe Kinder, dachte Dallow. Er starrte den Soldaten an, der offenbar Mühe hatte, die Augen offenzuhalten. Er stellte sich vor, der Junge würde die Gewalt über den Panzerwagen verlieren. Er sah, wie der Eisenkoloß plötzlich aus der Reihe brach und sich mit schlingernden Bewegungen auf ihn zu bewegte. Die riesigen Reifen rollten langsam heran und drückten die Fensterscheiben des kleinen Autos ein. Das Panzerfahrzeug schob Dallow in seinem Wagen vor sich her, stieß ihn in den Straßengraben und überrollte ihn schließlich. Er sah sich selbst zu, wie er in seinem sich überschlagenden Wagen ruhig sitzen blieb, die verkrampfte, schmerzende Hand um den Lenker gekrallt, bis er, noch

immer lächelnd, in dem Auto zerquetscht wurde. Dallow träumte mit offenen Augen, während die Armeefahrzeuge bereits wieder weiterfuhren. Er stellte sich die Szene so lebhaft vor, daß er schwitzte. Er bemerkte das Zittern seiner rechten Hand und nahm sie vom Steuer, aber schon nach einigen Sekunden ließ das Zittern nach, der befürchtete Krampf blieb aus.

"Das hätte es sein können," sagte Dallow laut zu sich und massierte die Hand, "vielleicht wars meine letzte Chance." (*DT* 204–5)

[A light attack tank stopped thirty feet away from him; he could see the young soldier's face, made pale by lack of sleep. They're practically children, thought Dallow. He stared at the soldier, who seemed to have trouble keeping his eyes open. He imagined the boy losing control of the tank, he pictured the iron colossus suddenly breaking away and swerving right in his direction. The giant treads slowly rolled onto his little car, shattering the windows. The tank shoved the car forward, plowing it into a ditch, and then rolled on over. He saw his car caving in while he quietly sat inside, his hand cramped with pain, clawing the steering wheel until he was finally crushed, still smiling.

Dallow sat dreaming with open eyes as the army vehicles continued on their way. He had imagined the scene so vividly that he broke out in a sweat. He noticed that his right hand was shaking and he took it off the steering wheel, but it only took a few seconds before the shaking subsided; the cramp he so feared never came.

"That could have been it," Dallow said to himself aloud and rubbed his hand, "maybe it was my last chance."] (*TTP* 218–219)

Like Claudia's remembered tank, this errant "light attack tank" stands unambiguously for socialism's "final argument" — brute force. It has just returned from Prague, where individuals had dared exercise autonomy, and having put a stop to that, it now threatens Dallow, confronting him with a clear illustration of the absolute state power he has been rather foolishly toying with. Dallow may debate with himself whether or not to seek work, whether or not to forget the wrong done him, but his body knows the truth: the paralyzed right hand is the physical counterpart to his loss of autonomy, which, as always in Hein, is both state- and self-imposed. The "last chance" that Dallow almost passes up is the chance to bend in the appropriate direction before the prevailing political wind. Such an accommodation to power is no guarantee of personal security (after all, a tank rolls over whatever is in its path, arbitrarily), but it is nonetheless safer than rebellion (as Horn's fate proved). Such a precarious pragmatism proves far more reliable than the rigid, ideologically guided rationalism of Roessler, Dallow's successor and rival at the institute. Thinking himself safe from a fall because of his faithfulness to the Party line, Roessler misunderstands the essence of his society: it is founded on force, which is irrational, not on ideology, which serves only to rationalize brutality. Roessler may be a better historian than Dallow (he remembers the socialist regime's public statements and points to Germany's experience as an aggressor in the Second World War as evidence that the GDR would never invade its neighbor), but he fails miserably as an opportunist. Greed, fear, and the hunger for power, not ideology, are the operative historical forces in Hein's GDR; with belief in the officially promulgated ideology in fact a pitfall to which intellectuals are prone, the truly prudent intellectual learns to emulate rationality without either believing in it or acting upon it.

When Dallow overcomes his paralysis and sits down to play the piano once again, his autonomy, his physical freedom to act, is really a mockery of freedom. He is once again, and now for the first time consciously, "just the tango player," accommodating himself to history and its political vicissitudes. Physically he escaped being crushed by the tank, but spiritually he dreamed the plain truth. With his reinstatement and his new attitude, he can count on living happily ever after, a good citizen of the GDR. Of course, good citizenship means complete, agile obeisance to authority, and the utter renunciation of a personal viewpoint. Dallow, always detached, always apolitical, has had the potential all along, like Claudia, to be an ideal citizen. But where Claudia is almost purely reactive to her society, virtually its logical consequence, Dallow is the more ominous representative of perverted intellect in the active service of power. He is a historian of forgetting, the faithful lackey of power, whatever power. Even Dallow's resentful memory of the wrong done him reveals an attitude surprisingly close to the desires of the government: if he gets his job back, everything is forgiven and forgotten; no broader social questions need be raised. Thus the regime functions on a wholly corrupt basis, ruling by bribes and terror, and so requiring individuals to accept willingly the bribes and endure the terror as the price of possible success. The individual who plays along best with this game of self-interest prospers; one who resists it on principle gets nowhere, or ends up like Horn.

Hein's narratives about history, historians, and historiography portray individuals forced to act against a historical background they would, in most cases, prefer not to acknowledge, and it is precisely this yearning to disengage from society, politics, and history that guarantees the recurrence of history as a nightmare of repression and war. To assist the powers that be in tailoring history for political ends is the greatest and most nearly suicidal crime that intellectuals can commit. Hein's writings, along with those of such diverse authors as Christa Wolf, Heiner Müller, and Günter de Bruyn, played an inestimable role during the waning years of the GDR in creating the *Öffentlichkeit*, the atmosphere of dialogue and multiple viewpoints, that would have fateful political consequences in the fall of 1989. As the messy, confusing, and disillusioning job of rebuilding Eastern Europe proceeds, and the political exigencies (and score-settling) of unified Germany generate new distortions of that country's catastrophic recent history, it should not be forgotten that the artists and intellectuals of East Germany were among those who sparked and led the revolution that ended Communism in Europe. Hein's parables of corrupt socialist intellectuals surely deserve credit for keeping alive the possibility of an alternative. His determination to chronicle rather than spin ideological fantasies remains instructive for intellectuals of the post-socialist world, the chronicle of which must also one day be written.

Notes

[1] In the epigraph to his story, Hein notes: "Zum Lever, der Zeremonie des königlichen Aufstehens, geladen zu sein, galt als besondere Gunst am französischen Hof" [To be invited to the Rising, the ceremony of the royal getting-out-of-bed, was a mark of special favor at the French Court: *NUFM* 118]. The "Lever Bourgeois" to which the reader is invited is presumably another matter.

[2] See also "Anmerkungen zu *Cromwell*," 173–74.

[3] "In schools and universities, and in our daily newspapers, history has been and still is conveyed to us in just one way: Everything that happened in the past was a necessary, purposeful expression of the historical world-spirit, leading ultimately to this state [that is, the GDR], to this society, to us. We are the victors of history, we heard through long years of schooling. The associated thrill of victory and joy was counteracted not solely by a number of unpleasant everyday realities; what truly astonishes is the lack of dialectical thinking in this account of history that claims to invoke dialectic" (Hein, "Die fünfte Grundrechenart" 62).

[4] A principle source of biographical information on Racine is his son, Louis, who was a young boy at the time of his father's death, and "whose laudable aim" in his *Mémoires* "was to whitewash his father" (Brereton 154) by emphasizing his virtues.

[5] Hein even exaggerates the gulf between the two phases in Racine's life by avoiding mention of the two late plays, *Esther* and *Athalie*, which were commissioned in the late 1680s by the king's morganatic wife, Madame de Maintenon, for her girls' school. Saintsbury notes that this late productivity

was the result of a "conjunction of the two reigning passions of the latter part of [Racine's] life — devoutness and obsequiousness to the court" (208).

[6] Meanwhile, doctrinaire Marxist criticism of "Einladung zum Lever Bourgeois" accused Hein of identifying with Racine by himself relying on "an insinuation, an ironic remark, a despairing laugh" to make his points. Krumrey scolds him disingenuously for employing this "exceedingly deformed type of communication" (145) instead of expressing himself directly (and thereby precluding publication in the GDR altogether, one imagines).

[7] Fischer even sees the anti-government pamphlet Racine allegedly wrote toward the end of his life (and which Hein includes in his story) as a symptom of the courtier's spiritual illness: "Racine's revolutionary act is that of a sick and bitter old man who at the end of his life is seeking to find some value in it after the many political and personal sacrifices he has made..." ("*Einladung*" 128).

[8] Hein acknowledges similarities between Racine's situation and his own: Racine "is dependent on patrons, and in order to do the work that is really important to him, he has to accept some unbearable things. Restrictions that conflict with his planned life and work. This surely applies to us in our time as well. If I am to accomplish certain important things — important to me, but larger than me as well — then I have to accept certain things that are unbearable, or let's say, not accept, but endure them" ("Wir werden es lernen müssen" 58). This succinct description of the position of the artist in an oppressive state applies even better to Hein than to his version of Racine, whose work actually seems to dry up as a consequence of his accommodations with power. Hein, however, successfully took on the task of the chronicler once circumstances temporarily forced him to abandon the stage.

[9] Cf. Sevin, who ties the narrative complexity and ambiguity of *Horns Ende* directly to the level of historical consciousness possessed (or lacked) by East Germans in the 1980s. The task of the reader, when confronted with the fragmentary picture of Guldenberger crimes such as the murder of Frau Gohl, the denunciation of Herr Horn, and the persecution of the Gypsies, is to investigate in him- or herself continuities with the German past (203). However, I would resist Sevin's near-dismissal of Kruschkatz's historical relativism, which, though entangled with the Bürgermeister's destructive opportunism, I think is not wholly discredited by events in the novel. As will become clear from the explication below of Horn's and Spodeck's views about history, Hein does not oppose relativism to absolute truth. Though no relativist in a moral sense, Hein seems to propose an understanding of history that emphatically renounces any appeal to absolute reality. "History" is always something more relevant to the present than the past; consequently its "truth" is a political construct, a space for the working of *Öffentlichkeit*.

[10] Yet Spodeck's admiration for Horn exists side by side with the conviction that he died a coward, in disgrace (*HE* 193). Kruschkatz and Thomas also label Horn a coward, a fact discussed below.

[11] Perhaps deadline pressures accont for the far simpler view of the reviewer at the *Frankfurter Allgemeine Zeitung*, who describes Kruschkatz as one who "always represents as political necessity that which furthers his career" (Wittstock).

[12] McKnight similarly describes Kruschkatz as a would-be materialist who cannot escape some taint of idealism, as opposed to Spodeck, a pure idealist who thinks (falsely) that he can detach himself from society, that is, the material world ("Ein Mosaik" 421).

[13] Hein fully endorses this declaration by Horn ("'Wir werden es lernen müssen'" 65–6).

[14] Claas notes that the mirror metaphor in Spodeck's remarks recalls Thomas's attempts to see past his own gazing eye into the infinite series of images produced by a pair of mirrors: "'It didn't work. I always ended up looking myself in the eye.' Only the perspective of the viewer, leading back to the viewer, can be seen on the direct path of the reflection." Analogously, Spodeck believes that the partial view afforded us of history always will be taken falsely as the whole truth, the holes filled in according to individual predilection. "The perspective puzzle occupying the half-grown Thomas turns up again in this conversation as a problem of historical truth" (17).

[15] This view of history as an interpretive activity may indicate how Hein understands the assumption by Benjamin that the photographs occupy a special status as "pieces of evidence about the historical process": Benjamin is not naively assuming that photography objectively records historic fact, rather he senses the importance of the *illusion* of objectivity it offers, and perceives in the habits of moviegoers a critical consciousness capable of resolving that illusion into technique, and thence into historical process, that is, class struggle. For Benjamin, photography is merely the most shameless attempt to date to present a historically conditioned worldview as "objective" and "natural." The question remains, as Hein shows in his essay, of whether or not a new critical consciousness necessarily accompanies the new technical medium.

[16] Münz harshly condemns Schlötel for this anarchistic stance (300–301), but in that play as well as in *Horns Ende*, Hein seems to take a more complex view of his idealist-anarchists. Their status as victims is real, regardless of the degree to which it is self-victimization. Indeed, as the discussion of *Der fremde Freund* showed, characters' motivations are sometimes inseparable from the historical and social realities that shape them.

[17] Löffler warns his East German readers (and more importantly, his ideologically-minded colleagues) against misunderstanding Horn as a model for Thomas or anyone else:

> The task of remembering Horn, used as a way into the process of remembering generally, inclines the reader to directly and constantly infer a connection between Horn and the biography of the narrator. The danger lies in mistaking Horn, who is seen only through the eyes of others, for a

moral and political standard by which these others can be judged. He is
no such standard. His retreat into truth as an abstraction not only renders
him incapable of resisting the political intrigues against him, it also renders him incapable of forming human bonds. As if the character who disappoints both Thomas and Gertrude could be taken for a role model. Of
course, the radical consequences of his life do compel the others to look
more sharply at themselves — but not to measure themselves against him!
(1486)

Horn is, of course, a more complex and contradictory character than Löffler indicates; he is indeed *partly* a model. Löffler, however, probably wants to mollify the hostile authorities who had largely succeeded in keeping mention of *Horns Ende* out of the East German press.

[18] Darnton gives an interesting description of the behind-the-scenes maneuvering that led to the book's publication (213).

[19] It is interesting to note how Milan Kundera handles such a confrontation with the meaninglessness of imprisonment. In *The Joke*, the protagonist suffers through a similar incident and similar imprisonment, except that for Kundera, the joke really is meaningless, really is a joke, and the attempt to get revenge boomerangs into a joke on the perpetrator. In Hein, the joke is that there is no rationality to this society (including at the end, when a rational man loses and Dallow wins). Only the reader becomes aware of the joke, which is what makes this book a satire while Kundera's is a farce. Yet both writers are talking about the same thing — the impossibility of being rational, of making sense, of living in a meaningful way in a society based on arbitrary power. Even a joke needs a reference point of rationality to be effective.

5: Chronicling the Cold War's Losers and Winners

Christoph Hein's *Wende*

IN RETROSPECT, THERE WERE SURELY SIGNS THAT the edifice of Soviet satellite states was growing unstable during the late 1980s, but nobody (save lunatics and visionaries) predicted the fall of the East Bloc anytime soon. I spent six months in the GDR during 1988 and witnessed a stable society in which most people had come to terms with the political system and were busily carrying on their lives much as they would in any industrialized society. The meagerness of the East German public sphere, of what is sometimes termed civil society, was counterbalanced in people's personal lives by carefully cultivated networks of friends and connections, draining energy, admittedly, from the economy and from the potential for political reform, but contributing to a rather benign coziness in everyday life that had (and has) no parallel in the West. The government, for its part, maintained a modus vivendi dependent on expulsion of the most annoying dissidents to a welcoming Federal Republic, combined with creeping liberalization at home in such areas as Western travel, artistic expression, and economic reform. Political life remained tightly controlled by the Socialist Unity Party (SED), as for the last four decades, and there was no organized political reform movement. The Lutheran church was a forum for such extra-governmental political discourse as was tolerated, most of it having to do with environmentalism and nuclear disarmament. The theater was the only other place where uncontrolled crowds of people gathered, and so it, too, was an oasis of independent thought, however cautious. Corruption and cronyism infested government and working life, but people responded for the most part with more cynicism and resignation than outrage. Political stability relied on an extensive system of secret police surveillance, but its scope was at the time unsuspected or at least disbelieved by all but the most paranoid citizens. All year people watched in disgust as the East German Politburo resisted the winds of reform blowing from Mikhail Gorbachev's Soviet Union, saying little and doing less, since public praise for Glasnost and Perestroika would have quickly interested the police.

When I returned to the GDR for a few weeks in the spring of 1989, I noticed at once a major change of mood. I heard complaints everywhere about shortages of consumer products, of food even, which seemed oddly to contradict my own observations. There was outspoken disgust about the government's business-as-usual handling of public life, particularly the planned "Pfingsttreffen," a huge, Party-organized youth rally, which was accurately described as a waste of time and generally spoken of with the nominal adjective "Scheiß-" affixed to it. At the May Day rally on Alexanderplatz in Berlin, I saw people in the crowds wearing Gorbachev buttons (like my own — a somewhat deflating experience), and at the university student club Moritzbastei in Leipzig, I was able to buy Gorbachev stickers for a mark apiece. Soon after my visit, the local elections held across the country provoked unaccustomed outrage when the usual vote tallies (on the order of ninety-nine to one in support of the regime) were made public.

What was new, in short, was a level of disgust that finally was overriding the decades-long cultivation of caution and silence characteristic of neo-Stalinist society. The complaints about shortages were indicative of a reduced tolerance for the shabby status quo, as confirmed by the willingness to openly support Gorbachev. People were so angry at the government that they no longer feared it. The anger, of course, was the product of another year's immobility in the GDR while the Soviet Union publicly redefined itself in ever more astonishing ways. The frozen conservatism of the Politburo, epitomized by its apparently senile chief Erich Honecker, was beginning to look too ludicrous to be taken seriously. The rules, clearly, were changing: the Soviets seemed to be proving that radical change *was* possible in socialism, and East Germans were anxious to take part.

The regime's death knell (though it was not immediately recognized as such) came in May 1989, when the Hungarian government announced it would open its border with Austria. Proving that they, too, had succumbed to a kind of malaise, the GDR authorities failed to halt tourist travel to Hungary (which would also have meant restricting access to *all* of the GDR's neighbors). Over the summer, a stream of East German refugees grew to a torrent as they took advantage of the new escape route to the West, bleeding the country dry of its labor force and disrupting the economy. The first organized opposition group, Neues Forum, was formed in September — and tolerated by a visibly helpless regime. With the arrival of autumn, peaceful weekly demonstrations began in Leipzig and spread to other major cities. Television audiences around the world watched as hundreds of refugees sought asylum in the West German embassy in Prague; to stop the humiliating spectacle, the GDR eventually granted them safe passage to the West. The GDR's fortieth anniversary celebrations were capped on October 6 with a visit by Gorbachev, whose show of support for Honecker consisted of an assurance that German problems would be solved in Germany — an ambiguous stance, implying that no Soviet military backing could be expected, and that Honecker was on his own. The presence of the highly popular Gorbachev, combined with public contempt for the scripted jubilation accompanying the anniversary celebration, swelled the ranks of street protestors and drew worldwide press attention, greatly embarrassing the regime. In response, police beat and arrested peaceful demonstrators in Berlin and elsewhere on October 7 and 8 in the worst civil unrest since the failed workers' revolt of 1953 (which had been quelled with Soviet armor). Growing dissension within the Politburo brought a halt to these aggressive police interventions before the next planned demonstration in Leipzig, on October 9, though Honecker remained adamant in his opposition to reform. Ultimately, under circumstances that will likely remain mysterious, the Politburo removed Honecker from his leadership position on October 18 and installed the younger Egon Krenz. The new, more liberal regime entered into talks with Neues Forum and allowed a million-participant demonstration to take place unmolested on Alexanderplatz on November 4. Tentative moves toward relaxation of the hated travel restrictions led to the sudden and unplanned collapse of border controls on the evening of November 9, marking the effective end of the Berlin Wall. No longer isolated from the capitalist world by troops and concrete, the GDR would cease to exist inside of a year, as it was absorbed by its Western neighbor.

Christoph Hein played an important role in the *Wende*, as the GDR's largely peaceful revolution came to be called. A beneficiary of the 1980s' gradual loosening of censorship, Hein was also partly responsible for the change, having remained in the scant but courageous ranks of critical GDR artists who refused during the dark days of the late 1970s to be silenced or hounded into exile. As early as 1982, with the lecture later published as "Öffentlich arbeiten," Hein was using meetings of the state-sanctioned Schriftstellerverband [Writers' Union] as a forum to attack the GDR's repression of free speech, citing not the violation of any abstract or unalienable right, but the damage done to society by such policies. His books continued to appear throughout the decade, and by fall of 1987 his new play *Passage* was enjoying a triple premiere in Dresden, Essen, and Zürich, yet, at that very moment, he was again lambasting the regime in a speech before the tenth Writer's Congress of the GDR titled "Die Zensur ist überlebt, nutzlos, paradox, menschenfeindlich, volksfeindlich, ungesetzlich und strafbar" [Censorship is outdated, useless, paradoxical, anti-human, anti-social, illegal, and punishable.]

In early 1989, two major events in Hein's career took on larger significance as the political ground began to shift. The first was the publication of *Der Tangospieler*, a book that would have stood out as a remarkable event even had it not been Hein's last novel of the GDR era. The novel's most obvious message was its condemnation of a now-familiar Hein figure, the *Aussteiger*, the social outcast or drop-out — the sort of person, usually an intellectual, who becomes the perfect servant of the state precisely because he thinks himself "free" from political entanglements. But *Der Tangospieler* was also problematic for other, more pressing reasons: it shows a pair of Stasi agents going about their unsavory business, and it contains an account of the Warsaw Pact invasion of Czechoslovakia in 1968, making it the first — and last — novel published in the GDR dealing with that event. The book had survived stiff resistance in the Culture Ministry. In his remarkable account of the inside workings of East German censorship, historian Robert Darnton describes how mid-level East German literary officials managed to get *Der Tangospieler* into print only by issuing an authorization on their own initiative, creating a *fait accompli* while preserving their sympathetic boss's "deniability" in dealings with his superiors in the ministry and the Party Central Committee (213). The story of the book's publication indicates how far Mikhail Gorbachev's reforms had tempted even the guardians of the East German social order to stretch the existing political limits. It could never have been published if the author had been less prominent or the narrative style less couched in satirical indirectness, which Hein disguised as objective description of a bygone era. Hein plainly had conceived of *Der Tangospieler* as a perestroika piece and had designed it to straddle the precise limit of what could be openly said. The events of the novel are a veiled commentary on the arbitrariness of the SED regime, coupled with a searing portrayal of the complicity of GDR intellectuals in their country's crimes. In choosing the end of the Dubček regime as the historical background for the novel, Hein was also returning to the formative event in his own political life, the moment at which he claims to have lost faith in the promise of a just socialism (Hein, "Kennen"). Thus the book recapitulates and interprets Hein's twenty years as a politically engaged writer, while diagnosing the ills that would lead to the GDR's collapse sooner than anybody, including Hein, imagined.[1]

The other, equally portentous event was the production of *Die Ritter der Tafelrunde* in Dresden. The play revisits the legends of the Arthurian knights and their search for the Holy Grail, focusing this time on the aftermath of the grand early exploits, once the heroes and heroines have grown old and quarrelsome. The play is a farce at the expense of the old warriors whose view of reality has become fossilized, hence a commentary on the fate of ideologues and their ideologies. The action takes place in the room housing the Round Table, which is now in disrepair and nearly deserted. The knights bicker among themselves about how to carry on, and some have given up the quest completely. The women bemoan the stupidity of the men and the loss of their own beauty. The younger generation, represented by Arthur's son Mordred, appears destined to overturn all of Arthur's achievements once it assumes power, yet Mordred has no idea what changes he might institute. And we learn that meanwhile, outside Camelot, Arthur and his knights have become objects of contempt instead of awe. Not even the threat of impending ecological disaster can rouse the embittered old men from their paralysis in the face of outcomes they never anticipated. The play ends with Arthur resignedly acknowledging that Mordred's day has come, and that, like it or not, it will be his responsibility to find a path into the future. The central philosophical burden of the play is the nature and meaning of the Grail, which appears to signify any ideal or utopia toward which human beings must strive in order to remain human, even when they know they can never attain it. The failure of Arthur and his knights to locate the Grail thus appears less tragic than merely inevitable, but so too is it inevitable that the whole process of pursuing the ideal, whether understood as social justice or personal fulfillment, will continue. The desperation of the knights, their fear that everything they have lived for is slipping away, turns out to be a parochial, if understandable, illusion based on limited perspective. Thus the play is at once an allegory for the moribund state of the GDR in the late 1980s, and an exploration of the role of utopian thinking in human experience, regardless of time or place. As such, it might be understood to speak to the fortunes of political idealism and social justice in the West as well as the East, and to the cyclic struggles that result when one generation must hand over power to a new one with wholly different experiences and views.[2]

    Hein himself, meanwhile, found himself lionized in the waning months of 1989 as a public spokesman for reform. Following the Politburo shakeup on October 18, demonstrations across the GDR had grown ever larger, culminating in the November 4 demonstration on Alexanderplatz that by some estimates drew more than a million people. Hein was one among a decidedly mixed crowd of orators (ranging from reform leaders to Christa Wolf to Politburo spokesman Günter

Schabowski to former espionage chief Marcus Wolf). He staked out a position in support of democratic socialism:

> Dear no-longer-voiceless fellow citizens!
>
> We all have a lot of work to do, and little time for it. The structures of this society must be changed if it is to become democratic and socialist. There are no alternatives.
>
> We must also speak of dirty hands, of dirty histories. Here, too, is work for the society and the media. Featherbedding, corruption, misuse of office, theft of public property — all this must be investigated, and the investigation must extend to the leadership of the state. That is where it must begin.
>
> Let us be careful not to confuse the euphoria of these days with the changes that we still have to make. The enthusiasm, the demonstrations were and are helpful and necessary, but they are not substitutes for the work at hand. Let us not be fooled by our own enthusiasm: we haven't yet succeeded. The cow still isn't off the ice. And there are sufficient forces that oppose change, that fear a new society and have reason to fear it.
>
> I wish for us to think now of an old man, an old and probably very lonely man. I am speaking of Erich Honecker. This man had a dream that he was ready to go to prison for.[3] Then he was given the chance to make his dream a reality. It was not a very good chance, because its midwives were defeated fascism and victorious Stalinism. A society took shape that had little to do with socialism. Instead, it was — and remains — distinguished by bureaucracy, demagoguery, spying, abuse of power, passivity, and crime. A system took shape before which many good, intelligent, honest people had to abase themselves if they wished to continue living here. And no one knew any longer how to proceed against this system, how to dismantle it.
>
> And I believe that even for this old man, our society is scarcely the fulfillment of a dream. Even he, standing at the helm of the state, responsible above all others for its successes but also for its mistakes, its sins of omission, and its crimes — even he was virtually powerless when confronting its encrusted structures.
>
> I call this man to mind for one reason: as a warning, lest we now also create structures before which we will someday find ourselves powerless. Let us create a democratic society founded on the rule of law and subject to the review of law. A socialism which doesn't make the word into a caricature. A society tailored to human beings, not one where human beings are subordinated to the system. This will mean a lot of work for all of us, much of it tedious detail work, worse than knitting.
>
> One word more. Success, as the saying goes, has many fathers. Obviously, there are many who believe that the changes in the GDR

are already successful, because many are now revealing themselves as the fathers of this success. Peculiar fathers, reaching high into the leadership of the state. I think, however, that our memory is not so bad that we have forgotten who really did begin dismantling the all-powerful system. Who ended the sleep of reason. It was the reason of the streets, the demonstrations by ordinary people.

(Hein, *Als Kind* 175–177)

Hein's independent leftist position, which called for the people of the GDR to confront and solve their own problems and to preserve the positive features of their society, and which combined rage at the SED leadership with strong suspicion of the West, was typical of the intellectual and artistic class that founded the Neues Forum. As the GDR's first officially recognized independent political organization, Neues Forum participated in the rump SED government in the "round tables" that briefly governed the country, and made up the constituency of the vaguely socialist coalition "Bündnis 90" that was soundly thrashed in the 1990 elections that installed a pro-unification GDR government. Hein's political views amid the whirlwind of the *Wende* were entirely consistent with his essayistic remarks over the previous ten years, in which he had been calling for a more democratic socialism instead of a rapprochement with what he saw as a rapacious and militaristic West. The realization during November and December 1989 that a majority of the citizens of the GDR no longer wanted socialism in any form, and wished to join economically and politically with the Federal Republic as quickly as possible, came as a huge disappointment, though it can hardly have been a surprise to the playwright who had imagined the disaffected post-socialist youth Mordred in *Die Ritter der Tafelrunde*.[4] Hein persisted gamely in his assertion of his right, as a citizen of the GDR, to participate in the writing of his own history and in arraigning the crimes mentioned in his speech; most notably, he served on the Ausschuß zur Ermittlung der polizeilichen Übergriffe vom 7. Oktober 1989, the citizens' committee investigating the violence of police authorities against peaceful demonstrators.[5] But clearly, Hein's own dream of a free, self-determining GDR — politically tempered by the experience of forty years of Stalinism, and free of the overwhelming force of West German materialism and its supporting capitalist ideology — would never be realized. With unification, the social position and role of the artist (like every other aspect of East German society) would be radically revised, from that of uniquely positioned social critic and public intellectual, to, on the face of it, a supplier of products utterly beholden to market forces. Changed, too, for an East German critic of ideology in the new whole-German state, was his primary subject matter: Stalinism was replaced by capitalism, a much more complicated target, and one with which he was less intimately familiar. Like his fellow citizens, Hein had no choice but to reinvent himself and his social function.

Against the new victors of history: Hein's attack on the West

Clearly, with capitalism triumphant, it was hazardous for writers (or critics) to show sympathy with the losers of history, as shown by the journalistic campaign against Christa Wolf (which was exacerbated by proof that she had herself written reports on fellow writers for the secret police in the early 1960s). This was merely the first of many similar attacks on the reputations of prominent figures of the GDR.[6] Although Hein's integrity remained untouched by any such allegations, his outspoken anti-Western sentiments, his uncompromising calls for social justice (which he was not afraid to label "socialism"), and the long-term anti-ideological project of his writing were poorly suited to resonate with the newly-dominant orthodoxies. (However, this dissonance was nothing new — it was, after all, as an opposition figure, as a challenger of political limits, that Hein made his mark in the GDR.) Certainly the prevailing German political mood had a distorting effect on the way Hein's most recent work, *Die Ritter der Tafelrunde*, was received in late 1989 and early 1990. Even before the *Wende*, and despite the general applicability of the themes of idealism, delusion, and disillusion evident in the play, *Die Ritter* was understood too frequently as a straightforwardly hostile allegory of the GDR's leadership. Governmental permission to produce the play had come only at the last minute after a delay of many months; Hein defended himself against suspicions that the knights were modeled on Communist Party Secretary Erich Honecker and his cronies by denying that he would have stooped to the flattery suggested by such an analogy ("Das Geld," 226). Nevertheless, the timing of the play's premiere did nothing to discourage the view that Arthur was Honecker, and the Round Table was socialism. The desire of some of the knights to solve their problems by killing off the younger generation was horribly paralleled in Tienanmen Square in May 1989, just a month after the play opened, and the impotence of an aging, doctrinaire leadership would be copied by the reality of the GDR in October and November. Hein soon acquired the status not just of political dissident but of prophet — a mixed blessing, since the immediate result was a great deal of public interest in the play, but at the cost of it being understood in rather crude terms. Karla Kochta, a dramaturge at the Dresden State Theater where the play was first produced, relates how a group of West Berlin literature and theater students came in early 1990 to what they expected to be the GDR's "perestroika play," hence an already musty bit of history, only to be puzzled that the East German audience was responding to the issue of utopia as though it were still a living concern. The Western students were also surprised that Mordred didn't smash the table to pieces at the end of the play, thereby announcing the end of a failed ideology. Kochta's answer, like Hein's, is that the failure of an ideology does not mean the end of hope for a better world (Kochta, 225).

The aspects of *Die Ritter* that have relevance to the post-Cold-War era are precisely those which early critics of the play ignored or failed to grasp. The reviewer for the West Berlin *tageszeitung* was typical in judging the play a political allegory pure and simple, and then criticizing it for datedness and inadequacy to the torrent of real political events sweeping Germany in the fall of 1989 (Mehr). *Theater heute* complained that the allegory was too heavy-handed, but that, puzzlingly, the Dresden audiences seemed to respond to it (Krug). The problem in each case may be traceable to inattention to Hein's other plays and novels, in all of which the place of action, often enough the GDR, is partly incidental: the popularity of *Der fremde Freund*, for example, resulted not from any West German taste for GDR-exotica, but from shocked recognition of the book's depiction of alienated life in a modern urban-industrial society. Similarly, Hein's novel *Horns Ende* explored the German, not just the East German, willingness to forget history, and Hein's most successful play to date, *Ah Q*, has been produced throughout Europe because of its insights about the fate of individuals in all revolutions, not just German or even socialist ones. *Die Ritter der Tafelrunde* is likewise a play about a society without a future, where old values have ceased to be relevant, the ruling class lacks the flexibility or creativeness to change, and the younger generation is plagued by hopelessness. It doesn't take a sociologist to point out that these are also characteristics, to varying degrees, of West German and American society, not just endemic maladies of the defunct East Bloc. Thus West German critic Antje Janssen-Zimmermann has argued cogently that the play should be seen as a meditation on the fact that material prosperity does not necessarily result in happiness; alienation is always with us, and Hein expects members of his audiences to apply the questions raised in the play to *themselves now*. The readiness of West Germans to ignore the contemporary relevance of Hein's concern with idealism and personal moral choices speaks volumes about the reactionary political climate of unified Germany in the early 1990s. The notion that the end of the Cold War somehow meant the end of ideological struggle merely reflects the Western point of view: ideology no longer exists, because what we do isn't ideology, it's just the plain, practical truth, like, for example, the practical need to seal our borders against the immigration of poor people.[7]

Hein's first post-*Wende* work was a collection of *Wende*-era speeches and essays, *Als Kind habe ich Stalin gesehen* (another and partly overlapping collection, *Die Mauern von Jerichow*, followed in 1996). Meanwhile, readers and critics waited expectantly to see what his post-GDR fiction and plays would look like. To many, the first indications were a bitter disappointment. It had been imagined that Hein would dust off all his formerly unpublishable manuscripts and treat the reading public to some serious postmortem muckraking about the evils of the GDR. However, as one eastern German weekly noted, "Hein settled his accounts with the GDR during its lifetime" (Kopka). True to form, Hein's new efforts concerned the West and the present-day East. And these treatments of new material proved as annoying to the establishment critics of the West as the earlier works had to the establishment critics of the East, even eliciting similar charges: that Hein doesn't really know what he is talking about when he describes the West so unflatteringly; that he is dreaming up wayward fantasies; that his characters are unrealistic, implausible, atypical.[8] Where Hein once risked being accused of anti-socialist provocation when he depicted alienated, unhappy citizens of the GDR, he now risked being accused of anti-Western stereotyping for depicting successful western Germans as arrogant, greedy, and ruthless.

The first piece of fiction Hein wrote after the *Wende* originally bore an English title, "Bridge Freezes Before Roadway" (1990), a phrase Hein doubtless noted during his visit to Kentucky in 1987. Amid political change such as the GDR was experiencing, it is tempting to read the title as a metaphor of a hazardous transition between the neo-Stalinist past and an uncertain future. The content of the story, however, makes it difficult to apply such a convenient political interpretation. In the story, a young female academic interviews a middle-aged former economist about his memories of a recently deceased mutual colleague. The men had been friends and rivals during their student days, and ultimately we learn that Rieder, the subject of the interview, had authored an anonymous letter of denunciation against his friend in order to secure for himself the post of institute director. This piece of workaday GDR office politics backfired, with the rival getting the institute job and pursuing a brilliant career, and Rieder leaving academia.

After emigrating to the West, Rieder becomes a successful businessman, and a thoroughly unpleasant person: bitter, vulgar, self-important, misogynistic, manipulative, and unscrupulous in evading his interviewer's questions while he tries to seduce her. The story ends with the tables turned: Rieder learns from the interviewer that his and his rival's shared mentor had privately determined that Rieder should be rejected for the institute job because of unspecified weaknesses in his character. Rieder is left trying vainly to convince the woman (and himself) that his luxurious lifestyle is sufficient recompense for his ruined scholarly career and distorted personal relationships.

Rieder is like a number of earlier Hein characters who struggled to deny or justify a failed life by pointing to their successful adjustment to society or their material comfort. He lives in splendid near-isolation, cut off from his past, from friends and family, and from society — a condition that Hein regards as pathological and even dangerous. He is also the first of a series of evil-capitalist-caricatures that would dominate each of Hein's next two post-*Wende* works, the novel *Das Napoleon-Spiel* (1993) and the play *Randow* (1994). The conjunction in "Bridge Freezes Before Roadway" between old and new emphases may illuminate the meaning of the seeming caricatures in subsequent works. The socially isolated characters of Hein's GDR-era writing translate easily into criminal freebooters in a West dedicated to the maximization of profit. As the title of the story suggests, all transitions are hazardous, and therefore the transition from socialism to capitalism can be expected to produce monsters. Rieder's own life serves as a bleak emblem of the *Wende*: the most corrupt and antisocial socialists have the best qualifications for success in the West, where greed and self-interest have the status of civic virtues. The capitalist takeover of the East will make good use both of those who emigrated and of the weak who stayed behind.

Hein's 1993 novel *Das Napoleon-Spiel* presents an even more scandalous picture of capitalism and one of its indigenous characters — this time a genuine monster.[9] Hein's protagonist, Manfred Wörle, also was initially an East German, his family having settled in Thuringia as refugees after the war, but Wörle eventually moves to West Berlin in order to study law. He builds a successful practice and later becomes a legal advisor to the West Berlin city government. Though Wörle is intensely involved in civic affairs, he always functions at a psychological remove from other people, who never suspect that the devoted public servant is actually a self-consciously nihilistic adventurer. Wörle describes himself as a "player" or gambler. Oppressed by the meaninglessness of his life, an emptiness that cannot be filled by women, money, or success, Wörle finds satisfaction only in the excitement of "games." Wörle's games start small but become more elaborate. He is a small-time black marketeer in the GDR, he experiments with the gamesmanship inherent in trial law, and he advances to the playing field of politics. Finally, he decides to kill a man for sport. Wörle is evidently mad: he fancies himself a modern-day Napoleon, playing dispassionately with peoples' lives, hence the murder he plans is to be deliberately random, its victim analogous to an impersonal casualty of war. The narrative itself is Wörle's explanation of his actions to his lawyer while he awaits trial. As in Hein's earlier first-person narratives, much of the narrator's energy is devoted to specious rationalization of his outlook and behavior; one valid criticism of the book may be that the reasoning is less seductive here than in some of the other examples, so that Wörle strikes one merely as a monster, not as an object of ambivalent sympathy like Claudia or Kruschkatz.

Hein himself objects to any such dismissal of Wörle, returning to the notion of chronicling (that is, of objective, dispassionate description *sine ira et studio*) to argue that Wörle is due something more complex than simple moralizing:

> When I have a choice between precise chronicling and moralizing, I will always choose precision. Even when there may be immorality involved. There is great value in being asocial. The readers can moralize if they wish. I present the matter, and I entrust any judgments to the reader. Including the judgment of this character [Wörle]. I just find it boring to invent a character simply to condemn him. It seems stupid.
>
> (Hein, "Kennen")

Hein puts himself in the same category with Wörle when he equates chronicling with being "asocial," rather as a wartime photojournalist is asocial when he stands and photographs a dying person rather than helping him. Such immorality is not without its uses, he points out. The detached chronicler Hein sympathizes, then, with Wörle's detachment (as with Claudia's, etc.), and as this quotation further suggests, he even sympathizes with Wörle's fear of boredom, and the "games" he plays as ways of fending it off. Being a moralist is "boring" to Hein; having a moral, conventional life is "boring" to Wörle. As always, though, the claim of moral indifference is slightly disingenuous. An essential difference between Hein and Wörle is surely that Hein has a social and moral conscience lurking behind his actions and his work, whereas Wörle is totally empty. But more importantly, Hein refuses to exempt himself from whatever pathology plagues Wörle and, by extension, Germany as a whole:

> The man acts out of boredom. This is increasingly a problem in these wealthy societies and can only be explained by looking at the deformed state of civilization. The more basic needs are met, the more boredom. I am not interested in the moral aspect, but in how he got into this, and what interests him about it. How can it come to this. For a person out of the lower orders, as they say, this wouldn't have been a problem. (Hein, "Kennen")

Accordingly, the novel culminates in a brilliant scene where Wörle's individual act abruptly takes on socio-political significance. Wörle commits his murder while on a West Berlin subway train passing through one of the "ghost stations" lying below the streets of East Berlin. These stations were sealed at the time the Berlin Wall was built, in August 1961, and their ground-level entrances sprouted again through the pavement of East Berlin only after the *Wende*. The setting is particularly arresting for any of the millions of passengers who experienced that same train ride past those empty platforms: it was the experience of being in two worlds at once, but also in neither. The rationally planned irreality of this twilit no-man's land that thousands briefly inhabited every day is a more telling symbol of Germany than the more obvious Berlin Wall: what better place for an act of mad arrogance? It is tempting, furthermore, to interpret this scene as an allegory of the fascist past underlying both Germanies, the site of atrocities that have been pushed out of the consciousness of the divided, speciously rational daylight world.

Hein's use of Wörle as an exemplar of Western values and ugly German history was clearly meant as a provocation to a western German public burdened with invincible confidence in its economic and cultural superiority. It provoked howls of displeasure from critics who dismissed Wörle as an aberrant figure who, though *possible*, was in no way *representative* of Western society.[10] (The argument perfectly mirrors complaints by advocates of Socialist Realism that Hein's unhappy East Germans were atypical of the New Socialist Man.)[11] A minor perversity introduced at the end of the novel — after the *Wende*, Wörle hires his abused, disinherited, and professionally failed brother, who had stayed in the East, as an all-purpose goon — points to the next step in Hein's critique of Western Man: the post-*Wende*, colonialist phase. Having established the nature of the West, he sets about describing its conquest of the East. McKnight suspects an allegorical aspect to the novel (*Understanding Christoph Hein* 114), which would make it something of a departure from Hein's earlier work, and sees a connection between the book and the political activities in which Hein was involved during its writing, particularly the investigation of police attacks on peaceful demonstrators in October 1989:

> In such a context, the novel is a commentary on unscrupulous and arrogant behavior by men in power, presented as symptomatic of the time in which we live. Hein had always written about victims in the past and had usually done so with humor. This time, he turned his attention to a perpetrator, and his portrayal is totally devoid of humor. (133)[12]

Hein's first play written and produced after the *Wende,* a dramatization of a shady East German property transaction entitled *Randow,* also provoked loud charges of stereotyping, anti-Western bias, and crude tendentiousness. Eastern reviews were sympathetic to the play if sometimes critical of the production, while Western reviews were flatly hostile on both counts. The play juxtaposes two initially unrelated settings: first, the Randow Valley border region with Poland, where the local authorities are pressuring an artist, Anna Andress, to sell her choice piece of land, and where two illegally entering asylum-seekers turn up murdered; and second, Cologne and Berlin, where we see a lawyer, Fred P. Paul, guiding his right-hand-man in the East (Peter Stadel, a former Stasi officer) in the acquisition of potentially lucrative Eastern property. After an inconsequential attempt by a Western-born officer of the Federal Border Patrol to acquire Andress's property for himself, as well as other forms of harassment against her, such as the poisoning of her dog, Andress sells out, and the plot culminates, predictably enough, in the takeover of the Randow property by Paul and his shadowy backers, who have promised to use the land to create new jobs.

The critical response to the play was mixed. Some reviewers dismissed it as simplistic stereotyping and saw it as proof of the ongoing decay of talent from the former GDR. The *tageszeitung* described the play as preachy and boring, declaring it "not a comedy, but a blunder" (Walther), while *Die Zeit* panned it as a *Dallas*-style soap opera suffering from bad dialog and built around commonplaces such as "When two fight, the third wins" and "It's a thankless world" (Engler). The *Tagesspiegel* summed up the matter revealingly:

> The catastrophe of this play, an attempt to come to grips with hard reality that ends up merely serving the Eastern Anti-*Wessi*-Complex, has its parallels in the aesthetic debacle signified by the end of the GDR: namely, the disappearance of the drive toward innovative devices of encryption, an ugly and beautiful system of signs that existed between the author and public. All that remains now is an excessive obviousness that serves as compensation. As in this play: the *Ossis* are

wounded seekers, dubious victims even when perpetrators as well. They are represented by the exploded and dispersed family that ultimately is robbed of its house, or by pawns of the West like Voß [the Bürgermeister] or Stasi-Stadel. The *Wessis* themselves are either greedy scoundrels or barely-disguised Nazis — ideally, both at once.

(Schulz-Ojala)

The most striking feature of this particular critique is its longing for the Cold War game of interpretive hide-and-go-seek, an old favorite of Western critics which, by the way, Hein has repeatedly denounced. (Whatever one thinks about Hein's politics or art, nobody can accuse him of being nostalgic for the Cold War and it cultural arrangements!) The best rejoinder to this late echo of the *Literaturstreit* appeared in the *Deutsches Allgemeines Sonntagsblatt,* which characterized *Randow* as an irritating and uncomfortable play, but interpreted this merely as being Hein's procedure: refusing to approve the status quo, describing it dispassionately as a chronicler, and offering no solutions. The play represents a new phase in Hein's work only insofar as the end of the Cold War facilitates more nuanced reading than was formerly possible:

> This would be a good time to reconsider Christoph Hein's complex fictions, particularly his theatrical work, since Hein as a writer was never a mere GDR-phenomenon. They reveal surprising insights and new connections, precisely because they always used to be read one-dimensionally in light of circumstances in the GDR. The alienation effects have in fact sharpened. (Klunker)[13]

The complaints about stereotyping are, again, new versions of the earlier, GDR-era complaint that Hein peopled his works with unrepresentative (hence meaningless, insignificant) figures. After all, if one admits that monsters like *Das Napoleon-Spiel*'s Wörle are possible, it is hard to maintain that the characters in *Randow* are either impossible or particularly unusual. The two stock GDR figures, Bürgermeister Voß and Andress's estranged husband Rudi Krappmann, are scarcely implausible, the one being a small time politician with a talent for bending before every political wind, the other a drunken ne'er-do-well baffled by the post- (as by the pre-) *Wende* world. The Western villain, Paul, likes to minimize German historical guilt, uses the word "patriotism" as though it meant *Führerprinzip,* and denies that anything as mundane as love of money motivates his Eastern undertakings — again, none of these characteristics is very remarkable. And even if we grant that Paul is one-dimensional, a definite bad guy, how much do we really care about his inner life? Externally he is a cynical, pompous opportunist, and for the Eastern citizens touched by his financial machinations, the external is what matters. Hein is perfectly capable of rounding-out characters like Paul or Voß, as his earlier works prove, but here he has decided not to. In an interview, when asked about the harshness of the play and its lack of hope, he replied:

> That obviously means a gain in realism, then. Hope has something to do with utopia, of course, and when that's all over, lost, irrecoverable, then we draw closer to a hopeless, utopia-free reality. Which is also an advantage, a genuine advance. I think that the play corresponds to the present situation — as I see it. ("Mit etwas Rückgrat")

Hein's claim of increased realism might well be taken with a grain of salt, for it can be argued that the apparent realism of his prose was never realistic at all. "Realism" is founded on an assumption that reality is directly accessible through surface detail, and that this detail is ultimately the only truth. Hein, on the other hand, provides a painstaking depiction of reality in order to show that the truth is hidden, elsewhere, obscured by ideological illusion and the universal desire to forget unpleasant memories, either in individuals or by whole societies. The GDR, for example, could not be depicted realistically, because it never "really" existed: it was an ideological construct through and through, and its truth was not to be found in surface details. Hein's prose attempted to capture and reveal the ideological fantasies inscribed in those surface manifestations. And as it turns out, this method can also be fruitfully applied to less obviously ideological societies. If all social experience is mediated by ideology, the realistic depiction of a western German character is no less ideologically interesting than that of an eastern one.

Reactions to *Das Napoleon-Spiel* and *Randow* suggest that Hein's writerly project has collided with the Western project of erasing all things Eastern, a process that often resembles the consolidation of a colonial hegemony. Events in Germany are showing how culture enables, enacts, and reflects the structures or mechanisms of power at a moment of revolutionary change. As the process of colonization proceeds, ideology must deflect real though arbitrary differences of power by allegorizing and rationalizing them in a manner that favors stable colonial rule. Through the sixties, seventies, and eighties, Eastern dissident or quasi-dissident intellectuals were understood in the West as members of a common humanity, or at least a common Germanness, which was embodied in Western democracy and suppressed by Soviet Communism. The Western political and economic triumph following 1989 necessitated a redistribution of symbolic categories: the *difference* which had been denied during the Cold War (when all differences were subsumed by the controlling one of Democracy vs. Communism, with

Germany as a special and tragic case) suddenly became useful, once reified as a stereotype, as a tool for exploitation. Just when one could have reasonably expected the East-West difference to become irrelevant, it was in fact rediscovered and exaggerated for new political profit. The East quickly and bizarrely became a site of absolute difference (figured, indeed, in all the ways that the West has traditionally figured the East, whether the Muslim world, or the Far East, or even Russia — as passive, effeminate, sentimental, irresponsible, irrational, feckless, evil.) In this figural world, the failed culture of the East had to be completely discredited and annihilated from memory, clearing space for the superior, successful culture of the West that had so long battled the decadent Russian influence on its eastern flank, and effecting a symbolic implementation of simultaneous economic and political shifts. At the same time that Christa Wolf was being portrayed as a Communist stooge and a literary hack, East German agricultural production was left rotting in the fields and East German industrial capacity was being liquidated by the Treuhandanstalt (the federal agency commissioned to privatize publicly-owned East German property), making room in both cases for the expansion of Western production into the new Eastern market.

After the fall:
Hein's recent short fiction

Hein's *Wende*-stamped writing (notably *Das Napoleon-Spiel* and *Randow*) has been succeeded by fiction that appears to seek a new equilibrium after the tumultuous events immediately following the collapse of the East Bloc and the sharp literary response to them. If Hein can be accused (perhaps with some justice) of vilifying the West *mit Haß und Eifer* through the creation of characters like Manfred Wörle or Fred P. Paul, the same cannot be said of the most recent books, *Exekution eines Kalbes* (1994) and *Von allem Anfang an* (1997), which take stock of Hein's pre-existing repertoire of chronicling techniques, and begin to apply them to the cultural scene of post-Cold War Germany. Beyond this, Hein has begun experimenting with surrealist allegory in his short fiction, while returning even more recently to the autobiographical material that informed the picture of 1950s GDR life in *Horns Ende*. This simultaneous exploration of past material and future forms has met with considerably more positive critical response than the more obviously topical work from the early nineties, solidifying Hein's reputation as the dominant literary voice of Germany's new federal states.

Hein's collection of short fiction *Exekution eines Kalbes* provides an interesting comparison to his earlier short-story volume, *Einladung zum Lever Bourgeois*. The collection is composed of stories written between 1977 and 1990, arranged in roughly chronological order, and thus providing an extraordinary literary-historical document across two decades of turbulent political change. The early stories look, indeed, as if they could have appeared in *Einladung,* while the later ones explore new possibilities opened by the collapse of the GDR and its system of censorship. The unusual diversity of the pieces set a difficult task for reviewers struggling to find a contemporary cultural framework in which to place (or entomb?) such a historically tortured book.

After the extreme annoyance provoked by *Das Napoleon-Spiel* a year earlier, *Exekution* appeared to slightly warmer reviews, a fact which can profitably be viewed in light of Hein's dictum that criticism is primarily self-disclosure. What the West German critics hated (insolent criticisms of the West by an Easterner) was less in evidence, and what they loved (confirmations of the miserable state of GDR society) was again a major theme. Yet despite a consensus that the stories were technically masterful, for most reviewers the book was either too political or not political enough, with little agreement as to specifics. What unfolded was a series of attempts to map Hein across some available historical/political grid, and when this failed, to blame the author. The *Süddeutsche Zeitung* tried to fit Hein within a literary version of convergence theory (the view that the two Germanies had become less different through time) by characterizing Hein as a Protestant counterpart to the Catholic West German novelist Heinrich Böll, both of them "old-fashioned social critics" (Krumbholz). Betraying an extreme insistence on the difference of the GDR and the interpretive centrality of the *Wende*, *Der Spiegel* complained that the dating of the stories was too coyly imprecise, "As if today, in 1994, it were already a matter of complete indifference whether an East Berlin writer wrote down his stories in 1977 or 1991" ("Ein Leben"). The *Neue Zürcher Zeitung* argued the opposite view, that the before-and-after question is no longer of much interest, the East German milieu of the stories is a mildly exotic but non-essential background, and that literature of "artistic quality" displayed classical technical virtues free from place and time (von Matt). This view led to special praise for the collection's most surreal stories, "Ein älterer Herr, Federleicht" and "Moses Tod," yet these same stories came in for sharp criticism from the *Frankfurter Rundschau* as excessively symbolic, even though the reviewer also plays down the importance of the stories' East Germanness or lack of it (Hüfner). The *Frankfurter Allgemeine Zeitung* dismisses Hein as an unoriginal imitator of Boccaccio, Kleist, Hebel, and Brecht, whose only real stylistic innovation is boredom; moreover, the reason that Hein is so boring and humorless is that he learned to write in an "unfree situation" (Seibt). *Die Zeit* renders a similar verdict, calling the stories "lifeless," and complaining that Hein is too much the (again) Protestant moralist. The reviewer sums up with this muddled assessment:

> He tells too little of politics and history to make us interested in lingering there, and too little of the abjectness of his heroes to make us care about them. One cannot help suspecting that we are dealing with an author who is more interested in the existential state of depression than the depravity of politics . . . . He should give it a rest . . . . He should worry less about his convictions and more about aesthetics.
>
> (Isenschmid)

The one clear conclusion to draw from all this is that the critics know not what they want. In the uncertain post-Cold War cultural landscape, first there was reaction (the *Kritikerstreit*), and later, as that venom faded in strength, puzzlement as to what happens next. Someone who writes like Hein is an embarrassment: he carries over too much from the GDR to be politically trustworthy, and too much from the nineteenth century to be aesthetically trustworthy. The critics seem unable to find the point of most of the stories — what, then, should a point look like? Baffled by a loss of old ideological and literary categories, conservative critics in particular demand an aesthetically pure, apolitical literature (as if such a thing were possible or desirable), while continuing to read Eastern authors exclusively as political allegorists, and blaming *them* for it.

The stories of *Exekution* fall into several categories. The title story is a lengthy *Novelle* and perhaps the GDR's last piece of production-prose. There is also a Hebel-like stylistic set-piece titled "Ein sächsischer Tartuffe," which seems akin to the stylistic experiment of "Der neuere (glücklichere) Kohlhaas"; a set of ten brief stories that could be justly described as additions to the album of "Berliner Stadtansichten"; "Die Krücke," a monologue by a mentally deficient boy, somewhat reminiscent of Marlene Gohl's passages in *Horns Ende*; one *Wende*-piece, the previously-published story "Auf den Brücken friert es zuerst" (Bridge Freezes Before Roadway), discussed above; and two stories unlike anything in Hein's oeuvre to date: "Moses Tod," a satiric allegory about the promised land of communism, and the concluding piece, "Ein älterer Herr, federleicht," a surreal fantasy set in gritty East Berlin.

The title story, its composition presumably dating to 1977, takes up once more the Schlötel syndrome, in which the ambition and talent of an individual worker (this time a cattle producer in an LPG, a Soviet-style cooperative farm) leads to his ruin. Other issues familiar from Hein's writing in the seventies and eighties include jail, emigration/exile, damaged family relations, and the poisonous bureaucratism of the East German system. The story is set up as a *Novelle*, with its "unerhörtes Ereignis" (the bizarre public "execution" of a calf) announced after an opening in medias res, in which the protagonist, Gotthold Sawetzki, is expelled into West Germany. The *Novelle* describes Sawetzki's struggle to raise LPG cattle amid unrealistic production requirements from the Party bureaucracy, incompetent management, and catastrophic reductions in fodder allotments. His heroic efforts to perform his job increasingly tax his family life, which collapses in adultery and divorce. When his protests and complaints to the administration of the LPG fail to achieve any effect, he slaughters, then buries, a healthy calf in front of the cooperative office to dramatize the mismanagement of the cattle operation. Hein encourages a reading of Sawetzki's protest that recalls animal sacrifice in the ancient sense. The whole affair is surrounded with suggestions of the supernatural, beginning with the rather unprovoked descriptions of Sawetzki's act as "widernatürlich" [unnatural: *EEK* 12] and "verwunderlich" [astonishing, odd: 65], very much in the Kleistian manner. Similarly, the commentary of the local shopkeeper, who is reputed to be a witch, adds to the mystical atmosphere by whipping up superstitious dread. Hence in a story centering on cattle and shortages, even the simplest material truths are hidden in a fog of mystery that cloaks the incompetence and self-interest of the management, and their accomplices among the workers and the community. The dilemma formulated in *Schlötel* (How does one live realistically without becoming a collaborator in corruption? How does the virtuous man act within an evil system?) receives the usual official answer, the voice of cynical common sense that recommends conformity. The prison official who informs Sawetzki he is to be expelled from the GDR tells him that "er hoffe, Sawetzki werde es in Zukunft besser verstehen, sein Leben nach den Gegebenheiten einzurichten" [he hoped that in the future Sawetzki would better understand how to arrange his life according to the prevailing circumstances: 11] — good advice East or West, though certainly open to divergent interpretations.

The brief stories that follow are prefaced by "Ein sächsischer Tartuffe" [A Saxon Tartuffe], an odd, ribald, mock-moralistic, Hebel-like sketch combining several narrative registers, obviously ironically, that range from fairytale formulations to patriotic jargon: the story centers on "ein böses Weib" [a wicked woman/wife: 75–76] and takes place in "unseres beliebten Vaterland" [our beloved fatherland: 73], and so on.

Ten of the next twelve pieces are recognizably of the same class as the "Berliner Stadtansichten," although Hein doesn't label them as such. Like their counterparts in *Einladung*, they turn on various large and small ironies of life in the East and West, in war and peace, and under changing legal and political circumstances. These stories may be summarized as follows.

"Der eine hauet Silber, der andere rotes Gold" [One Man Works Silver, Another Works Red Gold] juxtaposes the shabby cover-up mentality of many postwar Germans with the moral clarity possessed by the victims of the Nazi atrocities. A roomful of jewels and precious metals smeared with blood and hair is found in the cellar of the Finance Ministry. The officials responsible for dealing with it decide to quietly nationalize it instead of seeking the heirs of the murdered owners. Later, a German-born American identifies his family's property in a jeweler's window. When the jeweler claims to have a respectable pedigree for the items, the man declares, "Es sind nicht nur Mörder... es sind auch Räuber und Lügner" [They aren't just murderers... they are thieves and liars as well: 83]. With its frank assertion of East German complicity in Nazi crimes, the story would obviously have been unpublishable in the GDR.

"Der Name" [The Name] is a semi-amusing story about the craziness of the Nazi regulations concerning Jews. An old, half-senile woman refuses an official's order that she accept (like all the other Jewish women) the new middle name "Sara." Meeting official irrationality with her own, she insists that if she is to have a new name, it will be Miriam, a name she has always liked. Later, after informing an uncomprehending and then furious police officer that her papers have the wrong name on them, she dies contentedly the very same night.

In "Der Krüppel" [The Cripple], a return-from-Soviet-imprisonment story, a man missing an arm comes home from Siberia in 1952, and finds that his family doesn't need or want him. After three months they throw him out.[14]

"Zur Frage der Gesetze" [A Question of Law] portrays a virtuous abortion doctor. First in Weimar Germany, then under the Nazis, and finally in the GDR, he performs illegal abortions as a public service and political protest, free of charge. In each instance he is eventually caught and punished, the final time because of his refusal to perform what he regards as an "unnecessary" abortion, which leads to him being denounced and to the revocation of his license. He dies working as a doorman, having refused to clear his name even after the GDR legalized abortion in 1972. His motives are unclear, but the suggestion from his left-wing/independent political background seems to be that in a society *too* favorable to abortion, he again feels obliged to resist. He remains his own man, choosing the GDR regime to live in, but keeping it at arm's length from his own political center of belief.

"Jelängerjelieber Vergißnichtmein" [The longer the better Forget-me-not], a love story ending in old age and self-denial, takes up the familiar topic of loveless marriage and extra-marital affairs.

"Unverhofftes Wiedersehen" [Unhoped-for Reunion] narrates the tale of a man who re-encounters his Eastern nemesis in the West, after both have fled the GDR. The old enemy has not changed, however, and again tries (though unsuccessfully) to block the man's career. Thus the story depicts an ideological fanatic who is ultimately indistinguishable from a simple opportunist, always adopting the necessary beliefs and always landing on his feet — on the side of authority.

"Matzeln" [Wood Scraps] is another Hebel-like, tongue-in-cheek anecdote. An inexperienced gatekeeper at a coal mine halts a miner's departure with a sack of wood scraps, accusing him of "fortgesetzten und widerrechtlichen Aneignung von Volkseigentum" [long-term illegal appropriation of the people's property: 129], even though private use of the scraps is common practice. Hein is satirizing the Prussian love of rules and the letter of the law, as opposed to such qualities as mercy or human sympathy; there probably also is a comment on the cumulative effect of the quiet accommodations that made socialism function. At the conclusion, the *Matzeln* are symbolically equated with sins — let's all hope there isn't a Prussian *Advokat* who will total up our accumulated venialities.

"Die Vergewaltigung" [The Rape] has the earmarks of a "Berliner Stadtansicht," but with an unusual passage that gives a synopsis of East German history during the *Aufbau* and fifties almost in the manner of a fairy tale, as in this summation about the rebuilding of central Berlin:

> So entstanden die [Karl-Marx-] Allee und die Stadt neu aus Trümmern, und das Leben ging seinen Gang in dieser schönen und grimmigen Welt, und die Zeitungen des Landes berichteten von der schönen Welt und schwiegen über die grimmige. (135)

> And so the [Karl-Marx-]Allee and the rest of the city rose out of the ruins, and life went on in this beautiful and savage world, and the newspapers of the land reported the beauty and said nothing of the savagery.

This, along with such passages as the one explaining historical details like the *Arbeiter und Bauern Fakultäten* of the *Aufbau* period (the Worker and Peasant Faculties established to bring class diversity into higher education — a sort of socialist G.I. Bill) imply an expected audience broader than just East Germany. Hein's role as chronicler, strongly visible in the story, assumes in retrospect an almost elegiac character, as the peculiarities of the GDR are summed up for posterity. This historical background prepares for the main theme of the incompatibility between socialist propaganda (e.g., the lionizing of the Soviet "liberation" troops) and the fact of Soviet wartime atrocities. The contradiction occurs here in the rape of a woman's grandmother by Soviet soldiers in 1945, an event the woman seemingly forgets as she pursues a successful career, benefiting from the most admirably progressive policies of the socialist system. In 1983, the woman gives a speech at a *Jugendweihe* (the secular equivalent of a church confirmation) portraying the Soviet occupiers as kind benefactors and generally piling on the official East German clichés concerning relations with the Soviet Union. Her husband criticizes her afterward for having told one side of the truth and not the other, whereupon she breaks down and screams that he is a fascist. The official ideology that requires such a radical compartmentalization in the woman's mind (as in the whole society) has left her with no other category than "fascist" to accommodate unpleasant or contradictory facts. As a portrait of the intellectual trauma suffered by a whole generation of East Germans, the story is unsurpassed in Hein's writing.

"Ein Exil" [Exile] looks at the plight of an expatriated Paraguayan artist who finds that his politically-engaged work has gone out of style. He feels cut off from history, as from his homeland, a silent victim of his country's regime. Recognizing that neither his art nor his engagement has meaning anymore, he hangs himself.

In "Eine Frage der Macht" [A Question of Power] a regime-oriented hack writer throws his weight around and gets some drunken detractors hassled by the police. A visiting foreign colleague remarks that one doesn't *do* such things, and the writer replies that here (in the GDR), "we" have the power, and "we" intend to hold onto it. This "we" is worth reflecting on. Does the writer deceive himself, or is he in fact part of the despotic regime? In any event, the point seems to be to show an outsider's view of the despotism and ideological arrogance of "intellectual workers" in the GDR.

The remaining stories, "Die Krücke" [The Retard], "Moses Tod" [Moses' Death], "Auf den Brücken friert es zuerst" (discussed above), and "Ein älterer Herr, federleicht" [An Old Man, Light as a Feather] depart from the familiar ground of the "Berliner Stadtansichten"-like sketches. In "Die Krücke," a feeble-minded boy plots the murder of his teacher, who also is his mother's lover and ostensibly the impoverished family's benefactor. He is actually a physically and morally repellent extortionist who takes advantage of the mother's financial vulnerability and threatens the boy, whom she loves, with institutionalization. Like the unreliable narrators in *Horns Ende, Der fremde Freund*, and *Das Napoleon-Spiel*, the boy is not altogether wrong in his judgments about the world, and one is both horrified by the boy's crude (but not inaccurate) assessment of power relations, and somewhat gratified to anticipate his murder of the evil old man.

"Moses Tod," a satiric parable about socialist utopia, resembles nothing else Hein has published. As in the Biblical story, spies are sent to inspect the Promised Land, and the Israelites are afraid to enter it. In Hein's version, however, it is not the giants and other hostile inhabitants that inspire fear, but the report that the Promised Land has no heaven over it. Caleb, the only spy who remains faithful to the Lord, explains that this is not a problem: "Kaleb verspottete die Ängstlichen und sagte ihnen, daß im guten Land der Himmel auf Erden sei. Und Jahwe fand Gefallen an ihm" [Caleb mocked the fearful ones and said, in the Promised Land, Heaven is on Earth. And Caleb found favor with the Lord: 122]. The doubters (including Moses) are mercilessly punished (Moses is left unburied, to be eaten by animals), and after the whole generation (save Caleb) has died out, the Israelites happily occupy their promised homeland, unconcerned that "sich kein Himmel über ihrem Land wölbt. Denn keiner vermißt ihn, wo der Himmel auf Erden ist" [that no Heaven stretched above them. For no one misses it, where Heaven is on Earth: 123]. One reading of this might be that Socialist idealism (with heaven *over* the earth — the normal situation, one would think) is traded (unwisely) for *Realsozialismus* (heaven *on* earth, lost transcendence). Is fun being made of utopia or the fear of utopia? Or both? In the end, the Israelites get their heaven-on-earth — what does this mean? The parable also foregrounds the figure of the chronicler once more: we learn of this heterodox account only by way of certain lost, forgotten writings of a discredited chronicler. They were publicly burned after the establishment of the Israelite state, which has, like all states, no love for revisionist accounts of its origins.

The last story in the collection, "Ein älterer Herr, federleicht," is even more peculiar and much more difficult to classify, though Kafka comes to mind as a model. Squatters breaking into a run-down Berlin apartment building discover an old man living there; one of them, a young woman, returns later and begins taking care of the man, who calls himself Noah and claims to be 940 years old. She eventually finds him dead, and moves into the apartment herself. At the end of the story, a social worker comes to the apartment and has a conversation through the door with someone who appears to be the old man, and on the way out passes the women, who is just coming home. This surreal conclusion adds to the strangeness of Noah's stories about his past and his equally strange chronology (why is he aged 940, similar to Methuselah, and not 3000-plus?) to yield an unsettling but pleasant ambiguity. The concrete setting of the story and the stretch of history it purports to reveal might cause one to seek a historical or political interpretation, reading the story as an allegory, but Hein provides no secure interpretive foothold for such a procedure. The story appears to be rather an anti-history, a fulfillment of Spodeck's advice to distrust one's memories.

The detachment of the chronicler in *Von allem Anfang an*

In his most recent book, *Von allem Anfang an* [Right from the Start, 1997], Hein stunned the critics with his stylistic polish, his warmth, and his apparent renunciation of contemporary political commentary. The book describes the life of a 13-year-old boy living in the GDR in 1956, recounting his home life as a minister's son in a large family, his parents' marital discord and reconciliation, his school experiences, his vacation visits to the LPG managed by his grandfather (who is later sacked for refusing to join the Party), his sexual awakening, his dreams of escaping the small town where he lives (by running away with the circus, no less), and his first visit to West Berlin, where he is destined to attend high school in a few years. Much that occurs in the book will be familiar to Hein's longtime readers: the narrator Daniel resembles Thomas of *Horns Ende*, and the town where he lives is indistinguishable from Bad Guldenberg. Further, the parallels between Daniel's life and Hein's are overwhelming and precise, lending credibility to the assumption that with its first-person narration, the book is in fact a thinly-disguised autobiography. Hein, however, has rejected any such literal equation of himself with Daniel, asserting instead that the work is a "fictive autobiography," a work of fiction employing the genre of autobiography (Krusche; also personal interview, 18 July 1998). The ambiguity of the author's relation to the protagonist here is reminiscent of the subtle stance taken by James Joyce in *A Portrait of the Artist as a Young Man*, which uses extensive parallels to Joyce's own life in the construction of the protagonist Stephen Dedalus. In both books, the reader must be unusually cautious when ascribing authorial intent; despite the intimacy of the portrayal, an abyss of irony yawns beneath the central character, with the narration shuttling erratically between contemporaneous immediacy and implied post facto judgments by an adult Daniel. And like Joyce's *Portrait*, *Von allem Anfang an* attempts to capture the formative experiences that lead the protagonist to become the writer he is. In Hein's case, this means discovering the detached, dispassionate chronicler's stance, which evolves as a means of mastering the vicissitudes of adolescent life. When viewed thus as an account of the author's emerging aesthetic and moral position — emerging moreover from a specific historical context — *Von allem Anfang an* evinces as much political heft as any of the earlier books.[15]

Initial critical reaction focused on the fact that the political per se is conspicuously downplayed in this book, which foregrounds instead the universal discoveries and experiences of an adolescent boy who could be living anywhere. For most of the reviewers, this was a welcome escape from topicality into the purely aesthetic. "This book deliberately escapes every politically-oriented reading, for instance as an autobiographical reminiscence of the early GDR, in which Hein grew up. 'Right from the start,' historical thinking is an illusion" (Langner). Strong words about the author of *Horns Ende*![16] Baier, writing for *die tageszeitung*, contends that the important thing about Daniel is that he is a youth, not that he is a youth in the GDR, and further argues that the book is not so much about the GDR as about the disappearance of an "agrarian petty-bourgeois way of life" (Baier, "Nackte Brüste"). Peter von Matt's especially glowing review in the *Frankfurter Allgemeine Zeitung* praises Hein for his "Gerechtigkeit" [fairness] in dealing with his characters, congratulates him for having thrown away his "pocket guillotine" (presumably employed on Westerners in a book like *Das Napoleon-Spiel*), and describes at length the advent of a new style that transforms banalities into art. The most straightforwardly political readings, not bothering to hide behind notions of transcendently apolitical art, simply praise Hein for showing, once again, how bad the GDR really was ("Leuchtschrift am Kudamm"; Raddatz). Largely missing from these readings is an awareness of Hein's rigor in representing the political through the personal, with the personal thus becoming a key to the society at large. The infrequent intrusions of politics into the events of the book (such as the Grandfather's trouble with the Party, or Daniel's trip to West Berlin) do not exhaust the political implications of the book. These, rather, are best sought in the motif of detached observation that unifies the seemingly random selection of scenes from Daniel's life.

Applying his narrative method of chronicling without passion or prejudice to Daniel, Hein perfectly captures the naive crassness of childhood that his narrator often embodies. Here is Daniel describing the fashion shows that occasionally relieve the boredom in his small town:

> Die Modevorführungen waren langweilig, aber ich ging dennoch jedesmal hin, weil es etwas Besonderes war und weil Mutter mitkam und den Eintritt spendierte. In der Schule hatte einer erzählt, dass es in Leipzig Modenschauen gebe, wo Damenunterwäsche vorgeführt werde. Die Frauen marschieren über die Bühne mit fast nichts an und wenn man einen guten Feldstecher dabei habe, könne man alles sehen. (*VAAA* 39)

> [The fashion shows were boring, but I always went because they were something different and because mother came along and paid the admission. At school someone had reported that there were fashion shows in Leipzig for ladies' underwear. The women would march across the stage with almost nothing on, and with a good pair of binoculars you could see *everything*.]

The objective presentation of Daniel's 13-year-old sensibility amuses without provoking any sort of judgment; this is simply how a child thinks and talks, even if the child is an alter ego for the author. Similarly, Hein's dialogues often approach the high comic standard set by plays like *Ah Q*, while managing to remain entirely convincing as documents of childhood. One of the best examples of this successful blending of the documentary function of fiction with the humor seen in his plays is the conversation following Daniel's ejection from a lecture/demonstration on liquid air. His companion Bernd blames the lecturer and enlightens Daniel as to the man's sexuality:

> "Und alles wegen dieser schwulen Sau," sagte er . . . .
> "Wieso schwule Sau?"
> "Hast du das nicht gemerkt? Der ist doch stockschwul, der Kerl."
> "Dieser Doktor?"
> "Natürlich. Das ist eine Tunte."
> "Woher willst du das wissen?"
> "Das sieht man doch. Schon wie der angezogen ist! Und wie der läuft! Du kennst doch den alten Barmer?"
> "Den vom Friedhof?"
> "Ja, von eurem Friedhof. Das ist auch eine Tunte. Der läuft so schwul, als ob bei ihm die Beine verkehrtrum eingeschraubt sind. Mein Vater hat den sogar schon mal in Frauenkleidern gesehen."
> "Ist das wahr?"
> "Meinst du, mein Vater lügt? In Frauenkleidern, mitten in der Stadt!"
> "Aber warum denn in Frauenkleidern?"
> "Das machen die Schwulen so. Haben wohl Spaß daran, die Leute zu erschrecken, oder so."

"Mit Frauenkleidern könnte mich keiner erschrecken. Da ist doch eine Maske besser, so eine richtig gruselige Maske. Ein Mann, der in Frauenkleidern rumläuft, das ist doch eher zum Totlachen."

"Vielleicht wollen die das. Die sind doch nicht ganz richtig im Kopf."

"Und der in der Aula, das ist so einer? Du meinst, der läuft in Frauenkleidern herum?"

"Nicht immerfort. Aber das ist ein Schwuler, das kannst du mir glauben."

"Woher willst du das wissen? Er hat doch einen ganz normalen Anzug an."

"Die trägt er natürlich nicht am Tage. Aber wenns dunkel wird."

(*VAAA* 47–48)

["And it's all because of that damn queer," he said . . . .

"What damn queer?"

"Didn't you notice? He's totally queer, that guy."

"That doctor?"

"Of course. He's a faggot."

"How do you know that?"

"You can see it. Just look at the way he's dressed! And the way he walks! You know old Barmer, don't you?"

"From the cemetery?"

"From *your* cemetery. He's a faggot, too. He walks so queer you'd think he had his legs screwed on backwards. My father even saw him dressed up in women's clothes once."

"Is that true?"

"Are you calling my father a liar? In women's clothes, in the middle of town."

"But why in women's clothes?"

"That's just what queers do. Maybe they like to scare people or something."

"Nobody can scare me with women's clothes. A mask would be better for that, a really creepy mask. A man running around in women's clothes would make me die laughing."

"Maybe that's what they want. They aren't quite right in the head."

"And the guy in the auditorium, is he like that? You think he runs around in women's clothes?"

"Not all the time. But he's queer, you can be sure of that."

"So how do you know, then? He was dressed in a regular suit."

"He doesn't do it in the daytime. But when it gets dark . . . ."]

Despite the absurdity of Bernd's adduced evidence for the professor's homosexual behavior, the attitudes expressed are realistic enough and lead in the book to a further exploration of sexual attitudes in the GDR of the 1950s, with Daniel consulting his more charitable father on the subject and being advised even by him not to shake hands with "sick" Herr Barmer (*VAAA* 54). Even in the most absurd moments of Daniel's non-academic education, the humor and seriousness are perfectly balanced, providing opportunities for contemplation of the irony rather than pursuing any specific moral or political program. The finest example of this distanced yet fair stance comes when Daniel tries to reconcile his luminous vision of the older girl Pille with her clothes off and the news that she plans to join the Party, which, in Daniel's family, represents nothing but worldly corruption. But how bad can the Party be if this beautiful girl (without clothes) is in it? "Ich hatte ihre Brüste gesehen, die großen roten Brustwarzen, das feuchte Schamhaar, von dem die Wassertropfen herabrollten. Diese Bilder mischten sich in meinem Kopf mit der Partei, und ich war verwirrt" [I had seen her breasts, her large red nipples, the wet pubic hair with water dripping off of it. These images got mixed up in my head with the Party, and I was confused: 99]. Hein's detachment allows him to capture such ambiguous states of consciousness without giving up the potential for showing how politics impinges on individual lives, whether absurdly or tragically.

Versions of this same Olympian detachment are also found in many of the book's characters and even its symbols. Their common domain is Daniel's consciousness, which, like his creator's, relentlessly seeks out examples of composure and objectivity in the face of suffering, fleeing the self-deluding delights of partisanship and creating the possibility of real mastery over events. This search for models of detachment begins with the allegedly homosexual professor already mentioned. His deportment, which Daniel finds extremely peculiar even before it is explained to him by Bernd, suggests a kind of freedom from the banal struggles of schoolboy life, the petty tyranny of teachers over students that reflects the oppressive conformity of East German society. Even though he scarcely hides his condescension, the demeanor of the "little man" who give the physics lecture recalls Hein's many descriptions of the chronicler's stance: his movements have an "eigentümlichen Ruhe" [extraordinary composure: 41], "Manchmal streifte sein Blick über uns, ohne uns wirklich wahrzunehmen" [His gaze would sometimes sweep the room without really seeing us: 41], "Sein ganzes Benehmen war etwas grotesk, verwies jedoch auf Distanz zu uns" [His whole manner was slightly grotesque, yet it attested to his distance from us: 42]. Daniel and the other students are spellbound, oddly, by the utter disinterest or even contempt the professor seems to have for their world:

> Jede Geste verdeutlichte seinen herablassenden Stolz, seine Scherze und ironischen Bemerkungen waren nicht eigentlich heiter und führ-

> ten bei uns nicht zu einem ausgelassenen oder zumindest befreienden Lachen. Auch sein Humor hatte etwas Übellauniges und seine heitere Stimmung war eigentlich verdrossen.... Sein Benehmen hatte zur Folge, dass eine eigentümlich fiebernde Erwartung entstand (*VAAA* 42)
>
> Every gesture revealed his haughty pride, his jokes and ironic asides were not really amusing and they gave no occasion even for tension-breaking laughter. His humor had something mean-spirited about it and his high spirits were a cover for sullenness.... The effect of his manner was that a peculiar, feverish expectation arose.

The professor's detachment fascinates because it promises something outside the constricted range of possible thought and action familiar to Daniel and his fellow students. The most effective subversion of totalitarian Stalinist society (or of conformism in bourgeois society) comes from the violation of its taboos, the speaking of what cannot and must not be imagined from within it; hence the homosexuality of the lecturer has a subversive effect — it is an eruption of the unspeakable within a closed discourse, a disclosure of distance and difference, and consequently a portent of a more general liberation.

Two less peripheral characters, Tante Magdalena and Daniel's grandmother, model for Daniel more positive versions of the professor's *Gelassenheit*, or composure, when they describe for him their ways of dealing with painful events in their lives. Tante Magdalena is a more lovingly developed version of Gertrude Fischlinger of *Horns Ende*, sharing her clear-eyed stoicism in overcoming vast personal loss. Tante Magdalena's fiancé was lost at sea during the First World War, and she has led a life of quasi-widowhood ever since. Daniel, at the age of 13, may see every new experience as unique and catastrophic, but Tante Magdalena knows that catastrophes are anything but unique, and she exhibits Hein's favorite virtue — stoic endurance of tragedy — by surviving the most dreadful experiences and laughing where once she cried. Daniel finds in Tante Magdalena both a refuge from the turbulence of his own life and an education in how to master it. It is she who delivers the advice that provides the title of book. When Daniel's sister Dorle complains that her mother and grandmother (who has recently moved in with the family) are always fighting, Tante Magdalena says:

> Dem Leben muss man von allem Anfang an ins Gesicht sehen. Ihr seid jetzt alle zusammen, das ganze Jahr über. Ihr müsst euch nicht mehr trennen, ihr könnt euch jeden Tag sehen. Das ist einfach so schön, dass man sich manchmal streiten muss. (*VAAA* 140)
>
> [You have to look life in the face right from the start. Now you are all together all year long. You don't have to say goodbye, you can see

each other every day. That is simply so wonderful that you need to have a fight once in a while."]

As in Hein's essays, Tante Magdalena's stoic embrace of the truth, no matter how painful, includes the rejection of ideological cant, an unsentimental self-discipline she learned from her almost-mother-in-law after her fiancé's death:

"Ich weinte immerzu. Sie kochte uns schweigend einen Kaffee und wir setzten uns ins Wohnzimmer. 'Hör auf zu heulen,' sagte sie zu mir. Und dann: 'Ich verfluche den Krieg, der mir meinen einzigen Sohn genommen hat. Und dieser Dummkopf hat sich freiwillig gemeldet. Wer soll nun den Hof übernehmen?' Sie verzog keine Miene, ihr Gesicht war wie erstarrt. Ich sagte ihr, was Bernhard mir aufgetragen hatte, dass sie stolz sein solle und dass ihr Sohn verboten habe, um ihn zu klagen, weil er für das Vaterland gestorben sei. Sie erwiderte nichts, sie weinte keine Träne. Nur ich heulte. Sie sah mich mit ihrem starren, harten Gesicht an, dann stand sie auf, kam auf mich zu und haute mir eine runter. Mann, hat die zugehauen. Ich heulte gleich noch mal so laut. Aber sie sagte nur: 'So, Anna Magdalena, soviel dazu. Und wenn Bernhard noch leben würde, bekäme er die doppelte Portion'" (*VAAA* 195–196)

["I cried and cried. She made coffee without saying a word and we sat down in the living room. 'Stop crying,' she told me. And then: 'I curse the war that took my only son. And that blockhead enlisted voluntarily. Now who will take over the farm?' Her face had no expression, it was like stone. I told her what Bernhard had instructed me to say, that she should be proud and that her son forbade her to mourn, because he had died for the Fatherland. She didn't answer, and didn't shed a tear. I was the only one crying. She looked at me with her frozen, hard face, then she stood up, walked over to me and slapped my face. Man, did she hit hard. Now I was crying twice as loud as before. But she just said, 'There, Anna Magdalena, that's what you get. And if Bernhard were still alive, he'd get a double portion.'"]

"Magdalena," a fallen woman, an every-woman, a universal figure with a modest but real fund of wisdom, connects the chapters to one another through commentaries like these. In the closing lines of the book, Daniel states that when she died (he was in West Berlin at the time and unable to attend the funeral), he inherited nothing from her, not even a photo. Of course, he did inherit something extremely precious: a narrative stance. Similarly, Daniel learns from his grandmother that the passage of time brings distance from suffering, and hence allows one to look back at it with a cooler and more comprehending gaze. Her son, Daniel's uncle, had been killed in the Second World War:

> Weil sie nie weinte, wenn sie von ihm berichtete, fragte ich Großmutter einmal, ob sie nicht traurig wäre, dass ihr einziger Sohn im Krieg umgekommen war. Großmutter sah mich überrascht an und dachte nach. Und dann sagte sie: "Natürlich bin ich traurig, Junge, aber es ist lange her. Aber wenn ich an ihn denke, sehe ich nur den kleinen Jungen vor mir, der er einmal war. Und dann bin ich nicht mehr traurig. Es ist merkwürdig, nicht wahr, aber das machen die vielen Jahre, die seither vergangen sind. Jetzt tut es nicht mehr weh." (*VAAA* 138)

> [Because she never cried when she talked about him, I once asked Grandmother whether she was sad that her only son had been killed in the war. Grandmother looked at me with surprise and thought for a while. Then she said: "Of course I'm sad, boy, but it was a long time ago. But when I think about him, I only see the little boy that he used to be. And then I'm not sad any more. It's strange, isn't it, but that's what happens over the years. Now it doesn't hurt anymore."]

The book's most striking example of the dispassionate chronicler's stance emerges from Daniel's interpretation of the altar painting in his church, which depicts the Four Evangelists flanking Jesus on the cross. Daniel is fascinated by how unmoved they appear as they witness the crucifixion:

> Jeder von ihnen hielt ein aufgeschlagenes Buch in der Hand, das wohl die Bibel sein sollte, und zeigte mit einem langen und eigenartig gebogenen Finger auf den Text, während er teilnahmslos und ohne Erregung oder erkennbares Mitleid auf den Gekreuzigten blickte oder zu dem Betrachter des Bildes . . . . Und Lukas hatte mich besonders beeindruckt. Mir gefiel sein Evangelium besser als das der anderen, ich fand es einleuchtender, und seine Worte waren einprägsamer. Viele seiner Sätze kannte ich sogar auswendig, obwohl ich sie nie gelernt hatte und nur gelegentlich zu hören bekam. Ich glaube aber, seine grünen Augen waren es vor allem, die mich für ihn und seine Schrift einnahmen. Durch seine Augen war er vor allen anderen hervorgehoben und durch seinen besonders gelassenen, gleichgültigen Blick, den er auf den blutüberströmten, mit Nägeln durchbohrten Jesus warf. Jedesmal während des Gottesdienstes hatte ich genügend Muße, ihn zu betrachten und meinen Gedanken und Vermutungen freien Lauf zu lassen. Mir gefiel, dass er bei der entsetzlichen Szene so lässig dabei stand, die Hinrichtung scheinbar unbeeindruckt zur Kenntnis nahm, nicht gewillt, einzugreifen und zu helfen. (*VAAA* 109 110)

> [Each of them holds an open book in his hand, the Bible no doubt, and points with a long and strangely bent finger at the text, while

looking impassively, unmoved and without any noticeable sympathy, at either the crucified Christ or the viewer of the painting .... And I was especially impressed by Luke. I liked his gospel better than the others, it made more sense to me, and its words were more memorable. I even knew many passages by heart, although I had never tried to learn them and only occasionally heard them read. I think, though, that it was most of all his green eyes that drew me to him and to his writing. He stood out from all the others because of his eyes, and because of the calm, indifferent gaze he cast at the figure of Jesus dripping with blood and pierced with nails. During every service I had lots of time to study him and let my thoughts and conjectures run free. I liked the way he stood next to the horrible scene so casually, unimpressed by the execution he was witnessing, unwilling to intervene or give assistance.]

Though the Evangelists are indeed chroniclers in a sense, they can hardly be accused of being non-partisan and indifferent; this is Daniel's adumbration, or rather Hein's. Daniel's interpretation enables him both to deconstruct the religious cant that he endures as the son of a minister, and to reapply its moral imperatives to his own contradiction-filled life. His situation parallels the position of various Hein characters as they struggle to escape, conform to, or improve society, and like Claudia or Herr Horn, he runs the risk of withdrawing altogether at the very moment he achieves the distance necessary for effective intervention. Hein's elucidation of this paradox is his most important contribution to the Brechtian tradition of privileging political-moral-aesthetic intellect over emotional self-indulgence in response to tragedy.

The culminating moment of Daniel's evolution as a future chronicler of himself and his society occurs during his visit to West Berlin. The double-edged nature of impassive detachment *sine ira et studio* is fully in evidence as Daniel notes the indifference of West Berliners toward the events of the 1956 Hungarian uprising, yet integrates this response into his developing ideal of calm, composed conduct:

> Verwundert beobachtete ich die anderen Gäste des Cafés. Sie warfen nur gelegentlich einen Blick auf die Leuchtschrift und beobachteten offensichtlich weder die Nachrichten noch die Werbung. Sie plauderten miteinander, schauten sich aufmerksam die vorbeiflanierenden Passanten an oder starrten in die Luft. Auch die Passanten blickten nur selten zu den Meldungen hoch. Sie sahen sich die Auslagen der Geschäfte an, musterten eindringlich die hinter den Glasscheiben sitzenden Gäste des Cafés und schauten sich unbefangen an, was serviert worden war. Diese Gelassenheit beeindruckte mich. Neugierig geworden, teilte ich meine Aufmerksamkeit zwischen der flim-

mernden Schrift und den Passanten, ihren Gesichtern und der Art ihres Reagierens. Da ich mir nicht vorstellen konnte, dass diese Nachrichten für sie ohne Bedeutung waren, erschien mir ihr Verhalten ein Ausdruck der Großstadt zu sein. Nur wenn man vom Leben einer Weltstadt geprägt war, konnte man sich selbst bei den schlimmsten Schreckensmeldungen so lässig und ungerührt geben. Wie die vier Evangelisten bei der Kreuzigung auf dem Bild in unserer Marienkirche. (*VAAA* 185)

[I watched the other cafe guests in amazement. They glanced only occasionally at the illuminated letters and evidently paid no attention to either the news or the advertisements. They chatted with each other, watched the passers-by, or stared off into space. The passers-by, too, seldom looked up at the messages. They looked at displays in the shop windows, or studied the seated cafe guests through the glass, showing no embarrassment as they ascertained what was being served. This composure impressed me. Growing curious, I divided my attention between the flickering letters and the passers-by, their faces, and their way of reacting. Since I couldn't imagine that the news was of no importance to them, their behavior appeared to me an expression of big-city life. Only people shaped by life in a world city could appear so indifferent and unmoved by reports of the most terrible events. Like the Four Evangelists in the crucifixion scene in our Marienkirche.]

The critics who imagine that Hein has left pro-Eastern political positions behind, and who read *Von allem Anfang an* as a denunciation of the GDR, are applying only the most superficial analysis to scenes such as Daniel's visit to West Berlin. It would be obtuse to agree with Daniel's own assessment of evident Western indifference, taking it to be a sign of an achieved state of sober and worldly composure in the face of terrible events: "Since I couldn't imagine that the news was of no importance to them, their behavior appeared to me an expression of big-city life." As the detailed description of the strollers and window shoppers makes abundantly clear, the West Berliners are not just pretending to be indifferent — they really *are* indifferent, and not out of some moral imperative, but out of pure consumer intoxication. Daniel is simply not materialistic enough to suspect that wealth could blind people to any sense of social or political solidarity. The oblivious passers-by and cafe guests represent the exact opposite of what Daniel is here inferring from their behavior, just as Claudia's rationale for her isolation completely misses its real causes and real meaning. West Berlin is not a paradise; it is nothing more or less than a background for Daniel's invention of himself. The West per se is treated with the same distance and neutrality as the East. Hence both in theme and in narrative strategy, Hein's latest book is of a piece with its predecessors both before and after the Wende, not the departure or change of direction some have hailed it as.

At the end of the Communist century

Hein's decade of work since the opening of the Berlin Wall can now be viewed with a requisite degree of distance and perspective. Its general outline becomes clear. In the months leading up to the *Wende*, Hein was turning to political allegory on the stage *(Die Ritter der Tafelrunde)* and minimalist/realist satire in his fiction *(Der Tangospieler)* to directly challenge the GDR's cultural and political establishments. These efforts showed a serene and sovereign command of materials and a profound intimacy with both the GDR's ideological contortions and its everyday realities. Next, in the immediately post-*Wende* works — consisting of socio-political fables of a somewhat shrill and utterly humorless cast, represented by "Bridge Freezes before Roadway," *Das Napoleon-Spiel*, and *Randow* — Hein appears to briefly abandon the stance of *Gelassenheit* so carefully cultivated in his earlier work, perhaps (judging from these works' subject matter) out of anger or despair at the grotesque lies and injustices that must be counted among the dislocations of the unification process. Such a shift was probably inevitable given the ideological confusions of the early nineties, including the end of the East/West dualism, and, for artists, the loss of a clear (though not particularly pleasant) niche in GDR society as the main promoters of *Öffentlichkeit*. The imbalance of the early-nineties work surely derives from the ambiguity and even absence of a stable social context. Finally, the recent appearance of *Von allem Anfang an* announces a return to Hein's earlier proven strategy of resolutely dispassionate social chronicling, adapted now to a much more ambiguous political situation than that of the GDR. In other words, a narrative stance developed as a weapon in the ideological struggles internal to the GDR has now been transplanted into a fully post-Communist context, with future consequences yet to be assessed. Critics glad to see Hein abandon his direct criticisms of the West overlook the critical potential of exploring transhistorical issues of personal loss, official stupidity, and moral hypocrisy. In other words, the real subversiveness of Hein's recent writing lies in his treatment of the GDR as a typical case of humanity in general, a provocative enough notion, if reflected upon, for the complacent denizens of consumer capitalism: it may not be welcome news that East Germans, too, led fully human lives. Hein appears intent on naturalizing East Germany into the contemporary world, and retroactively into its own Cold War landscape, revising our attitude away from the ideological demonizing of the past toward a more normal, even banal recognition of it as a particular, but not particularly extraordinary, time and place. The process is similar to what must ultimately take place in the Federal Republic of Germany if it is to become a nation rather than a territory divided into antagonistic eastern and western sections. For that to happen, the human reality of the GDR will have to be assimilated — not repressed, not refuted as ideologically unsound, but made part of the totality of twentieth-century German consciousness.

The great question for observers of East German literature has been: How will former GDR writers represent their political sea change and their subsumption under Western ideology? A latent strength or potential of the old, ideologically constrained literary strategies of the East Bloc may be emerging: the invisible critique of a highly visible ideology (neo-Stalinism) has been turned inside-out, yielding a highly visible critique of an invisible, because perfectly internalized ideology (consumer capitalism). The appeal of such a strategy is that it strikes at the heart of a social arrangement that offers itself as utterly natural, inevitable, and hence non-ideological. The Western response to East German ideological critiques since 1989 has been to complain of stereotyping, over-simplification, prejudice, ignorance — anything, in short, that challenges the naturalness of capitalism, and with it, the rightness of capitalism. Hein continues to violate expectations whenever and wherever he writes. When Socialist Realist dogma demanded stereotyped, historically situated heroes that could function as role models, Hein created tortured, repellent individuals shut off from society. Now that Western ideology posits individual uniqueness and free will as basic human truths in our millennial post-history, Hein is creating stereotypes utterly trapped within themselves by historical circumstance. Hein's deconstruction of East Germany can therefore be understood as part of a larger anti-ideological project that continues unabated.

Hein's emergence as a German writer — rather than an East German one — comes as no surprise after his decades-long critique of German society and its characteristic accommodations with power. In politics as in art, each historical moment sees the proscription of certain thoughts as unthinkable. The integrity of Hein's writing has been proved by the fact that both East German and West German ideologues have decried it as wrongheaded. In literary terms, Hein is treading a path comprehended by neither of the historically competing literary canons, based in the East on a partisan, idealized, social subjectivity, and in the West on an ahistorical, reified subjectivity. His characters are always simultaneously victims and agents of history, trapped in society and trapped in themselves; the undialectical categories of West and East (we now call them winners and losers) are discarded in the effort to discover materially real historical facts — beginning with fascism, but extending also to the authoritarian roots of fascism, and ultimately taking in the conditions of modern industrial society. Hein's literature of dissent from ideological univocality promises to find ample raw material as Germany struggles toward self-definition.

Notes

[1] An interesting footnote to Hein's novel came after the collapse of the GDR, when the soon-to-be-defunct DEFA movie studios produced a feature film of *Der Tangospieler*. By the time Roland Gräf's rigorously faithful adaptation premiered at the 1991 Berlin Film Festival, the events of 1989 seemed no less like ancient history than those of 1968. Critics of the film seemed unable to look at it as anything other than a historical document of a lost world, or worse, a nostalgic monument to that world. The alternative Berlin daily *die tageszeitung*, for example, accused Gräf of turning an absurdist parable into a sentimental look at eternal inner crises, and ridiculed the film for trotting out the usual East German clichés: "crumbled buildings, wretched apartments, dingy shades of gray" (quoted in "Letzter Tango"). The film seems to have fallen to the wrong audience at the wrong time.

[2] See Robinson, "Christoph Hein between Ideologies, or, Where Do the Knights of the Round Table Go after Camelot Falls?"

[3] Honecker was arrested by the Nazi authorities in 1935 for his activities in the Communist underground and spent ten years in prison (Turner 175).

[4] As early as mid-December 1989 Hein remarked despairingly, "I am spending little or no time at my desk, but it is all for nothing: probably within a year . . . Germany will once again be Greater Germany. But there will be no reunification, just an annexation. McDonald's wins" (Letter to the author, 16 Dec. 1989).

[5] For a more extensive treatment of Hein's political activities in 1989 and 1990, see Andress, "Christoph Heins Weg durch den Herbst 1989" and Meyer-Gosau, "Christoph Hein, Politiker." See also the illustrated chronology of Hein's life in Baier (ed.), *Christoph Hein: Texte, Daten, Bilder* 101–118.

[6] For further reading on the *Kritiker-* or *Literaturstreit*, see chapter 1, note 1.

[7] On this subject see Hein's essay, "Eure Freiheit ist unser Auftrag: ein Brief an (fast alle) Ausländer — wider das Gerede vom Fremdenhaß der Deutschen" [Your Freedom is our Mission: A Letter to (Almost All) Foreign-

Deutschen" [Your Freedom is our Mission: A Letter to (Almost All) Foreigners — Challenging the Prattle About German Hatred of Foreigners]. In this "letter," Hein assures the world that Germans have nothing against foreigners per se; rather, it is *poor* foreigners that they can't abide.

[8] In response to such accusations, Hein maintains he is simply reporting what he has seen, even in the case of the monstrous West Berlin lawyer Wörle in *Das Napoleon-Spiel*: "I situated him in the West because that is where I saw this 'player.' I saw him many times. The essentials were comparable to what I have described. The rest is borrowed from my own vita" (Hein, "Kennen").

[9] See McKnight, *Understanding Christoph Hein*, for a detailed English summary and discussion of the novel (113–135).

[10] The irritated reviewer for *Der Spiegel* announces that Hein had "squandered" [*verspielt*] his status of being the "hope" of East German literature (Hage 235), and dismisses Wörle as a "mere assertion, a prattling cardboard figure invented solely to lecture us about what Hein thinks freedom can lead to" (239). Literary pundit Marcel Reich-Ranicki, writing for the *Frankfurter Allgemeine Zeitung*, employs words like *Blödsinn* [idiocy] and *Albernheit* [silliness] in the course of judging the book a failure, meanwhile reading it so sloppily that he confuses Wörle with another minor character. By contrast, the *Frankfurter Rundschau* (Böttiger) and *Süddeutsche Zeitung* (Baier) reviewed the book largely positively, the latter noting that "To the one-time 'GDR-bonus' there now corresponds a 'GDR-malus'" among the critics.

[11] See for instance the review collection "*Der Fremde Freund* von Christoph Hein: Für und Wider" for several examples such as the one contributed by Rüdiger Bernhardt, who diagnosed "the author's deficient ability to keep in view the development possibilities of society while describing the individually possible experiences of his characters" (1638). In other words, Hein was waywardly ignoring the obvious truth of the matter, that the society of the GDR was a *good* society.

[12] McKnight also recommends considering "Hein's intellectual activity during the writing of *Das Napoleon-Spiel* and his reaction to the neo-Nazi activity on both sides of the Elbe, especially his concern that the outgrowth of the long-lasting *Historikerstreit* would overturn national guilt and awareness about the past," and offers the following political allegory:

> Wörle, who always let the "bastard" [that is, Wörle's East German brother] take the blame, might symbolize the specter of fascism (always linked with capitalism in socialist ideology) raising its head again in Germany during and after unification, a ghost of the Nazi past who succeeds in duping the Germans (Fiarthes) into defending him and who is found not guilty (on legal technicalities) by the judges (historians), setting the monster free once again.... The consequences of a successful manipulation of history and people's knowledge of and attitudes towards history are embodied in the disturbing figure of Wörle and his justification of

[13] Other relatively positive assessments of the play similarly emphasized the continuities with his earlier work. *Neues Deutschland*, while judging the Dresden production itself to be rather weak, places Anna Andress in the same class as Hein's alienated Claudia. Anna's attempt at withdrawal from the world (after the exhilaration of the *Bürgerbewegung*), her "Nein!" to the various people importuning her, is akin to Claudia's "I'm fine." She is living in a kind of fool's paradise and must be driven out of it by outside forces (Pfützner). The *Neue Zürcher Zeitung* similarly noted that the play addresses Hein's oldest theme, "how state power and individual fate were interrelated in the GDR," only now the power involved is now that of the dog-eat-dog West where the right of the wealthier prevails. The characters themselves, as in Hein's earlier work, "are ordinary and monstrous at the same time" (Zimmermann).

[14] John Bornemann's interviews for his anthropological study *Belonging in the Two Berlins: Kin, State, and Nation* reveal how archetypal this sort of story is for the self-definition of East Germans who lived through the war and its aftermath (124–54).

[15] Because of the circular chronology of the chapters (the first chapter must be reread after finishing the last in order to be fully understood), we know from the outset that Daniel, like Hein, is destined to escape the stultification of rural life in the GDR by moving to West Berlin. Given that the book is to some extent a memoir, it is remarkable for its refusal to foreshadow Hein's ultimate return to the GDR in 1961. Daniel's trajectory offers no hint of such a return being likely. Similarly, the adult political convictions held by Hein himself are scarcely anticipated. Thus the book is a highly disciplined exercise in the chronicling of one personal and historic moment, undistorted by teleologies of foreknowledge and retrospection. Hein avoids constructing (however covertly) a basis for the overall development of a life, with its rounded narrative contours and evident significance waiting at the end. (The blatancy of Wörle's life, his long career of self-promotion, stands in stark contrast.)

[16] Langner adds that Hein's style benefits from the changed circumstances for East German writers, who need no longer fulfill a "compensatory function as critical moralists." Hein himself seems to agree, saying that he is relieved now that he can just be a writer, not a political seer (Personal interview with author, 18 July 1998). However, even being a mere writer involves a historical and moral context, as all of Hein's writing shows.

Works Consulted

Adling, Wilfried, and Renate Geldner. "Zur Bedeutung des Konflikts für unsere sozialistische Gegenwartsdramatik." *Einheit: Zeitschrift für Theorie und Praxis des wissenschaftlichen Sozialismus* 20.7 (1965): 95–103.

Althusser, Louis. "Ideology and Ideological State Apparatuses (Notes towards an Investigation)." *Lenin and Philosophy and other Essays.* New York: Monthly Review Press, 1971. 127–186.

Andress, Reinhard. "Christoph Heins Weg durch den Herbst 1989." *Chronist ohne Botschaft: Christoph Hein: Ein Arbeitsbuch: Materialien, Auskünfte, Bibliographie.* Ed. Klaus Hammer. Berlin & Weimar: Aufbau, 1992. 158–172.

Anz, Thomas, ed. *"Es geht nicht um Christa Wolf": Der Literaturstreit im vereinten Deutschland.* Munich: Edition Spangenberg, 1991.

Baier, Lothar, ed. *Christoph Hein: Texte, Daten, Bilder.* Frankfurt/M: Luchterhand, 1990.

Baier, Lothar. "Jenseits von Gewinn und Verlust: Falsche Erwartungen und Christoph Heins neuer Roman." Rev. of *Das Napoleon-Spiel. Süddeutsche Zeitung* 31 March 1993.

———. "Nackte Brüste und die Partei der Bestimmer: Eine frühe Jugend in der DDR: Christoph Hein erzählt listig und mit doppeltem Boden *Von allem anfang an.*" *die tageszeitung* 15 Oct. 1997.

Bathrick, David. *The Powers of Speech: The Politics of Culture in the GDR.* Lincoln: U of Nebraska P, 1995.

Behn, Manfred. "Christoph Hein." *Kritisches Lexikon der deutschsprachigen Gegenwartsliteratur.* Ed. Heinz Ludwig Arnold. Nachlieferung 34. March 1990.

Benjamin, Walter. "Theses on the Philosophy of History." *Illuminations.* Trans. Harry Zohn. New York: Harcourt Brace & World, 1968. 255–266.

———. "Kleine Geschichte der Photographie." *Das Kunstwerk im Zeitalter seiner technischen Reproduzierbarkeit.* Frankfurt/M: Suhrkamp, 1963. 45–64.

———. "The Work of Art in the Age of Mechanical Reproduction." *Illuminations.* 219–253.

———. *Das Passagen-Werk.* 2 Vols. Frankfurt/M: Suhrkamp, 1982.

Bernhardt, Rüdiger. "*Der fremde Freund* von Christoph Hein. [Für und Wider.]" *Weimarer Beiträge* 29 (1983): 1635–1638.

Bornemann, John. *Belonging in the Two Berlins: Kin, State, Nation*. Cambridge: Cambridge UP, 1992.

Böttcher, Brigitte. "Diagnose eines unheilbaren Zustands." *Neue deutsche Literatur* 31.6 (1983): 145–153.

Böttiger, Helmut. "Das Amoralische hat Hochkonjunktur: Blick auf den realen Kapitalismus: Christoph Heins Roman *Das Napoleon-Spiel*." Rev. *Frankfurter Rundschau* 3 April 1993.

Brereton, Geoffrey. *Jean Racine: A Critical Biography*. London: Cassell, 1951.

Claas, Herbert. "*Horns Ende* in gebrochenen Spiegeln: Gesellschaftsroman mit historischem Stoff von Christoph Hein." Rev. of *Horns Ende*. *Deutsche Volkszeitung / die tat* 4 October 1985: 17.

Corin, Karl. "Liebe zu Möbeln statt zu den Menschen: Das Maß der Kunst ist der gellende Schrei — Christoph Heins Novelle *Drachenblut*." Rev. of *Drachenblut [Der fremde Freund]*. *Stuttgarter Zeitung* 10 Dec. 1983: 50.

Darnton, Robert. *Berlin Journal 1989–1990*. New York & London: Norton, 1991.

"DDR-Literaturentwicklung in der Diskussion." Round table discussion with H. Haase, W. Hartinger, U. Heukenkamp, K. Jarmatz, J. Pischel, and D. Schlenstedt. *Weimarer Beiträge* 30 (1984): 1589–1616.

de Bruyn, Günter. *Neue Herrlichkeit*. Frankfurt/M: Fischer, 1986.

Deiritz, Karl, and Hannes Kraus, eds. *Der deutsch-deutsche Literaturstreit oder "Freunde, es spricht sich schlecht mit gebundener Zunge."* Hamburg and Zürich: Luchterhand, 1991.

Drommer, Günter. "Typische Bemerkungen zur untypischen Texten." Afterword to *Einladung zum Lever Bourgeois*, by Christoph Hein. Berlin & Weimar: Aufbau, 1980. 185–190.

Duclaux, Mary. *The Life of Racine*. Port Washington, New York, and London: Kennikat Press, 1972.

Eberlein, Sybille. "Claudia und kein Anfang." Rev. of *Der fremde Freund*. *Tribüne* 25 March 1983: 13.

Engler, Wolfgang. "Froschs Ende: Theater: Christoph Heins Komödie *Randow* in Dresden uraufgeführt." Rev. *Die Zeit* 30 Dec. 1994.

Feix, Ingrid. "Eine Art, nicht wirklich zu leben: Ein aufregendes und anregendes Gegenwartsbuch." Rev. of *Der fremde Freund*. *Junge Welt* 31 May 1983: 11.

Fischer, Bernd. *Christoph Hein: Drama und Prosa im letzten Jahrzehnt der DDR*. Heidelberg: C. Winter, 1990.

———. "*Einladung zum Lever Bourgeois*: Christoph Hein's First Prose Collection." *Studies in GDR Culture and Society 4: Selected Papers from the Ninth New Hampshire Symposium on the German Democratic Republic.* Ed. Margy Gerber et al. Lanham: UP of America, 1984. 125–136.

Franke, Konrad. "Spiegelungen: Christoph Hein stellt sich als Prosaautor vor." Rev. of *Nachtfahrt und früher Morgen*. *Süddeutsche Zeitung* 6 October 1982: 3.

"*Der fremde Freund* von Christoph Hein: Für und Wider." *Weimarer Beiträge* 29 (1983): 1635–1655.

Freud, Sigmund. *The Standard Edition of the Complete Psychological Works of Sigmund Freud*. 24 vols. Trans. and ed. James Strachey. London: The Hogarth Press and the Institute of Psycho-Analysis, 1961.

Fukuyama, Francis. *The End of History and the Last Man*. New York: Free Press, 1992.

Funke, Christoph. "Monolog einer Ärztin." Rev. of *Der fremde Freund*. *Der Morgen* 12/13 Feb. 1983: 5.

———. "Spiel mit Geschichte." *Neue deutsche Literatur* 29.10 (1981): 149–152.

Grünenberg, Antonia. "Geschichte der Entfremdung: Christoph Hein als Autor der DDR." *Michigan Germanic Studies* 8.1–2 (1985): 229–251.

Haase, Horst, et al., eds. *Literatur der DDR. Geschichte der deutschen Literatur*. Vol. 11. Berlin (East): Volk & Wissen, 1977.

Hage, Volker. "Glückliche Knechte." Rev. of *Das Napoleon-Spiel*. *Der Spiegel* 12 April 1993: 235+.

Hammer, Klaus, ed. *Chronist ohne Botschaft. Christoph Hein. Ein Arbeitsbuch: Materialien, Auskünfte, Bibliographie*. Berlin & Weimar: Aufbau, 1992.

———. "*Der fremde Freund*." Rev. *Sonntag* 10 April 1983.

Hebel, Johann Peter. *Aus dem Schatzkästlein des rheinischen Hausfreundes*. Stuttgart: Reclam, 1950.

Hein, Christoph. *Als Kind habe ich Stalin gesehen: Essais und Reden*. Berlin (East) & Weimar: Aufbau, 1990.

———. "Der alte Mann und die Straße: Ansprache zur Demonstration der Berliner Kulturschaffenden." *Als Kind habe ich Stalin gesehen*. 175–177.

———. "Die alten Themen habe ich noch, jetzt kommen neue dazu": Gespräch mit Sigrid Löffler (März 1990)." Interview. *Christoph Hein: Texte, Daten, Bilder*, ed. Lothar Baier. 37–44.

———. "Anmerkungen zu *Cromwell*." *Schlötel oder Was solls: Stücke und Essays*. Darmstadt & Neuwied: Luchterhand, 1986. 173–176.

———. "Anmerkung zu *Lassalle fragt Herrn Herbert nach Sonja. Die Szene ein Salon*." *Die wahre Geschichte des Ah Q: Stücke und Essays.* Darmstadt & Neuwied: Luchterhand, 1984. 76–80.

———. "'Ansonsten würde man ja aufhören zu schreiben . . .': Mit Christoph Hein sprach Gregor Edelmann." Interview. *Theater der Zeit* 10 (1983): 54–56.

———. "Auf den Brücken friert es zuerst." *Exekution eines Kalbes.* Berlin & Weimar: Aufbau, 1994. 145–180.

———. "Aus: Ein Album Berliner Stadtansichten." *Nachtfahrt und Früher Morgen. Prosa.* Munich: Deutscher Taschenbuch Verlag, 1987. 68–93.

———. "Cromwell." 1981. *Schlötel oder Was solls: Stücke und Essays.* Darmstadt & Neuwied: Luchterhand, 1986. 87–172.

———. "Eure Freiheit ist unser Auftrag: ein Brief an (fast alle) Ausländer — wider das Gerede vom Fremdenhaß der Deutschen." *Chronist ohne Botschaft*, ed. Klaus Hammer. 51–55.

———. "Bridge Freezes Before Roadway." Berlin: Berliner Handpresse, 1990. Reprinted as "Auf den Brücken friert es zuerst." *Exekution eines Kalbes.* 145–180.

———. "Charlottenburger Chaussee, 11. August." *Nachtfahrt und früher Morgen:* 82–84.

———. *Cromwell und andere Stücke.* Berlin (East) & Weimar: Aufbau, 1981.

———. *Einladung zum Lever Bourgeois.* Berlin (East) & Weimar: Aufbau, 1980.

———. "Einladung zum Lever Bourgeois." *Nachtfahrt und früher Morgen.* 118–134.

———. *Exekution eines Kalbes.* Berlin & Weimar: Aufbau, 1994.

———. "Die Familiengruft." *Nachtfahrt und früher Morgen.* 79–82.

———. "Frank, eine Kindheit mit Vätern." *Nachtfahrt und früher Morgen.* 90–93.

———. "Friederike, Martha, Hilde." *Nachtfahrt und früher Morgen.* 68–77.

———. *Der fremde Freund. Novelle.* Berlin (East) & Weimar: Aufbau, 1982.

———. "Die fünfte Grundrechenart." In *Die Geschichte ist offen: DDR 1990: Hoffnung auf eine neue Republik: Schriftsteller aus der DDR über die Zukunftschancen ihres Landes.* Ed. Michael Naumann. Hamburg: Rowohlt, 1990. 59–70.

———. "Das Geld ist nicht der Gral." Interview with the creators of the TV adaptation of *Die Ritter der Tafelrunde* (1990). *Chronist ohne Botschaft*, ed. Klaus Hammer. 226–229.

———. "Die Geschäfte des Herrn John D." Unpublished play. 1979.

———. "Gespräch mit Christoph Hein." Interview with Klaus Hammer (1982). *Öffentlich arbeiten: Essais und Gespräche.* Berlin (East) & Weimar: Aufbau, 1987. 120–129.

———. *Horns Ende. Roman.* Darmstadt & Neuwied: Luchterhand, 1987.

———. "Ich kann mein Publikum nicht belehren." Interview with Hans Bender and Agnes Hüfner (1984). *Christoph Hein: Texte, Daten, Bilder*, ed. Lothar Baier. 68–75.

———. "Ein Interview." Interview with *Theater der Zeit* (1978) *Öffentlich arbeiten.* 97–107.

———. "Kennen Sie eigentlich noch Leute, die Bücher lesen?: Der Schriftsteller Christoph Hein über Spieler in der Gesellschaft und über den fortschreitenden Analphabetismus." Interview with Cornelia Geißler. *Berliner Zeitung* 1/2 May 1993: 56.

———. "The Knights of the Round Table. A Comedy." Trans. David W. Robinson. In *No Man's Land: East German Drama after the Wall.* Ed. David W. Robinson. *Contemporary Theatre Review* 4.2 (1995): 87–123.

———. "Lassalle fragt Herrn Herbert nach Sonja. Die Szene ein Salon." 1981. *Die wahre Geschichte des Ah Q: Stücke und Essays.* Darmstadt & Neuwied: Luchterhand, 1984. 7–75.

———. "Leb wohl, mein Freund, es its schwer zu sterben." *Nachtfahrt und früher Morgen.* 94–101.

———. "Linker Kolonialismus oder Der Wille zum Feuilleton." *Öffentlich arbeiten.* 135–153.

———. "Lorbeerwald und Kartoffelacker: Vorlesung über einen Satz Heinrich Heines." *Öffentlich arbeiten.* 5–28.

———. "Maelzel's Chess Player Goes to Hollywood: Das Verschwinden des künstlerischen Produzenten im Zeitalter der technischen Reproduzierbarkeit." *Öffentlich arbeiten.* 165–194.

———. *Die Mauern von Jerichow: Essais und Reden.* Berlin: Aufbau, 1996.

———. "Mit etwas Rückgrat durch die Zeitläufe kommen: Gespräch mit Christoph Hein vor der Premiere von *Randow, Eine Komödie.*" Interview with Karin Großmann. *Sächsische Zeitung* 17 Dec. 1995.

———. "Mut ist keine literarische Kategorie': Gespräch mit Alois Bischof: Aus Anlaß einer Aufführung von *Die wahre Geschichte des Ah Q* in Zürich (1985)." Interview. *Christoph Hein: Texte, Daten, Bilder,* ed. Lothar Baier. 95–100.

———. "Nachtfahrt und früher Morgen." *Nachtfahrt und früher Morgen.* 84–90.

———. *Nachtfahrt und früher Morgen: Prosa.* (Modified version of *Einladung zum Lever Bourgeois* [1980].) 1982. Munich: Deutscher Taschenbuch Verlag, 1987.

———. *Das Napoleon-Spiel. Ein Roman.* Berlin & Weimar: Aufbau, 1993.

———. "Der neue Menoza oder Geschichte des kumbanischen Prinzen Tandi: Komödie nach Jakob Michael Reinhold Lenz." *Cromwell und andere Stücke.* 225–297.

———. "Der neuere (glücklichere) Kohlhaas." *Nachtfahrt und früher Morgen.* 102–117.

———. *Öffentlich arbeiten: Essais und Gespräche.* Berlin (East) & Weimar: Aufbau, 1987.

———. "Öffentlich arbeiten." *Öffentlich arbeiten.* 34–38.

———. *Passage.* Darmstadt: Luchterhand, 1988.

———. *Passage.* Program pamphlet for Dresden production. Ed. Karla Kochta. Staatsschauspiel Dresden, 1987.

———. Personal interview with author. 9 May 1988.

———. Personal interview with author. 4 May 1989.

———. Personal interview with author. 18 July 1998.

———. *Randow. Eine Komödie.* Berlin: Henschelschauspiel, 1995.

———. *Die Ritter der Tafelrunde und andere Stücke.* Berlin & Weimar: Aufbau, 1990.

———. "Die Ritter der Tafelrunde." *Die Ritter der Tafelrunde und andere Stücke.* 131–193.

———. "Die russischen Briefe des Jägers Johann Seifert." *Nachtfahrt und früher Morgen.* 7–67.

———. "*Schlötel oder Was solls.* Darmstadt & Neuwied: Luchterhand, 1986.

———. "Schlötel oder Was solls." *Schlötel oder Was solls: Stücke und Essays.* 21–85.

———. *The Tango Player.* Trans. Philip Boehm. New York: Farrar, Straus & Giroux, 1992.

———. *Der Tangospieler. Erzählung.* Berlin (East) & Weimar: Aufbau, 1989.

———. *The True Story of Ah Q.* Trans. Anthony Meech. Unpublished.

———. "Vom hungrigen Hennecke." Unpublished play. 1974.

———. *Von allem Anfang an.* Berlin: Aufbau, 1997.

———. *Die wahre Geschichte des Ah Q.* Darmstadt & Neuwied: Luchterhand, 1984.

———. "Die wahre Geschichte des Ah Q." *Die wahre Geschichte des Ah Q: Stücke and Essays.* 81–135.

———. "Waldbruder Lenz." *Öffentlich arbeiten.* 70–96.

———. "'Wir werden es lernen müssen, mit unserer Vergangenheit zu leben': Gespräch mit Krzysztof Jachimczak." Interview (1986). *Christoph Hein: Texte, Daten, Bilder,* ed. Lothar Baier. 45–67.

———. "Die Witwe eines Maurers." *Nachtfahrt und früher Morgen: Prosa.* 77–78.

———. "Worüber man nicht reden kann, davon kann die Kunst ein Lied singen: Zu einem Satz von Anna Seghers." *Öffentlich arbeiten.* 43–56.

———. "Die Zensur ist überlebt, nutzlos, paradox, menschenfeindlich, volksfeindlich, ungesetzlich und strafbar." Speech delivered before the tenth Writers' Congress of the GDR, November 1987. *Als Kind habe ich Stalin gesehen.* 77–104.

Heukenkamp, Ursula. "Die fremde Form." *Sinn und Form* 35 (1983): 625–632.

Hörnigk, Frank. "Christoph Hein." *Literatur der Deutschen Demokratischen Republik: Einzeldarstellungen.* Vol. 3. Ed. Hans Jürgen Geerdts et al. Berlin (East): Volk & Wissen, 1987. 101–116.

———. "'Texte, die auf Geschichte warten . . .' Zum Geschichtsbegriff bei Heiner Müller." *Heiner Müller Material.* Ed. Frank Hörnigk. Leipzig: Reclam, 1990. 123–137.

Hüfner, Agnes. "In den Gegebenheiten: Christoph Heins gesammelte Erzählungen *Exekution eines Kalbes.*" *Frankfurter Rundschau* 16 March 1994.

Isenschmid, Andreas. "Nachrichten vom beschädigten Leben: Nicht tot und nicht lebendig: Christoph Heins protestantische Kalendergeschichten aus Deutschland." Rev. of *Exekution eines Kalbes. Die Zeit* 18 March 1994.

James, C. Vaughan. *Soviet Socialist Realism: Origins and Theory.* London: Macmillan, 1973.

Janssen-Zimmermann, Antje. *Gegenwürfe: Untersuchungen zu Dramen Christoph Heins.* Frankfurt: Peter Lang, 1988.

———. "'Subjektiver Objektivität': Drei Theatertexte Christoph Heins — 'Trilogie des Sozialismus'?" *Chronist ohne Botschaft,* ed. Klaus Hammer. 184–194.

John, Erhard. "Einführung." Introduction to *Der sozialistische Realismus in Kunst und Literatur: Eine empfehlende Bibliographie.* Ed. Gottfried Rost and Helmut Schulze. Leipzig: VEB Verlag für Buch- & Bibliothekswesen, 1960. 5–8.

Kändler, Klaus. "*Der fremde Freund* von Christoph Hein [Für und Wider]." *Weimarer Beiträge*, 29 (1983), 9:1639–1642.

Kleist, Heinrich von. *Sämtliche Werke und Briefe*. Vol. 2. Darmstadt: Wissenschaftliche Buchgesellschaft, 1970.

Klunker, Heinz. "Gegenwart hat Zukunft: Im Dresden uraufgeführt: *Randow* von Christoph Hein. Ein politisches Porträt des Schriftstellers, der auch im neuen Deutschland nicht aufhört, unbequem zu sein." Rev. *Deutsches Allgemeines Sonntagsblatt* 23 Dec. 1994.

Kopka, Fritz-Jochen. "Reicher Irrer: Christoph Heins Nachwende-Buch hat die Kritik sich anders vorgestellt." Rev. of *Das Napoleon-Spiel*. *Wochenpost* 29 April 1993: 26.

Kochta, Karla. "Austreibung des Grals?" *Chronist ohne Botschaft*, ed. Klaus Hammer. 223–225.

Krug, Hartmut. "Ritter von der traurigen Gestalt." *Theater heute* 7 (1989): 26. Quoted in *Chronist ohne Botschaft*, ed. Klaus Hammer. 258–59.

Krumbholz, Martin. "Eine Frage der Macht: Erzählungen Christoph Heins aus den Jahren 1977–1990." Rev. of *Exekution eines Kalbes*. *Süddeutsche Zeitung* 17 March 1994.

Krumrey, Marianne. "Gegenwart im Spiegel der Geschichte: Christoph Hein, *Einladung zum Lever Bourgeois*." Rev. *Temperamente* 4 (1981): 143–147.

Krusche, Friedemann. "Meergrüner Erlöserblick: Ein Bißchen Wehmut, kein Bißchen Nostalgie — Christoph Hein schaut auf die DDR zurück: *Von allem Anfang an*." Rev. *Das Sonntagsblatt* 17 Oct. 1997.

Kuczynski, Jürgen. "Gesellschaftliche Widersprüche." *Deutsche Zeitschrift für Philosophie* 20.10 (1972): 1269–1279.

Kundera, Milan. *The Joke*. Rev. ed. New York: HarperCollins, 1992.

Kunze, Reiner. *Die wunderbaren Jahre: Prosa*. Frankfurt/M: Fischer, 1976.

Langner, Beatrix. "Kleine Schnitte in der Haut: Eine ostdeutsche Kindheit in den fünfziger Jahren — neun Geschichten von Christoph Hein." Rev. of *Von allem Anfang an*. *Süddeutsche Zeitung* 15 Oct. 1997.

"Ein Leben mit der Lüge: Christoph Hein hat seinen Schreibtisch aufgeräumt — und eine Reihe hervorragende Erzählungen aus der DDR-Zeit gefunden." Rev. of *Exekution eines Kalbes*. *Der Spiegel* 28 Feb. 1994: 212+.

Leistner, Bernd. "*Der fremde Freund* von Christoph Hein [Für und Wider]." *Weimarer Beiträge* 29 (1983): 1642–1645.

"Leuchtschrift am Kudamm: *Von allem Anfang an* heißt das neue Buch des Schriftstellers Christoph Hein — ein gar nicht nostalgischer Rückblick auf die frühe DDR." *Der Spiegel* 25 Aug. 1997: 178.

Liebmann, Kurt. "Über die Methode des Sozialistischen Realismus." *Aufbau* 13.9 (1957): 323–327.

Lindner, Gabriele. "*Der fremde Freund* von Christoph Hein [Für und Wider]." *Weimarer Beiträge* 29 (1983): 1645–1648.

Linsel, Klaus. "Vollendet ausgesdachte Wirklichkeiten: Zu den erstaunlichen Prosatexten Christoph Heins." (Review of *Einladung zum Lever Bourgeois.*) *Die Tat* 22 Jan. 1982: 11.

Löffler, Dietrich. "Christoph Heins Prosa — Chronik der Zeitgeschichte." *Weimarer Beiträge* 33 (1987): 1484–1487.

Marx, Karl, and Friedrich Engels. *Ausgewählte Werke*. Moscow: Verlag Progress, 1986.

Matt, Beatrice von. "Spröd und meisterlich: Christoph Heins Erzählband *Exekution eines Kalbes*." Rev. *Neue Zürcher Zeitung* 11 Feb. 1994.

Matt, Peter von. "Fort mit der Taschenguillotine: Christoph Hein schreibt ein Meisterwerk nicht nur der Tantenkunde." Rev. of *Von allem Anfang an*. *Frankfurter Allgemeine Zeitung* 14 Oct. 1997.

McKnight, Philip S. "Alltag, Apathy, Anarchy: GDR Everyday Life as a Provocation in Christoph Hein's Novella *Der fremde Freund*." Studies in GDR Culture and Society 8. Margy Gerber. Lanham, MD: UP of America, 1988. 179–190.

——. "Alltag oder Anarchie: GDR Everyday Life as a Provocation in Christoph Hein's Novella *Der fremde Freund*." Unpublished version of conference paper. 17 pp.

——. "Ein Mosaik zu Christoph Heins Roman *Horns Ende*." *Sinn und Form* 39 (1987): 415–425.

——. *Understanding Christoph Hein*. Columbia: U of South Carolina P, 1995.

Mehr, Max Thomas. "Eine Zukunft, die keiner haben will." Rev. of *Die Ritter der Tafelrunde*. *tageszeitung*. 26 Oct. 1989. Quoted in *Chronist ohne Botschaft*, ed. Klaus Hammer. 258.

Meyer-Gosau, Frauke. "Christoph Hein, Politiker." *Chronist ohne Botschaft*, ed. Klaus Hammer. 173–183.

Michaelis, Rolf. "Aus der Geschichte des Schweigens: Ein Buch aus der DDR erzählt von Verletzungen, die Menschen einander und sich selber antun: Leben ohne zu leben: Christoph Heins erstaunliche Novelle *Drachenblut*." Rev. of *Drachenblut* [*Der fremde Freund*]. *Die Zeit* 11 Nov. 1983.

Mudrich, Heinz. "Ärztin, geschieden, keine Klagen: Novelle aus der DDR, im Westen ausgezeichnet: Christoph Heins *Drachenblut*." Rev. of *Drachenblut* [*Der fremde Freund*]. *Saarbrücker Zeitung* 8 March 1984.

Müller, Heiner. "Der Auftrag." *Herzstück*. Berlin (West): Rotbuch, 1983. 43–70.

——. "Der glücklose Engel." *Theater-Arbeit*. Berlin (West): Rotbuch, 1975. 18.

——. "Der Horatier." *Mauser*. Berlin (West): Rotbuch, 1978. 45–54.

——. "Leben Gundlings Friedrich von Preußen Lessings Schlaf Traum Schrei." *Herzstück*. Berlin (West): Rotbuch, 1983. 9–40.

——. "Der Lohndrücker." *Geschichten aus der Produktion 1: Stücke Prosa Gedichte Protokolle*. Berlin (West): Rotbuch/Verlag der Autoren, 1974. 15–44.

——. "Wolokolamsker Chaussee III: Das Duell." *Shakespeare Factory 2*. Berlin (West): Rotbuch, 1989. 239–244.

Münz, Rudolph. "Nachwort." *Cromwell und andere Stücke*. By Christoph Hein. Berlin & Weimar: Aufbau, 1981. 299–320.

Pfützner, Klaus. "Dünnes Eis über dem Brackwasser: *Randow* von Christoph Hein — eine Uraufführung am Staatsschauspiel Dresden." Rev. *Neues Deutschland* 24 Dec. 1994.

Plenzdorf, Ulrich. *Die Neue Leiden des jungen W*. Frankfurt/M: Suhrkamp, 1976.

Postl, Gertrude. "The Silencing of a Voice: Christa Wolf, Cassandra, and the German Unification." *Differences* 5.2 (1993): 92–115.

Racine, Jean. "Britannicus." Trans. Christoph Hein. In *Die Ritter der Tafelrunde und andere Stücke* by Christoph Hein. 195–263.

Raddatz, Fritz J. "Besonnte Vergangenheit: Christoph Heins wenig nette Märchen." Rev. of *Von allem Anfang an*. *Die Zeit* 19 Sept. 1997.

Reich-Ranicki, Marcel. "Der Billardmörder: Christoph Heins *Napoleon-Spiel*." Rev. *Frankfurter Allgemeine Zeitung* 10 April 1993.

Reinhardt, Stephan. "Vom Schweigen und Verschweigen: Christoph Heins wichtige Novelle *Drachenblut*." Rev. of *Drachenblut* [*Der fremde Freund*]. *Frankfurter Rundschau* 8 Oct. 1983.

Robinson, David W. "Abortion as Repression in Christoph Hein's *The Distant Lover*." *New German Critique* 58 (1993): 65–78.

——. "Christoph Hein between Ideologies, or, Where Do the Knights of the Round Table Go after Camelot Falls?" *No Man's Land: East German Drama After the Wall*, ed. David W. Robinson. 79–85.

Romanowski, A. "Zur Geschichte des Terminus 'Sozialistischer Realismus.'" [*Sowjetwissenschaft*.] *Kunst und Literatur* 6.2 (1958): 159–166.

Saintsbury, George. "Racine, Jean." *Encyclopedia Britannica*. 9th ed.

Schachtsiek-Freitag, Norbert. "Erinnere dich: Das Vergangene ist nicht tot." Rev. of *Horns Ende*. *Deutschland Archiv* 5 (1987): 540–542.

Schiffer, Wolfgang. "So möglich gewesene Geschichte: Lesestücke von Christoph Hein." Rev. of *Einladung zum Lever Bourgeois*. *Deutsche Volkszeitung* 26 March 1981.

Schulz, Helmut H. "Schriftsteller über Schriftsteller: Jedes gelungene Kunstwerk nutzt: Helmut H. Schulz zu Büchern von Brězan und Hein." Rev. of *Drachenblut* [*Der fremde Freund*]. *Berliner Zeitung* 21 April 1983.

Schulz-Ojala, Jan. "Biederfrau und die Brandstifter." Rev. of *Randow*. *Der Tagesspiegel*. 23 Dec. 1994.

Seibt, Gustav. "Krach in der Mastrinderbrigade: Und doch kein Anlaß zum Literaturstreit: Christoph Hein erzählt." Rev. of *Exekution eines Kalbes*. *Frankfurter Allgemeine Zeitung* 19 February 1994.

Sevin, Dieter. *Textstrategien in DDR-Prosawerken zwischen Bau und Durchbruch der Berliner Mauer*. Heidelberg: C. Winter, 1994.

Sieg, Katrin. "The Poets and the Power: Heiner Müller, Christa Wolf and the German *Literaturstreit*." *No Man's Land: East German Drama After the Wall*, ed. David W. Robinson. 151–158.

Stephan, Erika. "Das Kammerspiel *Passage* im Verständnis des Theaters." *Chronist ohne Botschaft: Christoph Hein,* ed. Klaus Hammer. 213–222.

Tacitus, Publius Cornelius. *Annales*. Vol. 1. Ed. Gabriel Brotier. Paris: Typographia Ludovici-Francisci Delatour, 1771.

"Thesen zum sozialistischen Realismus." *Neue Deutsche Literatur* 6.3 (1958): 120–132.

Turner, Henry Ashby, Jr. *The Two Germanies Since 1945*. New Haven & London: Yale UP, 1987.

Walther, Peter. "Mutter heißt jetzt Mum: Christoph Hein hat ein Stück über den Alltag im vereinten Deutschland geschrieben. Eine Komödie ist es aber leider doch nicht geworden." Rev. of *Randow*. *tageszeitung* 15/16 April 1995.

Wilke, Ursula. "*Der fremde Freund* von Christoph Hein [Für und Wider]." *Weimarer Beiträge* 29 (1983): 1652–1655.

Wittstock, Uwe. "Der Mann mit dem Strick um den Hals: *Horns Ende* — der erste Roman des in Ost-Berlin lebenden Autors Christoph Hein." Rev.. *Frankfurter Allgemeine Zeitung*, Literarische Beilage, 19 Nov. 1985.

———. "Letzte Liebe in der Seelenwüste." Rev. of *Drachenblut* [*Der fremde Freund*]. *Frankfurter Allgemeine Zeitung* 17 March 1983.

———. "Michael Kohlhaas als Buchhalter: Der erste Prosaband des DDR-Dramitikers Christoph Hein." Rev. of *Nachtfahrt und früher Morgen*. *Frankfurter Allgemeine Zeitung* 5 Oct. 1982: 5.

Wolf, Christa. *Nachdenken über Christa T.* Halle (Saale): Mitteldeutscher Verlag, 1968.

———. *The Search for Christa T.* Trans. Christopher Middleton. New York: Farrar, Straus, & Giroux, 1970.

———. *Was bleibt. Erzählung.* Frankfurt/M: Luchterhand, 1990.

Wörterbuch der marxistischen-leninistischen Philosophie. Berlin (East): Dietz, 1987.

Zimmermann, Stephan. "Zwischen Angst und Hingabe? *Randow* von Christoph Hein in Dresden uraufgeführt." Rev. *Neue Zürcher Zeitung* 25 Dec. 1994.

Index

Adling, Wilfried, 6, 7
Adorno, Theodor, 19
Althusser, Louis, xvii, 153
America, United States of, xi, xiv, 47, 49–50, 69–70, 189, 201
Andress, Reinhard, 217
Aragon, Louis, 67
Aristotelianism, 7, 61
Auschwitz, 64

Baier, Lothar, 206, 217
Baudelaire, Charles, 21
Behn, Manfred 55, 72
Benjamin, Walter, 66–70, 106–107, 155–56, 179
Berlin Wall, xi, 4, 14, 183, 193
Berliner Ensemble, 4
Bernhardt, Rüdiger, 81, 123
Besson, Benno, 4
Biermann, Wolf, 1, 4
Bismarck, Otto von, 17, 18
Boccaccio, Giovanni, 199
Boehm, Philip, xviii
Boileau, Nicolas, 130
Böll, Heinrich, 198
Borges, Jorge Luis, 32, 33
Bornemann, John, 219
Böttcher, Brigitte, 124
Braun, Volker, 9
Brecht, Bertolt, 4, 6, 12, 20, 33, 38, 199, 213
Brereton, Geoffrey, 130, 136, 177
Bundesrepublik Deutschland, see Federal Republic of Germany

Champmeslé, Marie de, 130, 135–36
China, xii, 2, 18, 63–64
Claas, Herbert, 179
Cold War, xiii, 3, 181–219

Communist Party, East German, see Socialist Unity Party
Corin, Karl, 123
Cromwell, Oliver, 13ff, 72
Czechoslovakia, xiii, 161–63, 169–70, 172–75, 182, 184

Darnton, Robert, 72, 180, 184
DDR, see German Democratic Republic
de Bruyn, Günter, 177
deconstruction, xii–xiii, 25, 32, 68, 70, 126, 164, 213, 216
Derrida, Jacques, 106
Deutsche Demokratische Republik, see German Democratic Republic
Deutsches Theater, 18
Dresden State Theater, 183, 189
Drommer, Günter, 71
Dubček, Alexander, 4, 173, 184
Duclaux, Mary, 130, 136

East Germany, see German Democratic Republic
Eberlein, Sybille, 79
Engler, Wolfgang, 194
Enlightenment, the, xii, xiii, 57
epic theater, 12, 20, 38
Fanon, Frantz, 25
fascism (see also National Socialism), xii, 123, 138, 186, 193
Federal Republic of Germany: attitudes toward East Germany, xi, xiii; national identity of, xi, 137–38
Feix, Ingrid, 78
Fischer, Bernd, 56, 67, 71–72, 178
Franke, Konrad, 72–73

Freud, Sigmund, 90–95, 114–15, 121, 123
Fukuyama, Francis, xi
Funke, Christoph, 56, 72, 78

Garcia Marquez, Gabriel, 32–33
GDR, see German Democratic Republic
Geldner, Renate, 6–7
German Democratic Republic (GDR, East Germany): as literary period, xii; cultural policies and practices, xv, 1, 4–8, 30–33, 76–77, 179–80, 184, 198; dissolution of, see *Wende*; founding of, 96, 140, 197, 202–203; national identity, xi, 3, 48–49, 75, 82–83, 95, 137–38, 181; role of artists in, 1–3, 30–31, 178, 181, 183, 215; role of churches in, 1–2, 181
Germany, East, see German Democratic Republic
Germany, Federal Republic of, see Federal Republic of Germany
Germany, West: see Federal Republic of Germany
Gestapo (Nazi secret police), 35, 62–64, 66, 73
Goethe, Johann Wolfgang von, 34, 60–61,
Gorbachev, Mikhail Sergeyevich, 181–84
Gorky, Maxim, 5
Gräf, Roland, 217
Grünenberg, Antonia, 71

Hacks, Peter, 9
Hage, Volker, 218
Hammer, Klaus, 79–80
Hebel, Johann Peter, xiv, xv, 32–33, 38, 71, 199–200, 202
Hegel, Georg Wilhelm Friedrich, 12, 147

Hein, Christoph:
attitude toward the West, 2, 187–97;
background and childhood, 3, 197, 205;
censorship, opposition to, 37, 72, 128–29, 183–84;
education, 3–4;
literary influences, xiv, xv, 12, 32–33, 198–99;
persecution by regime, 3–4;
political views and activities, 2, 184, 185–89
post-*Wende* significance, xii, 3, 215–17;
subversive literary tactics, xii, xii–xiv, 1–2, 7–8, 30–31, 33–34, 36–37, 127, 139, 150, 183, 206;
theatrical apprenticeship, 4
Hein, Christoph: themes, motifs, and concepts important in his works:
abortion, 119, 201–202;
anarchy 19–20, 23–25, 57, 160, 179;
chronicling, concept of, xiii–xiv, 26, 30–34, 42, 52, 66, 126–29, 143, 151, 157, 171, 177, 192, 197, 203–204, 206–216;
didacticism, rejection of, 19, 21, 31, 48, 76, 81, 85–86, 127;
history, xiii–xvii, 4, 9, 11, 12–26, 34, 38, 40, 42, 60–62, 66–70, 75, 85, 96, 102, 112, 125–180, 205, 217;
Jesus, 11, 25, 212–13;
Jews, 16–17, 36–37, 39–44, 52, 62–65, 70, 73–74, 166–67, 201;

INDEX

modernity, treatment of, xi, xiii, 8, 26, 29, 59, 75, 96, 114–15, 189, 217;
Öffentlichkeit, concept of, 37, 72, 128, 137, 138–39, 176–77, 178, 215;
realism, stage and prose violations of, 12, 21–24, 64, 70, 137, 196–99, 205;
revolution, depictions of, 12–14, 21–24, 55, 62, 70
Hein, Christoph, works by, plays:
Cromwell, xv, 9, 12–14, 23, 26, 36, 55, 62–63, 70, 129;
Lassalle fragt Herrn Herbert nach Sonja. Die Szene ein Salon, xv, 9, 12, 14–18, 26, 36, 45, 62;
Passage, xv, 9, 31, 62–70, 133, 136, 151, 166, 183;
Randow, xv, 191, 194–97, 219;
Die Ritter der Tafelrunde (The Knights of the Round Table), xvi, 9, 63, 184–85, 187–90, 215;
Schlötel oder Was solls, xv, 9–14, 26, 55–56, 61–63, 66, 120, 129, 151, 160, 179, 199–200;
Die wahre Geschichte des Ah Q, xiv, 9, 12, 18–26, 62–63, 68, 133, 189, 207
Hein, Christoph, works by, prose fiction:
"Bridge Freezes before Roadway," 190–91, 199;
Einladung zum Lever Bourgeois (Nachtfahrt und früher Morgen; including "Aus: Ein Album Berliner Stadtansichten" and "Der neuere [glücklichere] Kohlhaas"), xv–xvii, 30, 34–61, 125–126, 129–136, 151, 160, 129–136, 151, 160, 178, 198–199, 201, 203–204;
Exekution eines Kalbes, xvii, 197–205;
Der fremde Freund (Drachenblut, The Distant Lover), xiv–xv, xvii, 8, 23, 36, 45, 68, 72, 75–124, 129, 132–133, 136–137, 140, 143, 145, 149–150, 162–163, 174, 176, 179, 189, 192, 204, 213–214, 219;
Horns Ende, xvi, 36–37, 42, 45, 66–67, 82, 125–126, 129, 133, 136–61, 164–165, 167, 171, 174–76, 178–80, 189, 197, 199, 204–205, 213;
Das Napoleon-Spiel, xvii, 191–98, 204;
Der Tangospieler (The Tango Player), xvi, 36, 125, 133, 144, 149, 161–77, 180, 184, 215;
Von allem Anfang an, xvii, 197, 205–215
Heukenkamp, Ursula, 60, 72
Historikerstreit, xi
Hitler, Adolph, 13, 138
Holocaust, the, 14, 17, 30, 67
Honecker, Erich, 16, 182–83, 186, 188, 217
Hörnigk, Frank, x, 32, 69–70, 85–86
Hüfner, Agnes, 198
Humboldt, Alexander von, 34ff, 72

ideology, xii–xiii, xvii, 1–3, 7, 9, 11–13, 19, 24, 26, 32–34, 36, 38, 52, 56–57, 61–62, 70, 76–86, 80, 82, 84–85, 97–98, 116, 125–29, 147–53, 165, 168–69, 175–77, 179–80, 185, 187–90,

196–97, 199, 203, 211, 215–18

Jachimczak, Krzysztof, 96, 137
James, C. Vaughan, 5
Jannsen-Zimmermann, Antje, 74, 189
John, Erhard, 5
Joyce, James, 205–206

Kafka, Franz, xiv, xvii, 32–33, 38, 204
Kändler, Klaus, 81
KGB (Soviet secret police), 35
Kierkegaard, Søren, 49–50
Kirst, Klaus Dieter, 74
Kleist, Heinrich von, xv, xvii, 32–33, 38, 44, 54ff, 71–73, 170, 199–200
Klunker, Heinz, 195
Kochta, Karla, 189
Kohl, Helmut, xi
Kopka, Fritz-Jochen, 190
Krenz, Egon, 183
Kritikerstreit, see *Literaturstreit*
Krug, Hartmut, 189
Krumbholz, Martin, 198
Krumrey, Marianne, 32, 134, 178
Kuczynski, Jürgen, 6
Kundera, Milan, 36, 180
Kunze, Reiner, 73

Lang, Alexander, 18
Langner, Beatrix, 206, 219
Lassalle, Ferdinand, 9, 14ff, 72
Leistner, Bernd, 123
Lenin, Vladimir Ilich, and Leninism, xii, 5, 7, 13, 31, 44, 76, 98
Liebmann, Kurt, 5
Lindner, Gabriele, 123–24
Linsel, Klaus, 72
Literaturstreit, xi, 27, 195
Löffler, Dietrich, 84–85, 179–80

Louis XIV, 125, 129, 130, 133–34
Luxemburg, Rosa, 97–98
Maintenon, Madame de, 177
Man, New Socialist, 5, 11, 56, 62, 162, 170, 193
Mann, Heinrich, 67
Marx, Karl, and Marxism, xii, xvii, 6, 31–32, 42, 44–45, 48, 56, 82, 127, 145, 147, 156, 162, 178
McKnight, Phillip, 4, 73–74, 96, 106, 124, 138, 144, 147, 149, 157, 160–161, 179, 193–94, 218–219
Meech, Anthony, 28
Mehr, Max Thomas, 189
Meyer-Gosau, Frauke, 217
Michaelis, Rolf, 123
Mudrich, Heinz, 123
Müller, Heiner, xiv, 1, 4, 7–9, 25, 27, 31, 55, 68–72, 97, 99, 176–77
Münz, Rudolph, 179
Matt, Beatrice von, 198
Matt, Peter von, 206

National Socialism, xi, 3, 18, 23, 30, 39–44, 49, 52, 65–66, 74, 84, 118–19, 133, 137–142, 149, 161, 166, 195, 201, 203, 217–218
Nazi, Nazism, see National Socialism
Neues Forum, 182–83, 187
Nietzsche, Friedrich, 49–50

Party, see Socialist Unity Party
Pascal, Blaise, 107
Pfützner, Klaus, 219
Poland, xiii, 14, 170, 194
production plays and prose, 10, 55, 199

INDEX

Racine, Jean Baptiste, 34, 38, 71–72, 125, 129ff, 177–78
Racine, Louis, 130, 177
Raddatz, Fritz J., 206
Realsozialismus, or *real existierender Sozialismus,* 10, 48, 53, 55, 57, 59, 170, 204
Reich-Ranicki, Marcel, 218
Reinhardt, Stephan, 123
Robinson, David W., 124, 217
Romanowski, A., 5
Romanticism, 55, 57, 61, 89
Russia, xii, 4–5, 25, 28, 30, 34–37, 40, 44, 49, 96–102, 111, 118, 181–83, 196–97, 199–201, 203

Saintsbury, George, 130
Sartre, Jean-Paul, 49–50
Schabowski, Günter, 185–86
Schachtsiek-Freitag, Norbert, 137
Schlenstedt, Dieter, 83–84
Schultz, Helmut H., 78
Schulz-Ojala, Jan, 195
SED, see Socialist Unity Party
Seghers, Anna, 72
Seibt, Gustav, 199
Sevin, Dieter, 178
Shakespeare, William, 12–13, 21, 33
Sieg, Katrin, 27
Socialist Realism, xiv, xv, 4–12, 26, 33, 48, 61, 78–80, 82–83, 127, 162, 193, 216
Socialist Unity Party (SED), xii, 3, 8, 10–11, 31, 97, 137–38, 144–45, 148, 162–63, 181–84, 187–88, 200, 205–206, 209
Soviet Union: see Russia
Staatssicherheitsdienst (Stasi, East German secret police), xi, 3, 35, 133, 162, 168, 172, 181, 184, 194–95

Stalin, Joseph, and Stalinism, xiv, 1–2, 4, 13, 31, 42, 51, 75, 79, 82–84, 95–96, 97, 144, 182, 186–88, 190, 210, 216
Stasi, see Staatssicherheitsdienst
Stephan, Erika, 73
Surrealism, 49–50

Tacitus, Publius Cornelius, xiii
tanks, symbolism of, 97–102, 111, 113, 117–118, 124, 174–76
Tienanmen Square Massacre: xii, 188

Ulbricht, Walter, 118, 162
unification, German, xi–xii, 2–3, 181–88, 215–17
Union of Soviet Socialist Republics, see Russia
USSR, see Russia

Volksbühne, 4, 12, 30

Walther, Peter, 194
Warsaw Pact, 4, 161–62, 169
Wende, die, xi–xii, xvi, 2–3, 161–62, 176–77, 181–88, 190–95, 197–99, 215
Wilke, Ursula, 81
Winston, Krishna, xviii
Wittstock, Uwe, 73, 123, 179
Wolf, Christa, xiv, 1, 3, 8, 27, 71, 176, 185, 188, 197
Wolf, Marcus, 186

Zimmermann, Stephan, 219
Zola, Emile, 46